BY THE SAME AUTHOR

FICTION

Mirror

The Dossier
(with Pierre Salinger)

Mortal Games
(with Pierre Salinger)

NONFICTION

God and Freud

The Last, Best Hope

1985

The Great Wall Street Scandal
(with Raymond L. Dirks)

The Last Jews in Berlin

How Much Is Too Much?

STRANGERS
AT THE GATE

RANDOM HOUSE NEW YORK

STRANGERS
AT THE GATE

LEONARD GROSS

IN MEMORY OF
CLARA ROER
AND
ELIZABETH PAIGE

San Francisco, open your golden gate
You let no stranger wait outside your door.

—Lyric by Gus Kahn from official city song

When I was a freshman at Berkeley in 1970, we talked about the likelihood that urban America was transforming itself into two societies, one enclosed behind heavily secured urban fortresses, the other ruling the streets and plotting ways to scale the fortress walls.

I begin this chronicle twenty-five years later, sequestered in my home. An armed off-duty policeman stands by my front door, another sits in a car parked across the street and a third brings food to my study so that I don't have to pass through my living room, where I might provide a target to a sniper stationed in any of the several apartment buildings within rifle range of my windows. My three guardians belong to the San Francisco Police Department's Gang Task Force, as I once did myself. All three are volunteers, having refused my offer of payment. They work from eight until four, rotating stations every two hours. Another three volunteers guard me between four and midnight, and a two-man shift works from midnight until 8:00 A.M.

Very soon now—as soon as I've recovered sufficiently from my wounds—I intend to leave my sanctuary to tell a story one man has already tried to censor with a bullet. My guardians have no idea of what that story consists. Their only concern is that I remain alive to tell it.

January 2, 1995

I

NOVEMBER 5–11, 1994

I t had happened, Maggie explained from her hospital bed, as suddenly and smoothly as the passing of a baton, and somewhat in that manner. She'd just stepped from her Divisadero Street apartment on the evening of her twenty-sixth birthday and begun a gingerly descent down the hill to her car, en route to an opera and supper celebration with her parents, her trench coat buttoned against an early November mist, when a man crept up behind her, covered her mouth with his right hand, grabbed her left wrist, wrenched it tight against her back, and threw her into the open door of a dark sedan that came abreast of them at that instant. He followed her into the car and shoved her to the far side of the seat, behind the driver. "You no scream," he said, showing her a cleaver. Its blade was longer and thinner than the cleaver she'd used in her Chinese cooking class to chop through poultry and meat bones, but its wooden handle and rectangular shape were the same. The man was Asian, slight, in his mid-twenties, and he reeked of tobacco. To emphasize his point he ran the edge of the cleaver lightly across the top of the front seat. The upholstery parted like a banana skin.

As waves of fear engulfed her, it occurred to Maggie that the car must be stolen. "Take my money," she said, trembling so badly she could hardly get the words out. "Just don't hurt me."

The man beside her laughed. He spoke to the driver in what sounded like Chinese. Whatever the man said, it made the driver laugh. His response was equally unintelligible. Their dialect was neither the one she'd studied in college nor what she heard in the home of her best friend, Barbara Woo. All she could understand was that for the first time in her life she was frightened in the presence of Asians.

When they got to Lombard Street, San Francisco's Motel Row, the driver turned his head to the right to check the traffic and she could see that he was at least fifteen years older than the man who had seized her, and extremely heavy. When the light changed, he turned left onto Lombard and headed west toward the Golden Gate Bridge. She concluded that they were taking her to Marin County, but a block farther on, instead of angling right onto Richardson Avenue and the approach to the bridge, the driver jogged left onto the Lombard continuation and drove into the Presidio, the historic army post that had recently become a national park. Then he curved around the Letterman Army Medical Center and began to weave through a warren of streets, past a series of aged one- and two-story cream-colored wood frame buildings and into the center of the army post. He seemed to know exactly where he was going. Just past the former Officers' Club, now the Community Club, he turned left onto Arguello Boulevard and began the steep ascent to Presidio Heights on a curving road bordered by stands of trees so thick at times they seemed, in the faint light from the streetlamps, like walls of wood. Only a single car passed them going down the hill.

Near the top of the road was a parking area Maggie had often passed on hikes along one of the many trails that meandered through the preserve, and she thought the men would surely stop there. "When they didn't," she recalled, "I had this sudden dread that it was going to be something worse than rape, that they were taking me to some big-shot triad leader who'd been ticked off by my series, and I was too petrified to even imagine what he'd do to me." The series she referred to, about the huge influx of Asians to the Bay Area, had run in five parts the week before on our most popular TV station, KUBC.

But at the top of the hill, instead of continuing on Arguello, the older man drove onto a narrow road that took them past the Presidio Golf Club and down a bumpy street bordered on the right by the course and on the left by private homes. The last streetlight was a few hundred yards below the clubhouse; as soon as he passed it, the driver turned off the car lights. He drove until they were past the homes and alongside a stone wall, then turned the car around so that it pointed back up the hill. Then he killed the engine.

Part of Maggie's stock-in-trade—more memorable, even, than her fair-skinned, lightly freckled and irresistibly comely if not quite beautiful face—was a vibrant voice, the kind you recognize, the moment you hear it, as having been meant for broadcasting. But the fright she'd experienced had diminished that voice as effectively as a mute muffles a trumpet. "We just sat there," she recalled, speaking so softly I had to lean close to hear her. "It was probably seconds, but it seemed like minutes, and it was so quiet I could hear people in their homes and kitchen noises and music and television programs. I figured these guys were waiting to see if anyone had heard them. Or maybe they were waiting for someone."

But moments later, Maggie continued, the man beside her spoke quietly to the driver, and the driver got out of the car. The interior light did not go on. He closed the door but not completely. Maggie figured it was to avoid the noise. "They were real pros. They'd thought of everything," she said. Then the driver opened the door next to Maggie. "Outside," the young, thin man whispered. "You scream, you die."

She placed her feet outside the car, but before she could stand the driver yanked her upright, spun her around, pinned both of her arms behind her and jammed her against the car. With his left hand he grabbed her hair and pulled it so hard she thought it would separate from her scalp. She gasped with pain, the sound dying in her throat as she remembered the young man's threat. With one hand tugging her hair and the other holding her left arm in a hammerlock, the older man then marched her through an opening in the rock wall and to a dense clump of tall bushes. There he turned her so that she was facing the younger man. "You scream, you die," he repeated as he approached her. In her horror, time seemed to elongate and her assailant to move in slow motion. She knew that something awful was about to happen to her, but she couldn't imagine what it was. "Please," she whispered.

And then the younger man raised his arm, and she saw that he was holding the cleaver. Her knees sagged. The older man straightened her in a hurry, tugging harder on her hair and putting even more pressure on her left arm. Once again she gasped with pain, and once again stifled an outcry. "Please," she whispered again.

As the younger man placed the cleaver close to her face, he was grinning. He ran the edge of the cleaver deftly along her right cheek several times, making crisscross strokes. The pain took a second to register, as did the unthinkable thing he was doing. He made the same pattern on her left cheek, but that she neither felt nor thought about, because by then she'd fainted. Neither did she feel herself falling when the driver let her go, nor the kicks the two men must have delivered, judging by the injuries to her ribs.

When she came to, her face was on fire and slick with blood. But the men were gone. Even so, she felt too terrified to scream. She struggled to her feet and stumbled toward the nearest lights, as unsteady as though she had just stepped from bed after a weeklong bout of the flu.

The lights were coming through a set of leaded windows of a three-story shingled house. Inside, a couple sat at dinner. They were in their seventies, with the look of people who had thoroughly enjoyed their lives. A bottle of wine stood on the table between them. Although they were dining alone, the man wore a jacket and tie, and the woman a dress. When Maggie rapped on the window, their heads jerked instantly toward the noise. She saw the woman's mouth fly open, but heard no sound. The man leaped to his feet, his napkin dropping from his lap. As he began to rush toward her, she fainted a second time. Her next memory was of paramedics lifting her onto a stretcher and carrying her past a small crowd. In moments, she was in an ambulance and on her way to San Francisco General Hospital.

In twenty years with the San Francisco Police Department, I've made so many professional visits to every hospital in the city that I know which one I'd send my mother to for every conceivable condition. SF General is not a place I'd send her for an elective procedure, but if she was hurt in an automobile accident or poisoned or shot, it would definitely be my hospital of choice. Big cities have long since discovered that survival rates are highest if all trauma cases are funneled to one place, and in San Francisco, SF General is that place. Its highly regarded trauma unit is staffed twenty-four hours a day by residents in training and members of the hospital's faculty, who are either on duty or on call.

The one thing I have against SF General is that, although they'd never admit it to outsiders, they won't touch you until they know who you are. Maggie had no purse—she'd either left it in the car, or her assailants had taken it—and no other identification, and after briefly describing the attack to the paramedic as they sped to the hospital, she'd been too dazed to do more than give him her name. So precious minutes passed while several residents stood a few feet from the gurney on which she was lying and spoke in low voices about what to do. At last one of them detached herself from the group, walked over, looked at Maggie, then turned abruptly to her colleagues and said, "Wait a minute, I know this woman." In telling me the story, Maggie recalled that the resident looked like a high school dropout and sounded as though she hadn't spent a week of her life outside her barrio. Maggie would never have taken her for a college graduate, let alone a graduate of a medical school. The resident turned back to Maggie, squeezed her arm and said, "I'm Dr. Velasquez. Have I seen you on the news?"

"Yes."

"Which station?" Her question sounded like a challenge.

"KUBC."

Dr. Velasquez grabbed the paramedic's work sheet and glanced at it. "Maggie Winehouse," she read out. "Holy shit." She wheeled around to face her colleagues. "Who's on call for plastic surgery?"

"Mooney," someone answered.

"Get him over here, pronto."

Dr. Mooney arrived within minutes. He was extremely tall and lean and already stooped from his labors, and, Maggie later learned, in his third year of postgraduate training. "Oh, God," he said when he saw the wounds. "What sick son of a bitch did this? And why didn't you call me sooner?"

A moment later, another resident hovered over her. "I'm Dr. Taper, your anesthesiologist," he said. He ran rapidly through a series of questions about illnesses and allergies, which Maggie tried to answer just as rapidly, despite her shock and pain. "I'm gonna give you something to make you more comfortable," he said then. Seconds later, she felt a sensation sweep through her body, miraculously erasing the pain. In another moment she felt nothing.

The call for a city ambulance had been noted at the Hall of Justice at 850 Bryant Street. The investigation was assigned to the Richmond Station. Two uniformed officers from that station, one a man, the other a woman, both in their early thirties, arrived at the hospital emergency room just as the surgery began. From the chief nurse they learned the victim's name, that she was a reporter for a major San Francisco television station, and that she'd told the paramedic who'd tended her in the ambulance that her attackers had been Asians. Within another thirty minutes, this information had passed through the entire police chain of command, first to the field supervisor at the district station, a sergeant, then to his lieutenant, then to operations center at 850 Bryant, whose inspectors immediately referred the matter to the on-call crew of the General Works Detail, the catchall unit for cases that don't fall readily into special categories. The head of that detail called the chief of police, Jerome Doyle, away from a dinner party to be certain he'd be informed before the inevitable call from Mayor Putnam.

In an age when chiefs of police of major cities come to their jobs with graduate degrees in sociology and criminology and are more often than not black or Latino, Chief Doyle was a throwback, a beat cop of Irish descent who'd joined the force out of high school and made it through the ranks all the way to the top, where he'd remained now for a decade. He was a hulking, beefy man with a voice made raspy from too much bourbon and an ample nose that had been flattened when he was an all-city end and face guards were optional equipment. Although he was pushing seventy, he still possessed great stamina and vigor, and he was thoroughly accustomed to deference. His immediate subordinates took care not to arouse what even he referred to as the Irish in him. Doyle could be imperious and insensitive, and, based on his barely contained resentment of me, I'd always suspected he was a closet bigot. But no one could ever call him stupid, particularly when his own survival was at issue.

Although the chief's official responsibility was to maintain law and order and the safety of his city, his de facto priority was never to embarrass his boss, Mayor Putnam. Jerry Doyle hated criminals and pursued them with a vengeance, but it was his deftness at protecting mayors that had kept him in his job through two City Hall administrations. Given the ingredients of this case, he'd immediately appreciated its ominous potential. Not only was Maggie visible in her own right; she was the daughter of Mike Winehouse, the columnist the Eastern press refers to as the Jimmy Breslin of San Francisco. When, to these factors, you added the huge demographic changes that had literally transformed the city's face over the last twenty-five years, and the inevitable tensions that change had produced, the mutilation of a Caucasian by Asians had crisis written all over it—a crisis that could only profit Harold Halderman, a xenophobic, close-the-gate district attorney who would almost certainly be Mayor Putnam's principal opponent in the upcoming election, now just a year away.

Rather than wait for the mayor's call, Doyle immediately telephoned him at Ernie's, the landmark North Beach restaurant where Putnam dined with his wife every Saturday night. They spoke for five minutes. The moment they finished, the chief called me.

I was at home that evening. My hours are so long and uncertain and I'm out so often at night that it takes a promising concert, ballet, opera or play to get me out of my apartment on my evenings off. It's on the eastern slope of Russian Hill, on the top floor of a fifty-year-old three-story building I bought in 1990 and improved with tender loving care and a disturbing amount of cash. I rent out the apartments on the first and second floors. My apartment has five large rooms, an ample terrace and a wide-angle view of the Bay Bridge, Telegraph Hill, San Francisco Bay and portions of the East Bay. On those weekend days when I'm not windsurfing on the bay or skiing at Squaw Valley, there's no place I'd rather be than in my favorite living-room armchair, surrounded by my books and paintings, half listening to a tape I made of the slow, melodic second movements of my favorite concertos and looking up occasionally from the book in my lap to savor the panorama. This is a cop? you're probably asking at this point.

The chief didn't apologize for calling—I'd never heard him apologize for anything—but then I wouldn't have expected him to even if we were on good terms. As the captain of the SFPD's Special Investigations Division, I wanted to be informed. In that especially brusque and strained manner he always used in his conversations with me, he quickly gave me the highlights, filling me in on his conversation with Mayor Putnam, whose thoughts, predictably, had gone immediately to the crime's potential for racial repercussion, and how such repercussions could cost him the election. "He wanted to know if I'd seen the series the girl did last week on Asians moving into the area," the chief said. "I didn't. Did you?"

"Of course."

"And?" he said, his voice rising.

"A solid job. Mostly basic stuff. A few tough hits on the triads for buying local real estate with dirty money."

"Could that be it?"

"It *could* be, Chief. But it strikes me as a stretch."

"Why?" he said, as though daring me to prove it.

"Because she didn't name any names."

"You sure?"

"I would have remembered if she had."

"Not good enough," the chief said brusquely. "I want you to review those programs first thing tomorrow morning. Call me as soon as you've finished."

"They'll be reviewed by the time you get up. What's the earliest I can call?"

"Seven. In the meanwhile, get over to the hospital right away and talk to the girl."

That stopped me. Captains run departments. They almost never investigate crimes. I wasn't happy about that, but it came with the territory. Even as the chief was filling me in, I'd been thinking about which of my inspectors could best handle this investigation. Given the chief's antipathy toward me, he'd just paid me a backhanded compliment—not one I welcomed, however.

"You want me to handle this myself?" I asked with just enough doubt in my voice to encourage him to think again.

"You got a problem with that?" The question implied that there was only one possible answer: "No."

"It could send the wrong message to my division."

"Yeah, well, fuck the messages, Tobias, and get your ass over to SF General."

I took a moment to calm myself. "If Maggie Winehouse is in surgery, Chief, she won't be doing any talking for a while. If it's okay with you, I'd like to finish my dinner."

"It's not okay with me," the chief said, biting off the words. "If you didn't want your dinners interrupted you should have gone into the family business."

That did it. "And missed the pleasure of working for you?" I said, not caring what it might cost me.

In the moment of silence that preceded his curt "Get to work," I could hear Doyle inhaling through his nostrils and exhaling through his mouth, as I'd seen him do in moments of anger. One of the many things he dislikes about me is that I don't show him that deference he's so accustomed to getting—my personal defense against his verbal, innuendo-tinged hectoring, of which his last remarks were a mild example. While he'd had it in for me ever since I joined the force, his antagonism had intensified each time I moved up the promotion ladder. Given his age, there'd inevitably been talk within the police department—and, according to the media, at City Hall as well—that he was dated and ought to retire. That, in turn, had provoked speculation in the media about his successor, and most of the speculation, to my discomfort, had centered on me. I was, those stories said, young, sharp—their word—well educated, proactive in police work, had made captain in record time, and was well connected politically, exactly the kind of police chief the city needed to deal with its proliferating problems. As you can imagine, publicity like this had created a working relationship between myself and Jerry Doyle for which "dysfunctional" is a tame description.

Years before, the chief had approved my transfer to the Asian squad of the Gang Task Force, thinking that would bury me. But my years on that detail had turned out to be my happiest on the force. "Tell me one thing, Tobias," he'd asked me once, "what is it about Asians that you like so much?"

"It's the food, Chief."

"The food? What the fuck are you talking about?"

"Jews love Chinese food. Every Sunday night, half the Jews in

America eat in Chinese restaurants, and the other half order takeout. If you associated with Jews you'd know that."

So. I'm a rich Jewish cop—to Chief Doyle, as well as to many others, I'm sure, a double oxymoron. Zachariah Tobias, my paternal ancestor, who came to California from Prussia in 1849, when revolutionary reforms failed to produce the freedoms Jews had coveted for so long, and in whose memory my parents named me Zachary, believed that there were two ways to get rich in a gold rush. You could prospect for gold or you could sell provisions to the prospectors. Like his contemporary Levi Strauss, Zachariah did the latter, with stunning success, and ensuing generations of Tobiases built on his accomplishment, taking Z. Tobias and Company into banking, shipping, fur trading and construction.

When I was born, my father's parents set up a million-dollar trust fund for me, just as they had for my sister, Sari, born two years earlier. The rich *do* get richer; through the miracle of compound interest, the original million has multiplied so many times that I live without regard to money—one reason I don't have to take guff from the chief—and enjoy the sweet pleasure of dispensing every penny of my salary to charity. There's more: on the death of my mother—assuming my sister has not conned her by that point into disinheriting me, a definite possibility—I'll inherit half her assets. All of which makes me one of the wealthier single men in town, and thus, theoretically, a catch. But in the affluent San Francisco Jewish society in which I was raised—the one that gave me my taste for the arts—a cop, no matter how wealthy, is not considered a proper match for an eligible young woman. A district attorney, yes. Not a cop.

So why did I become a cop? One October night in 1971 my parents were taking an after-dinner walk along the Presidio Wall in Presidio Heights, a few blocks from our home, when two teenagers approached them. "Gimme that watch, mothahfuckah," one of them said to my father, pointing a small handgun at him. My father, a big man who had played tackle for the University of California when the first string still played offense and defense, been an infantry captain in World War II and fought for Israel's independence in Palestine in 1948, said, "Go to hell," and reached for the gun. My father must have figured that the two kids would have only one gun between them. He was wrong. Just as he wrested the first kid's gun from him, the second one drew his gun and shot him in the heart. While my mother screamed, the two kids took my father's watch and wallet and ran off into the night. They were never caught.

I was nineteen at the time, a sophomore at Berkeley, enrolled, by default, as a business administration major, for lack of a true calling. But I'd never wanted to enter the family business. I had many reasons; for now, let's just say that spending my life making money when I already had infinitely more of it than I could ever use struck me as ridiculous. So, taking my father's death as a sign, I switched my major to police science, as certain as only nineteen-year-olds can be that one day I would not only take charge of the protection of my city but reverse the social conditions that turned boys into criminals.

For a moment after Chief Doyle's call I stood at the telephone, adjusting to what he'd told me. You see terrible things in police work, to the point that you sometimes have to joke about them in order to deal with them, but this was the first time in my years on the force that anything bad had happened to someone I knew. Maggie and I weren't friends, but she'd called me several times while researching her series, and interviewed me twice in person, the second time from the backseat of a patrol car as a cameraman sat beside me, recording a drive along Clement Street, in the heart of what has come to be called New Chinatown. Once an unremarkable shopping area patronized mostly by Caucasians, Clement Street is now the bustling commercial and social center for thousands of immigrants from Hong Kong and China who have settled in a mile-wide corridor extending west from Arguello Boulevard to the ocean.

Those two encounters with Maggie had convinced me that she was a comer, at least as much because of her acute, incessant questioning as her physical presence. I could visualize not only her freckles and striking green eyes but also her vivacity, so fresh and strong it communicated itself even through a picture tube. And now? Where was the television station that would have the courage to broadcast her scarred face—assuming she would eventually have the courage to brave the camera lens? Had I been a religious man, I would have prayed for her. Instead, I offered a silent wish for some medical miracle that would restore her. Then I returned to the living room, where

Britt sat exactly as she had before Chief Doyle's call had interrupted us, half reclining on the sofa, her blouse unbuttoned, her skirt raised almost to the tops of her athletic legs. She looked at me despondently. "Do you have to go?"

I nodded sadly.

"Damn," said Britt.

"I'm sorry," I said. Was I ever. Britt and I had been about to culminate the most sustained and provocative prelude to sex I'd ever experienced. It was Britt who'd orchestrated our daylong tease, but as aroused as I was, I still couldn't turn off a little red light in my brain that was warning me, Watch out, there's something behind this.

Britt made me promise to awaken her when I returned, no matter what the hour. I kissed her good-bye, grabbed a warm jacket and headed for my car, my groin heavy with expectations thwarted by the chief's call, my mind heavy with suspicion that something more than sex was involved in that buildup.

Weekends are the only time I drink, and only then when I know I won't be driving. Dealing professionally with the consequences of drunken driving does that to you. Intellectually I knew I shouldn't be behind a wheel, that though my blood-alcohol level might be below the legal limit, even a small amount of alcohol can impair my coordination and perception because I drink so little. But physically I felt capable of flying my Toyota 4Runner, if necessary, to SF General, and because the alcohol had temporarily immobilized that portion of my brain that knew better, I sped down Russian Hill so fast there were seconds, as I shot across the rounded lips of the intersections, when the car did seem to be airborne. Moments later I was racing through the Mission District, ignoring the startled looks and protesting horns of competing motorists.

Maybe it was the alcohol enriching my perceptions, but driving to the hospital that misty November evening, I felt I was the surrogate of those kinsmen of mine who had crossed the Atlantic in steerage in 1849, trudged across Panama and sailed up the Pacific to San Francisco, from where they set out at once for such mining towns as Gold Camp and Angels Camp and Sonora and Mokelumne Hill, their wagons filled with food and clothing they'd purchased in San Francisco for resale to the prospectors. Once the stores they built in the Mother Lode had prospered, they returned to San Francisco to create factories and department stores and ultimately museums and parks in gratitude to a city that had embraced them as Jews of the *Diaspora* had never been embraced before. Five generations of my ancestors had lavished their love on San Francisco, helping in the process to make it the most humane and civilized of cities, but now, driving through that city—its streets filthy and overrun with homeless panhandlers, its criminals rampant, its centerpiece, Union Square, a nightly haven for pushers and addicts, its payroll padded, its treasury depleted, its tax base eroded by corporations fleeing to more tranquil and less expensive venues, its social fabric rent, a majority of its residents convinced that its best days are behind it—I believed that unless people like myself intervened, the heritage my forebears had bequeathed me might not survive my generation. I knew in my bones that the attack on Maggie Winehouse could trigger more than mass protests and turn more than an election. It could destroy the sympathy for human diversity that proclaims San Francisco to the world.

For me, there was an added problem: I knew that once the alcohol left my bloodstream, I would have zero confidence that I could affect the outcome.

At the hospital, I parked near the emergency entrance and walked swiftly inside, trying—and, as usual, failing—to still my demons. The association of this place with my past was so powerful that no matter how many times I entered those glass doors and no matter how many years went by I could never repress the images of that evening when I'd come home from work and found my wife, Elaine, unconscious. Ten minutes afterward I was in the passenger seat of an ambulance while it raced toward this very hospital, and then at this same emergency entrance, where the stretcher, with Elaine still motionless on it, disappeared into a labyrinth of treatment and surgical rooms. I had waited—not very long—in the same square, bare-walled, oppressive waiting room I was entering now, until a young doctor appeared and said, "She's gone."

I had no time to dwell on my memories. My size—I'm big like my father, six feet four and 220 pounds—doesn't exactly permit me to slip in and out of buildings, so a moment after I walked through the glass doors, I was pulled harshly into the present by reporters, photographers and television crews, the reporters all shouting questions at once, the photographers and camera crews jockeying for my picture, which quickly told me that no one more pertinent to the story had arrived. "Give me a chance," I said. "I just got here." I pushed past them to the triage desk just off the waiting room, where a nurse told me that Maggie was still in surgery. I went looking for the paramedics who'd brought her to the hospital, talked to them for ten minutes, interviewed three residents, Dr. Velasquez among them, and finally and reluctantly returned to the waiting room. The moment I reappeared, the reporters were on me again. At the sides of the scruffy room, slouched in battered chairs, a half-dozen indigents who'd sought refuge from the damp night looked on in dazed perplexity. In a corner a television set broadcast to no one.

"Did she tell you anything, Zack?" the reporter with the loudest voice asked.

"I haven't spoken to her," I answered, my volume deliberately just above a whisper.

"What? I couldn't hear that," one of the reporters said.

"Hold it down, you guys," another said. And suddenly the reporters were silent, waiting for me to speak. It always worked, and they never caught on.

"I said I haven't spoken to her. She's still in surgery."

"Is there *anything* you can tell us?" a young reporter asked. I'd never seen him before. He looked no more than twenty-four. I would have bet that this was one of his first assignments.

"Only what she told the paramedics who brought her here," I said.

"Which was?" he pressed.

"That she was abducted from in front of her apartment by two men."

"Did she identify the men?" the same young man demanded, his persistence cutting off questions from other reporters.

"No."

"She couldn't even describe them?" he asked incredulously, as if to suggest that I was holding back on him.

"Yeah, she described them," I said as kindly as I could. "You asked if she identified them. I don't mean to embarrass you, but there's a difference."

"Okay," he said uncomfortably, "what description did she give?"

"That they were Asians—"

"Nothing more specific? Chinese? Japanese? Korean?"

"No," I said. By now the other reporters were casting dark looks at the newcomer.

"Anything else?" he kept on, either unaware of or indifferent to the reaction he was provoking.

"One mid-twenties, the other forty. They spoke to each other in a foreign language."

"Which one?"

"She wasn't sure, but she thought it sounded like Chinese. Now, if it's okay with you, I'll answer some of the other reporters' questions."

"Zack," Sherman Sproul, a reporter for KUBC, asked, "does the police department consider the attack on Maggie Winehouse a retaliation for our recent series about Asian migration to San Francisco?"

It was the logical question for Sherman, a ten-year veteran at KUBC who'd impressed me before with his thoroughness. "First of all, Sherman," I said with a shake of my head, "this crime is three hours old, so I'm sure the department hasn't had time to consider anything. Secondly, I don't speak for the department. And third, if my opinion's of any use to you, I'd say you're really putting yourself out there with that kind of speculation." The truth was that at the moment the speculation had an irresistible logic to it, but I hated to have it broadcast to a public that was going to be plenty upset with this crime as it was.

It was then that I saw Mike Winehouse.

He came through the door with faltering steps, and stood for a moment, looking dazed and lost, a small man with a balding head, droopy posture and slight belly. Behind him was his wife, Bess—save for her auburn hair, undoubtedly dyed, his feminine counterpart in appearance and manner. Perhaps they'd been attracted to each other initially by some unconscious recognition of their similarities, or perhaps their years together and shared reaction to life had imposed identical expressions on their faces. Whatever the reason, someone who didn't know them might easily have taken them for brother and sister.

Few members of San Francisco society didn't know the Winehouses at least well enough to recognize them on sight. They were at the top of every invitation list, not because of who they were but because of what Mike represented. He wasn't popular with our establishment, but he seemed necessary to them, as though their existence wasn't fully validated until it was acknowledged in his feisty column. I'm certain that the day Mike retires, the invitations will stop; I'm equally certain he'll be relieved. I'd seen him at parties over the years, on several occasions in my mother's home, invariably standing off to the side, looking almost as lost as he did at this moment. But pity the person who mistook shyness for timidity, and reticence for lack of enterprise. Mike Winehouse feared no one, and would walk to the North Pole for a story. Behind that humble countenance was the toughness and savvy of a poor kid raised on the immigrant-rich southwest side of Chicago. San Francisco was his adopted city—he'd fallen in love with it as he sailed out the Golden Gate on a troopship during the Korean War—and he defended it with the zeal of a convert.

The reporters and cameramen must have seen my eyes move to the door, because an instant later they turned as one, saw the Winehouses and raced to them, shouting questions as they went. In seconds Mike and Bess were bathed in television lights. If they had looked bewildered on entering, they now appeared frightened as well. Bess moved closer to Mike, who seemed to clutch her as much for his own reassurance as for hers. I pushed my way to their side.

"Hello, Mike," I said. For a fraction of a second, he looked at me vacantly, his small hazel eyes pinched, lines creasing his high forehead. Then he recognized me, and his look changed to relief. I turned to the media. "Excuse us for a minute, will you, guys?" I said. Then, taking each of the Winehouses by an elbow, I guided them past the triage desk and down the corridor, where they leaned against a wall. I stood next to them, with my back deliberately toward the media, hoping to screen them from view. "I'm really sorry about this," I said, bothered, as usual, by the inadequacy of words at such times.

"Have you seen Maggie?" Mike asked piteously. He looked as mournful as a basset hound.

"No. But I talked to several doctors who saw her when she was brought in." I put a hand on each of them. "I want you both to understand that her life isn't in danger."

"What did they do to her?" Mike said insistently, his eyes pinched once again. "The news reports didn't say."

"You should get that from the doctor." I tried to sound as convincing as I could, but I could see his eyes harden as they had so often in the past when he was after information, and I knew he wasn't going to let me off the hook.

"I want to know," he said.

I sighed. "Apparently, they cut her face pretty bad."

Bess wailed, and sank against the wall. "Oh, Jesus," Mike said. His legs buckled, and he would have fallen if I hadn't grabbed him. There was a rush of footsteps. Within seconds the cameramen and photographers were upon us, and all three of us were suddenly the focus of their paralyzing lights.

"Come on!" I shouted. "Can't you even show some consideration for a colleague?"

"A story's a story, Zack," one of the photographers said coolly.

There was nothing I could do. They had every right to be there. They took their shots, then backed away. It was over in a minute.

A nurse who must have been watching came out from behind the triage desk and led us to a small alcove around the corner from the desk, where the Winehouses sank into chairs. I gave them time to compose themselves. "How did you hear about it?" I asked at last, not because the information was of any consequence but because I hoped to ease them as gently as possible back to the reality of the moment.

"We were at the opera," Mike said. "Maggie was supposed to meet us. When she didn't show, I called KUBC, but they hadn't heard from her, or anything about her. We stuck it out through the first act, but then we went home, thinking she'd call. We were watching KUBC when Gordon Lee broke in with a bulletin."

"He's Maggie's boyfriend, isn't he?" I knew this because San Francisco, as cosmopolitan as any city in the world, has the familiar aspects of a small town, with an elite almost as well known to newspaper readers as its members are to one another.

"Supposedly," Mike said quietly.

You didn't have to be a detective to draw an inference from that remark.

Barely thirty and with less than five years' experience in a metropolitan area, Gordon was already the showcase reporter of KUBC, the station Maggie worked for, as well as the weekend anchor. Like Peter Jennings, on whom he appeared to have modeled himself, he seemed perfect for television: good-looking, poised beyond his years, quick, decisive, articulate, and at once urbane and warm. Watching Gordon, you didn't need to be told that he had Jennings in his sights; you sensed his impatience for the summons to network he seemed to consider his due. Did it distress Mike that Gordon was earning twice as much as the top reporters on the *Dispatch* for disseminating the same news they did? Was he resentful that print journalists like himself had spent their best years climbing the wrong mountain, that they lived in an era when not just fame and fortune but consequence as well were gained through the abominable tube? Or was it that Gordon was Chinese? Perhaps a combination of all three.

"Do you feel up to answering a few questions?" I asked Mike.

"I'll try," he said without enthusiasm.

I pulled a chair close to him and sat. Bess turned her head to the side, as though she didn't want to participate in the interview. "Did your daughter talk to you about that series she was doing?"

"Of course."

"Did she say anything at all that stuck in your mind?"

For a moment he stared at me vacantly. "Not that I recall," he said, his voice flat.

"Did she mention anyone being unhappy with it?"

"Not that I recall."

"Did she mention receiving any threats?"

"Not that I recall."

I paused, puzzled. "You keep saying, 'Not that I recall.' Are you trying to tell me she might have said something about these matters but that you don't recall what she said?"

"That's certainly possible, isn't it? I'm trying to give you as careful an answer as I can."

"Did you see the series?"

"Every segment."

"Was there anything in the series that you thought might offend any parties?"

"Not that I recall."

"Yeah, that was my impression." I looked at Bess. She was no longer crying, but she had a fist in front of her mouth and a handkerchief in her fist. Her eyes were red. "How about you, Bess?"

"No. Nothing. But what do I know?"

And what did *I* know? That rush-into-battle euphoria I'd felt as I was racing to the hospital had ebbed as surely as the alcohol in my bloodstream and in inverse proportion to my increasing awareness of how little I had to go on. For the next hour, I waited with the Winehouses, suffused with a feeling of helplessness that overwhelms me at the outset of every case. Two Asian men, identities unknown, had committed a crime and then vanished. By now they could be anywhere. I could only pray that Maggie might have seen or heard something that would at least point me in the right direction.

At eleven o'clock, hearing the familiar theme music of KUBC's late-evening newscast, I rose and walked back into the waiting room. The few media people remaining were clustered around the set. In a moment, Gordon Lee—an obviously shaken and distracted Gordon—filled the screen. He led with the story of Maggie's abduction. His words told us nothing we didn't know, but the pictures shot an electric current through me. They were like a thirty-second highlights film of the last two hours of my life: my entry into the hospital, the arrival of the Winehouses, their collapse as I told them about Maggie's wounds, my anger at the cameramen as they moved in for the kill.

As I watched I heard a soft moan to my left. Turning my head, I saw Mike. He was staring at the screen, his eyes narrowed, his skin taut and turning red before my eyes. "Sonofabitch, sonofabitch, sonofabitch," he mumbled, so softly that I was sure no one else could hear him. I sensed that he felt violated in some primordial way. Reporters reported news; they weren't supposed to make it. The moment Gordon turned to the next story, Mike walked slowly back to the alcove. I followed him. He sat close to Bess, took her hand, and stared blankly at the wall opposite him. It was obvious that neither one of them wanted to talk anymore, at least not to me. I returned to the waiting room to give them some privacy.

Twenty minutes after finishing his broadcast, Gordon, still wearing his makeup but bereft of his trademark poise, burst through the glass doors of the emergency room and came straight at me. "Where are they?" he said. He was media, but he was also Maggie's boyfriend; I led him to the alcove. Seeing him—and in him, perhaps, a target for his anguish and frustrations—Mike exploded. "You people know nothing about this business," he shouted. "I told you it was wrong to put an inexperienced reporter on such a story."

For a moment, Mike's attack seemed to confound Gordon. His head jerked back and he stood frozen for several seconds. "And I told you I don't make the assignments," he said finally, biting each word.

"Then you should have told her not to take it!" Mike cried, blood darkening his skin once again.

Gordon threw up his hands. "Where've you been the last thirty years? Maggie's a grown woman. She makes her own decisions." He was breathing hard. "Look, I'm sorry for you, and for you, Bess, but you're not the only ones hurting here. Christ!" He turned away, walked to a wall and stood there, his back to us. Finally, he turned around, walked slowly back and took a seat.

A few minutes later Dr. Mooney, the young plastic surgeon, appeared, looking as though he'd left all his energy in the operating room. "We've put her back together," he said, speaking carefully. "I know that's not much comfort."

"Can we see her?" Mike said.

"When she's out of recovery. That shouldn't be more than an hour."

I stepped forward. "I'm Zack Tobias, SFPD, Dr. Mooney. Would it be all right if I went along? I won't ask any questions, but she might say something helpful."

"That's up to the parents. I have no objection."

I looked at Mike. He shrugged. "Whatever," he muttered.

It was well past 1:00 A.M. before we saw her, if that's the right verb. Only her eyes, nose and mouth were visible. The rest of her face was swathed in bandages, leaving us to imagine what awful destruction lay beneath them. Gordon and I stood back while Mike and Bess moved to the bed, once again clutching each other. Either Maggie heard them, or else she sensed their presence, because a moment later she turned toward them. Even from my vantage point, I could see her eyes fill with tears, which caught the light from the door. "What did I do?" she beseeched them. "I don't know what I did."

An hour later, I was in an editing room at KUBC's all but deserted studios, trying to answer her question.

Maggie's series had run in five parts under the title *The Bay Area's Changing Face.* I shuddered at the irony as I began to watch the tapes. Part One, focusing on the arrival of immigrant groups to the area from unstable parts of the world—a contingent of Russians, most of them Jews, prominently among them—came quickly to the theme of the series. Standing in the heart of Chinatown, Maggie declared, "In 2028, according to projections of the Demographic Research Unit of the State Department of Finance, Asians will become the largest ethnic group in San Francisco."

Part Two focused on the city's Asian population—28.41 percent of the total as of the 1990 census, and rising every day—and showed how these Asians, the overwhelming number of them Chinese, were transforming several of the city's neighborhoods, particularly the Richmond and the Tenderloin. There were problems, Maggie said, but mostly the Chinese were assimilating well, with only minimal expense to the city.

Part Three dealt with the considerable impact of this migration on the local housing market, particularly during the buying frenzy of the late 1980s. "There were never any official numbers," Maggie said from a residential street in the Richmond, "only anecdotal evidence, stories of Chinese ringing doorbells in neighborhoods like this one and saying to the homeowners, usually through an interpreter, 'I know your house isn't for sale, but what would it take for you to sell it?' " At this point, McGuire & Company's Malin Giddings, one of the city's leading residential realtors, appeared on the screen, recounting how Chinese newcomers would sometimes arrive at the closing of expensive home purchases with bundles of cash in brown paper bags.

By the late eighties, Maggie went on, residential real estate had become more expensive in San Francisco than in any other metropolitan area in the United States. Not even the recession of the early nineties had deprived the city of that dubious distinction, she observed almost wistfully over pictures of fine homes in Atlanta that could be bought for less than a two-bedroom apartment in a marginal San Francisco neighborhood. Today, with the volume of emigration from Hong Kong increasing in anticipation of the takeover of the territory by the Communists in 1997, industry watchers were expecting the pace of real estate transactions to pick up once again.

Part Four jumped to Hong Kong, and to interviews with Chinese there, many of whom had families already in and around San Francisco and planned to join them. In one shot Maggie held up a Chinese newspaper filled, she said, with advertisements offering to assist residents of Hong Kong in finding homes in San Francisco. The next shot was a close-up of the ads. The text was in Chinese, but the photographs conveyed the message. Maggie interviewed officials of the Hong Kong government who, despite evidence to the contrary, insisted that the flight of people and capital from Hong Kong was more a media event than a real one. They pointed to the great investment of capital in the city by major firms, the vast new $21 billion airport complex under construction. "That much is true," she said against a background of the city's famous skyline, "but experts also point out that the profit cycle in Hong Kong is a short one, as short as three years, so there's still just enough time for investors to make big profits before abandoning ship."

Part Five dealt with the potential consequences of Asian migration to the Bay Area. Into this final part—the one in which I'd made a brief appearance—Maggie had folded a two-minute segment on the Hong Kong–based triads and their efforts to form a base in San Francisco.

"The triads are Chinese criminal societies," she said to the camera, looking young and fresh against the backdrop of bustling Hong Kong Harbor. "They came into being three hundred years ago as underground resistance organizations formed to fight oppressive rulers. The triads were extremely popular with the people, and they put up a good struggle, but ultimately they had to accept that they were fighting a losing battle. From then on they put their manpower and organization to more profitable use. Today, the triads dominate every phase of illicit activity in Asia—drugs, contraband, money laundering, prostitution, extortion, murder. In Hong Kong it's illegal to gamble anywhere but at the city's two racetracks, yet gambling goes on all over the city and the triads control most of it. All this criminal activity generates a lot of money, and with the takeover of Hong Kong by the People's Republic of China now just three years away, that money has to go somewhere. Authorities are convinced that a good bit of the money has found its way to the Bay Area." That's where I came in, riding in a patrol car and talking to Maggie about the increase in extortion, gambling, loan-sharking and prostitution among the city's proliferating Asian communities.

The final setup had Maggie on a corner of Clement Street in the heart of New Chinatown, its sidewalks overflowing with shoppers, most of them Asians. "Ironically," she said, "a good portion of that triad money may have been gained illicitly right here at home through the sale of drugs. The drug money is exported from the United States, laundered abroad, then returned here illegally, usually through wire transfers to local banks, from where it finds its way into investment, mostly in real estate. If the amounts the authorities talk about are accurate, the Bay Area could one day be owned by gangsters."

It was, I had to acknowledge at the end of the third screening, a solid piece of work, almost seamless in its structure, well reported and shot. But where was the incitement? There seemed to be nothing in the piece to provoke anyone to attack Maggie. True, its portrait of the triads had been tough and uncompromising. But no names had been named. No specific crimes had been alleged. No finger had been pointed.

It was 4:30 A.M. when I left the station, no wiser than when I had entered. Twenty minutes later, after setting my alarm for 6:50, I slipped into bed next to Britt, trying, in spite of my promise, not to awaken her.

Britt Edström had been my lady for almost a year, a bright, thoughtful, engaging woman of forty-three who looked much younger than I did even though she was a year older. She'd come out from New York two years earlier to set up a gallery specializing in the works of artists from underdeveloped countries, and had quickly prospered. We'd met when, like so many other well-to-do San Franciscans, I'd gone to her gallery in the city's South of Market district to see the huge, explosive oil paintings she was offering at bargain prices—art that had the critics raving.

Britt had come to the States in the late seventies in the company of an American who'd moved to Stockholm during the sixties to avoid the Vietnam war draft. They weren't married but they had a child, a three-year-old boy. Not marrying had been Britt's idea. She's not a radical, not even an activist; she simply possesses a clarity about how she wants to live, and the equanimity to pull it off. She believed that if and when two people tired of each other, they ought to be able to part amicably without the stress of divorce—exactly what had happened in her case eleven years after arriving in New York, where she'd managed to arrange a permanent resident's visa thanks to an auctioneer who'd convinced the Immigration and Naturalization Service that her knowledge of European art and antiques was indispensable to his business. For me, she'd been a godsend.

My ideas about relationships were as singular as Britt's, but where hers flowed from a reasoned viewpoint, mine were a consequence of trauma. I was married at twenty-seven to Elaine Bassett, a lanky, blond English major I'd met at Berkeley who'd warned me at least a hundred times that she wasn't fit to be any man's wife. But I loved her so much that I was certain I could support her through her intermittent bouts of depression. Late one afternoon, in the sixth year of our turbulent marriage and in her thirty-first year of life, she wrote me a four-word note—"I tried. Forgive me."—and swallowed a bottleful of sleeping pills. The experience had left me with such a profound sense of guilt and uncertainty about my qualifications to be a husband that I'd not only been incapable of considering a second marriage, I'd been unwilling to set up house with any of the women with whom I'd been involved in the nine years since Elaine's death. Weekend arrangements, such as the one I'd maintained for the last five months with Britt, had been the best I could manage.

While our weekends together were invariably physical, this particular weekend had been supercharged from the moment she'd walked through the door. She'd arrived, as usual, at seven-thirty on Friday evening, after bicycling from her house on Belgrave Street at the base of Twin Peaks, where she'd dropped off her car, changed from her gallery clothes and picked up her backpack. It's a half-hour ride, with a steep hill at the end, but Britt, a cross-country skier and tennis player as well as a cyclist, had steadfastly turned down my offer to pick her up so that she might shed the week's cares with a workout. I met her at the door, marveling, as I always did, at her face, a testament to the rejuvenating benefits of exercise, the skin smooth and tight, the brown eyes clear, the chin firm. Britt had that wholesomely compelling look you find in advertisements for face soap rather than in high-fashion spreads in *Vogue*. But the real marvel of her face was its genetic mystery. When you learned she was Swedish, you would say, ah, yes, of course, because her hair was light and her skin was fair, but later you might notice that the hair wasn't *that* light, and the skin had a tint of olive, and that the markedly oval shape of her face and her thin, straight nose made her look as though she had just stepped out of a Modigliani portrait, and you wondered if some male ancestor on a trip to Italy hadn't conned some Mediterranean maiden into returning to Sweden with him to lighten the long, dark winters.

But what had driven me to Britt the instant I saw her, even more than her features, was the combination of openness and peacefulness I saw in her face. It was a look that seemed to express not only her acceptance of whatever hand life dealt her but her delight in simple pleasures. And that was exactly the woman she'd turned out to be. Week by week, my affection for her had deepened until I'd realized it was approaching a full-blown love. The deeper my feelings, the greater my problem, because Britt obviously cared for me as well, which made our living arrangement increasingly frustrating. Even her son was no longer an impediment; after living with Britt while he finished high school, he'd gone east to Kenyon College, and spent summers in New York with his father. Only my fears had kept Britt and me from joining forces. How much longer she'd tolerate my anxieties I didn't know.

The moment she entered the apartment I'd sensed that this weekend would be different. It was the way she'd kissed me, not the normal hello peck but a deep, lingering kiss, her mouth fully open, her lips yielding and sensuous, her tongue exploring my mouth. When it finally ended, she took my hand and led me to bed. There, again, she set the pace, favoring me with her hands and lips and tongue, pushing me back onto the pillow each time I tried to enter her. Only when I started to moan did she finally mount me, and even then she made it evident that my gratification was paramount. But when I'd reached for her on awakening Saturday morning, determined to reciprocate, she'd resisted me, saying she wanted us to save ourselves for the evening. Throughout the day, she'd played with me, kissing and stroking me at every opportunity, priming me, she swore, for what would be an unforgettable night. That evening, she'd cooked a Swedish dinner: *gravad lax* with a dill mustard sauce, and then *pytt i panna*, a roast-beef hash that most Swedes deride but I devour, the *gravad lax* accompanied by aquavit, the hash by a huge California cabernet. As I swallowed my last bite, she rose and held out her hand. "I'm dessert," she said with a smile. In the year we'd known each other, we'd probably made love more than a hundred times, but her remark sent tremors into my fingertips.

We took our wineglasses, turned out the lights and moved into the living room. Arms around each other, sipping the last of our wine, we regarded the view down Russian Hill to the bay, diminished yet strangely enhanced by the mist. Then I took Britt's hand, intent on leading her to the bedroom.

"Let's start here," she said, and pulled me to the couch.

We were ten minutes into the sort of inflammatory petting I hadn't done since high school when the telephone rang. "Oh, no," Britt said, and cast me a stricken look as I detached myself from her arms.

Seven hours had passed since my abrupt departure. The moment I settled beside her, she turned and took me in her arms and held me for several minutes, stroking my head and neck. My grunts and murmurs told her how good it felt.

With that encouragement, she pushed me onto my stomach, hiked her nightgown, straddled me, and proceeded to knead the big muscles in my shoulders and back. After several minutes, she moved to my butt, and then my legs, her hands working closer and closer to my groin. By the time she turned me over, I was stiff and ready. "Ah," she said, with a smile. But she didn't touch me there, moving instead to my chest, her fingers kneading my pectorals until they relaxed. In this manner she passed to my arms and then my stomach and once again to my legs, her face at times within inches of my cock, her eyes wide with anticipation. I tried several times to reach for her breasts, but each time I did she pushed me away. At last, she removed her nightgown and lay on top of me, kissing first my eyes, then my ears, then my lips. And then she began to move down my body, kissing and gently biting my nipples until I moaned, then moving her tongue along my sides and my stomach and finally to my cock. "Oh, my God," I cried, wanting it to continue, but fearing the consequences. Finally, unable to stand it, I pushed her off me and, putting her first on her stomach and then on her back, returned her favors in every manner I could think of. When I finally went inside, she was as ready as I was. "Go!" she cried after a few dozen strokes, and we did, together.

We stayed together for several minutes afterward, kissing lightly and gazing at each other. "Without diminishing all the sex that's preceded it," I said at last, "that *was* unforgettable."

"That was the idea," Britt said.

"What's going on? What's this all about?"

"Sleep," she said, gently pushing me away. "We'll talk at break-fast."

She slept at once. But I stayed awake. In spite of the sex I was still wired. I thought about poor Maggie Winehouse, traumatized and disfigured, undoubtedly for life. I searched my memory for crimes of this nature, and couldn't come up with one. And then I thought about Britt, breathing deeply and evenly beside me, and the mystery of her actions since Friday night. At six-thirty I finally gave up and slipped out of bed. At seven, I called Chief Doyle on the kitchen phone. "I hope I didn't wake you," I began.

"The mayor did," he said. His voice sounded like a gravel mixer. "At six o'clock. He's really shook. Keeps talking about '77: 'I don't want a repeat of '77. I don't want a repeat of '77.' "

"Who does?" I said. It was on a summer evening in 1977, four years after I'd joined the force, when members of a Chinese gang burst into the Golden Dragon restaurant in San Francisco's Chinatown and opened fire on the patrons, believing many of them to be members of a rival gang attempting to break *their* gang's monopoly on the sale of firecrackers within the Chinese community. Five people were killed, another eleven injured, not one of them connected in any way to the rival gang.

Until the Golden Dragon Massacre, as the newspapers immediately tagged it, the San Francisco Police Department had maintained an arm's-length policy toward Chinatown, preferring to let the community—which it didn't pretend to understand—police itself. Given the tremendous influx of Asians into San Francisco and a concurrent increase in Asian crime, the massacre obliged the SFPD to acknowledge the existence of a problem that had been building for a long time. Overnight, the chief of police, Jerry Doyle's predecessor, ordered the formation of a Gang Task Force within the police department's Intelligence Bureau, its immediate task to investigate the massacre and stop the revenge killings taking place in its wake. Everyone in the department had expected the task force to dissolve once those missions had been completed, but seventeen years later it was still in business, its work expanded to include black and Latino gangs as well.

"Did you look at those programs?" the chief asked.

"I did."

"And?"

"As I remembered them. Competent but innocuous."

"No clues?" A life on the police force had trained the chief to detach his work from his feelings. But he asked the question as though he knew the answer would disappoint him.

I didn't let him down. "None."

"Then keep looking until you find something," he said grimly. "In the meanwhile I'm putting two dozen Chinese cops in Chinatown tomorrow morning, wearing plain clothes, to see what they can pick up. I need something by Tuesday morning."

"What's happening on Tuesday morning?"

"The mayor's inviting a group of civic leaders to his office to tell them everything he's doing to head off trouble, and to ask for their help." His voice lowered as he spoke, each word like the next note in a descending scale. "He'll be an unhappy mayor if I haven't got something for him by then, which will make me an unhappy chief, which will make you an unhappy cop, I promise you. So get your ass in gear." With that he hung up.

If the chief was threatening me, he had to be truly scared. I'm the nearest thing to a sacred cow on the force, not so much from my political connections as from my mother's. Sadie Tobias, a vigorous, youthful sixty-seven, is arguably the most influential woman in San Francisco and a testament to how well Jews are integrated into the city's society. She's certainly the best connected, on the boards of the city's two most important cultural organizations—the opera and symphony—as well as a heavy supporter of the ballet and our several art museums. But most important, Sadie is the maker and keeper of The List, that collection of names from which guests are drawn for any major event hosted by the city. The prince and princess of Japan are coming to San Francisco? The List determines who's invited to the official reception. That assignment, which carries no title and pays no salary, had come from Mayor Putnam, a friend and legal counselor of forty years, in whose behalf Mother had organized yearly fund-raisers since his belated entry into politics. Once a month the mayor and his wife ate dinner at our family home in Pacific Heights. As long as the food agreed with him, I figured, my job was secure. I was too tired, in any case, to take the chief's threat seriously. I returned to bed, curled up next to Britt and slept at last.

When I woke up it was nearly noon. I took a long hot shower, shaved, put on jeans, a work shirt and sneakers, my favorite Sunday attire, and went to the kitchen. Britt, dressed almost identically, her long, light brown hair pulled back in a ponytail, smiled, kissed me, handed me a glass of freshly squeezed orange juice and pushed me onto a counter stool. Then, using an omelette pan, she cooked Swedish pancakes, my favorite, and presented them to me along with a rasher of bacon. "Now I *know* something's up," I said. "Are you going to talk, or do I have to give you the third degree?"

She sat on the stool next to mine, covered my left hand with her right hand, and said with more sadness than I'd ever heard in her voice, "What's up is that I won't be spending weekends with you any-more."

I put my fork down and stared at her, my appetite gone. She stared back, her brown eyes locking with mine. "Do I get an explanation?" I said.

"Of course," she said at once, as though she'd expected to be asked and wanted to supply it. "After trying not to for almost a year, I've fallen in love with you."

In the quiet that followed, I could hear our breathing. "Why would that change things?" I asked, although I was sure I knew the answer.

She squeezed my hand, and then released it. "It makes weekends inadequate," she said softly but definitively. Then she took a breath and sighed. "Which means that I have to extricate myself before it's terminal. It's not quite terminal yet."

I felt dismayed and cornered and frightened all in the same moment. Part of me wanted to preserve my independence. The other part of me suspected that this could be my last and best chance to have a life with a loving woman. "So the sex and the meals and the special attention—"

"Were to give both of us a wonderful memory."

I took some time to formulate my next question. "What is it you would like to have happen, Britt?" I asked. I had to force myself to say the words.

Her look seemed to blend tenderness, concern and perplexity. "I can't answer that question. I can't ask you to be one thing or another thing. I can only accept what you are." She looked at me intently, her brow compressed, her eyes seeming to beg me to understand her. "You know how strongly I believe in the right of people to live as they wish, so long as they don't hurt other people, but I never told you where the conviction came from or why I feel it so strongly. It came from an indelible, quite terrible lesson I learned as a child."

She paused then, I supposed to gird herself for the obviously painful memory she was about to resurrect, and in that moment, I reminded myself how dearly I loved the way she spoke English—all but sang it, really—so formal and correct and exact, and yet so melodious and lightly tinged with a Swedish accent, and I realized how unimaginable it was that I would not have that voice in my life.

"Your food's getting cold," she said, glancing at my untouched plate.

"Never mind my food," I said. "Go on."

She took a deep breath, exhaled and said, "Ah, God," the sorrow in her voice a match for the look in her eyes. "My parents were the classic story of two good people not being good with each other. The physical part was fine—too fine actually, because they were both striking and their chemical attraction kept them together when they should have parted. You'd hear them arguing, saying the most terrible things to each other, and half an hour later, you'd come into the kitchen or the living room and there they'd be, holding on to each other as though each would fall if the other let go. Within minutes they'd be in the bedroom."

She nodded now, as if to reinforce the truth of her memory. "It was Mother who initiated the arguments. At some point after they married, she'd decided that my father wasn't sufficiently bright or creative or lively for her, and that she'd made a mistake. Instead of leaving him, as she should have, she remained with him, but she let him know in every way she could that he didn't measure up. He lived a wretched life, drank a great deal—as unhappy Swedes are apt to do—and died before his time."

She paused for a moment, her expression intent, her absorption so complete it seemed as though her words had carried her back to that time. "My father was a kind and decent man, gentle and thoughtful and quiet," she said, expressing each of those qualities as though she had given them long and careful consideration. "Many other women would have cherished him. My mother had no right to punish him for being who he was. No one has a right to do that to anyone."

She sighed yet again, and looked away for a moment, as though searching for some missing thought, and then looked back at me and, raising her right hand, gently touched my cheek. "You are who you are for a very good reason, and I have no right to ask you to change." Then she dropped her hand to the counter.

I could hardly claim that I hadn't seen it coming. "Are you sure you know who I am?" I asked, for lack of a better defense.

"No," she said emphatically, her eyes enlarging as if to punctuate her statement, "I'm not sure at all, and that's part of the problem. I know what *kind* of a man you are—gentle, in complete contradiction to your size, unselfish in your lovemaking, thoughtful and decent and determined to save the world all by yourself. But those are descriptions, not explanations. I know nothing about what made you the way you are."

"I can't believe that," I said, my voice betraying my bewilderment. "I've got nothing to hide."

"Oh, Zachary," Britt said, tilting her head and looking at me as though I'd just told a fib. "You are a closed book. When I try to talk about such things, you change the subject. You've never talked about your childhood. You've never talked about your family. You've never talked about why you continue doing what you're doing when you find it so dissatisfying so much of the time and you don't need the money. As for Elaine and your marriage . . ." She stopped, threw up her hands and shook her head. After a minute she reached for my hand and looked into my eyes, and spoke with quiet urgency. "I know how much you loved Elaine. Maybe you're the kind of man who has only one love in his life. And maybe the reason you're unwilling to live with another woman is that doing so would require you to acknowledge that your one true love is dead. That's something only you can answer."

She kissed me lightly on the lips, and left the kitchen. A few minutes later I heard the front door close. And then I heard the roar of emptiness.

3

Elaine.

I saw her one crisp fall morning of my senior year, a month after the start of classes, as I was entering the Berkeley campus through Sather Gate. She was walking with a loping stride, her straight, light, shoulder-length hair bouncing with each step, her books held against her breasts, her achingly mournful eyes resolutely focused on her path—a defense, I was certain, against the stares she'd surely evoked from men since she became a teenager. She was tall—something that attracts me because of my own height—and lean, as distinguished from thin, which told me that she liked to be active. Much later I would discover that she took daily solitary walks in the Berkeley hills. I judged her to be not more than nineteen, which proved to be true, but the seriousness with which she regarded the world from behind that heart-stopping face suggested the concerns and understanding of a person twice her age. I was immediately smitten.

I'd become a minor campus celebrity by that point, the centerpiece, it was said, of a defensive line that, along with an offense led by Steve Bartkowski and Chuck Muncie, was giving Cal—the University of

California, Berkeley—some of its best football in years. For that reason I'd been featured on the sports pages of the Bay Area's newspapers, which, not surprisingly, had identified me as a descendant of
Gold Rush pioneers, the son of a leader of San Francisco's Jewish
community—an oddity in itself, they might have added had it been
politically correct to do so, since not many Jewish kids played college
football—and a future cop, dedicated to eradicating the conditions
that had indirectly led to my father's death. The weekend following
his murder, the *Dispatch* had run a feature about him, with side-by-
side pictures of the two of us in our Cal football uniforms, minus hel-
mets. We looked like twins: tall, muscular but lean, with thick, wavy
black hair, big-boned faces, broad noses and smiles so wide and seemingly friendly that more than a few readers must have wondered why
we'd elected to play such a brutal contact sport.

Had Elaine read the stories, which it turned out she hadn't, only
my choice of career would have impressed her. She took no part in
campus life, had no interest in football, and was as indifferent to my
wealth as she was to my history. Her own family had been in California almost as long as mine, her forebears having migrated from Illinois in the 1870s. Her father was a fourth-generation cattle rancher
and farmer, with huge landholdings in the San Joaquin Valley and
the deltas west of Sacramento. The oldest of three children, she was a
source of dismay, even anguish, to her father. Rather than thank her
lucky stars for her privileged birth, she had renounced all claim to the
family fortune, rejected her father's help and struck out on her own
the morning after graduation from high school, carrying little more
than the clothes she was wearing—jeans, a work shirt, a denim
jacket and sneakers, the standard uniform of the era.

If the flower child movement hadn't already existed by that point,
Elaine would have invented it. She believed her father's generation had gotten it all wrong—a belief for which, even then, there
was more supporting evidence than at any time in our nation's history. The war in Vietnam was about to end, but the emotions it
had aroused had polarized the country, and the money to pay for
it had been diverted from domestic programs. However justly her
father had come by his wealth, however hard he'd worked to increase
it, Elaine could not bear the burden of being rich in a country in
which nearly forty million people lived below the poverty level. She

had set forth believing she could right such wrongs by example and protest. When she discovered she couldn't, she decided to become a writer in the hope of communicating her concerns to others. That's what had finally gotten her off the road and onto the Berkeley campus, and persuaded her to accept tuition money from her maternal grandmother.

Technically, she was already a writer when she enrolled at Berkeley, because she'd been writing almost since she could hold a crayon. She'd written her first story at seven, her first book at ten. It couldn't have been more than two thousand words, but it was divided into chapters, and it told a complete story of a girl and her mother. It ended with the mother's death, by suicide, when the girl was six. Autobiographical, of course, in every respect save the names.

Elaine's mother, Allison Patten, a Sacramento merchant's daughter, had not simply been adjudged not good enough for Samuel Barrett by his parents and three sisters, she'd been virtually shunned. The consequence was a feeling of unworthiness that produced an intractable depression. A year after her marriage, Allison, then twenty-three, had committed herself to a live-in clinic run by a woman psychiatrist. She'd emerged a year later better but not cured. Both the psychiatrist and Samuel Barrett had thought children would be the answer; they couldn't have been more wrong. Rather than give her a sense of worthiness, the act of bringing children into a world she perceived as so ineradicably unjust had only deepened Allison's depression. After struggling through her twenties, and dutifully bearing their three children, she'd written a poignant farewell and swallowed two dozen sleeping pills. She was thirty-one.

I didn't learn any of this until well after Elaine and I finally met, which didn't occur until six months after that first sighting. I'd never before been shy with women. To the contrary, I'd already imagined myself in love half a dozen times, aggressively courted the objects of my ardor and managed to awaken their passions in all but one case. But with Elaine I'd found it impossible to walk up and introduce myself, let alone ask for a date. There was a sternness to those elegant features, seemingly frozen into a state of perplexed concern, that broadcast a "No trespassing" warning. Whenever I saw her on campus, I could only follow her in a daze.

I came to know her schedule as well as my own: the times and locations of her classes, her study hours in the library, where she had morning coffee, where she ate lunch. Whenever possible I would race from my own classes in order to be outside hers when they broke, or arrange my library visits to coincide with hers, or eat where she ate. As big as I am, you would have thought she'd have noticed me. But she never looked at me; she never looked at anyone. She seemed to exist in a constant state of suspension from the reality around her, as though whatever was going on in her mind had preempted other concerns. Except for a coincidence, I might have graduated without speaking to her.

Late one rainy Friday afternoon in April I set out from the campus for a dinner date with my mother. As I drove onto University Avenue and turned toward the bay there was Elaine, holding a sign in one hand that said SF, and a small duffel bag in the other. I braked abruptly, too startled to be nervous, unable to believe my luck. "Thanks," she said as she got in the car, her voice tinged with melancholy, as I'd somehow known it would be. For a moment I was so mesmerized by those mournful eyes, which I now saw were blue, that I did nothing. The honk of a horn behind me broke the spell. As I drove down University Avenue, Elaine explained that she was going to the city to spend the weekend with friends in the Haight-Ashbury. She spoke softly, and with a slightly patrician accent that suggested some years at a private school. As we crawled along the Eastshore Freeway and then onto the Bay Bridge in the usual Friday-afternoon traffic jam, she answered my questions with such reluctance it dawned on me that she wasn't haughty at all. She was simply, painfully shy. Never before had I been grateful to be stuck in traffic; it took us half an hour to get across the bridge. By the time we reached the city I knew I was in love in a way I'd never been before.

Elaine finished her freshman year still hopeful that she could eventually involve herself in the work of the world. During her sophomore year, my first out of college, she would spend weekends at my apartment in the city, and I could almost measure the drop in her confidence level from week to week. By her junior year she sensed that she was neither exceptional nor bold enough to make a difference. She was no more religious than I was, but she came to believe that her fate had been predestined, a consequence of a gene map as precise and comprehensive as a computer program, and that there was nothing she could do to alter it. Like her mother, she developed feelings of unworthiness, feelings her professors reinforced by giving her Bs and Cs. "You're wasting your time," one of them, a newly tenured English professor in her late thirties whose stories had been published in obscure but prestigious literary magazines, wrote on one of Elaine's stories. "You'll never be a writer. If you want to save the world, as this content suggests, I suggest you change your major from English to sociology."

I tried to convince Elaine that the professor didn't know what she was talking about. I even suggested that since she was an exceedingly heavy and homely woman, she resented Elaine because she was so beautiful, and took unconscious satisfaction in disparaging her intellectual qualifications. But nothing worked.

By Elaine's senior year I'd asked her to marry me at least fifty times. She, of course, had refused, citing her supposed unworthiness. She knew I loved children and would want to have some, and she used that as another argument against marriage. In no case, she said, would she consider bringing children into a world as unredeemed as the one we lived in. I was afraid to point out to her that if her mother, who'd harbored those exact feelings, had acted on them, we would not be discussing children of our own.

It wasn't until a year after Elaine graduated that I was able to persuade her to move in with me. By then, having abandoned all thoughts of writing, she'd found a job at a free clinic south of Market Street, in the seamiest part of downtown San Francisco. I hoped the work would produce in her that sense of validation she'd sought for so long, but the malnourished and diseased junkies who staggered through the clinic only reinforced her convictions about the basic inhumanity of our social system. She wasn't a communist or even a socialist; her argument was that *nothing* worked. Nothing I could say or do could persuade her otherwise. If anything, my own working experience underscored her argument.

That experience, for the most part, had been dismal, despite my well-publicized climb through the ranks. I'd entered the police academy immediately after graduation to the kind of publicity that had me cringing: JOCK TO COP and SON OF S.F. SOCIALITE CHOOSES LIFE ON THE BEAT. That sort of thing. The attention doomed me with my academy classmates, some of whom accused me of grandstanding, and, far more seriously, of taking a spot that might have gone to someone who needed the money. That slumming rich-guy image, which bothered me far more than the inevitable half-joking, half-serious slurs against Jews, pursued me onto the force. Wherever I was assigned, my commanding officers—one of them Jerome Doyle, son of a laborer—made certain I got the worst hours and details. It was mostly grunt work involving traffic, petty crime and auto theft; it had nothing whatever to do with the lofty objectives that had motivated me to choose police work in the wake of my father's murder.

I like to think of myself as resolute, but my mother calls me stubborn and she's probably right. Whatever the truth, I stuck it out on the force, moving quickly up the promotion ladder in spite of the strikes against me. Regulations mandated periodic increases in rank and salary, except for cause, to those who passed the qualifying exams, and I not only passed those tests, I made sure my work was blameless. The bottom line, of course, was that my superiors didn't dare hold me back, I was simply too visible—knowledge that only served to reinforce their feelings about me. But the work didn't change; I engaged no grand issues. Whatever my rank, I knew—as a friend once said in another context—that I was only failing on a higher level.

By this point, the mid-eighties, Elaine was failing in a far more serious manner. She'd finally married me in 1979—the only way, she'd said, to get me to stop nagging her. But before another two years had passed, she'd become so depressed—"The world stinks and I can't change it," she'd repeat over and over—that she was convinced she would end her life as her mother had. The more depressed she became, the more bound up my life became in her salvation. I took her on study trips to Scandinavia, Germany, Japan, anyplace that showed promise of social or economic progress, clipped rare upbeat articles from newspapers and magazines, combed the reviews for books on social reform. Nothing worked. Late one evening in the fifth year of our marriage, as we sat in the dark in our apartment on the twelfth floor of 999 Green Street, gazing at the twinkling magic of San Francisco at night, Elaine, her voice soft and melancholy as always, delivered the ultimate crusher.

"How," she said, "can you ask me to believe that what I do could change anything when you can't change anything yourself?" It was the end of a long evening's argument, but also, I sensed, the end of the debate we'd been waging since her junior year in college. She spoke from behind a barrier so thick by this point that I knew I could never crack it. A coldness settled on my heart as I recognized my defeat, not against the inertia of the system, which in my stubbornness I would continue to battle, but against the despair that was destroying my wife. A year later she was dead.

The shock that permeated every molecule of my body in the hours after Elaine died wasn't from surprise, because I'd known intellectually that she'd eventually take her life, and had even sensed that she'd do it in her thirty-first year, as her mother had. What I felt was more like what one feels in the immediate aftermath of danger, when the adrenaline, no longer needed by specific muscles, races randomly through the system and shakes it uncontrollably.

My lieutenant on the Gang Task Force—where I'd been working since the early eighties—told me to take a week off, the first human gesture from a superior I'd been shown since joining the force. But I stayed on the job. I dreaded that moment in the day or night when, my duties finished, all other options gone, my system demanding sleep, I was compelled to return to our apartment high above the city. The magic of those views was gone; to me the world looked as lusterless and out of focus as it must to a nearsighted person without glasses. Wherever I turned, I visualized Elaine, curled into a corner of the sofa, or seated at the dining table, or at the kitchen sink, or in the shower, or, worst of all, in bed, where she had clung to me as though I were her only hope on earth. I thought her presence would diminish and eventually disappear; when I realized it wouldn't, I began to look for another apartment. But her spirit—and her challenge—remained with me even after I was resettled in my present place, and would have even if I had moved to Timbuktu.

Remembering all this now in the wake of Britt's departure, I wondered whether it was my doubts about my qualifications for mating that had kept me from committing anew, or whether my real fear was of being found out, once again, as a man who didn't matter.

Britt had brought the Sunday paper in and left it on the living-room coffee table, in front of my favorite chair. I turned on the stereo, sank into the chair, and picked up the front section. The story about

Maggie Winehouse was in the lead spot, under a two-column head-line: SAVAGE, MYSTERIOUS ATTACK ON BAY AREA NEWSWOMAN. It briefly described the abduction, the attack—mostly an educated recon-struction pieced together from interviews with the paramedics and myself—the scene at the hospital involving Mike and Bess Wine-house, Maggie's background and her series on Asian immigration to the Bay Area. There was no speculation about cause and effect, but the implication was there.

I leafed quickly through the rest of the paper, unable to concen-trate. When I finished, I stared at the bay. It seemed unusually calm, its surface looking on this overcast day like a gigantic piece of rolled steel. The only boats on the water were pleasure craft; the only ones making progress were powered; all of the sailboats seemed becalmed, their sails slack.

I called the hospital, and spoke to Maggie's nurse, who told me that Maggie was still being sedated, and would be out of it for hours. Orders or no orders, there was nothing to learn from her until we could talk to her, so I decided to remain where I was, figuring that given what I'd just been through, I needed some sedation myself. In that mood and for that reason, I turned on the TV, found nothing that grabbed me—not even a football game I cared about, the 49ers having already trounced the Redskins at RFK Stadium earlier in the day—and was about to turn off the set when the hourly bulletins came on. Not surprisingly, Maggie's story led the newscast, but with-out any new information.

At that point, some visceral response pulled me from my shelter and out into a world even more bleak than the one I'd returned from early that morning. The chief was on my back, I hadn't so much as a whiff of a lead on an explosive case, and I had lost my woman. My throat burned, my stomach was churning, and as I drove to the hos-pital my limbs jerked as though they were being manipulated by a puppeteer.

Almost as many reporters as had been there the evening before were in the hospital waiting room—a big crowd for a Sunday. They all started toward me, but I waved them off and headed swiftly for the elevators. I got off on the third floor and walked down the hall to Mag-gie's room. A guard was posted at the door, courtesy, I was sure, of Chief Doyle. Inside sat Mike Winehouse, for whom that gesture had surely been made, and, of course, his wife, both of them staring silently and uncomprehendingly at the bed on which their daughter lay in a drug-induced sleep. I could see that I wouldn't be talking to Maggie that day, which frustrated me, but I figured that for her it was something of a blessing. At least she'd be spared for another day from thinking about this hideous attack, and what it had done to her life.

Seeing me, Mike stood up quickly and tiptoed into the hallway. "Anything new?" he asked me hopefully. I'd seen that same look on a hundred different faces: victims and their loved ones eager for vengeance—not justice, vengeance—as though it were a miracle drug that could heal their wounds. And he was wounded, no question—not, God knows, as badly as Maggie had been, because his wounds were invisible, but they would scar him nonetheless and pain him for the rest of his life, and the suffering, already visible, would probably never leave his face.

"No," I said, wishing there were something, anything, I could give him, "nothing new."

He sighed, sagged against the wall of the corridor, and closed his eyes. Perhaps it was his day-old beard, but he looked exhausted, as though he hadn't slept more than a few hours, if that. His clothes—a pair of gray wool slacks, yesterday's shirt and a blue wool cardigan sweater I would bet he wore at home each morning when he wrote his column—hung on his slumping body.

I waited several seconds until he opened his eyes, then asked, "Has Maggie said anything?"

He shook his head slowly. "No," he said, "not a word."

With that, Mike walked slowly back into the room. I followed.

Bess was in a corner of the darkened room, so obviously weary that even sitting seemed like an effort. She was wearing a black warm-up suit and sneakers—another around-the-house getup, I figured—which testified to her own harried state, because she'd always struck me as the kind of woman who would normally never leave her home, not even to buy groceries, without careful grooming.

I walked up to her, squeezed her shoulder, then looked toward the bed. Maggie was breathing deeply. I waited another minute, then, suddenly oppressed by the overwhelming sadness in the room, nodded good-bye to Mike and Bess and tiptoed into the corridor.

Five minutes later, having evaded the reporters by using a side door, I was in my car, weaving impatiently through the Sunday traffic toward Crissy Field, just inside the Presidio at the north edge of the city, where windsurfers launch their rigs into San Francisco Bay. Feeling a breeze as I walked to my garage, I'd strapped my board and sail onto my 4Runner's roof rack and thrown my wetsuit into the back, in the hope that I might get an hour on the bay. But the serene view I'd contemplated from my apartment had been the proverbial calm before the storm. As I stepped from my car and walked to the beach, I could feel a wind roaring in through the Golden Gate, heralding an approaching front, the first of the rainy season. The sky was a jumble of contrasts, clear patches surrounded by huge black clouds racing toward the city. In the distance the sun was descending behind the Golden Gate Bridge. The southern half of the bridge was backlighted by shafts of light so brilliant they shrank one's pupils to pins; the northern half of the bridge disappeared into dense fog. The bay was flecked with whitecaps, giving the windsurfers all they could handle as they beat it to shore. Sailboats, too, were tacking toward their harbors.

Disappointed, but desperate for some exercise, I turned my back to the wind and jogged east to the Marina Green and then along the jetty beyond the St. Francis Yacht Club. At the end of the jetty is a wave organ, a series of pipes set vertically into cement and down close to the waterline in a way that causes each pipe to emit different sounds, depending on the wave. Usually on a Sunday the seats built into the rocks are all taken. But the impending storm must have driven everyone off, because for the next several minutes I sat alone, marginally sheltered by the rocks, listening to a cacophony.

From my vantage point I could look across the inlet to the city, beyond the flatland of the Marina to the houses and apartment buildings climbing Telegraph Hill and Russian Hill, and the great mansions atop Pacific Heights. I suppose it was the state of mind I'd brought to the moment, but the city, still caught in the piercing shafts of the descending sun, and with pitch-black clouds racing toward it, seemed helpless to defend itself from the approaching storm.

I got to my car just as the storm broke, and drove home in a rain so fierce that at one point my wipers were unable to clear the windshield and I had to stop my car.

A package, about the size of a shirt box, awaited me at my door. It was wrapped in brown paper obviously torn from a shopping bag, and addressed in large, crude capital letters, the kind made by people who learned to write the English alphabet as adults.

A combination of instinct and training directed me away from the package and back to my car, from where, it being Sunday, I called Pat Stacker of the bomb squad at home. Pat was one of the few in my class at the police academy who'd been on my side.

"I'm gonna feel pretty stupid if I get your detail all excited and this turns out to be a false alarm," I said after I'd described the package.

"Why don't I handle it myself?"

I faltered. "I hate to ask that," I said.

"You didn't. I suggested it."

"Can whoever's on duty keep his mouth shut?"

"He will if he wants to keep his job."

Pat arrived in half an hour—a tall, slim, soft-spoken Irishman who'd married his high school sweetheart, produced five children and probably wasn't finished. I thought about his family as he removed the package to his truck, did whatever crazy things demolition experts do and waved me over. "Someone sent you a present," he said, holding up a large white T-shirt. An inscription was printed across the front: *You can't be first, but you can be next.*

I stared at the T-shirt in silence. "I don't get it," I finally said.

"Take a look in the box," Pat said.

I did. At the bottom of the box was a cleaver, its rectangular blade long and thin.

4

The first time I saw the T-shirt it was being worn by a full-figured woman in her mid-thirties walking on Fillmore Street in Pacific Heights, a shopping and restaurant area popular with yuppies and affluent older couples. I smiled at the implied invitation, wondered what the world was coming to and passed her by. Then, on an impulse, I turned and followed her, curious to see how others would react. It was vastly entertaining: men *and* women glancing at the woman, then looking quickly and guiltily away, then doing a double take, glancing back once again to read and contemplate the message. One couple in their seventies stared in astonished disapproval at the woman, but most of the passersby at least managed a smile, some grinned and one couple laughed out loud. The woman kept walking, acknowledging none of the reactions her T-shirt had inspired.

This time the message shrank my scrotum. I stared at the open box for a moment before turning to Pat. He was frowning, looking quizzically and apprehensively at me. He knew a threat when he saw one, even if he didn't know the details. "Any idea who sent it?" he asked.

"None," I said. "Any chance this can be between us?"

"You got it, Zack," he said. He looked at me for another moment, then stuck out his hand. "Take care of yourself," he said.

"You, too," I said.

He climbed into his truck and was gone.

I hadn't lied to Pat—I *didn't* know who'd sent the package—but I hadn't told him the truth, either, because I had several ideas about the kind of person who might have sent it.

It figured that whoever had ordered the hit on Maggie had seen me on television, knew I was in charge of the case and was trying to scare me away. Assuming this person had addressed the package himself, he was foreign-born, writing in a second, newly familiar language, but had a sufficient command of English to appreciate the humor of the message on the T-shirt. Most important, this person had access to at least one of the Hong Kong triads or was a member himself—the only deduction possible given the inclusion of the cleaver. In my years on the force, there hadn't been a single instance of a San Francisco–based criminal using a cleaver. But triad hit men—usually operating out of Hong Kong—used them all the time.

You try hard in this business to avoid premature conclusions, but it was tough to resist the one that slipped into my mind: that Maggie's series had somehow, in some way, aroused a major triad figure. Since the mid-eighties, when the British government had agreed to relinquish control of Hong Kong to the People's Republic of China in July 1997, U.S. law enforcement officials had assumed that the various Hong Kong triads would install point men in major American cities to supervise the transfer and investment of their assets. These point men, it was further assumed, wouldn't be thugs; they'd be coat-and-tie business types or lawyers, men with ample education but few, if any, scruples, eager to enrich themselves in the process of investing the assets of their gangster bosses. With the hit on Maggie, and now this threat against me, I had my first intimation that at least one of these Chinese *consiglieri* had landed.

I'd been in threatening situations maybe half a dozen times as a cop, but the threats had been immediate and visible. This was the first time I'd been threatened by something I couldn't see. I didn't like the queasy feeling it gave me—undoubtedly what whoever was out there had intended.

The moment I entered my apartment I disarmed the burglar alarm.

Normally I didn't reset the alarm until bedtime, but this time I reset it at once. Then I went to the bureau in my bedroom, removed a .357 Smith & Wesson from the top drawer and took the gun with me to the living room—something I had never done before. Then I planted myself in front of the television set, if only to fill the apartment with the sound of human voices.

The absence of fresh material had not prevented the Maggie Winehouse story from spreading as insistently as an oil spill. That evening it made the newscasts of all the major networks. By the next morning, Monday, November 7, the question of what Maggie had done to provoke such a bizarre and cruel attack was being asked in newspapers and on television programs throughout the country.

Ultimately, I knew, everyone would look to me for the answer. As I thought about that, the terrible feeling I get at the start of every case swept over me once again, the conviction that I was not only not up to the challenge but wouldn't even know where to start. Unless the undercover work in Chinatown produced a lead or Maggie Winehouse had a clue, I had nowhere to turn—and in my mind, I'd already discounted the likelihood of any leads from Chinatown, no matter how many undercover cops Jerry Doyle put in there. If the hit on Maggie had been ordered locally, they might get word of it, but given the warning I'd received I didn't think they would. Even without that clue to go on, my gut had told me that the attack had been ordered from abroad. The criminal elements of San Francisco's Asian community live by a cardinal rule: Never fuck with the police or the press. Logic suggested that whoever had ordered the hit didn't know the second part of the rule, and was therefore from out of town.

That morning, more than ever, the drive to my office struck me as a quick descent from heaven to hell. It began at the top of Russian Hill, where immaculate, well-fortified apartment buildings and multimillion-dollar homes surround a block-square park built on top of an underground reservoir. I drove down Hyde Street, past clanging cable cars the first several blocks, each block lower than the last, the lower the block the lower its caliber, until I was in the Tenderloin, San Francisco's collecting place for the discards of our social system, no different, probably, from the rotting areas of every American city, yet more incongruous and disturbing in San Francisco because of its proximity to such wealth and beauty. As I passed through this down-

and-out neighborhood, I was less than a five-minute drive from my home, where I lived the American dream. Here, in the aftermath of the storm and the first light of day, homeless people, many looking exceedingly damp, were already lined up outside soup kitchens. On one corner, a Latino family—father, mother and four children—appearing stunned and lost, stood silently, unable, it seemed, to grasp how fate had brought them to a land so strange, so unpromising and so cold.

A mile southeast of the Tenderloin is the building where I work.

Among government buildings around the world, our Hall of Justice at 850 Bryant must set the standard for ugliness: a squat, unadorned, seven-story granite structure a block long and half a block wide, mercifully shielded along its south-facing length by eleven majestic sycamore trees whose tips, reaching to the fifth floor, sway in the ever-present breeze. In the lobby mottled green and black linoleum-tile floors clash with marble walls streaked with an unsettling color somewhere between red and rust, the unattractiveness of each material magnified by its proximity to the other. A makeshift screening system just inside the entry, more appropriate to a Third World country, suggests how quickly modern problems have outpaced designs to cope with them, and a sense of general scruffiness attests to the passage of the millions of unwilling visitors who have entered the building since its doors opened in 1960.

My office is in Room 558, a cheerless space ten feet high, forty feet wide and fifty feet long, crammed with cubicles—one of them mine—along three walls, and nineteen desks in the center, all separated by partitions, each covered with photographs, newspaper clippings and memoranda that summarize the professional and personal life of its occupant. Never in my life, not even playing ball at Cal, have I met a group of people more devoted to one another. Every one of them had been invited to join the Gang Task Force; every one was here because he or she wanted to be. Whatever racial or religious biases they had brought into this room had ultimately been preempted by the more pressing concern of keeping one another alive. Eventually, I had even been forgiven my wealth. If my years on the Gang Task Force had been my happiest as a cop, the members of that unit are the reason why. Not all of them are perfect; every so often, one of them disappoints the rest of us by succumbing to temptation—no surprise to the rest of the force. When it was formed in 1977 to deal with Asian gangs, the task force was regarded by most Caucasian cops as a blind alley, short and narrow and leading nowhere, just like Spofford or Waverly or any of those dark little streets in Chinatown. It was widely believed that the only reason a Caucasian cop would choose the task force was to get onto the take, shaking down illegal gambling operations, after-hours bars, prostitutes, health code violators and so on. When I joined the unit in 1983, there was one Caucasian who fit that description, a sergeant named Joseph Pendola, several years my senior, a bachelor of dark temperament and mysterious habits, one of which, it was rumored, was raising carrier pigeons and eating those that didn't perform to his standards. My first act on assuming command of the Asian squad six years later was to get him transferred. But Pendola had been an exception. On the whole, the members of the Gang Task Force bring an intense, dedicated and honorable attitude to work each day.

It was a few minutes after eight when I arrived. As usual, the office was empty, except for Jim Mich, a member of the Asian squad and one of the few original members of the Gang Task Force, the one man who invariably beats me to work. "Hey," he called out as I passed his cubicle. "Any breaks?"

"None," I answered, surprising as well as disappointing myself. If there was anyone I should have been willing to share my concerns with, it was Jim. He'd been the man most responsible for whatever gratification I'd experienced as a cop. I'd gotten to know him when I was still a patrolman, working in the Richmond district. The area was just then being settled by Chinese whose entry into the United States had been facilitated by a relaxation in the immigration laws. After all that grunt work, I'd finally managed to talk my way into a school car, which meant that most of my shifts were spent dealing with juvenile crimes and disturbances reported by teachers and principals. Because so many of the problems among Asian kids seemed gang-related, I'd called the Gang Task Force to see what I could learn. It was a cold call; I'd known no one in the unit. It was my good luck that the receptionist, after hearing what I was after, had transferred me to Jim. He not only became my mentor, he recommended my transfer into the unit when the first opening came up. Over the years he'd earned my trust. Not only would it have been comforting to share my burdens, it would have been wise as well. But I couldn't bring myself to do that, not even with him. I wanted to believe it was because I felt I should get a handle on what had happened before getting anyone else excited. But it also struck me that maybe Britt was right. Maybe I *was* a closed book.

Jim sprang from his chair and followed me into my cubicle. He was a man of fifty-five with the body of a forty-year-old, so light on his sneakered feet he seemed to be walking on air. Had Pablo Picasso run marathons, as Jim did, he would have looked like Jim's father. Same powerful face and wide-open, wondering eyes. Like most members of the Gang Task Force, Jim held two ranks: sergeant and inspector. Had he wished, he could have made captain long ago. But captains run departments—unthinkable to Jim. He was far happier making busts.

"I've been thinkin' about the Winehouse case," he said, a hint of promise in his voice.

"That's great," I said. "I need all the help I can get."

"Did it strike you as odd that these guys took her where they did?" A small, conspiratorial smile suggested he knew what I would answer.

"You bet it did."

"I mean," he asked, holding his hands out to me, palms up, "how many residents of this city know that road?"

"Not one in a thousand."

"So what does that tell you?"

"You tell me."

"That the dirtballs who hit Maggie Winehouse were put up by people who live in the Richmond."

"Exactly."

"So what's the point of putting undercover cops in Chinatown?" he asked rhetorically, with that same conspiratorial smile.

"Not much."

"Did you tell the chief that?"

I smiled—wanly, I'm sure. "I thought I'd give you the pleasure of telling him."

Jim laughed. He knew all about my problems with Jerry Doyle. But then his wide eyes narrowed to half their normal size, and he looked steadily at me. "You okay?" he said.

"Yeah," I said. "Why? Don't I look okay?"

"No, since you asked. You look like shit."

That morning, I sent two of my men, both Asians, down to KUBC to review Maggie's series, hoping they'd see something I might have missed. I spent the rest of the morning and half the afternoon inventing ways to tell several dozen callers that we were on the case but had nothing yet to report. At three-thirty, I finally received a green light from Maggie's nurse and left at once for the hospital.

Bess was with Maggie when I arrived, arranging one of a dozen bouquets of flowers whose collective aroma was almost as strong as the one that hits you when you enter a florist's shop. There was a lot more daylight in the room than when I'd been there on Sunday afternoon, which made the sight of Maggie, her face still covered with bandages except for the eyes and nose, a little less depressing. I said hello to Bess, then walked to the bed and squeezed Maggie's arm.

"Hi, Maggie, remember me?"

She looked at me in silence. As they had after her surgery her eyes filled with tears. I could imagine the train of thought I'd launched, one leading inexorably to those life-scarring minutes next to that dark road bordering the Presidio. "Be careful," I'd warned her perfunctorily as we parted that day we toured Clement Street. "You bet," she'd replied, her remark, I'm sure, as perfunctory as mine.

After a moment, Maggie nodded, took my hand and squeezed back. I turned to Bess. "I could use some time alone with Maggie," I said. "Would you mind getting yourself a cup of coffee?"

Without a word Bess left the room.

I drew a chair alongside Maggie's bed. "I'd like you to tell me everything you remember. Take it very slowly. Try not to leave anything out, even if it seems irrelevant. Do you feel up to doing that?"

"I'll try," she said, a tremor in her voice. Maybe it was the bandages, maybe the residues of shock, but she spoke with difficulty, as you do after a dentist has numbed your mouth with novocaine. "Where do you want me to start?"

"As far back as you can. Was the story your idea, or did someone hand you the assignment?"

"It was my idea," she said so softly that I leaned closer.

"What triggered it?"

She sighed, and looked at the ceiling. For some seconds those striking green eyes of hers shifted so rapidly that I thought she might be
following the flight of an insect. But then she looked at me, and when
she began speaking it was with great care, as though she too would
be searching among her answers for some clue to the attack.

"I've always been interested in Asians. My best friend growing up
was Chinese. She's still my best friend. Probably because of her, I
majored in Asian studies at Berkeley. For me, it's been very exciting to
see all these Asians settling in the Bay Area, but you hear people
grumbling about all the immigrants and how much it's costing us,
which I knew wasn't true of the Chinese because they're so industri-
ous and they always take care of their own. And then I found out that
Asians had hit thirty percent of the city's population, and I figured
there's gotta be a story there."

She paused. I sensed that she was watching me closely to see if I
would react to anything she was saying. "Anything else?" I asked. As
I waited for her reply I glanced out the window and noticed that a
light rain had begun to fall.

"I suppose what really triggered it," Maggie said after a moment,
"was that I'd been looking for a house, and even with my salary,
which is pretty good for a woman my age, I couldn't find anything I
could afford to buy. And I knew the Hong Kong Chinese had bought a
lot of property during the eighties, and I suspected that with '97
approaching they were still out there buying. So it was just all these
things." She trailed off. I was watching her closely as she spoke, looking and listening for any signs of fatigue. With her face covered with
gauze, I had only her eyes and mouth to go on, so the best indicator
was her voice. It lacked energy, but she didn't sound weary.

"What was the first thing you did when you got an okay on the
story?" I asked, settling into my chair, hoping to convey to Maggie
that she could talk as long as she wanted. For the next half hour, as
she led me through the story, I interrupted only to ask her if she was
getting too tired to continue. But the further she got into it, the more
eager she seemed to talk. Only when she came to the attack did she
falter, and then just for a moment. When she finished, I asked her if
she'd be willing to describe the attack again.

"If I have to," she said reluctantly, after a pause.

"It would help me a lot," I said. I didn't tell her why, that I'd be listening for a repetition of a single word she'd used twice in her first narration.

This time she used the word not twice but three times, and I was more convinced than ever that her assailants had been triad hit men.

The word she'd used was "cleaver."

It was nearly five o'clock when we finished. The room had darkened, and the rain sounded heavier. I stood and stretched. "Would you like me to turn on some lights?" I asked.

"No," Maggie said. Then, apparently sensing the hour through some inner clock, she said, "I'd like to watch the news."

"You're sure?" I said, thinking that was probably the last thing she should do.

"I'm sure," she said emphatically, and her steady gaze underscored her answer.

Using the control on a bedside table, I tuned into KUBC. Then I went to the door and looked into the hallway. Mike Winehouse was there with Bess. I motioned them inside. They entered just as Ida Parsons, one of KUBC's anchors, was finishing her lead-in to the day's top story. ". . . featured by outpourings of outrage from every segment of the Bay Area, and outbreaks of violence at two San Francisco high schools. For more on the story, here's Gordon Lee at SF General Hospital."

Suddenly Gordon was on the screen. He was standing just outside the hospital, holding a golf umbrella with one hand and a microphone with the other, the collar of his trench coat turned up against the rain. At the sight of him, Maggie inhaled audibly. Mike and Bess must have heard her as well, because they both looked guardedly at her, then at each other. I thought I knew why. Gordon had probably been in the vicinity of the hospital for some time but hadn't come to see her.

"Fights between Asians and Caucasians broke out this morning at Lincoln and Washington high schools," he began, as pictures of the events he was describing began to follow one another on the tube, "triggered, it's believed, by reports of the savage attack Saturday evening on Maggie Winehouse of KUBC. Riot police had to be summoned to both campuses before order could be restored. Winehouse, a reporter for this station, was abducted at about seven o'clock Saturday evening as she was leaving her home to attend the opera, and driven to a darkened area on the edge of the Presidio in the Richmond, where her abductors slashed her face." That area was briefly pictured, and then Gordon was back on camera. "Winehouse told the paramedics who brought her here to San Francisco General Hospital that her attackers were Asians, and that she believed they were speaking Chinese."

Was it my imagination, or had Gordon faltered as he said that? I looked out of the corner of my eye to see if Mike had picked up on it, but his eyes were riveted on the screen.

"In the absence of any other explanation," Gordon went on, "speculation about the motive for the attack centers on a series of stories reported by Winehouse and carried on this station the week of October twenty-fourth, dealing with the impact on the Bay Area of increasing migration here by Asians."

The picture then switched to the two officers I'd sent to KUBC. They were seated next to a TV set, watching a tape of Maggie's series. "But after two inspectors from the Gang Task Force, both Asians, spent several hours today at KUBC studying all five parts of the series," Gordon noted in a voice-over, "the SFPD released a statement saying that nothing had been found in the programs to which any Asian could take offense."

That surprised and disturbed me. The two officers still hadn't returned when I'd left for the hospital. I hadn't authorized the release of a statement, but someone else obviously had—someone, like Chief Doyle, anxious to do everything he could to defuse the explosive racial elements of this case.

Once again Gordon was back on camera. "In the meantime, Winehouse is recuperating in the building behind me from the attack as well as from surgery. Gordon Lee, reporting live from SF General Hospital."

Then the program cut back to Ida Parsons. "The mayor has asked a number of civic leaders to his office tomorrow to discuss—"

"Turn it off, please," Maggie said. I hesitated, thinking Mike would do it, then, seeing he hadn't moved, I walked over to pick up the remote.

"—what the city and police are doing to deal with this potentially explosive situation, and KUBC has offered a twenty-five-thousand-dollar reward for information leading—" As the tube died Mike and

Bess turned to Maggie, but she didn't look at them. She stared, instead, at the ceiling. They said nothing, probably not knowing what to say. I sensed that all three of them were asking the same question: Would Gordon come?

Minutes later he appeared, much to my relief, as I was racking my brain for a way to break the silence. He was carrying a bouquet of flowers, his darting eyes and quick steps broadcasting intense nervous energy. He nodded to all of us, walked to the bed, bent down and kissed the top of Maggie's head, and squeezed her hand. "Feeling better?" he asked.

"Now I am," she said. I could hear the pleasure in her voice.

"They asked me to take the story on," he said. "I didn't want to do it. If it bothers you, I'll beg off."

"It's okay," she said. "It's okay," she repeated firmly, as if to make certain he believed her.

A silence passed. Then Maggie turned to us. "Could we be alone for a few minutes?"

We went outside. I excused myself to go to the restroom, not wanting to talk to the Winehouses, and returned just as Gordon emerged from Maggie's room, looking upset. "I've got to get back," he said. "They want a new segment for the eleven o'clock." And then, with a nod to Mike, he turned for the elevators. Mike watched him for a moment, not even bothering to hide his contempt.

I followed the Winehouses inside. "He'll leave me," Maggie said matter-of-factly.

"If he does, he's not worth keeping," Mike said. Seeing the expression on his face, I guessed that some errant and terrible thought had just flown into his head—a thought about black clouds and silver linings.

5

F or Richard Putnam, the prospect of holding public office had been an afterthought to a long career in the private sector, albeit one with a lot of volunteer work thrown in. A third-generation San Franciscan and a member of one of the city's oldest law firms, he had been so horrified by the decline in the city's fortunes that he'd made a sudden decision to run for mayor eight months before the 1991 election. Our mayoral elections are officially nonpartisan, but everyone knows who's a Democrat and who's a Republican. It was a measure of both past and present in our city that Mayor Putnam, a Republican all his life, had now been outflanked on his right by an even more conservative opponent.

In happier days, even Putnam would have been too conservative for the majority of San Francisco's traditionally liberal voters, but given the increasingly unhappy state of affairs in our city, his promises to get the homeless off the streets, clean up the city and balance its budget had won over enough liberals to give him a close victory. The mayor's conservative head, however, was coupled with a humanist's heart—a familiar combination in our city. Once in office, he had tried to be an all-things-to-all-people mayor, respecting the city's consensus traditions and placating its ethnic and political groups each time one of them became aroused. The result was that while a few of our more glaring sore spots had been healed, and the most flagrant panhandlers had been tamed, the city still had a tawdry look, was still overrun with vagrants and had a bigger deficit than ever. Enter Harold Halderman, the brilliant forty-year-old homicide prosecutor, who had seized on immigration, the red-hot issue of the mid-nineties in every state with large immigrant populations—legal *and* illegal—in a manner that had the commentators and columnists going back to the anti-Chinese vitriol of the 1870s for comparisons. As of this moment, the first week of November, the mayor had a twenty-three point lead over Halderman in the polls, but six months earlier it had been thirty points, and he was now running scared.

On the few occasions when I'd seen the mayor in the morning, he'd positively glowed, the pale skin of his English ancestors highlighted by the kind of ruddy cheeks you associate with Cornwall squires who spend their days in windy fields and their evenings in toasty pubs. Putnam's shining face was invariably set off by a gleaming white button-down shirt made of the most expensive cotton, and his big, even teeth, uncommonly bright for a man in his early seventies, cast a conciliator's smile at everyone in range. But on Tuesday morning, Election Day, he neither glowed nor smiled. Seated behind his uncluttered desk at the eastern end of his roomy yet cozy office, its walls covered with photographs and paintings, its corners softened by big, leafy plants, he looked gravely at the twenty civic leaders seated in two crescent-shaped rows on the other side of the desk and said, "I've asked you here this morning, first of all, so that you could hear personally from Chief Doyle about what's being done in the wake of the attack on Maggie Winehouse."

Of the twenty—bankers, publishers, commissioners, the heads of advocacy groups and neighborhood associations, religious leaders— eight were Caucasians, seven were Asians, three were Hispanic and two were black. The division was not accidental; it was a close approximation of the city's evolving ethnic balance. The mayor, a meticulous man, left nothing he could control to accident. Ten civic leaders would have fit far more comfortably into the space, but ten could not have been apportioned into as accurate a reflection of the city's population. So half of the civic leaders were seated in dark wood and red leather armchairs, and the other half sat on folding chairs brought into the mayor's office for the meeting. Chief Doyle, John O'Hara (the SFPD's deputy chief of investigations) and I sat behind the visitors, our backs to the fireplace, along with John Lucero, the president of the Board of Supervisors; Tom Golden, the mayor's chief of staff; Dennis Jang, deputy mayor for minority relations; and Marilyn Glusker, the mayor's press secretary. Incredibly, Glusker and a representative of the Community United Against Violence, a coalition of gay and lesbian leaders, were the only women in the room; as meticulous as he was, Putnam, born in the twenties, still lived in the age of the double standard—which might be why he felt so comfortable with my mother, whose views on the roles of men and women were equally dated.

"I'm determined that those responsible for this despicable attack be apprehended as quickly as possible," Putnam continued, the sincerity of his expression a perfect match for the earnest tone of his voice. And what a reassuring combination it was, the voice a steady baritone, the expression a combination of focused eyes and a resolute mouth above a firm, prominent chin. "I'm equally determined that this issue not be used by opportunists to create larger problems in our community. The population of San Francisco is changing rapidly. Rapid change of any kind produces problems. It's our job—your job, my job—to identify these problems and deal with them before they get out of hand. This city has a well-deserved reputation for tolerance, but our Asian friends know better than I do that this wasn't always the case. I want to be sure that nothing happens to turn back the clock. In that spirit, let's hear from Chief Doyle."

The chief walked forward and stood next to the mayor, looming over him. Normally, he wore civilian clothes to work, but for this occasion he had worn his uniform, festooned with gold braid. I knew what he intended to say because, at his grudging request, I'd briefed him an hour earlier, and then rehearsed him as well. Had the occasion been a different one—a crime-prevention meeting, for example, rather than one to reassure a community upset by a savage attack on a prominent young woman—I might have enjoyed it, because each time I prompted him he'd looked balefully at me, and once when I corrected him he'd positively writhed. "You missed your calling,

Tobias," he'd said. "You shoulda been down in Hollywood with your people, directing movies." I'd let it pass because the deputy chief was with us; I talk back only when we're one on one.

"Gentlemen," Doyle began in his raspy, big drinker's voice, typically failing to acknowledge the presence of women in the room, "at this moment, we have more than two dozen undercover police officers in the Asian community attempting to elicit information about the attack on Miss Winehouse. Because of the nature of the attack, and because of what the victim has told us, we are as certain as we can be that robbery wasn't the motive. We also have ascertained that she was not sexually assaulted."

Listening, I shook my head in wonder—about an inch to each side. The man was a piece of work, all right. He was speaking in the arch language and controlled address he reserved for special moments. I'd heard him use this "correct speech" pattern perhaps two dozen times; whenever I did, it made me wonder whether beneath the tough-guy, pulled-myself-up-by-the-bootstraps image he'd cultivated throughout his career was a secret reader.

"So it's our impression," Doyle went on, "that the attack was personally motivated. What we are trying to determine is whether the persons involved were San Francisco–based or imported for the job. At this time, we have reason to believe that the latter was the case."

"How do you know that?" Sam Barnes said. He was the station manager of KUBC, a man of fifty whose slicked-back dyed black hair, manicured nails and department-store clothes gave him away as a nonestablishment San Franciscan.

The chief hesitated for a minute, seemingly surprised by the question. He couldn't say I hadn't warned him. Even though I'd said nothing about the threat I'd received—still sensing that it would be better to guard that information for the time being—I had told him about my interrogation of Maggie and her mention of the cleaver. But I'd also urged him to say nothing about it to the citizens' group. "I've got to give 'em somethin'," he'd growled. "Sir," he said now, "I'm not at liberty to disclose that at this time."

"Oh, bullshit, Chief. I'm the general manager of the station Maggie works for and—"

"I know who you are, Mr. Barnes, but I'm not going to release information at this time that might impede our investigation."

"I think the people of this city have a right to know where an attack like this came from."

"I'm going to have to be the judge of that, Mr. Barnes," the chief said, his skin by this point close to matching the red leather on the chairs.

"Gentlemen," the mayor interceded in his soothing conciliator's voice, "why don't we hold the discussion until the chief has finished? Okay?"

Barnes gave a curt nod to the mayor and settled back into his chair, missing the chief's contemptuous glance.

As the chief turned back to the civic leaders, his gaze swept over them, as though daring a further challenge. "In addition to our undercover surveillance in Chinatown," he went on at last, trying to regain the rhythm disrupted by Barnes's verbal assault, "we have put an extra contingent of uniformed officers into sensitive areas, particularly those with high rates of crime. As I'm sure you gentlemen can appreciate, a high police profile keeps your criminal activity low. I won't mince words," he said, his confidence now flooding back. "We're very happy about all these newcomers to our city, but there are bad apples mixed in with the good. We've got triads from Hong Kong trying to move in here, and we also have problems with Chinese gangs. In the latter case, they're mostly kids in their late teens and early twenties, and while they're not running around shooting at each other—at least not yet—they're into just about everything you can think of: street prostitution, gambling, loan-sharking and extortion."

Come on, come on, pick it up, I urged him silently, knowing what a tough audience the chief was playing to. Put a cop on the witness stand in most American communities, and a jury will assume he's telling the truth—one reason I hadn't been in the least surprised by the acquittal verdict of the first Rodney King jurors. In San Francisco, a city traditionally skeptical of authority, it's another story. A San Francisco cop testifying before a jury isn't necessarily taken at his word, and defense attorneys can often get their clients off just by raising the possibility of "police fallibility." For these reasons, I figured the chief had only so much time to convince his audience—fully half of them either members of minorities or veterans of the sixties protests or both—that the SFPD was doing all it could not only to solve the case but to maintain calm in the city.

But if the chief felt any sense of urgency, he didn't show it. He took a step to his right, his big body framed now by a huge glass door leading onto a balcony. Behind him you could see half a dozen flags in Civic Center Plaza, flapping in a brisk wind. It suddenly struck me that the chief was deliberately taking his time, the sense of calm he projected meant to have a calming effect on his audience.

"One other change that I'm sure some of you gentlemen here know about," he said finally, still ignoring the women. "These activities aren't confined to Chinatown any longer. They're in the Richmond, as well, extortion in particular. Within those communities, you've got your special tensions, because Hong Kong Chinese as a rule don't like Taiwanese Chinese and neither of them like mainland Chinese and none of them like Southeast Asian Chinese."

With that, the chief darted a quick, almost reflexive look at me, perhaps to check whether he'd got it right, because I'd gone over that point with him not an hour earlier. I nodded my assurance, at the same time signaling him with my hands to speed it up. Either he saw only my reassuring nod or chose to ignore my warning signal, because to my dismay he launched into a windy evaluation of racial tensions in the city, focusing at last on the situation in our high schools. "You'll always have conflict on the high school level," he said after several minutes, "because what they're fighting about is turf. Sensible whites in their twenties and thirties aren't going to go out and bash Asians, and Asians in the same age group aren't going to go out and bash whites."

"Is that right?" Sam Barnes broke in again. "Then prove it by telling me how you know that the attack on our reporter wasn't ordered by local people."

"Excuse me." It was Jimmy Chang, the dapper chairman of the San Francisco Port Commission and self-appointed spokesperson for first-generation Chinese immigrants, his round, middle-aged, normally ebullient face puckered into deep furrows. Jimmy had arrived penniless in the city in the early seventies from Hong Kong via Vancouver, or so the legend had it. Today, he owned half a dozen restaurants and as many commercial buildings, and ran several businesses. "You tell us, Mr. Barnes, why you say on your station Chinese people responsible for big increase in house prices," he said, his voice loud but unsteady, a giveaway to the indignation he seemed to be struggling to check. "People move here from all over, not just Chinese people. Come from East Coast, Midwest. Come from Mexico. Young people get married, wife work, they buy house. Not just Chinese people, like you say. But you say that on television, people believe you, Chinese people get blame."

"I believe our story went into those aspects, Mr. Chang," Sam said firmly.

"Maybe one line, two line," Jimmy insisted. "All the rest, Chinese people."

Now it was Sam's turn to burn. He clipped his words. "I'm not here to discuss the real estate market, Mr. Chang. I'm here to find out what the city is doing to apprehend the criminals who made a cowardly attack on one of our reporters, who happened to be a beautiful young woman, and who mutilated her in a manner that could ruin her personal and professional life."

"That's why *I'm* here," a new voice said emphatically.

Until now the room had been quiet. Suddenly it was *still.* Motion ceased, except for the turning of heads. Everyone looked at George "Bud" Donnelly, a tall, big-boned Irishman, the other character in the two-character play within a play that had been going on almost since the day Mayor Putnam took office—the first character, of course, being the mayor. It was the moment everyone in the room had anticipated, an epic moment in its way, years and years in the making.

Dick Putnam was Protestant, Bud Donnelly was Catholic, and Bud was the better athlete, but they'd been virtually interchangeable in all other respects: big, good-looking, well-behaved kids from established families, in the top 2 percent of their Lowell High School class, stars of the debating team, and as inseparable as the slices of a peanut butter sandwich. The day after Pearl Harbor they'd enlisted together in the Navy, eventually serving as officers on the same aircraft carrier in the Pacific. After the war Dick had gone to Boalt Hall, Cal's blue-ribbon law school, and Bud had entered the family construction business. Compared with what followed, those had been fairy-tale years in San Francisco, the air sweet, the streets clean, the society orderly everywhere but on the waterfront, everyone prospering from the postwar boom—or at least everyone they knew. Dick quickly became one of the city's more visible lawyers. Bud quadrupled the size of the family business. Then came the hippies and the Vietnam war, and for Bud, everything changed. First, his oldest son, George Jr., an infantry lieutenant, was killed. Then Bud's wife, Helen, shut herself up in their substantial St. Francis Woods home, all but dropping from sight and, rumor had it, drinking herself into daily stupors. Bud entered a world of his own. Enraged at those who protested the war for which his son had given his life, he lobbied his way onto the police commission, where he quickly gained a reputation as an advocate of tough justice. Within a few years he had become the most prickly, vocal right-winger in San Francisco, his scowling face radiating the frustration and hostility he expressed in his diatribes against panhandlers, homosexuals and immigrants.

Dick Putnam, on the other hand, had become the picture of establishment rectitude: thick white hair, that glowing face with its reassuring smile, Brooks Brothers clothes down to his shoes and the unwavering eyes of a careful listener. A reputation for fairness and good judgment, earned in dozens of civic and professional battles, accompanied the picture. Had a group of his peers, appalled by the slide of the city, not implored him to run for mayor, he probably wouldn't have, but once they did he agreed because he was as appalled as they were.

For Bud Donnelly, it was as though his brother had married his former girlfriend. He was enraged. Those men were his peers as much as they were Dick Putnam's, and he believed they should have come to him, not Dick, because he'd been so much more active in city life than Dick had been.

I knew all this about Bud because I'd known him all my life. He and my father had been teammates at Cal. After the war they'd put their respective firms into some joint business ventures. Our families got together several times a year, at christenings or confirmations, on July Fourth, over the Christmas holidays. There'd even been a period when George Jr. and my sister, Sari, had been smitten with each other. Interfaith marriages being increasingly common in San Francisco, neither set of parents had attempted to intervene, but I'm sure both were relieved when the relationship ran its course. When George Jr. was killed, our family grieved for him, his parents and his siblings.

After Dick Putnam was elected, he kept Bud on the police commission for the same reason his liberal predecessors had, as a sop to the city's most conservative elements. But Bud tested him to the limit. From the first day of the new mayor's term, he gave his childhood friend no quarter, criticizing everything he did as well as everything he didn't do. When Harold Halderman announced his candidacy, Bud announced that if Mayor Putnam didn't, at a minimum, get the homeless off the streets and reduce welfare costs, he'd throw his support behind Halderman. That automatically meant the support, as well, of SOC—Save Our City—a mushrooming, increasingly visible organization Bud had created in the late eighties to lobby for tough restrictions against the homeless population, combat illegal immigration and deny benefits of any kind to undocumented aliens. By the I-told-you-so look on his face as he rose to speak, he considered the attack on Maggie Winehouse by foreigners—the most likely scenario, according to Chief Doyle—as vindication for everything he'd been saying.

"This is the worst example yet of the state to which San Francisco has fallen," he said now, "and if the people who mutilated that beautiful young girl aren't promptly apprehended I for one am gonna damn well wanna know why." In the silence that followed, he glared first at the mayor, then at Chief Doyle, his sunken eyes set deeply into his face, and I had a moment to reflect on the irony of a poorly educated chief of police who affected lofty speech in public, and a superbly educated police commissioner who, in front of the same audience, tried to sound like one of the boys. "There is only one good thing we can get outta this," he went on, "and that is if it becomes a wake-up call to all San Franciscans—and I do mean *all* San Franciscans, whether they're white, black, brown, yellow or polka dot—to understand what we're doin' to ourselves by lettin' anyone and everyone who manages to get his body here suck our lifeblood. We used to call 'em illegal immigrants, which musta hurt their feelin's because now we gotta call 'em undocumented aliens. You can call 'em whatever you like, you can't get around that they've taken our jobs, filled up our schools and hospitals, fed off our welfare, used up our resources—"

"Bud, please," Mayor Putnam interjected softly, looking with concern at Donnelly, "this isn't the place—"

It was the worst thing he could have said. "This isn't the *place?*"

Bud bellowed, turning full at him. "Is that a fact? Then maybe you better tell all of us here in this room, and all the people of this city where the place *is* to get our problems solved if it's not the office of the mayor." His head seemed to push several inches toward Dick Putnam, whose features had suddenly turned to stone. "I'm here to tell you this *is* the place, or it damn well *oughta* be the place from which the word should go out that it's wrong when the people who helped build this city and kept it going and paid its bills aren't able to get the services they need because the funds that run these programs were all spent on illegal immigrants."

Everyone looked in unison at Mayor Putnam, expecting him to respond, but he just sat there in silence, his color a little deeper but his face expressionless, having obviously decided to let Bud talk himself out. I think Bud was as surprised as the rest of us, because he seemed to falter. I was baffled too until, looking around the room, I saw what the mayor must have seen, that while Bud's attack might have been pleasing the vintage San Franciscans, it wasn't sitting well with the newer arrivals and the special-interest groups.

"And now," Bud said, obviously groping, "if I'm understandin' Chief Doyle correctly, a coupla immigrants came in here and attacked a member of the media."

I looked at Jerry Doyle. He was squirming, caught between his boss, the mayor, and a police commissioner he'd worked with for a quarter century who'd also become a close friend. After an agonizing moment he held up a restraining hand and said, "Not necessarily, Commissioner. Our conclusion, based on the limited information available to us, is that the attack was mounted from abroad. The people who actually attacked Maggie Winehouse could have come in on tourist visas to do the job, and then left the country that night or the next day." He hesitated, then added, "I never said they were immigrants."

That stopped Bud Donnelly. Mayor Putnam threw Jerry Doyle a grateful look. In the silence that followed, Jimmy Chang spoke up. "Why she do story anyway?" he said, turning again to Sam Barnes. "How come you don't have Chinese reporter?"

"We have three Asian reporters," Barnes said. "Two are Chinese."

"Then how come they not do story?" Jimmy insisted, scowling uncharacteristically.

"Because the story was her idea." With that, Barnes turned away from Jimmy and began to address the others. "Maggie Winehouse has a degree in Asian studies from the University of California. She has done stories for us in the past on Asians in the Bay Area. She asked to do this story not only because of her ongoing interest in the subject but because of an unexpected personal involvement. Maggie earns an excellent salary, but even she was having trouble finding a house she could afford. She wanted, among other things, to find out to what extent the high cost of housing was related to the influx of Asians into the Bay Area."

"That not good enough reason to do story blaming Chinese, and talking so much about Chinese criminal come here," Jimmy said, his voice cracking with anger. His skin, still deeply furrowed, had darkened. His eyes had narrowed. He was, in that moment, a picture of livid righteousness.

"I'll be the judge of that, Mr. Chang," Barnes said coldly.

"Then let me be the judge of how much information we can release to the media," Chief Doyle said to Barnes.

"Gentlemen, gentlemen," the mayor said with a dark look at all three men. "This isn't going to get us anywhere."

They hadn't gotten much further half an hour later when the mayor disbanded the meeting with two requests: first, that the participants urge their respective communities to remain calm; and second, that none of the participants share any specifics of the meeting with reporters. Then the doors of the mayor's office were opened to the media, Marilyn Glusker issued a release announcing the formation of the mayor's ad hoc committee, and the mayor and committee members posed for the TV cameras and photographers. Everybody looked appropriately grim, the mayor especially, and I slipped away in the certain knowledge that a morning of all of our lives had been wasted.

I drove to San Francisco General, only to discover that Maggie had been transferred by ambulance two hours earlier to California Pacific Medical Center in Pacific Heights, the finest private hospital in the city, staffed by many of the city's best and most expensive doctors. A news release from KUBC later that day would note that the transfer had been arranged by Sam Barnes, and that KUBC would pay for all costs connected with Maggie's treatment that weren't covered by insurance. Presbyterian—as the hospital continues to be known despite a series of name changes—was where Maggie's personal physician practiced, the release also noted. What the release didn't say, of course, was that Maggie's presence in a public hospital did not befit the image of a thriving metropolitan television station it was Barnes's job to project.

Even though the use of a cleaver had convinced me that the attack on Maggie had been carried out by hit men from Hong Kong, I'd brought a mug book with me to the hospital. The pictures in the book were of known criminals, Asian men living in the Bay Area who fit the description of the hit men Maggie had given me. Her face was still bandaged, but her lackluster eyes and weak voice were enough to tell me that she was tired and depressed. She looked through the book apprehensively, as though sensing that even an encounter with a photograph of her assailants held some menace for her. It took less than ten minutes to establish that she'd never seen any of these men, and she came to the end of the book with obvious relief. That settled it in my mind. As to why someone from Hong Kong would reach all the way across the Pacific to attack a young street reporter for a San Francisco television station—particularly when her series had been so innocuous—I hadn't a clue.

I put the book on a table, walked back to the bed and put a hand on her arm, trying to communicate the compassion I was feeling. "Do you feel up to a few more questions?" I asked.

"Yes," she said, but with zero enthusiasm. I could only imagine what thoughts had been going through her mind as she lay alone in this small, square room, staring at the white ceiling or the bare, cream-colored walls or at the wall of the brick building visible through her window. None of the flowers that had decorated her room at SF General had been transferred to Presbyterian, and no new flowers had arrived, and the room, without them, seemed like a cell.

"Are you sure?" I asked. "I can wait if you don't feel up to it."

"I doubt that I'm going to feel any better for a very long time, and probably not ever."

I squeezed her arm. "I don't want to upset you, Maggie."

"It's all I think about, so there's nothing you could ask me that I haven't thought about already."

"Okay, good," I said, trying to sound positive. I moved a chair from the wall to the side of her bed, and sat beside her. "In all your thinking about what happened, have you come up with *any* reason why someone might have been offended by your broadcast?"

"No. None." Her voice still sounded muted.

"Who'd you see in Hong Kong?"

Maggie shrugged. "Just the obvious people you'd see for a story about people emigrating from Hong Kong. At least, they seemed like the obvious people to me."

"Tell me. Walk me through it."

"I started at the American consulate. Besides the public information officer, I saw the Immigration and Naturalization Service, and then U.S. Customs. Then I saw a bunch of people with the Hong Kong government, and a detective inspector with the Hong Kong police—"

I held up a hand. "Why him?"

"Because I thought he might be able to tell me something about the triads."

"And did he?"

"No way," Maggie said after a small, ironic laugh. "He said he was sick of American journalists coming to Hong Kong to talk about the triads."

"What was the inspector's name?"

"Desmond Smythe-Jones." She said the name contemptuously, obviously still smarting from the rebuff.

"Don't know him," I said, half to myself. "Anyone else?"

"A few local journalists. And then all those people I interviewed on camera who wound up in the piece. But none of them said anything at all deprecating about specific people." Her voice trailed off and she looked away, but not before I saw the despair in her eyes. I could relate to that: having gone through the same material over and over again, she'd come up with no more than I had.

I waited a good half minute to give her time to compose herself. "Did any of the people other than the police inspector give you a bad time?" I said then.

"Only him."

"Okay," I said. I squeezed her arm again and tried to manage a smile. "We'll figure this out." I could only hope I projected more confidence than I felt.

Mike Winehouse arrived just as I was leaving Maggie's room—the last man I wanted to see. We met in the corridor.

"Anything new?" he asked. His eyes were bloodshot. In the dull, even light of the corridor his skin looked pallid, and his expression was haunted.

"I wish there were, Mike," I said, trying to sound sorry without also sounding pessimistic. But my effort seemed to be wasted, because he plunged ahead as though I hadn't spoken.

"So what are the chances that you're going to catch those bastards?"

I knew I should say nothing, given who he was. But he looked so pitiful that I couldn't bring myself to cut him off. "Are you asking as Maggie's father or as a member of the media?" I said.

"Would your answer be different?"

"Has to be," I said as emphatically as I could without sounding officious.

"Okay, then answer me as Maggie's father."

"Off the record?"

"Off the record."

"I have your word?" I insisted.

"Yes, yes," he said, obviously annoyed.

"For the moment, the chances aren't great. We have almost nothing to go on, and you can bet the farm that the guys who hit Maggie are long gone from San Francisco."

He sagged visibly, leaned against a wall, and let out a prolonged sigh. "What makes you so sure?"

"Given what Maggie's told us, we're assuming they were Chinese. Chinese criminals are incredibly well organized. A guy shoots somebody here, they send him off to Uncle Louie in Los Angeles, or to Denver, or South America or Holland. They move people around all the time. We've got guys coming here who've just pulled a robbery in Vancouver. They'll pull another one here, then head for Monterey Park in East LA, where they'll do another one and then it's on to Houston or Boston. So the guys who made the hit on Maggie were probably out of here that night or, at the latest, Sunday morning."

Mike took a minute to digest that. It was obviously the last thing he wanted to hear. "What about the people who hired those guys? Have you got any theories on that?"

"Theories are the easy part," I said, then waited as two nurses, their eyes on us, took their time walking by. I supposed they had hoped to eavesdrop, but then it occurred to me what an eye-catching pair we made, the undersized columnist and the oversized cop. "Since we know that robbery and sex weren't motives, all that leaves is revenge. Question: When does an Asian seek revenge? Answer: When he's lost face. How was Maggie attacked? They carved up her face—"

I stopped in mid-thought, instantly regretting my choice of words. They'd made Mike recoil as surely as if Maggie's attackers had turned their blades on him. His eyes shut, and he turned his face away. I waited some seconds, then put a hand on his shoulder. "I'm sorry, Mike," I said. God, but I meant it. That was the moment, I think, in which I realized that this case had gotten to me more than any I'd handled—partly, I suppose, because the crime was so cruel, and partly because not only the victim but her loved ones were people I knew.

When Mike turned back to me, his face displayed neither anger nor sorrow, only resolve. "Go on," he said.

I did, carefully. "The Occidental interpretation would be that whoever did it didn't want her on television anymore. That may be true, but there's an Oriental interpretation as well: You cause me to lose face, I cause you to lose face. Theoretically, all we have to do is figure out who lost face because of those stories and we'd have our culprit. Practically, we've got nothing to go on, because there's nothing on those tapes. She didn't name any names."

"So what now?" Mike said, tilting his head back so he could look me in the eye.

It was as much a challenge as a question, and I dreaded the only true answer I could give him. "If no leads develop in the next few days, we close the case."

In an instant, that haunted face metamorphosed into a monster's mask. The eyes enlarged, the corners of the mouth curled down, the chin jutted so far forward that the lower teeth protruded beyond the upper teeth. "What do you mean, close the case?" Mike bellowed, his voice reverberating through the corridor. Moments later, patients were peering from their doors, and a nurse at the nurses' station was glaring at us and holding a finger to her lips. "There's nothing to go on, Mike," I said as gently as I could. "We've got no leads. We've had two dozen cops undercover since yesterday morning, and they've picked up zip. When you have no leads and you have no suspects, you have no case. So you put it on the inactive file, and you reactivate it if and when new information turns up."

"You don't get leads if you sit on your ass," he said, barely able to hold his voice down. His body quivered.

I had no illusions about how dangerous this man confronting me could be. For more than a year, he'd been after the mayor in his column because of the deplorable state of the city, and had shown increasing, if reluctant, sympathy for Harold Halderman's mayoral candidacy. If he got it into his head that the police department wasn't doing its job, I was certain he'd be merciless, and that I'd be blamed. But I was on edge from the threat I'd received, tired from all the sleep I'd missed since Chief Doyle's call, and frustrated by my lack of progress on the case, not to mention being heartsick over my break with Britt. I stared at Mike for a moment. "I'm gonna do you a favor, and pretend you didn't say that. For what it's worth, I'm sorry." Then I turned and walked away.

6

I drove home at six o'clock, put my car in the garage, walked up to Hyde Street and then down the steep hill—the one the cable cars descend on their way to Fisherman's Wharf—to my polling place, the Norwegian Seaman's Church between Chestnut and Francisco. Having listened on my car radio to the election results in the East, I cast my ballot convinced that I was backing a slate of losers, issues as well as candidates.

Ten minutes later, walking up the steps from the street to my apartment building, I heard a noise behind me, whirled, drew and crouched—only to see a black cat jumping onto the fence separating my building from the one to the east. Heart pounding, I put the gun back in its holster, and walked the rest of the steps feeling every pulse in my body, aware that I had a more acute case of the jitters than I'd ever had in my life.

Once again, I reset the burglar alarm as soon as I closed the door to my apartment, and spent the evening with a gun at my side, watching the election results until I couldn't take any more. I slept poorly. In the morning, it showed in my mirror. Sitting on a kitchen stool, my customary breakfast of granola and sliced bananas before me, I unfolded Wednesday's *Dispatch,* skimmed the depressing headlines and turned quickly to the editorial pages, expecting to be lambasted. To my surprise, I found not a Mike Winehouse column but a laconic note in boldface at the bottom of the page saying, "Mike Winehouse has taken a few days off." I let out a grateful sigh. Only as I felt the tension slip from my body did I realize how tight I'd been.

The morning paper did carry a statement from Harold Halderman ridiculing Mayor Putnam's appointment of the mayor's committee to oversee the investigation into the attack on Maggie. "What's needed is not another committee," the mayor's political opponent said, "but vigorous leadership combined with strong police work to combat those foreign criminal elements that are moving into our city and making it unsafe for law-abiding Americans." In a comment that sounded almost exactly like those made by Bud Donnelly the day before in Mayor Putnam's office, Halderman added: "This is one more example—perhaps the worst yet—of the degree to which our way of life is being threatened by people who have no right to be here and ought *not* to be here." I could almost hear the gratification in his voice as he added, "With the overwhelming victory of Proposition 187 in yesterday's election, we not only have a mandate from the people to do something about that problem but a tool with which to do it."

What Halderman neglected to say was that 70.5% of San Franciscans voting had voted against Prop. 187. If he was going to be the city's next mayor he had his work cut out for him.

At ten o'clock, seated at my office desk, I got a surprise: a call from Mike Winehouse. "I'm sorry about yesterday," he mumbled, his voice subdued.

"You're entitled. These haven't exactly been the best days of your life."

"There's something I'd like to talk to you about. You got a lunch date?"

I laughed. "Cops at my level don't have a lot of lunch dates."

"So you're free?"

"Sure."

"You willing to have lunch with me?"

"I'm more than willing to have lunch with you."

"Good. Pick a Chinese restaurant where a lot of Chinese eat."

After twenty years as a cop, there's not an awful lot that surprises me. But that left me speechless. Had *I* suggested a Chinese restaurant to a man whose daughter had, in all probability, just been mutilated by Chinese gangsters, I should have been handed a dunce cap and banished to a corner. "Are you sure you want to do that?" I asked him delicately.

"I'm sure," he said firmly.

"Then meet me at Yuet Lee, on the northeast corner of Broadway and Stockton."

I hung up, mystified. But I figured Mike had his reasons. For my part, I was triply pleased. I wasn't going to be lambasted. My time with Mike would divert me from my worries. And I was overdue for a fix at Yuet Lee.

I hadn't exactly been kidding when I'd told Chief Doyle how much Jews love Chinese food. Every Sunday evening when I was a child, my parents would take my sister and me to the same restaurant in Chinatown, where we were joined by relatives or Jewish friends. In the course of the evening, we would see half a dozen other Jewish families with their relatives and friends. Was it the tradition, or was it the food? Either way, I get the feeling when I go too long without a visit to a Chinese restaurant that my life is out of whack.

Even today, as familiar as this compact enclave adjoining downtown San Francisco has become to me, I have the same impression driving into Chinatown I had in those days: that I'm entering a foreign country. For every fancy curio shop for tourists, there are dozens of unadorned stores overflowing with goods in which commerce is carried on exclusively among Asians, the overwhelming number of them Chinese. And in spite of all the tourists, most of the faces are still Chinese, and the predominant sound remains the loud, incessant chatter of Chinese conversations, the sentences more sung than spoken. If you listen carefully, especially on those small side streets, you can hear the clatter of mah-jongg pieces being mixed in illegal gambling halls, most of them on the second floor of battered walkups. And the smells, ah God, the sweet smell of lacquered ducks and the briny smell of fresh seafood and, most especially, the zesty smell of ginger, garlic and scallion, the flavor base of so many Chinese dishes, stir-frying in a wok.

At twelve o'clock I stood outside Yuet Lee, my favorite Chinese restaurant, its name on a sign also advertising Coca-Cola that wrapped around the corner of the building. The exterior walls of the restaurant were painted an unfortunate but eye-catching chartreuse. To call the restaurant unprepossessing was a kindness, but you couldn't get a better Hong Kong–style meal in San Francisco. You couldn't beat the prices, either.

A moment later, I saw Mike crossing Broadway, his shuffling gait only marginally more vigorous than it had been when he'd entered the hospital on Saturday night, his trench coat, a size too large for his small frame, failing to conceal his droopy posture, which seemed to have sagged another few degrees. Whatever force he had summoned during our confrontation twenty-four hours earlier had completely dissipated. My heart went out to him; I couldn't conceivably be angry or even upset with a man so obviously crushed. He shook my hand limply, and looked doubtfully at the restaurant.

"Trust me," I said. At the door I hesitated. "Are you *really* sure you want to do this?"

"Yeah, I'm sure," he said just as firmly as before. But he spoke with the enthusiasm of someone agreeing to elective surgery.

The one thing that could be said for the interior of the restaurant was that its decor went well with the exterior. An open kitchen, stained from the preparation of several hundred thousand dishes, was just inside the door to the left. The dining area held only a dozen wooden tables, most for four people, two for eight or more, the ones near the door unguarded from the chilly wind.

The manager, a small, rotund man in his fifties, came up to greet us. He was beaming. He led us to my habitual table at the end of the room. I took my customary seat against the wall—cops are uncomfortable with their backs to a room—and gestured for Mike to sit across from me.

"Thanks for coming," he said. "After the way I mouthed off I wasn't sure you'd want to talk to me."

"Listening to people talk is what I do for a living," I said.

"Me, too," Mike said.

An awkward silence passed: two listeners, each waiting for the other to speak. "Some election," I said to break the impasse.

"That was no election," Mike said. "It was an uprising of elderly white men. They're the only ones who bother to vote anymore." Then he turned in his chair to observe the room, taking in the tables one by one, two thirds of them occupied by Chinese. He didn't seem in the least interested in the passage of the waiters or the preparations in the open kitchen. He appeared to be totally absorbed in the Chinese customers, as though he had never seen Chinese people before. At last he turned back to me. "How many of these people do you suppose are illegals?"

"No idea," I said.

"But some?"

"Oh, sure."

"What do you suppose will happen to them?"

"It's not them I'm worried about so much. It's their kids. No schools. No medical care." I shrugged. "Guess what they're going to grow up to be?"

Mike nodded. "I take it you were against One eighty-seven?"

"I don't know a cop who wasn't. It's going to create a whole new underclass."

Mike sighed. "Strange times," he said. He looked around the room again, then back at me. "You eat here a lot?"

"Whenever I can."

"The food must be good," he said indifferently, as though it really didn't matter whether it was or wasn't.

"You'll know soon enough."

A waiter brought tea to the table, and the rotund manager came back a moment later to take our order.

"Your restaurant, you choose," Mike said.

"Anything you don't eat?"

"Dog."

I would have laughed, but Mike didn't so much as smile. I realized that he'd made a statement, not a joke. It struck me then that not once in all the years I'd been reading him had he displayed the faintest humor. Had I questioned him, I was sure he would have told me he never ate Chinese food by choice, and that he'd either read a book or seen a film in which Asians ate dog. But I let it go. "Any preferences?" I asked.

He held out his hand, palm up. "Please."

I ordered as I usually do, in Chinese and without looking at the menu.

"I'm impressed," Mike said after the manager left.

I shrugged. "Comes with the territory."

"Was it difficult to learn?"

"Not as difficult as trying to understand the English spoken by the newcomers."

"That's quite an accomplishment," he said, nodding in agreement with his own statement.

"I don't know how else to do the job."

"Are you the rule or the exception?"

"You mean, am I the only Caucasian on the force who speaks Chinese?"

"Yeah." He regarded me intently, as though my answer to his question was of vast importance. It gave me a good feeling, and encouraged me to respond.

"There's one other officer who speaks more dialects than I do. On the other hand, we have some Chinese officers who never learned more than Chinese baby talk. They at least know the culture, though, which is more important than the language."

He nodded as though he understood and agreed. But then suddenly he frowned and said, "What do you mean by that?"

My mind flipped through pictures of long-ago incidents I hadn't thought of in years. "Let's say Caucasian or black or Latino officers respond to a wife-beating complaint at a Chinese household. They walk into the living room and there's the wife and the husband, both visibly upset, both hyperventilating, the wife with marks on her face, maybe some furniture overturned. No doubt they've been struggling. But when the officers try to question her, she won't say a word. Of course she won't, because they're trying to get her to talk in the presence of her husband, which traditional Chinese women never do. But take her in the next room and she'll talk her head off."

That seemed to make sense to Mike, because this time he nodded his head vigorously. "It sounds like you enjoy your work," he said then, watching me intently.

"I'm not sure police work is something one enjoys, but if you're a cop, it's the only game in town."

His eyebrows rose. "How so?"

"What the Mafia is to New York, Chinese criminals are to San Francisco. You media guys have been making a big deal about all the criminals coming here from Hong Kong, but the fact is that Chinese criminals have been in San Francisco since the Gold Rush."

Mike held up his hands. "Wait a minute, wait a minute, what are you saying? That the threat's been overstated? That not that many are coming? That they won't make matters worse?"

I took another sip of tea, noting as I did that Mike hadn't touched his. "That's three different questions," I said. "Let me back up a little. When the Communists ran the Nationalists out of China in the late forties, they followed with a merciless crackdown on the triads. No trials, just dragged them out into the streets and shot them. Those who could escaped to Hong Kong, where they set up with the triads already in place, which is the main reason why Hong Kong today is the base of Chinese organized crime in Asia. That won't be the case after '97. There won't be any shooting in the streets, but life will get very tough there for criminals."

Mike nodded. "I'll say one thing for those People's Republics. They know how to handle crime. Look at Russia—the safest place in the world under the Communists, and now you can't even go out at night."

"There was plenty of crime, Mike. You just didn't read about it." I took another sip of tea. "Would you like something else to drink?" I asked.

"No. Why?"

"You're not drinking your tea."

"Tea's fine."

"Good," I said, then quickly got back on track. "Let me amend what I said a minute ago. The People's Republic will let some criminals stay, because they have uses for criminals from time to time. But the rest will leave. Some will go to Australia and England, and a big contingent is already setting up in Canada. But the key figures will try to move to the States, primarily the West Coast, because that's where the biggest action is, and among that group the favorite choice by far is San Francisco."

"Ah!" Mike said. He pursed his lips and nodded, grimly satisfied, it seemed, that his fears had been confirmed, yet perversely pleased, I supposed, in that way reporters are when they sense a big story. The worse the news, the bigger the story—not their doing, but rather, the nature of the beast—analogous, in a way, to doctors' fascination with illness.

"So I take the arrival of these people very seriously," I went on. "My point is that they're not going to be bringing anything new with them in the way of criminal activities. For the most part, they're just going to augment what's already here. There'll be a struggle, because there are only so many businesses you can extort, so many nightclubs you can control or prostitutes you can run or dope you can sell or gambling you can skim. But I don't see an all-out war. The Chinese have a saying: 'Any business is better than no business.' If they fight one another, a lot of them will go out of business. I think what will happen is that instead of fighting the Asian-American gangs, the triads will co-opt them. In the late eighties, the triads invited a number of Asian-American gangsters to a summit meeting in Hong Kong. We understand they worked out some arrangements."

Mike's eyes narrowed, and he tilted his head, the way a dog does when something unfamiliar comes into its vision. "How'd you find that out?" he asked, an edge to his voice, as though he was challenging me to prove what I'd just said.

I shook my head. "Professional secret."

"Come on. Who am I gonna tell?"

I laughed. "Several hundred thousand readers."

"No way," he said. "You had to have had an informer, or someone undercover."

I smiled. "You said it. I didn't."

He measured me carefully, wondering, I supposed, if it was worth it to press me. "But the bottom line is that when the dust settles, Asian crime will be more entrenched here than ever," he said with finality.

"Unless we find a more effective means of combating it than we have so far."

"What do you think the chances are?"

"Off the record?"

"Yes, yes, off the record," he said impatiently.

"The chances aren't great. The problem isn't just the triads coming from Hong Kong. It's the kids the gangs are recruiting. A lot of them are good kids who come here already upset at being uprooted, and then when they get here they have trouble fitting in, trouble with school, trouble with the language. One day, some hood flashes a few dollars. He says, 'All you have to do is be a "look-see." If you're arrested, we'll take care of your bail, get you an attorney.' It's very attractive. Any kid who shows he can take care of himself is recruited for the gangs. They take him to nightspots, show him a good time, give him a feeling he belongs and that someone cares about what happens to him. There are a lot of kids who want to avoid the gangs, but they feel that once they're touched, that's it, this is their lot in life. They tell themselves, 'If I quit there'll be pressure and maybe some backlash and loss of money for sure, and my family will suffer.' "

Mike took a minute at that point to look around the restaurant again, as if to connect what I'd just said to real Chinese people. By then, there were lots of Chinese to look at. The restaurant had filled up; even the tables by the open door were occupied.

"So what can you do about that?" he asked, turning back to me.

"Try to change their minds."

Mike snorted. "You really think you can change kids' minds?"

"You obviously don't."

"All I know is I couldn't change Maggie's mind. She's been a handful since the day we got her."

He must have seen me frown because he answered my question before I could ask it. " 'Got' her's right. Maggie's adopted. I shoot blanks."

He spoke those last words matter-of-factly, as though they were a necessary part of the story. The disclosure put to rest two questions that had been hovering in my mind. Mike and Ruth, both in their sixties, seemed uncommonly old to be the parents of a twenty-six-year-old. And based on their appearance, neither parent had the genes to create such an attractive daughter, who resembled them not at all.

"She was a difficult kid," Mike went on, "stubborn as hell, the kind who if you said 'Don't do that, it's bad for you' would do it just because you told her not to. From the time she was thirteen, fourteen, I couldn't tell her anything. I'd express concern and she'd hear it as criticism. I'd suggest something and she'd reject it, not because she disagreed with the idea but because I'd suggested it. You'd think I'd catch on, but I didn't. I didn't want Maggie to go into television, and told her so. Me, I write well enough to do what I do. Maggie writes like a dream. She could write for the best magazines. She could write books. If she wrote for a paper, she could win a Pulitzer, because she not only knows how to dig out a story, she understands what she finds. Instead, she's writing these one- or two-page nothing stories that vanish into the air."

"Except for the last one," I said, and instantly regretted it. As an unfortunate remark, it wasn't in a class with my "carved up her face" gem of the previous day, but it was bad enough, and Mike had obviously felt it. His face had gone slack. He stared at me. "Yeah," he said dispiritedly.

At that moment, thank God, our food arrived: first, oysters in black bean sauce, then crab stir-fried with ginger and scallions, then steamed beancurd cakes stuffed with shrimp, served with onion and cilantro and soy sauce, all of the seafood fresh, all of the dishes as good as I had ever had them. I was sure that Mike, left to himself, would have ordered chow mein and sweet and sour pork, so I was mildly apprehensive about the outcome, but he attacked his plate with gusto. "Good," he mumbled with a nod. Spearing morsels with a fork, he ate rapidly and in silence for several minutes. The food seemed to revive him. He seemed, if not content, at least appeased for the first time since Saturday night. At one point he looked up from his plate, and stared at me. "Something wrong?" I asked worriedly, wondering what else I might have done to offend him.

"You're using a fork."

"Does that surprise you?" I said, puzzled.

"Yeah, given what you do."

"Why is that?" I couldn't imagine what he was getting at.

"Reporters learn to blend in with the people they want information from. Makes the source more comfortable. We're in the same business in that respect. We live or die on the basis of the information we get from people who know what we need to find out. You work with Asians, it makes sense you'd use chopsticks like they do."

"I did until four years ago," I acknowledged.

"Why'd you change?"

I smiled, remembering. "I had a late lunch one day in a Chinese restaurant with a Caucasian guy who'd spent a lot of time in China. He ate like they do there and first-generation Chinese do here, filling his rice bowl with food morsels, then holding the bowl just below his mouth, and shoveling the food in with chopsticks. At the time, I used chopsticks Western style, picking the food up from my plate. When we left that day it was so late that all the waiters were eating. There were nine of them at one table, and all of them were using forks. I had a good laugh, and I haven't used chopsticks since."

Mike didn't even smile. He took another bite, chewed for a moment, then said, "You make a habit of not doing things that people expect you to do?" It sounded more like a statement than a question.

I ate another oyster before replying, puzzling once again over his drift. "What do you mean?"

"You don't talk like a cop."

"In what way?" I asked, knowing the answer but needing a moment to adjust to his probing. In any one-on-one, I was invariably the one asking the questions; the attention Mike was giving me was flattering but too strange to be comfortable.

"Your grammar. Your vocabulary."

I filled my teacup and took a sip. The tea was tepid. I signaled for a waiter, and when I caught one's eye, pointed to the teapot. He immediately retrieved it.

"Most cops didn't go to private schools," I said. "I'm not going to change the way I speak just to sound like everyone else. That would be phony."

"Cops swear. You don't swear."

"I used to swear."

"Why'd you stop?"

"I realized the words were used so much that they'd lost their force. But when I'm provoked I swear, and then the words mean something—at least to me they do."

The waiter brought the tea. I checked Mike's cup, which was still full, then filled my own cup and took a sip. "Anything else?" I asked warily. Part of me squirmed under Mike's inquisition, but another part of me loved the attention as much as the actor who tells his listener, "Enough about me. What did *you* think of my performance?"

"You've never used your gun," Mike said.

That stopped me. Mike had obviously talked to people in the department. If he only knew, I thought, feeling the bulge on my hip. "Most cops never use their guns," I said after a pause.

"Maybe they've never had the chance. You have."

I picked up the last oyster shell, and speared the contents with my fork. "Who told you that?" I asked, trying to sound nonchalant, not wanting to give away how eager I was to know who his source was. I chewed the oyster slowly.

"Several people. They say you took unnecessary risks."

I waited to answer until I'd swallowed. "That's their opinion. I got the job done."

We finished the rest of the food, the chattering of the other customers and shouted orders of the waiters more than making up for our silence. When several minutes had passed without a question, I figured Mike had finished with his minor inquisition. I should have known better.

"Any reason why you didn't use your gun?" he asked abruptly, after finally taking a sip of tea. Maggie might not be Mike's natural child, but something had rubbed off. He was some kind of reporter. His face betrayed neither approval nor disapproval, only avid interest. He *made* me want to answer.

"I don't like to kill people. That's not so surprising, is it, even for a cop?"

"You tell me."

"I'd say most cops dread the thought. A few don't, and they're the ones you read about."

We sat in silence for a minute. Then Mike said, "Why are you still a cop if you don't enjoy it?"

I'd been about to pour more tea. Now I set the pot down. Britt had posed the same question.

"Did I say I didn't enjoy it?"

"What you said was 'I'm not sure police work is something one enjoys.' "

He'd quoted me word for word. Alarms went off. "Is this an interview?" I asked, suddenly upset.

He raised his hands, then dropped them. "What difference does it make?"

"I hate publicity."

"See? Most cops love publicity. They also enjoy what they do—"

This time *I* raised my hands, palms out. "Whoa! Wait a minute. *Some* cops enjoy what they do. Most cops *don't* enjoy what they do. They have a saying: 'It beats working.' Most cops are bored out of their skulls. They hang in there to get their pensions, then split for other jobs."

"The cops I've known enjoy what they do," Mike insisted.

"You've come to know them because they've done something newsworthy, which by definition means they're special."

"Whatever," he said with a wave of his hand. "They like being special. They like the power. They like the feeling that because of them, the world's a slightly better place."

"There are cops like that," I conceded. Mike had a point.

"But you don't feel that?"

I leaned back, trying, I suppose, to distance myself from this probing. As if on cue, four undercover cops from Central Station a block away came through the door. If you didn't know them, you would have guessed they were on their lunch break from a nearby construction job. All four were in their thirties, with stocky builds and incipient pots; all four were wearing jeans, work shirts, windbreakers and sneakers. They all saw me within two seconds of entering the restaurant, and acknowledged me with their eyes. These four cops would probably fall into the category Mike had just described. But not one of the four, I was sure, had entered the police academy with the expectations I had. "I don't feel that powerful, or special," I conceded uncomfortably, not because of the admission itself but because it was setting off memories of Elaine and that terrible night at 999 Green when she'd confronted me with my own ineffectiveness, "and I don't think that what little I've been able to do to date has made the world a better place." I thought for a moment, then added, not without bitterness, "I'm like a dermatologist who treats pimples without getting to the cause of the acne."

Mike took a second, slightly bigger sip of tea, then looked at me. "So if you don't enjoy it, why do you do it?" he insisted.

"I'm not saying I don't enjoy it, okay? But even if I didn't, I would do it because it needs to be done."

"But not by you," he said so strongly it surprised me.

"Why not me?"

"Because you don't need the money."

I stared at Mike for at least ten seconds. He had just rung my bell. But it didn't seem right to unload on him, given what he was going through. "Someday, when all this is behind you, I'd like to talk to you about that," I said, trying to keep my voice even.

"Talk to me about it now," he said at once.

"No," I said, fighting my temptation. "You've got enough to think about."

"Go ahead," Mike insisted. "I wouldn't mind thinking about something else for a few minutes."

Why not? I thought. When would I ever again have the ear of the Jimmy Breslin of San Francisco? "I'll keep it brief," I said. "What you've just said—that I shouldn't be doing what I'm doing because I don't need the money—you've got it backwards, Mike. What I'm saying is that I should be doing it *precisely* because I don't need the money."

This time Mike really frowned, wrinkling his nose and eyes and forehead. "What are you talking about?"

"The more I watch people, the more their lives seem to reduce to three stages: grow up, make money and die. I'm not just talking about working-class people, I'm talking about the so-called upper class, people with so much money they couldn't possibly spend it all even if they tried. And yet all they do, year in and year out, is apply themselves to making still more money. These are the people who call me a schmuck for becoming a cop."

He was looking at me intently for the first time since we'd sat down. "Go on," he said.

"*They're* the schmucks, those people. They don't understand that their home isn't just the house they live in, it's the *city* they live in— the place they enter when they walk out their door each morning, the place where their children go to school, where they buy their food and work and go to restaurants and movies and ball games. And every time they do, they have to drive over potholes, or walk down dirty streets, or run a gauntlet of beggars, or wonder if they're going to get mugged, or all of the above. They can see the city falling down around them as plain as the nose on their face, but they still think it's enough to write an annual check to charity and the rest will take care of itself. It *won't* take care of itself. What they've got to understand is that nothing's going to change until they contribute their time and their talent to solving the problem. If they were smart enough to make their fortune, they ought to be smart enough to fix their city. Instead of spending yet another year making yet another million they'll never possibly spend, they should give that year to their city."

Mike's eyes had shrunk. He looked down his nose at me as though trying to get a bead on this wild idea I was flying. "Doing what?" he said.

"Whatever they do in private life," I said, hearing the excitement in my voice. I'd tried the idea out perhaps half a dozen times, always at small gatherings, and always with the understanding that it wasn't to go further. Now here I was, laying it out for the most widely read man in town. "Only instead of getting paid for it," I went on, "they should give their expertise to the city. What I'm talking about is a cadre of professionals, an executive domestic peace corps, dollar-a-year men and women, like the executives who served our government during World War Two."

My heart was beating as though I'd just run a race. I watched Mike for a reaction. His eyes disconnected from mine. He seemed to look into the distance, nodding as he did. "You really think anyone would do that?"

"Why not?" I asked him, although I already knew his answer.

"People aren't like that."

"Oh, no?" I said, leaning toward him. "If that's the case, then tell me why you write your column. From what I understand, the pay isn't all that good."

"The pay's lousy, but the thought that I might be making a difference gives me a good feeling."

"Exactly my point," I said triumphantly. "I think if Mayor Putnam would offer some of his downtown buddies the chance to make a difference, they might go for it."

Mike stroked his chin, watching me closely. "Interesting," he said. "But this mayor would never do that. He's too bound up in the old ways."

I took a sip of tea to give myself a moment to think. Even as I was responding to Mike's explanation of his motivation for writing his column, two disconnected ideas had collided in my brain. A moment later I said as offhandedly as I could, "I'd imagine you've gotten some people sore over the years in the course of writing the column."

He stared at me for a moment, seeming to measure me in a manner and to a degree he hadn't done before, as though he was about to move us to a new level of trust and wanted to be certain I was worthy. I must have passed the test because he said, "What you're asking is whether I might have gotten someone so sore he decided to get even by hitting Maggie."

"That's right. The possibility just occurred to me."

"Then I'm ahead of you. That's one of the things I wanted to talk to you about." For a moment he dropped his eyes and stared vacantly at the table, still littered with our dishes and plates of unfinished food. Then he raised his eyes slowly, until he was looking at me again. "I get complaints every day. If I didn't, I'd be worrying that I wasn't doing my job. Threats are another matter. I get maybe half a dozen a year. The latest was about a month ago." He paused. "Do you read the column?"

"Of course," I said.

"Do you remember a piece I did last month about zoning?"

"I do, but refresh me."

"I wrote that the headlines these days are reserved for killers and dope peddlers, but that the biggest criminals in this city, the ones who are destroying it, are those who are perverting the city's power to regulate land use. Paying off politicians and bureaucrats for permits to put high-rises in undesirable places. Paying off building inspectors and fire inspectors and cops to look the other way while they ruin neighborhoods."

While he was speaking I happened to glance out of the corner of my eye. The four undercover cops had taken a table about ten feet from us and were giving their order to the manager. I'd seen them here before. I wondered if they paid their bill. In all probability they did. But you never know. "I remember that," I said to Mike. "Your case in point was the Tenderloin."

"Which twenty years ago consisted of a few porno movie houses and fleabag hotels where hookers took their tricks, and cheap boardinghouses, and today is teeming with Asians just off the boat, living eight to a room in tenements with dozens of code violations."

He had that right. "If I remember correctly, you didn't name any culprits."

"But I said I knew who they were," he said with a nod, "and that I was gonna name names if they didn't clean up their act."

"And?"

"And that day, I got a call from some guy with a foreign accent. He didn't give me his name."

"What kind of an accent?"

"It sounded Asian."

The restaurant crowd had thinned a little, and the noise level had diminished. Mike was speaking loud enough to be heard at nearby tables. But no one at those tables turned our way. I leaned close to Mike all the same and lowered my voice, hoping he'd take my cue. "Chinese? Japanese? Korean?" I said.

"I couldn't tell. They all sound the same to me."

It was a perfectly normal remark, considering the source, but it bothered me all the same. I let it pass. "What did this guy say?" I asked.

"He told me it would be a good idea for me not to write about that subject anymore."

Once again, I checked the nearby tables. We'd attracted no attention. "Did he threaten you?" I asked.

"Yeah. He said if I didn't lay off, he would cut my nuts off."

"That's just an expression."

"Not when it's your nuts, it's not."

Another time, I might have chuckled. Now, the sour taste of fear still a fresh memory, I could only sympathize. "You've got a point there. So what did you tell him?"

"I repeated what I'd said in the column, that if I didn't see some changes within the next few months, I'd name names. 'You'll be sorry,' the guy said, and hung up."

"So are you suggesting that whoever called you hit Maggie as a warning to you?"

"It's possible, isn't it?"

"Sure."

Just then the rotund manager came by, noted our empty plates and beckoned to a waiter. The waiter came over at once and cleared the plates.

"Everything okay?" the manager asked me.

"Outstanding," I said.

He picked up the teapot, felt it, and held on to it. "Your friend like the food?" he said, looking at Mike.

"Outstanding," Mike echoed.

The manager smiled. "I bring you hot tea," he said and walked away with the pot.

"You didn't use any names in the column," I said to Mike, "but did you describe anyone in a way that would make them recognizable?"

"Only to themselves," Mike answered immediately and conclusively, as though he'd not only anticipated the question but had already thought it through.

It took me a minute to frame my next question. "Were any of the slumlords in your column more identifiable than others—even to themselves?"

Same quick, decisive response. "Yeah," Mike said. "The biggest slumlord is an offshore corporation, registered in Curaçao. But four different sources told me the deep pocket is a man named Clarence Ho."

"Never heard of him. Did you check him out?"

"Yeah."

"And?"

"He's from Hong Kong, made his money in real estate there, and seems to have a lot of it."

"Does he have a criminal record?"

"None that I can find."

"Where have you looked?"

"Here and in Hong Kong." For a moment he faltered, then went on. "Clarence Ho, whoever he is, is only part of my problem."

"Go ahead."

A waiter brought tea and fresh cups to our table, and filled the cups. Over an hour had passed since our arrival. Most of the tables were still occupied, but with different sets of customers. The four cops were replenishing their plates from half a dozen dishes set on their table. They weren't doing much talking.

"You may have noticed that I haven't had a column in the paper this week," Mike said as soon as the waiter had left. "The editor told me to take the week off, more if I want it. But eventually I'm gonna have to get back to it." He turned for a moment and watched the traffic moving along Broadway. When he next spoke, his voice wavered. "And I'm gonna have to write about what happened." Then he looked at me piteously. "And I don't know how to handle it. I don't know shit about Asians. Except for Gordon, who's the Chinese equivalent of an Oreo—"

"The Chinese call them bananas, yellow on the outside, white on the inside."

"Whatever," Mike said, scarcely registering my remark. "Asians just haven't been part of my life. I don't write about them, and judging from the response, I doubt I have many Asian readers. Until that call, I'd never heard from an Asian either by phone or letter."

Mike sighed, picked up his teacup, seemed to study it for a few seconds, then raised it to his lips, staring over the rim before taking a sip. Then he put it down slowly and continued to stare at it. When he spoke next, it seemed to be with some difficulty. "I don't think of myself as a bigot, but the truth is I prefer it that way." And then he looked at me with an unspoken plea for understanding. "I was eleven when the Japanese bombed Pearl Harbor. Ten years later, I was an army war correspondent in Korea. Fifteen years after that, I did a tour in Saigon for the *Dispatch*. In twenty-five years, three wars against Asians." He paused. "That did something to me," he said after a moment, and then seemed to fight for his next words. "And now this." He sighed. "So I gotta write about it, and I don't trust myself to do it."

He sank back against his chair, seeming to diminish before my eyes. I could only imagine what he was thinking, this man who had written for so many years with such love and protectiveness and conviction about his adopted city and now, if the blank, uncomprehending look on his weary face was an indication, had to be telling himself that the city he served as watchdog had evolved into a place he no longer understood. Of the dozen or so print journalists I've come to know over the years, there is not one who, with good reason, doesn't consider himself or herself privy to some special knowledge about the workings of the world. It's this knowledge, gained through grinding experience, that helps them rationalize their generally underpaid existence. Take away the knowledge, and the understanding that goes with it, and you've taken the fight out of them. That was Mike in this moment, exhausted, depleted, helpless.

I understood now why he'd asked me to pick a Chinese restaurant in which he'd see Chinese people. It was the most basic beginning of his attempt to educate himself about Asians. "So how can I help you?" I asked.

"Reporters are only as smart as their sources. I thought maybe you could give me some perspective. You seem to genuinely admire Asians. Why?"

I smiled. "Funny you should ask. Chief Doyle once asked me the same question."

"What'd you tell him?"

"Nothing worth repeating. Let me think for a minute." Now it was my turn to study the traffic on Broadway. "Okay," I said after a while, turning back to Mike. "Let me start with a story. When I was in my mid-twenties, I developed excruciating pains in my ankles. It was all I could do not to scream when I got out of bed in the morning. It was agony just to walk, and running—the way I'd stayed in shape after I stopped playing ball—was out of the question. I went to every kind of doctor imaginable, orthopedists, neurologists, chiropractors, physiatrists."

"You mean psychiatrists?"

"No. Physiatrists, specialists in physical medicine."

Mike shook his head and pursed his mouth. "Never heard of 'em."

"Neither had I. They use nonsurgical methods to resolve physical problems. But they didn't help me, and neither did anyone else. The only thing that gave me any relief at all was an antiinflammatory medication, but it made me punchy and gave me stomach pains, and after a week the pain in my ankles would come back.

"So I finally went to see a Chinese acupuncturist, and she introduced me to a whole new way of thinking about the body, as an electric field with circuit breakers. The Chinese call it Ch'i. When one of those circuit breakers trips, the electric current that produces energy is interrupted, and the whole body suffers. You feel lousy overall, and you can have pain far removed from the site of the breakdown. She found my problem in my kidneys, the repository of energy, according to Chinese medicine. She took me off exercise, put me on a strict macrobiotic diet—no dairy products of any kind—and one day she stuck those famous needles in me. All of a sudden I felt this huge rush of energy pouring through me. It was warm and it tingled and I felt alive as I never had before. Within days the pain had subsided, and within weeks it was gone. Two months later, the acupuncturist gave me the green light to exercise. That day, I ran a mile in ten minutes. The next day I wasn't sore. The day after that I ran a mile in five:fifty, totally free of pain, and the only time I've had pain since then is when I eat food I shouldn't, or drink too much wine."

All this time, Mike had been listening intently, or so it seemed by his steady gaze and wrinkled brow. "So what's your point?" he said now.

"My point is that Asians address life differently than we do and in some ways better than we do, and it might help you to put your negative feelings about Asians into the context of a history that is a whole lot longer than ours and in some ways more successful. A second suggestion is that you stop thinking of Japanese, Koreans, Vietnamese and Chinese as one people. They're all Asians, but they're as different as Brazilians are from Argentines even though both are Latin Americans."

I sipped some tea. Once again, it was tepid. I looked around for a waiter, caught the manager's eye, and signaled for yet another pot. Then I turned back to Mike, who had slumped against his chair. By the look of him, he seemed satisfied with what I'd told him. I could have stopped right there, but I was revved up by this point, extremely conscious once again of whom I was talking to, and suddenly determined to say some things I'd kept inside me for years that might, through Mike, get to a huge audience of Caucasians.

"Since Chinese seem to be involved in the attack on Maggie, and since they're the ones I know the best, let me talk about them. They're great people, gifted, hardworking, inured to hardship—to other people, in other words, intolerable competitors. They practically built this state, and they were treated the way the Europeans treated the Jews in earlier centuries, and for the same reasons. If you ever want to read about a repressive society, read about California in the decades following the Gold Rush. The Chinese had no rights, none at all. But they kept coming because as bad as it might be here it was better than where they'd come from. That's still true."

Mike was staring at me, his eyes unblinking. If he wasn't listening to me intently, he was putting up a very good act. I pressed on.

"Today's Chinese immigrants aren't just victims of the political and economic circumstances that drove them from their homes, they're also victims of the people who came here before them, who began as victims themselves, fought their way out and up, and now want to take advantage of the latest crop of victims. As long as these people are in the victim pool, they're at the mercy of the people who profit from it. Only when they're free of the victim pool can they seek the benefits they came here to find."

The manager brought a fresh pot of tea to the table along with the bill, and filled our cups. I sipped from my cup, but Mike ignored his.

"What I hope is that when you do write about what happened, you'll keep it in perspective. The overwhelming majority of Chinese coming here are decent people. The day after they arrive, they're washing dishes in a restaurant, and three years later they own the restaurant. But there are bad people coming in at the same time—not many but enough—who are literally buying their way into every segment of society. That's much more insidious than out-and-out crime. One day the people of San Francisco will wake up and discover they're in competition with criminals, just as Maggie predicted. The attack on her could mean that day is imminent, and may have already arrived."

Mike cocked his head slightly to the side, and nodded several times, as though digesting what I'd said. I saw the four cops rise from their table. One of them was counting money. When he'd finished, he put it on the table. I was pleased. As they filed out each turned to nod at me, and I nodded back. But none of them came over. I was sure they'd recognized Mike, and had figured out why we were together.

I turned back to Mike. "Does any of that help?" I asked him.

"Yeah, sure. I'll have to think about it." He looked at me. "There's one other thing."

"What's that?"

"What makes you so sure the two men who hit Maggie were imported from abroad?"

I'd been against giving that information to the mayor's committee, but Chief Doyle had said he had to give them something. In the twenty-four hours since the meeting, someone had leaked the information, just as I'd predicted. "Where'd you get that idea?" I asked.

"Don't bullshit me, Zack." Unless I'd missed it, he still hadn't blinked.

I measured him for a moment. "If I tell you, and you use it, it could cause me trouble."

"I'm not gonna use it, I promise you. I just want to know." He said the last sentence slowly, emphasizing each word.

"Are you asking as Maggie's father?"

"Yes, yes, as Maggie's father, for Chrissake."

I took a breath, knowing that I wasn't using good judgment. But sometimes the "right" decision isn't the right decision. "Maggie told me that the man who slashed her used a cleaver, and then she repeated that fact twice without prompting. Asian-American criminals don't use cleavers. Triad hit men from Hong Kong do."

What happened next made me think of that opening scene in *The Hustler* where Paul Newman, pretending to be drunk, bets the guys in a small-town pool hall that he can make an impossible-looking shot. Once Newman's cohort has the wagers in hand, Newman, those famous blue eyes suddenly focused, takes the shot, then turns for the door without bothering to watch the foregone result. The moment I finished speaking, Mike's piteous expression vanished, his watery eyes turned dry and hard and his drooping mouth set in a thin, straight line. He glanced at the bill, took out his wallet, put thirty-five dollars on the table, tore off the receipt and put it in his wallet, pulled on his trench coat, shook my hand limply while mumbling his thanks and walked toward the door, his mind obviously elsewhere. As I watched him cross Broadway, his trench coat flattened by the wind against his skinny legs, it occurred to me that I'd just been hustled by the best reporter in town.

7

Mike had told me he'd checked out Clarence Ho with both the SFPD and the Royal Hong Kong Police, but on the off chance he'd been given a runaround, I typed Ho's name onto my computer screen as soon as I returned to my desk. Within seconds a message told me that as far as the SFPD was concerned, Clarence Ho didn't exist. I was disappointed but not surprised; if he'd been arrested in San Francisco, I would have known about him.

But I wasn't about to let the matter rest there. If Clarence Ho, whoever he was, had hit Maggie as a warning to Mike, he was undoubtedly the man who'd also threatened me. Minutes later, I sent a routine query by fax to Inspector Dennis Hampton, my best contact at the Royal Hong Kong Police. At six o'clock I received a long fax back from Hampton. Clarence Ho had no record, Hampton stated, but he was under investigation. To this terse message, the inspector had attached a confidential memorandum.

CRIMINAL INTELLIGENCE BUREAU
CRIME WING

POLICE HEADQUARTERS
HONG KONG

Illegal Immigration Syndicate

The Criminal Intelligence Bureau have recently been conducting enquiries into the activities of a syndicate which is arranging the passage of illegal immigrants from China through Hong Kong to the United States. As a result of these enquiries a number of personalities who are involved in these activities have been identified, as have a number of companies which are being utilized by the syndicate to carry out these activities. This report serves to apprise the reader as to the identity of the personalities and companies involved, as to the method employed by the syndicate and as to the identities of a number of customers of the syndicate.

The report then identified two travel agencies that booked illegal immigrants on Swissair flights from Hong Kong to El Salvador, from where they eventually made their way to the United States.

Both agencies provide the illegal immigrants with forged "two way" permits, enabling them to enter Hong Kong from China and ensuring a safe stay in Hong Kong whilst travel arrangements are being finalised. Forged travel documents and airlines tickets are then provided for the onward journey to El Salvador and the United States. The principals in said agencies will only deal with clients by way of introduction, so as to minimise the possibility of detection. All illegal immigrants should have a guarantor or relative in Hong Kong so that once the immigrant has arrived safely in the United States the outstanding finances can be settled.

One of the agencies, Sunset Travel Services Limited, the memo noted, was owned by Clarence Ho.

A sweet business. Ho not only maintained tenements in San Francisco for Chinese immigrants but recruited his tenants in Hong Kong and China. No wonder he was upset with Mike Winehouse. That, of course, didn't prove he'd arranged the hit against Maggie, but he was a man worth watching, and that was just what I was going to do.

I sent another message to Dennis Hampton—an Englishman my age whom I'd met at a conference on Asian crime in Honolulu several years before and who'd helped me ever since—requesting that I be kept informed, and sank back into my chair wondering what I could do next. It was when I realized there was *nothing* I could do that I was suddenly and violently hit, as surprisingly as by a blindside block, by exhaustion and despair in equal measure.

Since Chief Doyle's call the previous Saturday, I'd averaged less than four hours' sleep a night, kept awake by thoughts of my breakup with Britt, or of the case or the threat I'd received. I'd worked compulsively from seven each morning until late each evening, certainly out of a desire to get some momentum going on the investigation and to block out thoughts of who might be stalking my every move, but just as certainly to diminish the time in which my thoughts would dwell on Britt. Now, with the weekend only two days off, nothing could suppress the realization that, for the first time in half a year, she would not be walking through my door on Friday evening.

At seven o'clock I finally drove home, too weary to think of an alternative. To add to my gloom, it was yet another misty evening, not dense enough to be called fog but sufficient to spoil the view. The combination of the mist and my misery must have awakened long-ago memories, much as a remembered smell or sound will do, and I found myself thinking about that period fifteen years earlier when I was living alone at 999 Green and trying to persuade Elaine to move in with me. At that time, I'd taken to drinking to try to handle my loneliness, unaware that alcohol, while providing an almost instantaneous lift, eventually reinforces whatever mood the drinker brings to it. A happy drinker becomes happier, a sad one sadder. That was during my rookie days on the force, before the sight of alcohol-related automobile accidents had worked their cumulative effect on me. Every night I would drink, and wind up more miserable than when I began; the following night, knowing what the outcome would be, I would still drink again.

My drink in those days was the dry martini, which had lost favor in other regions of the country but remained the cocktail of choice among San Francisco men. I loved everything about the martini, its appearance and smell and taste and of course its instantaneous effect—the sense of blissful relaxation, the temporary suspension of the day's concerns—and even its ritualized manufacture. Now, missing Britt, doubting my ability to get the Maggie Winehouse case off square one, and depleted since the threat against me by a constant expense of nervous energy, it was a dry martini that was suddenly

uppermost in my mind, and to hell with the downstream consequences.

It had been years since I'd made a martini, but as I went into the
kitchen it was as though I hadn't missed a day. I took five ice cubes
from the refrigerator just as I had in those days—it was never four or
six—and put them into an oversized old-fashioned glass. Then I went
to the small dry bar between the kitchen and dining area and poured
one part Noilly Prat vermouth and four parts Gordon's gin—wet by
others' standards but not by mine—into the glass, not needing to
measure after all these years. After stirring for ten seconds, I removed
one of the ice cubes and swizzled it around a cocktail glass, then cut a
peel from a lemon, giving the mixture just enough time to cool further but not enough time to be diluted by the ice. Then I removed the
ice cube from the cocktail glass, poured the mixture into the glass
with the aid of a strainer, and twisted the lemon peel over it, watching
with satisfaction as oil from the skin of the fruit spread across the surface of the liquid. Then I went back into the living room, settled into
my favorite oversized armchair, and at last—anticipation being yet
another pleasurable part of this ritual—took my first sip.

In my drinking days I always drank slowly and carefully, feeling
my way through the familiar terrain, recognizing each signpost,
knowing exactly where I was going and how long it would take to
get there. There were never stops or detours. There was only the
steady progress toward the objective, the same one every day, and
that feeling of floating toward it, knowing that nothing would keep
me from it.

That's how I remembered it, but this time nothing happened. No
first, gratifying hit of the drink or increase in self-assurance that
inevitably accompanied it, no tingling in my limbs, no sense of peace
regained. I took another sip, and then another. A martini in those
days lasted twenty minutes, but this one was gone in ten.

I made another in exactly the same way, took a big sip, and
returned again to the living room. This time, rather than return to
my favorite chair, I picked up the binoculars I keep on the table next
to my chair in order to observe passing ships, turned off the lights,
walked to the windows and, careful to remain to one side, looked
down into Greenwich Street. There was just enough light from the
streetlamps to enable me to use the binoculars. Moving them slowly

from east to west, I inspected every doorway and parked car. Then I moved to the windows facing north, and trained the binoculars on that small portion of Hyde Street visible to me. There were no doorways to inspect because west of Hyde and north of Greenwich is Alice Marble Park. All I could see from my vantage point were two cars parked on Hyde, facing south.

A man was seated in the driver's seat of the car parked at the corner. And he was looking my way, with as clear a view of my building as I had of his car. In the darkness, relieved only by the light from the streetlamps, I couldn't make out his features, but I kept the binoculars trained on him anyway, hoping that he'd keep looking my way until a car moving north along Hyde would throw added light into his car. Ten seconds passed, then twenty, then thirty. Cars moved south, but not north. Finally, a car moved up Greenwich to Hyde, stopped, and then turned north. In the second that the car was turning, its headlights shone directly into the parked car, and I had a perfect view of its occupant.

He was Asian, about forty, and heavy.

I watched for another minute, then moved away from the window, retrieved my martini and swallowed half of it. Whatever soothing impact the alcohol was having had been tempered, if not canceled, by the adrenaline the sight of that man had triggered. I couldn't prove that he was a stakeout, but what else would he be doing there?

Cool it, I told myself. It's a lousy night. You're tired—tired, hell, exhausted. Pack it in. Make yourself some dinner.

Drink in hand, I walked to the kitchen, opened the refrigerator, found nothing to cook—Louisa Maria, my once-a-week Brazilian housekeeper, who also bought groceries for me, hadn't been in since the previous Friday—went to the pantry, found a can of salmon, walked to the counter and was about to open the can when I suddenly drained my glass, put the .357 into my hip holster, threw on a sportcoat and trench coat and raced out the door. All of this probably hadn't taken twenty seconds. In another twenty seconds, I was marching up Greenwich to Hyde. Whether it was pride or whiskey courage or a determination not to settle for canned salmon for dinner I didn't know, but I was damned if I was going to cower in my home.

He was still there, in his car, and he was looking straight at me. As

I got to the corner, he opened the door of his car. Trench coat and sportcoat opened, I watched his hands, ready to draw my gun.

Suddenly, he smiled. *"Hola!"* he called.

"Hola!" came a voice a few steps behind me.

In a moment a woman came up alongside me. She was Latina, in her thirties, and pretty. And she was smiling at the man, who was now crossing the street, obviously to greet her, and just as obviously with no interest in me.

He wasn't Asian. He was Latino, with the kind of almond eyes and other features that make you put stock in those theories about how it was Asians who first settled the Americas.

The man and woman—probably a domestic in a nearby household—kissed and, arm in arm, walked to the man's car, leaving me alone and feeling stupid.

In that mood I walked six blocks through the mist to the Hyde Street Bistro, where I'd been eating most nights I was alone since the restaurant had opened in 1988. A fresh wind drove the mist against my face and chilled my body. By the time I arrived I'd persuaded myself that the effect of the cocktails had abated, and following a brief inner struggle, I ordered a glass of red wine with dinner. If I was breaking my rule of not drinking during the week, I might as well do it in style, I told myself, and what difference did a one-night recess make anyway? I was surprised when Albert Rainer, the restaurant's genial young owner, a tall, good-looking transplanted Austrian who by this point considered me more a friend than a client, set a second glass of wine in front of me, because I hadn't been conscious of drinking the first and hadn't remembered ordering the second. By the time the third glass arrived I was more depressed than I'd been when I'd started drinking and, sure enough, I returned to my flat as though to a haunted house.

The sound of the telephone Thursday morning shocked me from a fitful, drug-induced sleep.

"It's Gordon Lee," the familiar voice said, the delivery quicker and pitch higher than normal. "I'm sorry to call you so early, but I didn't want to miss you. I've got something to show you, but I can't do it at the station. Have you got a VCR?"

"Of course," I said without enthusiasm. Years ago, believing that

people with an urgent need to talk to me ought to be able to find me,
I'd listed my telephone number. Feeling my throbbing head, I was
regretting that decision now.

"I can be at your apartment in fifteen minutes. Okay?"

"Make it twenty," I said groggily.

I put the phone down, and lay in my bed for another minute, recognizing that hungover condition I remembered so well from my
rookie-cop days, hating myself for what I'd done to myself. Neither a
hot shower nor a shave could erase the lines in my face.

Gordon and I really made a pair. He arrived exactly fifteen minutes
later, a haggard copy of the carefully composed man he projected on
television. His face was drawn and tinged with stubble, and his thick
black hair was uncombed. His eyes were bloodshot and rimmed with
shadows. His movements were abrupt; he punctuated every sentence
with nervous gestures and he couldn't sit still, rising every minute or
two to pace around the living room. He talked twice as fast as he
broadcast.

"Before I show you what I've got, I've gotta know something." He
paused for a deep breath, then exhaled slowly. "Can you keep it to
yourself?"

"If it's information dealing with the case, I'll have to report it."

Gordon bit his lip. "But what about the media? Will you have to tell
the media?"

"Of course not."

I'd been sitting in my reading chair, trying not to move. Now Gordon came close to me and stood over me, obliging me to tilt my head,
and instantly a stabbing pain shot through it.

"Can I have your word that you won't give anything about this to
the media?" Gordon pressed.

Too many secrets, I thought. I'd confided in Mike Winehouse. Gordon was confiding in me. "You've got it," I said, meaning it, yet
knowing that as a circle of confidentiality enlarges, its circumference
invariably weakens.

Gordon looked marginally better at once. "Good," he said, exhaling with relief and backing off, enabling me to return my head to
level, which must have made me look better as well.

"Are you under some kind of pressure?" I asked him.

"Pressure's not the half of it." For the next ten minutes, he must

have walked the equivalent of half a mile as he told me what had happened since Saturday night. He'd anchored the late-evening news on
Sunday, just as he had on Saturday, leading, of course, with the story
on Maggie, which, he said, had been a ghastly experience. How he'd
gotten through it he still couldn't figure. As he spoke, the memory
seemed to shake him. Monday was supposed to have been his day off,
but he'd been awakened shortly after eight by a call from the news
editor, Jim Smith, a former news editor at the *Dispatch* and one of the
more levelheaded veterans in town, asking him to be in the station
by nine-thirty. When he arrived, he'd found Sam Barnes, the station
manager—the man who'd complained so vociferously days earlier at
the mayor's meeting—in Smitty's office.

"They both thanked me for hanging in there over the weekend,"
Gordon related. "They said they wouldn't have blamed me if I'd
begged off. Then Smitty got to the point. He said that the station was
going to be under a lot of pressure in the coming days and for some
time to come. Everybody would be doing Maggie's story, but it was
our story, so everybody would be watching us to see what we did
with it. For that reason, he said, they wanted to put their best reporter
on it, which, he said, meant me. But they couldn't do that without
asking me how I felt about it, because of my relationship with Maggie.
I said I felt lousy about it. 'Then you tell me what to do,' Smitty said.
He said that network had called him at home at seven o'clock that
morning, asking him what he was planning for the story. Given the
connection, they said they'd like us to cover the story for them. Then
Smitty said to me, 'Whoever does our story will do the network
piece.' "

Gordon stopped pacing, and came close to me again. This time he
placed his hands on the arms of the chair and leaned down so that
his face was a foot from mine. "They were baiting me with network.
They know how much I want to move up. But they know just as well
as I do that I'm not the most qualified person to do Maggie's story. I
may be the best on camera at the station, but there's no way I'm the
best reporter. I told them there were at least three people who have
more experience than I do and would do a better job. I've done almost
no investigative reporting and I don't know squat about crime reporting. I told them that. 'Doesn't matter,' Smitty said. 'You'll learn.' And
he'd give me a strong producer."

At this moment he looked as if he'd need a Hercules. He was beginning to sag and move erratically, like a mechanical doll in need of rewinding. "Sit down, Gordon, before you fall down," I said. "And let me fix us some breakfast."

"You go ahead," he said, sinking into a chair. "I'm too upset to eat."

I put some coffee on and made myself a Virgin Mary, using twice as much Tabasco sauce as normal. That got my attention. Then I poured my usual granola into a bowl, topped it as always with sliced banana and returned to the living room, where Gordon was dozing. His haggard condition couldn't obscure the strong and harmonious features that had undoubtedly given him a leg up in television and just as undoubtedly drawn Maggie to him. "Gordon?" I said softly, hating to wake him, but knowing I had to.

He woke with a start, blanched at the sight of my cereal and sank back into the chair as I returned to my reading chair.

"Why do you suppose Smitty and Sam were so eager to assign you to the story?" I asked him.

Gordon nodded. "I was afraid you'd ask that," he said grimly. "I'm not very proud of the answer—or what I imagine the answer is. They're appalled by what happened, but I have a feeling that someone at the station—I'm sure it's Sam—decided that as long as it happened they might as well make the most of it. And the way to make the most of it for sure is to have me on the story because of my relationship with Maggie." Gordon took a nervous breath. "Whoever that someone is," he added bitterly, "he made sure the media knew about the relationship."

"You think Sam leaked it?" I asked between crunching bites that must have unsettled Gordon.

"Either Sam, or Smitty at the insistence of Sam, because Smitty on his own would never do something like that. He's too much of a pro. But I couldn't prove it. All I know is that on Monday afternoon the AP filed a story—a 'heart-wrenching' story, they called it," he said, a disgusted look on his face—"about the San Francisco television reporter who had set out to track down the men who abducted and maimed his girlfriend, and the story apparently ran all over the country. I've had calls from *People*, *McCall's*, *Redbook*, the *Ladies' Home Journal* and a dozen other magazines, all of them wanting interviews, and some of them wanting me to write a story for them."

Gordon raised his hands, then dropped them into his lap. "The worst part of it is that whoever leaked the story put out the wrong idea. Yes, we're sleeping together, but we're not living together like they say." He rose from his chair and began to pace again. "I mean, how can I make a commitment when my future's in New York—at least I hope to God it is—and Maggie wants to spend her life in San Francisco?" he said, seemingly needing to explain himself to himself as much as to me. "But now the whole country thinks I'm committed to Maggie, so if I were to break off with her for whatever reason, no matter how legitimate, I'm suddenly the all-American shitheel— which kills my chances with network. Even saying that makes me sound like a shitheel." At that, Gordon raised his arms up over his head and tilted his head back, as though beseeching higher powers. "Ah, God," he cried in despair. Then, dropping his arms, he held his hands out to me. "I *do* grieve for her. Christ, I go crazy thinking about what those fuckers did to her. But I've got my own life to live."

Gordon walked to the window and looked at the bay. "So I told them I'd give it a try." He turned back to me as I set my cereal bowl aside. "That was my mistake." He gave his head a violent shake before continuing, as if that might clear it of his unhappy memories. "Monday was difficult for me, but pretty routine, because there was a lot of breaking news. The riots. The reactions. The police reports. I thought I'd done okay. But when I got back to the station, Smitty called me into his office again and said that wasn't what they wanted. Anyone could do that. What they wanted from me was stuff on the investigation. If the police wouldn't give it to me, Smitty said, I should develop my own leads. I told him I wouldn't know where to start. And he said, 'Get us something, anything. We don't want this story dyin' on us.' "

Gordon stopped to catch his breath. "Are you sure you don't want a cup of coffee?" I asked, rising to refill my own cup.

"Nah," he said. "My stomach's an acid factory."

I took my dishes to the kitchen, poured the coffee and walked back to the living room. Gordon was talking and pacing before I'd resumed my seat. "Under the circumstances," he went on, "there was only one constructive thing I could do, and that was to study the tapes of Maggie's series. So that's what I did, until five o'clock yesterday morning. And I just couldn't find a thing. It just made no sense that anyone could be so provoked by that series that they'd do what they did to her."

I nodded. "I'm sure you know I reviewed the tapes myself, and I didn't find anything either."

"Yeah, they told me you'd been in."

"But there's got to be something there."

Gordon stared at me. "There is," he said. "But there's no way you would have found it." He paused, for emphasis, I was sure. His theatrics were wasted. By this point, my nerves were so raw that any glimmer of a clue, from any direction, would have caught my attention. "Do you know what outtakes are?" he said.

"Footage that doesn't get used?"

"Exactly. It's station policy to hold outtakes of every show for a month in case of any kickbacks. About four o'clock this morning, I was lying in bed, unable to sleep, when it suddenly hit me that I'd forgotten to look at the outtakes. I immediately got dressed and went to the station. And here's what I found." He went to his tote bag and removed two tape cassettes. He put one of them into my VCR, and turned on the television set. "Okay, now listen to what Maggie's saying, and watch what happens as she says it."

And suddenly, on the screen, there was Maggie, standing with her microphone somewhere on Clement Street, in the midst of her segment on the triads, reciting what had certainly been the hardest-hitting statement of her series: "Ironically, a good many of those triad millions coming into the Bay Area may have been gained illicitly right here at home through the sale of drugs. The drug money is exported from the United States, laundered abroad, then returned here illegally, usually through wire transfers to local banks, from where it finds its way into investment, mostly in real estate. If the amounts the authorities talk about are accurate, the Bay Area could one day be owned by gangsters."

"Here it comes," Gordon said, his voice rising like a sports announcer's.

Abruptly the camera zoomed past Maggie to a shot of a white two-story corner building, with a large black-and-white sign that said PACIFIC RIM BANK.

I felt my spine stiffen. "Ha!" I said. "That wasn't in the piece."

"That's right. But look."

Quickly Gordon ejected the outtake tape from the slot and replaced it with the tape of the actual broadcast, and hit the play button. And there it was, the Pacific Rim Bank in the background, not nearly so noticeable as in the outtake, but there nonetheless. "The non-Chinese viewer wouldn't know it's the Pacific Rim Bank," Gordon said excitedly, "but a discerning Chinese viewer who lives in the area would know it, and whoever owns the bank would sure as *hell* know it and figure that what Maggie's suggesting, without saying as much, is that the local bank receiving the wire transfers on behalf of the drug dealers is the Pacific Rim Bank." As he finished, Gordon's voice was trembling, either from fatigue or excitement or both. He fell into a sofa and watched me intently.

Don't jump to conclusions, right? A story on the evening news about triads moving big money to San Francisco, a bank in the background. It sounded pretty good to this target of some mystery man's cruel intrigues. Thoughts bombarded me. Had Maggie interviewed anyone at the Pacific Rim Bank? Had anyone in the course of her reporting mentioned the Pacific Rim Bank, or suggested she stand in front of the Pacific Rim Bank? Did someone at the bank decide that Maggie knew more than she was saying? Or was the Pacific Rim Bank's involvement completely inadvertent?

"It's slim," I said, trying to keep a poker face and the excitement out of my voice.

"But it's something, isn't it?" Gordon said, leaning toward me from the sofa, his eyes wide.

"Could be." I chewed on my lip for a minute. "Have you talked to Maggie?"

"Not yet," he said. His answer was a little quick, as though designed to head me off. I remembered his abrupt departure from the hospital two nights earlier. I decided that whatever friction existed between him and Maggie was not pertinent to the case, and was better left to them.

"So what do you want from me?" I said.

"You've already given me one thing, confirmation that I could be on to something. What I need now is help in following it through." He leaned forward, spread his arms and held his hands out, looking helpless. "I don't have a clue as to what to do next."

"What you do next, Gordon," I said, "is check out the Pacific Rim Bank."

"That much I figured. But how?"

"Would you like me to do it?"

Gordon sagged back against the sofa. "I thought you'd never ask," he said. "But I don't want to trouble you," he added quickly.

Not much he didn't. "It won't be any trouble," I said.

"Then could you do it right away?" That note of desperation had crept back into his voice.

I peered at him, incredulous. "Gordon," I said, "this case is my top priority. Of course I'll do it right away."

"And you'll tell me what you find?"

"I can't make any promises. It depends on what I find."

Gordon shot from his seat, straightening to his full height. "Wait a minute, wait a minute," he said. "That's not fair. Look what I've given you."

My hands shot out in front of me, a sign for him to back off. "What you've given me may be nothing, but even if it's something, there's no quid pro quo, and you've got to understand that. I'm a cop, Gordon, not your legman."

Gordon sat down heavily and fell against the back of the sofa once again. "I hate this," he said softly, his handsome face spoiled by misery.

I walked to him and put a hand on his shoulder. "I promise you, I'll do what I can. Now, will you have some breakfast? You look like you could use it."

I gave him some orange juice—he refused anything else—and sent him on his way. In my car half an hour later I imagined the scene between Smitty and Sam Barnes after Gordon had left Smitty's office. Smitty would have turned his chair around and stared at Sam. "Do I look like a piece of shit?" he'd have said. "I sure feel like one."

"Spare me," Sam would have said.

"He's right, you know. He *doesn't* know squat about crime reporting, and we do have three reporters with newspaper experience who could do a much better job."

"Doesn't matter. Just make sure the press finds out that Gordon and Maggie are lovers. And don't look at me like that. I've got a job to do."

8

As a member of the San Francisco Police Department, I was obliged to make a formal request before I could receive information from any other agency of the government. As a private citizen, I could often obtain the information directly, without paperwork or delay. Given Gordon's fragile condition and my own jeopardy, the more direct approach struck me as being in the public interest. So instead of driving to 850 Bryant, I drove to the State of California building at 455 Golden Gate to obtain a copy of the incorporation papers of the Pacific Rim Bank from the secretary of state's office.

A new weather front had moved in overnight, ushered in by brisk winds. Rain had begun to fall, the winds magnifying its force. The morning traffic crept along slick streets. I pulled into a parking space a block from the State Building and, head down and trench-coat collar up, jogged through the rain to the entry.

The main office of the secretary of state was in Sacramento. The San Francisco office, in Room 2236, seemed just big enough for its two employees. At least I figured there were only two, since the room held two desks. Only one person was there when I arrived, a trim, red-haired, pleasant-looking woman I judged to be in her late thirties. She turned to me with a smile, then unaccountably pinched her brow and tilted her head back. "What can I do for you?" she said. I wondered if my hangover had made me a little paranoid or whether there really was a challenge in her question.

"I'd like to see the incorporation papers of the Pacific Rim Bank, located in San Francisco."

"All I can do for you here is tell you whether the bank exists as a corporation. If you want a copy of the incorporation papers you have to get that from Sacramento. I can take your application if you like."

I shook my head, discouraged. "How long would that take?"

"A week, ten days."

"No good," I said, continuing to shake my head. "They couldn't fax a copy here?"

"We don't normally do that for the public. You'd have to be from a government agency." Was I imagining again, or was she trying to lead me somewhere? She was certainly watching me closely.

"I see," I said, not at all comfortable with where this was heading. "And if I *were* from a government agency?"

"If you *were,* and you had an urgent need, we do make accommodations for that sort of thing. But *are* you from a government agency?"

I sighed. "I'm a captain in the SFPD," I confessed.

"I knew it!" she said, her smile suddenly returning. "You're Captain Tobias. I saw you on TV."

I tried not to show my dismay. "I need those incorporation papers fast, as in right away," I said. "If I go through channels it could take days. I'll be happy to pay whatever charges there are."

She smiled. "I think we can help you, Captain, and there won't be any charges."

I smiled back. "When's your birthday?" I said.

"No, no, none of that," she said, coloring. "First, let's make sure the Pacific Rim Bank is a California corporation."

That took about a minute. A phone call to Sacramento took another three minutes. "It'll be about forty-five minutes," she said. "I hope that's soon enough."

"It'll have to be, won't it?" I said.

She bit her lip. "I probably shouldn't ask, but does this have anything to do with that horrible thing they did to that poor girl?"

Oh, boy, I thought, here we go. "Look," I said, "I assume you'd like us to find the guys who did it."

"Oh, would I ever," she said, her face turning grim.

"You could help us a whole lot if you said nothing about this visit."

She nodded. "There'll be paperwork. Your name'll be on it."

I sighed. "Just don't call anyone's attention to it, okay? If they say something, explain what I just told you."

In the hallway, I shook my head again. I hated having to take these bureaucratic risks. I worried about that for a minute, and then walked out into the rain.

Ideally, it would have been better to read over the incorporation papers before talking to Maggie, but I felt I knew enough to interrogate her. Back in my 4Runner, I set out for the hospital. In seven minutes I pulled into the covered alcove leading to the emergency room, put my SFPD parking card on top of the dashboard and went to Maggie's room.

I walked inside to find half a dozen men and women, doctors and nurses, standing at the foot of Maggie's bed. On the left side of the bed was a lean man of perhaps sixty with thick wavy hair, wearing a doctor's long white coat. A pair of glasses with magnifiers clipped to them perched on his nose. He had his butt on the bed, next to Maggie's right side, and as he bent to examine her his face was six inches from hers. His two delicate hands—a surgeon's, I was certain—moved lightly across her skin, which had been harshly illuminated with a portable light. Her eyes were shut to defend against the intense glare.

I'd tried to prepare for this moment by telling myself it would be awful. Nothing could have readied me for the reality. Half a dozen rows of small, precise, closely spaced black sutures ran vertically and horizontally on each side of her swollen face, some from eye level to her chin, others from her nose to her ears. The most aggravated areas were around those points where the wounds intersected. As I stood, appalled yet transfixed by the sight, a ball of rage shot from my stomach and through my throat. I had to clench my jaw to stop myself from crying out.

Until that moment I had never put any stock in the theory that energy fields exist between people who share a strong concern. But just then, as I could all but taste the bile of my anger, Maggie's eyes flew open and fastened onto mine. "Don't look," she begged.

In an instant all eyes were on me, pronouncing me an intruder. Without a word I fled into the hall, leaned against a wall and shook.

I take no special credit for my emotion. With the possible exception of Joseph Pendola, the dark-tempered, misanthropic sergeant I'd caused to be transferred from the Gang Task Force, I don't know another cop who wouldn't have reacted as I did to the sight of Maggie's mutilated face, not, perhaps, as intensely but enough to silently vow, as I did now, to find the perpetrators if it took a lifetime.

Only then, like the aftershock of an earthquake, did it hit me: whoever had done that to Maggie had promised to do the same to me. I pressed my back more firmly against the wall.

Moments later Mike and Bess arrived. Mike was carrying a small overnight case. He peered at my face through narrowed eyes and said, "What's wrong? What's happened?"

"Nothing," I said quickly, upset that I'd let my emotions show. "Maggie's being examined by a bunch of doctors."

Mike immediately began to propel Bess toward the door. "Better wait," I said. "They don't want anybody in there."

"We're not anybody," Mike said gruffly, urging Bess forward.

"I don't think *Maggie* wants anyone in there," I said as emphatically as I could without also sounding alarming.

That stopped them. We waited in the hall together. A few minutes later the doctors and nurses filed out of Maggie's room, talking among themselves. Mike made no attempt to stop them. He took Bess's arm, and walked her into the room. I waited a minute, then followed them inside.

One parent was on either side of the bed, clutching Maggie, whose face had mercifully been swathed once again in bandages, held in place by a gauze mask with holes for her eyes, nose and mouth. All three of them were crying. I immediately began to back out of the room, but Maggie saw me and motioned me to stay.

"That man who was examining me was Dr. Soskin, the chief of plastic surgery," she said in a quavering voice, trying to compose herself. "He said . . . he said . . ." For a moment I thought she wouldn't be able to continue. "He said he could make the scars practically disappear." At that, she burst once again into tears.

It took her another several minutes to report what the doctor had said. Through a process called dermabrasion, and using a machine that looks like a handheld drill, with a sandpaper disk attached, he would sand the scars away. For weeks, her face would be covered with scabs; when the scabs fell away, the abraded areas would initially be pinker than the rest of her face, and then whiter, but in time they would blend in. If they didn't, the surgeon could employ another process called repigmentation, in which the white skin is tattooed the same shade as the rest of her face. "He says that when it's over, and with the proper makeup, no one will be able to see the scars unless they're looking for them."

It sounded almost too good. I wondered if Dr. Soskin had been trying a little too hard to reassure Maggie. But I wasn't about to say so. "That's great," I said instead, my voice suddenly so shaky and my throat so tight you would have thought Maggie was my kid sister. "That's just great." As Mike and Bess clutched at Maggie once more, I reminded myself that regardless of the outcome, there would be no way of abrading the internal scars inflicted on her by this outrage.

A few minutes later, a nurse came in to tell Maggie that she'd been discharged. Mike and I stepped into the hallway so that Maggie could dress. "There's a mob of reporters in the lobby," Mike said. "Is there any way to avoid them?"

"I could take her," I said. "I parked in the emergency entrance, and there were no media people there. Give us a ten-minute head start."

"Good," Mike said. Without another word he turned and walked slowly to the restroom.

Minutes later a husky young orderly who sounded Jamaican arrived with a wheelchair and went into Maggie's room. When he reappeared, Maggie was in the chair, dressed in sweats and sneakers, which I assumed had been in the overnight case, looking absolutely normal except for her gauze mask. The orderly pushed her to the elevator. I followed behind. Everyone in the corridor stopped to watch her leave, but no one said a word.

In another minute we were in the emergency room and headed for the exit. We both saw it at once: a pack of reporters, photographers and camera crews, gathered just outside the door. "Oh, no," Maggie whispered.

"Someone on the inside got paid to alert them," I said.

The orderly looked at me. "Not me, *mon*," he said.

I looked at Maggie, squeezed her shoulder and said, "Let's go."

The moment we emerged, all hell broke loose. There was pushing and shoving and cursing, as well as blinding light. At least a dozen reporters shouted questions at the same time.

Maggie seemed to shrivel before my eyes, trying, turtle-like, to sink her head into her shoulders. "I'm sorry, but I have nothing to say," she repeated half a dozen times, but that didn't stop the questions or the shoving.

"What a horrible experience," she said as I drove away from the hospital. "I'm ashamed to think of all the times I've been on the other side."

"Someone has to do it," I said.

"But I don't have to be that someone." She spoke slowly, and with a finality suggesting that she'd been rehearsing the line—or some equivalent—for days.

"What do you mean by that?"

"I mean," she said in those same measured tones, "that I've decided not to go back to the station. I don't want to be a journalist."

I suddenly felt very paternal. "This is no time for decisions, Maggie. It's a time to heal, and to be grateful it wasn't worse than it was."

Maggie uttered a sharp, bitter laugh. "What could be worse than this?"

"They could have killed you."

"I think I might have preferred that," she said after a moment, her voice barely audible.

I could feel my insides shrivel. "Don't even say that," I said.

I drove a roundabout route to Maggie's apartment to make it difficult for anyone who might try to follow us. It was a waste of time. "Oh, no," Maggie moaned as I turned onto Divisadero and started down the hill. In front of her apartment building were three mobile television units and the same small media army she'd had to deal with at the hospital.

I parked in a red zone, got out, then helped Maggie out. She clutched me, and once again seemed to try to hide her head between her shoulders. "Give us a break, Maggie," someone shouted as we pushed through to her door. Maggie turned and cast a stricken look in the direction of the voice. Moments later we were inside the building.

The living room of Maggie's apartment had views to the west and north. To the west lay the Presidio, to the north the bay and the Golden Gate Bridge and, across the bay, Sausalito, Tiburon and Belvedere. The views this day were obscured by the rain, which had lost its force but still persisted. "It must be gorgeous on a clear day," I said to Maggie, who had sunk into a deep armchair. "Dead people don't get to see that."

"Shall I tell you what I see?" she asked quietly. Without waiting for a reply, she pointed at the Presidio, its tall forests covering the slopes rising to the northwest portion of the city. "There, in there, that's where they drove me. I'll never be able to look at the Presidio again without thinking of those men."

There was no answering that remark. I could do nothing more than stare at her, my mind once again processing the knowledge that someone somewhere in the world had scarred not just the face but the life of this young woman, and had threatened to do the same to me. "Can you take a few more questions?" I asked.

"Go ahead," she said, her voice resigned.

Before I could begin, Mike and Bess arrived. I stepped into the kitchen to give them some time alone with Maggie, and to drink some desperately needed water. Then I returned to the living room. "I need to have a few more minutes alone with Maggie," I said to her parents. "Could you excuse us?"

As they turned and walked into the kitchen, I moved a dining-table chair next to the armchair in which Maggie was seated, sat beside her and spoke just above a whisper. "Your father will probably want to know what we talked about. It's important to both of us that what passes between us stays between us. Okay?"

"Sure, okay," she said at once. "I can understand that."

"Good," I said, my voice still low. I looked toward the kitchen to be certain Mike was out of earshot. Satisfied that he was, I said, "When you did that wrap-up segment about the triads and money laundering, was there any particular reason why you stood where you did?"

"You mean the stand-up on Clement Street?" Taking my lead, she kept her voice as low as mine.

"Yes."

"I didn't choose the location. It was either the producer's choice or the cameraman's."

"There was no special reason why you wanted to have the Pacific Rim Bank in the background? No point you were trying to make?"

Maggie drew her head back. "I don't remember the Pacific Rim Bank or any other bank being in the background and, no, I wasn't trying to make a special point."

I thought for a minute, my eyes wandering around the room. Someone—either Maggie or whoever had helped her decorate—had good taste. A small sofa covered with a subtle gray and white stripe— the same fabric as the chair she sat in—was placed along the wall, centered on the fireplace. A glass coffee table was next to the sofa, its base a piece of free-form iron sculpture painted light blue. Under the coffee table was an off-white rug, resting on the gleaming hardwood floor. Two huge ferns sat in large terra-cotta pots on either side of the window. Half a dozen framed gallery posters hung on the walls. It was the room of a successful, competent woman who had her life together—its only incongruous element at the moment the woman herself, with her bandaged face.

"Producers have a lot to do with the content of a story, don't they?" I said then.

"That's putting it mildly," Maggie said, her voice tinged with irony.

"Do you know whether the producer on your series was trying to make a special point?"

She shook her head. "If he was, he sure didn't tell me."

"Did you ever have any dealings of any kind with the Pacific Rim Bank?"

"I've never *heard* of the Pacific Rim Bank."

"You never interviewed anyone connected with the bank?"

"No."

"Are you sure?" I said, trying not to sound disappointed.

She hesitated before answering. "I may have conceivably inter- viewed someone who had a connection to the bank, but I certainly didn't know of the connection at the time of the interview, and the connection would have had nothing to do with my wanting to inter- view that person."

"That seems definitive enough," I said with a sigh.

"Why all these questions about the Pacific Rim Bank?"

I hesitated. "You haven't spoken to Gordon this morning?"

Maggie seemed to sink further into the armchair. "I spoke to him at nine o'clock," she said flatly.

"What did he have to say?" I asked carefully.

"He wanted to know if I felt up to doing an interview for the station."

"What did you tell him?"

"That I didn't." Because of her bandages, I could only guess what kind of a look she had on her face, but I could imagine it from her tone of voice: weary, angry.

"How did he take it?"

"Not very well. He sounded weird, as if he was under a lot of pressure."

"He is. Anything else?"

"No. Why? Was there something he was supposed to tell me?"

"It was probably better that he didn't, but I'm going to tell you because you of all people have a right to know." After extracting a promise of secrecy, I explained about the outtakes and the Pacific Rim Bank's presence in the background.

Maggie shook her head. "Pure coincidence."

I pursed my lips. "Maybe there's someone out there who doesn't believe in coincidence."

By the time I got back to the secretary of state's office, the fax had arrived from Sacramento.

"Good luck," the pleasant woman said. "I hope you find whoever did it, and put him away till he rots."

"You can help me do that by keeping our little secret," I reminded her.

"With great pleasure," she said grimly. "Put it out of your mind."

I read through the papers the moment I got to my office.

The Pacific Rim Bank had been capitalized at five hundred thousand dollars. The low figure surprised me, but when I thought about it I realized it wasn't surprising at all. Banks were in the business of risking other people's money, not their own.

As I read the list of corporate officers, that familiar feeling of trepidation began creeping back into my system. The names meant nothing to me. It would take weeks just to identify these people; it could take months to discover which of them, if any, had ties to the triads. If they'd been clever, we might not discover that at all. The question I had to answer was whether it was worth all the effort, given the circumstantial nature of the lead and the minuscule chance of a payoff, and considering that the Asian detail, which would do the work, was already overextended.

Oh, shit, I suddenly thought. It's happening. You're thinking exactly the way whoever threatened you wants you to think. You're backing off.

And then, just as suddenly, before I'd had time to berate myself, I saw a name I knew: Jimmy Chang, the mayor's dapper, hail-fellow appointee to the Port Commission, the self-appointed spokesperson for Chinese immigrants who had complained so passionately at the mayor's office about the bad rap they were taking for the rise in real estate prices.

For a cop, I have an unusually positive attitude about people. It's not just a matter of giving them the benefit of the doubt or believing that a person is innocent until proven guilty, it's a conviction, as basic as DNA, that, deep down, the overwhelming majority of people are decent and well-meaning. You'd think that by this point I'd have known better, given the work I do, but for some reason my faith in people persists. Seeing Jimmy Chang's name on those incorporation papers, I immediately rejected the thought that this committed, enterprising, outspoken man could conceivably be involved in anything remotely shady. I recalled the legend: how he'd come to San Francisco from Hong Kong via Canada in the early seventies with little more than the clothes he was wearing, and how, twenty years later, his restaurants and other investments had made him a multi-millionaire. Through his assiduous contributions to charities and campaign war chests, he had, moreover, ingratiated himself with the city's establishment. Appointments had resulted: first to steering committees, then to chairmanships. His crowning achievement had been his recent appointment by the mayor to head up the San Francisco Port Commission, his all but hopeless task to persuade shipping lines from the Pacific Rim to off-load in San Francisco instead of Oakland, San Pedro–Wilmington or San Diego.

All this I knew because Jimmy Chang—unlike most Chinese, especially first-generation immigrants—loved publicity. "Chinese want to be in control, but don't want to be in the limelight," Jim Mich, my mentor on the Gang Task Force, had told me within weeks after I'd joined the Asian detail. "They've always had to manipulate. They've survived because they've always known how to find the back door."

Jimmy Chang used the front door. It was not enough that his work in both public and private sectors merited legitimate coverage by the media; he also employed a public relations man to get his name in the columns. A self-proclaimed Horatio Alger, he was highly regarded in the Chinese community, not only for his phenomenal career but for his efforts in its behalf. Want an inspiring speaker for your function? Call Jimmy Chang. The gist of his statement was "If I can do it, you can do it," exactly what newcomers from Asia wanted to hear. His advice they didn't want to hear, but they listened. "Assimilate," he told them. "Learn language. America your country now."

Jimmy was married, had three children and was by all accounts a devoted family man. There wasn't the slightest whiff of a problem. That his name had turned up on the incorporation papers of a new and modest bank owned and operated by Chinese meant absolutely nothing—unless that five hundred thousand dollars had been put up by the triads and the bank was being used to launder triad money.

Was Jimmy Chang a triad point man? I'd always wondered how he'd become so prosperous in such a relatively short time. It takes money to make money, and it was Jimmy himself who boasted that he'd had nothing when he got here. It was conceivable that he'd done it all on his own, but it was more likely that someone had helped him. If he'd been helped, the odds were that it had been with tainted money, because with a past like his, Jimmy didn't exactly fit the profile of a man with an abundance of legitimately wealthy friends. In the context of the present situation, that possibility should now be explored.

As should the possibility that it was Jimmy Chang—affable, gregarious Jimmy—who'd sent me the package with the warning message and the cleaver, as far-fetched as that seemed. I'd figured that the man who'd addressed that package had been foreign-born, was writing in a language acquired as an adult, yet knew English well enough to get the humor of the message on the T-shirt. Jimmy fit all those criteria.

But I knew that neither of these possibilities would be investigated. In a city in which Asian voters could turn an election, they were political dynamite. Permission to investigate Jimmy Chang would not be forthcoming from the man I worked for, whose mandate from the mayor was "Do whatever you have to do not to embarrass my administration." A finding that Jimmy Chang was even peripherally associated with the hit on Maggie' would reflect very poorly on the man who had appointed him to the Port Commission.

Still, I was obliged to report Gordon Lee's discovery, as well as my follow-up, to Chief Doyle.

The chief's office is on the fifth floor of the Hall of Justice, about fifty yards from mine. Compared with every other office in this ill-conceived and cheerless building, it isn't bad. A large reception room manned by two policemen leads to the main office, a spacious rectangle furnished with dark mahogany desks and tables and brown leather chairs and sofas, with windows looking east directly at the Bay Bridge. A trophy case filled with memorabilia is set into the west wall, which is paneled in pine and covered with plaques. There is a large full bathroom, a small room equipped with a cot, where the chief can get some rest when he's obliged to man the fort around the clock during crises, and a private door through which he can flee when someone he doesn't want to see is in the waiting room. Because I more or less fit into the category of someone he doesn't want to see, I try to do as much of my business with him as possible on the phone, even though his office is half a minute's walk from mine.

His reaction was exactly what I'd expected, and then some. He glowered when I knocked, waved me inside impatiently, then listened in silence as I made my report, his face darkening before my eyes. When I tried to place the copy of the incorporation papers in front of him he waved it away. "Get it out of here," he said, back once again in his normal tough-guy idiom. "I don't want shit like this on my desk."

"Excuse me, Chief," I said, trying to keep my voice neutral, "what happens if KUBC follows this up on its own, gets something on Jimmy and then reports that they approached us with the information but we did nothing?"

Doyle looked at me as though I'd just said the dumbest thing he'd ever heard. "What are they gonna get on Jimmy, fer Chrissake? The man's a fuckin' angel. I don't want you touchin' this, you hear?"

"Then what do I tell Gordon Lee?"

"That's your problem," he said, dismissing me with a wave of his hand.

"Excuse me again, Chief," I insisted, "it's not just my problem. He didn't come to Zack Tobias, private citizen, he came to a representative of the SFPD. He expects a response from the SFPD. And he didn't come as Gordon Lee, private citizen, he came as a representative of the most popular television station in San Francisco."

The chief glared at me in silence, as though the problem was entirely my creation. "Just get rid of it, Tobias," he said impatiently. "And then go out and make some busts."

"What?" I was so startled that my question sounded like an accusation.

"You heard me."

"Who am I supposed to bust?"

"Chinese dirtballs, that's who," he said, his always limited patience clearly exhausted. "It's been five days since the Winehouse assault and we haven't made a bust. We're way overdue. We've gotta show some action."

"We've got nothing, Chief. We've got nobody."

He wasn't listening to me. "How many Asian dirtballs are there in this town? Five hundred? A thousand? Take your pick, but bring half a dozen of 'em in for questioning before the sun goes down, and that's an order."

That was the moment when, at long last, my stubborn faith in the basic goodness of people finally cracked. I'd opted for police work in a flush of youthful idealism, believing—unlike my more fervent contemporaries—that the only way to change the system was to work within it. My father's murder had been the catalyst, but the idea had already been percolating in my brain. A month before his death I'd been to a raucous campus meeting featuring a speaker from the New York City Police Department. He'd let the audience chant "Pig, pig, pig" until it finally tired out, and then he'd offered the audacious proposal that if we liked the idea of seeing a problem on the street and being able to correct it, we should consider becoming cops. Imagine, he'd said to his disbelieving audience, totally silenced by surprise, every one of you can combine your own agenda with the public agenda. Don't think of the cops you've seen. Think of *yourself* as a cop—a modern knight.

In my twenty years on the force, that mating of personal and public agendas had happened at most half a dozen times. Looking at Chief Doyle now, his contempt for due process as ineradicable as an oil stain, a man who considered every lawbreaker a bad seed, who, deep in his heart, did not believe that criminal behavior could be a consequence of social and environmental causes, I recognized what I'd denied for so long, that I, not he, was the misfit, not just a double but a triple oxymoron, a rich *and* Jewish *and* progressive cop. "That's an order I won't obey," I said as calmly as I could.

For a moment the chief stared at me. And then he smiled. "That's insubordination, Tobias, and that's your ticket out of the force."

"You couldn't bring charges and you know it."

"Don't bet on it."

"The order's illegal."

"That's not for you to determine."

"I'll take my chances," I said.

Doyle smiled again, like a man sitting down to dinner who's presented his favorite food. "Good," he said.

9

The first of Gordon's calls had come in before noon. I hadn't taken it. By two o'clock he'd called half a dozen times. At two-thirty, Martina, our young but experienced receptionist, who has a feel for trouble, stuck her head inside my office, a look of concern on her face.

"Him, again?" I said.

She nodded. "I think you better talk to him. He sounds real strung out."

I did my best to stall him without actually lying. "These things take time, Gordon," I said. "I've read the incorporation papers, but there's nothing in them that suggests the kind of link you're looking for."

"Is there anything, anything at all?" he said. Martina had been right; he was strung out, all right, speaking in a new, higher register, as though the tension he was under had tightened his vocal chords.

"To answer that question truthfully," I said carefully, "I would have to have IDs done on every officer and member of the bank's board."

"Well, are you looking into them?"

" 'Looking into them,' as you put it, would take weeks."

"Can I say you're investigating?"

A little chill invaded me. "Gordon," I said, trying to drive the words home with the same force and rhythm you'd use to pound a nail, "you *can't* use this. There's nothing to it."

I've owned dogs who were less single-minded. "I've got to have something, anything," Gordon pleaded. "They're on my back over here."

I blew out my breath. "All I can tell you is that if and when I develop something substantial, and it's something I can let you have, I'll give it to you. You want to tell your bosses that, go ahead."

"That's not going to be good enough," Gordon muttered, and hung up.

For the next minute I sat at my desk, Gordon's last remark in my head, wishing mightily that there was something I could do to make this investigation move forward. Four days had passed since my own safety had been threatened. I was tired of looking over my shoulder and jumping at the sound of every unexpected noise, tired of worrying, tired of being tired. I wanted desperately to be someplace where no one could get me. Unable to bear my frustration, I walked across the office to a window. Seeing that the rain had stopped, I returned to my cubicle, put on my trench coat and left without even bothering to tell Martina where I was going.

In praising the attributes of San Francisco, everyone speaks of its beauty, but almost no one mentions its size. Here's a metropolis with all the commerce, culture, sophistication and amenities you could want, and yet you can get from one end of the city to the other in twenty minutes, and to most places a lot quicker than that. By three-fifteen, I'd been to my home, checked for stakeouts and, finding none, collected my gear and was at Crissy Field with my wet suit on and my sailboard assembled. As I prepared to launch I scanned the choppy waters for other windsurfers. It didn't surprise me that I saw none. This wasn't prudent windsurfing weather, and I knew it. But I was captive to the need to solve a problem, and before I could do that I had to create one.

Within minutes I was well out into the bay, in the heaviest wind I'd ever experienced, a full sail wrenching my arms, my legs working like shocks to absorb the waves. If a thought crossed my mind, I don't recall it. I was aware of nothing but wind and water and how I could use them to propel myself in the fastest possible manner. As I reached the center of the bay a gust of wind pouring through the Golden Gate hit my sail. The mast dipped toward the water, carrying me with it. I pulled against the force with all my strength. Just as I thought I was going in, the wind eased so quickly that I not only righted but almost lost it the other way. As the board and sail rocked out of control, first one way, then the other, I was a helpless passenger. I'd never been in conditions like these. If I got into real trouble, my chances of being spotted were nil.

I saw the boat before I heard it, only because the cardinal rule of windsurfing on the bay is to be constantly on the lookout for freighters passing in and out of the Golden Gate. It was a power-cruiser, big enough to pull water-skiers, heading out into the bay from somewhere on the San Francisco side, possibly the St. Francis Yacht Club. My first thought was that whoever was at the helm was as crazy as I was, because he was hauling so fast he cleared the water each time he hit a wave. By the time I could hear his engine, I realized that his course would take him uncomfortably close to me. I'd been on a starboard tack, heading south toward the city at something like eighteen to twenty knots, my back to the Golden Gate; quickly I eased the sail, and changed my course 180 degrees, in the direction of Sausalito. While doing this I turned my head to check the power-cruiser, and saw to my surprise that its skipper had also changed course, and was now bearing straight at me. Seconds later the pow-ercruiser came up on my starboard side, so close it all but brushed me. I screamed in rage, and then in fear, as the wake from the cruiser threw my board into the air. An instant later I was in the water.

I came up, shook my head, grabbed my board and maneuvered myself so that I was between the rig and the Golden Gate. An instant later the wind began to flow under the sail and the sail rose from the water, pulling me with it. Seconds later I was back on the board.

I had one moment to be aware that I was hyperventilating and to feel my heart thumping my ribs before I saw the cruiser—once again, it was heading straight for me. I assumed the skipper had put about to apologize and to make sure I was all right. It took me about one sec-ond to realize that I was dreaming. Whoever was piloting that cruiser was trying to kill me.

I pulled on my sail with all my might, turning my board just in time to miss the cruiser's bow by no more than a yard. Again the wake flipped my board, and again I found myself in the water. I came up panting and weak, and had to hold on for a minute before starting my remounting maneuvers. The instant I was up I pointed my board toward Crissy Field, more than a mile away. Then I began to tack to and fro, turning my head every few seconds to watch for the cruiser.

It had come about and was on my tail. In moments it was so close that for an instant I could see the man at the helm. He was Asian. His mouth was open. I could see his teeth. I couldn't hear him, but I was sure he was laughing.

Seconds later he caught me, coming up this time on my port side. Once again he passed within a yard, and once again the cruiser's wake set my board bucking, but this time I miraculously managed to stay upright. I had no time to note the cruiser's name, let alone its progress. I had everything I could do to keep from flipping.

Never had I felt more helpless or vulnerable. I discovered a degree of fear worse than fear: terror. Only my rage held me together. But I was sure I couldn't survive another pass.

And then, just as suddenly as it had appeared, the cruiser vanished.

At last I managed to regain control, and continue toward Crissy Field. I beached, exhausted, a few minutes later, as the last light of day glimmered in the sky. For five minutes I sat, shaking too hard to stand, processing the understanding that someone out there not only knew my every move and intended to hurt me unless I heeded his warnings, but could kill me at his whim. For the moment, at least, that wasn't his objective, because he could have done that easily, either ramming me or shooting me, certain there'd be no witnesses. But my disappearance would arouse the SFPD, and he obviously didn't want that. What he wanted was to make the cop in charge of the Maggie Winehouse case fold it.

With this comforting thought in mind, I rose and staggered to my car through the gathering darkness. By the time I'd changed from my wet suit, stored my board and sail and strapped them to the roof of the car, it was almost five o'clock. Once in the car, I began to shake uncontrollably, as you do when a high fever breaks. Driving home, I might as well have been attempting to fly a helicopter, for all the assurance I had about getting there.

At last I made it to my flat. My answering machine was signaling a single message. It was from Gordon. "Zack, I've *got* to talk to you before the five o'clock broadcast. Please call me the minute you hear this. It's now four-thirty." He sounded desperate and rattled.

"Oh, Jesus," I said aloud. I turned on the television set. The broadcast had just started. I watched the introduction with impatience. At last, the image of Ida Parsons came on the screen. Her first sentence set me on edge. "A possible break in the Maggie Winehouse case," she said.

"Come on, come on," I called out as she continued her summary of the day's top stories. And finally there was Gordon, standing on Clement Street in front of the Pacific Rim Bank, reporting that tape found in the KUBC archives had raised questions about a possible connection between the bank and the attack, five days earlier, on Maggie Winehouse. And there, on the screen, was the tape, the very tape Gordon had shown me that morning, and there was Maggie, on Clement Street, talking about the triads. And then the clip from the outtakes. And then Gordon, once again in front of the bank. "A copy of the bank's incorporation papers, filed with the secretary of state, lists Jimmy Chang, Mayor Putnam's appointee to the San Francisco Port Commission, as a director of the bank. The Special Investigations Division of the SFPD is pursuing this and other leads. Gordon Lee, reporting live from Clement Street in the Richmond."

"Oh, my God," I cried, wondering if I'd just heard my death sentence.

Mature judgment would have compelled me to stay where I was, but judgment of any kind was no longer in command. Rage and fear in equal measure had taken over. I showered in two minutes, dressed in three, ran from my apartment, climbed into my car and raced it through a series of side streets to avoid the rush-hour traffic. In another ten minutes I was at the KUBC building across from the Embarcadero. A uniformed guard sat behind a marble counter in the lobby. "Can I help you?" he said.

"Has Gordon Lee come in yet?"

"He just got back."

"Good," I said, and strode toward the elevator.

"Hey, you can't go up there."

"Oh, yes, I can." I showed him my badge.

The guard shrugged. "Third floor," he said.

A minute later I was in the newsroom. It looked just like the city room of a newspaper—dozens of desks in clusters, each desk with a computer monitor. The only difference was the television camera affixed to a rolling pedestal in front of Ida Parsons's desk. Behind the camera was a cameraman, and behind him the floor director, cuing the closing minutes of the newscast.

Then I saw Gordon. He was seated at a desk twenty feet beyond Ida. I half ran to him, grabbed him by the shoulder and turned him around. "Are you out of your mind?" I shouted. "Have you taken leave of your senses?"

Instantly Gordon was on his feet. "Please," he whispered, holding up his hands.

"Please, my foot," I shouted.

"Shut him up," someone hissed. Several men were approaching on a run.

"For Christ's sake, we're broadcasting," Gordon whispered to me.

"I don't give a damn," I snapped back, making no attempt to whisper.

"Please," Gordon pleaded. He motioned me into an office separated from the newsroom by a glass partition. "I called you," he said the moment he shut the door. "I wanted to explain what happened. Smitty demanded to know what I'd been doing, so I had to show him the outtake. And then one of the other reporters got a copy of the incorporation papers and we found Jimmy's name, and then Smitty told me to use it."

"I can't believe that," I said. "Smitty knows better than that."

"You don't understand the pressure we're under, Zack." At that moment, his strong face looked positively craven. "It's coming all the way from network. We had to put something on the air."

"And blow the only lead we've got?"

Gordon suddenly straightened, and regarded me defiantly. "It was *my* lead. I'm the one who found it. Look, I'm sorry, but there was nothing I could do."

"Yes, there was. You could have kept your mouth shut, no matter how much pressure there was. And you had no right to say that the SFPD was investigating."

"You investigated, didn't you?" he said in a tone that implied he had me.

For a moment, I stood there, fury jumbling my thoughts. "Watch what happens," I said at last. I turned for the door, then turned back. "And don't call me again." With that I stormed from the newsroom through a corridor of Gordon's gaping colleagues.

For an hour after that encounter I walked the Embarcadero. For the first half hour, I was so incensed that I was completely unaware of my surroundings. Only gradually did it begin to register on me that all these piers, once loaded with freighters and passenger ships belonging to Matson and Pacific Far East Lines and Pacific Orient Express and others whose very names conjured images of romantic voyages to intoxicating ports, were now empty of anything save seagulls and the occasional homeless person willing to brave the damp and cold in exchange for a night of solitude. "Come on," I shouted into the silence, "you want me, here I am." At last, I drove home, my fear and anger diminished but far from discharged.

My phone was ringing as I walked into my apartment. I let the answering machine take it. A minute later I heard Chief Doyle's raspy voice. He didn't bother to identify himself. "Be in my office at nine o'clock tomorrow morning," he said. The sound of his handset dropping into its cradle was as definitive as a gunshot.

There'd been three calls before the chief's, all from reporters. In the next hour I received another six calls, one of them from Mike Winehouse. His voice sounded ominously curt. His suggestion that I return his call seemed more for my benefit than his. But I couldn't bring myself to talk to him or any of the others.

It was ten o'clock before my stomach seemed receptive to food. I fought off the craving for a drink, and made myself an omelette. At eleven o'clock I fought another craving: to watch the local newscasts and see what damage Gordon had caused. I knew that I'd be up all night if what I saw disturbed me, so I went to bed and tried to read myself to sleep with the latest *New Yorker*. It didn't work. My mind kept drifting from the printed page to the day's events. My muscles kept firing, as though I was still out on the bay. In the moments when I wasn't replaying that deadly game of water-tag, my mind leaped from Maggie to Mike to Gordon to Chief Doyle to that wretched and seemingly insoluble crime of the previous Saturday night and finally to thoughts of what would happen when I stood before Chief Doyle the following morning.

I didn't have the slightest doubt that the chief would attempt to use Gordon's dangerous gaffe to get me in some way, but I tried to persuade myself that he wouldn't be able to do much damage. A reprimand, perhaps, but certainly not a suspension. One didn't, willy-nilly, suspend an officer with as good a record as mine. No question, I hadn't followed the book in my dealings with Gordon. I should have listened to what he had to say and watched what he had to show me and then sent him on his way, giving him no encouragement whatever. I certainly shouldn't have given him a pretext for saying the SFPD was investigating *anything.* So I'd been indiscreet with the media—once. But that alone would be insufficient grounds for a suspension. Besides, I reasoned, Gordon and his station had proceeded on their own. In any case, I was entitled to a hearing; if the chief proposed to suspend me, he'd better have some good hard facts to support his case.

At midnight, I tried to sleep, but I was still too shaken. At 2:00 A.M., I gave up, turned on my light and tried *The New Yorker* again. When I turned off the light an hour later, I'd read more than half the magazine, but had I been tested on the content, I wouldn't have been able to answer two questions in ten.

Sometime before four I must have fallen asleep. The alarm woke me at seven. By eight o'clock, I knew that the Jimmy Chang story was the lead item on all the local newscasts, and had made page one of Friday morning's *Dispatch.* But the news stories weren't half as bad as Mike Winehouse's long column, his first since the attack six days before, which the editors commemorated by breaking it on page one.

It began innocently, even touchingly, and, to judge by its quality, sounded as though Mike had been working on it for days:

> Maggie's not quite four when I hear her screaming for help in the backyard of the house we've rented for the summer at Lake Tahoe. I rush outside to find her hanging on for dear life to the arm of two-year-old Larry, son of friends, who's found a way to crawl beneath a fence and is about to tumble over a thirty-foot drop. It's the first sign in Maggie of a powerful nurturing instinct.
>
> Throughout her childhood, she plays with younger children, pretending she's their mother. Because her own mother gave her up for

adoption at birth—a fact we shared with her as soon as she could understand it—I figure that she's compensating in some inner way.

But pretty soon I realize this mothering instinct in her is just that, an instinct. Each year it grows stronger. Mothers recognize it, and entrust their kids to Maggie, who has a thriving baby-sitter business going by the time she's twelve.

It's not just younger children Maggie nurtures. Children her own age cast aside by their peers become part of her family. One is Barbara Woo, who arrives from Taiwan with her father, a doctor, and mother, a teacher, when Maggie's nine, and moves into our neighborhood.

Barbara speaks little English, so none of the schoolgirls play with her. None of them but Maggie.

Somehow they communicate. Maggie coaches Barbara in English, and learns bits of Chinese. Before long there's a place at the Woo family's dinner table for Maggie anytime Bess and I are out for the evening.

Maggie grows up older than her years, always comfortable in the presence of adults. In our house that means fellow scribes, or city officials, or attorneys plugged into the city's life.

From the time she's seven we let Maggie stay up through the cocktail hour. Dressed in pajamas and robe, she sits quietly, usually at my side. I think maybe she's not listening. She never says a word, but the next morning she asks me a dozen questions about matters we discussed.

Of all those matters, the one she cares most about is the increasing presence of Asians in the city. She perceives them as underdogs, needing her help. In high school, she organizes a welcome committee, designed to ease the adjustment of newcomers.

At Berkeley, Maggie majors in Asian studies, then gets a master's degree in journalism. During her graduate studies, she interns at KUBC. They tell her she's got a job as soon as she finishes school.

I'm not happy with her choice, and tell her so. I hope she'll be a print journalist because I believe her gift with words will be wasted, that television's time constraints won't give her the chance to express her knowledge and understanding. But Maggie tells me she'd be trading on her father's name if she went into the newspaper business in San Francisco, which is where she wants to make her life. She won't do that.

Maggie's assignment on the impact of Asian migration to the Bay Area is her first big project. I'm worried that she doesn't have the seasoning for such a sensitive story, and tell her so. I should know better. At 26, Maggie has yet to find a challenge she doesn't like.

Maggie argues that, with the exception of their three Asian reporters, she's as aware of Asian sensibilities as anyone on the KUBC staff, and she promises to produce a measured story.

I think she does. Apparently someone thinks she doesn't.

Early Sunday morning, she's in a bed in San Francisco General Hospital, her head encased in bandages. She looks at me with tears in her eyes and says, "What did I do? I don't know what I did."

At this point, the column turned so sour and vindictive it seemed as though another writer had finished it.

The police think Maggie's series upset some Asians. They don't know who. Too bad the investigation is being conducted by the SFPD's Gang Task Force, a gang of misfits with a reputation for being more interested in the amount of money and personal favors they can shake out of Chinatown than in the amount of protection they can give it.

Working on a lead developed with the help of the SFPD—undoubtedly someone in the Gang Task Force—the television station Maggie works for broadcasts a story alleging that one of our city's most valued Asian citizens was somehow involved in the criminal attack against her. The flimsiest, most poorly documented, irresponsible story I have seen or heard in nearly forty years of reporting about this city.

The SFPD has concluded—on the basis of a coincidence it is passing off as evidence—that the attack on Maggie was carried out by triad goons from Hong Kong. Now, I've learned, the police are shutting down their investigation, for lack of further clues.

Sure, I'm Maggie's father. But I'm also a citizen of this city, suddenly and deeply ashamed of its police department.

I would have bet anything that Mike Winehouse had written the column in advance, and put a new, bitter ending on it after watching Gordon's story. In the process, he'd violated our confidence. He hadn't said "cleaver," but he might as well have. Now every reporter assigned to the case would demand to know what the SFPD was "passing off as evidence." And I would have to revise my self-appraisal: not a double or a triple but a quadruple oxymoron—too soft to be a cop.

A few minutes before nine, trying to hold up a head that felt like it weighed fifty pounds, I walked into the Hall of Justice, took an elevator to the fifth floor and stepped out into a darkened, deserted corridor. For about one second I was mystified. Only then did I remember what it was that preoccupation had obviously caused me to forget. It was Veterans Day, Friday, November eleventh. Except for the Southern Station, Traffic Bureau, Operations Center and jails, the Hall of Justice was closed.

At nine sharp, I entered Chief Doyle's office. Al Gomez, his driver, an officer big enough to stop an intruder from bursting into the chief's office, was seated at his desk in the reception area. He stood when he saw me—why I didn't know, maybe to express his condolences for what was about to happen to me. He said nothing, but he didn't have to; his commiserating expression said it all. He was wearing weekend clothes—a sweater over a sport shirt, and jeans—which told me that he'd received an unwelcome summons from the chief, just as I had. It crossed my mind that the chief had committed yet another thoughtless little act—he could have driven himself in—but I didn't have time to dwell on it. I walked on, into Doyle's office.

He was seated at his desk, wearing a red sweater over a red polo shirt, the color as obvious as his mood, and a perfect match. It was a golfing outfit, I was sure, and it occurred to me that among the many things he must have held against me this morning was that the need to deal with me had made him lose his tee time at the Olympic Club. The *Dispatch* was on his desk, folded to Mike Winehouse's column. His scowl dug deep furrows into his ruddy face, into which anger seemed to have infused new life. His body was ramrod-straight from the waist up. He did not invite me to sit down.

"I have just come from the mayor's residence," he began, lapsing at once into that polished, careful language he retained not only for public appearances but for moments of special fury. "I was summoned there at seven o'clock this morning. The mayor informed me that he had been on the phone last night and this morning with Jimmy Chang. It should not surprise you that Mr. Chang is extremely upset. He is threatening to sue, not just KUBC but the city, for defamation of character and grievous damage to his earning power. He believes that the SFPD leaked a story to KUBC—a story without foundation—that has irreparably damaged not only his reputation but the reputation of a bank in which he has invested a considerable sum of money and from which he stood to make a considerable sum of money. He indicated to the mayor that unless something is done to redress this matter he intends to charge the SFPD with anti-Asian bias *and* to take his case to the Asian community in pursuit of appropriate political reprisals."

I tried to speak, but the chief held up his hand. "When the mayor finished telling me what Jimmy Chang had told him, he asked me if I knew what percentage of the city's population was Asian. I told him I thought it must be close to thirty percent. 'That is correct,' he said, and then he asked me how good I felt his chances for reelection would be if he were to alienate thirty percent of the city's population. 'Not good,' I said. 'Impossible,' he said. And then he reminded me that if he lost the election I would lose my job."

Whenever the chief had spoken to me in the past, I'd always detected a wariness in his eyes. Now they were pools of pure malevolence. "I did not need to be reminded," he added, his voice laden with irony.

Once again I tried to speak, and once again Doyle held up a warning hand. "I blame you for this, Tobias. I ordered you to get rid of it." With a flip of his wrist, he gestured at Mike Winehouse's column. "Not only did you not get rid of it, you made it worse."

"KUBC got nothing from me," I said before he could stop me.

In all our previous verbal sparring the chief had listened to my words with the same wary attention a boxer gives the other fighter's fists. This time, it was as though I hadn't spoken. It dawned on me then that I was fighting an opponent transformed by the knowledge that whatever I might throw at him wasn't going to hurt him. The protection I'd enjoyed as the son of an important political supporter of Mayor Putnam had been cast aside by this sudden new threat to his reelection, of which I was being portrayed as a principal cause. The time had come, I decided in a flash, to tell the chief about the threat I'd received, as well as my close call on the water. But as I began to do that he cut me off.

"As of this moment," he said, in that same portentous manner, and speaking, it seemed, with more gratification than wrath, "you are relieved of command of the Special Investigations Division. As of Monday morning, you are assigned to the Records Division."

For a minute, I was too stunned to reply. In all my reckoning about what sort of move the chief might make against me, the one thing I hadn't considered was a transfer to the SFPD's equivalent of Siberia.

Unlike formal charges or a suspension, this was not something I could fight.

And then, more swiftly and mysteriously than the response of a computer program to the stroking of a single key, my mind processed half a dozen related ideas, and Jimmy Chang materialized on my brain's equivalent of a computer screen as a man who had lost face.

How many times have you said something so suddenly and unexpectedly that it's out of your mouth before you've had time to consider it? "As of Monday morning," I said, completely surprising myself, "I'll be on vacation." With that, I saluted the chief, did an about-face and walked toward the door.

"Just a minute," the chief ordered. I stopped, turned and stared at him. For a moment he glared at me in silence. "Officer Gomez!" he shouted. Seconds later, Al walked swiftly through the door. "You're a witness to what I'm telling Captain Tobias," the chief said, inadvertently clarifying why he'd asked Al to drive him in instead of driving himself. Then those malevolent eyes moved back to me. "You're off the Maggie Winehouse case," he said. "And stay the hell away from Jimmy Chang. Those are orders. Now get out of here."

I'll say this much for fear. It takes you places you've never been before. For one fleeting moment, I had a glimpse of the sweet side of surrender: an end to anxiety, risk, responsibility. I could walk the streets again without looking over my shoulder—and with my head held high. *I* hadn't flinched or bolted; it was the chief who'd removed me from the case.

And then, just as suddenly, I saw surrender's sour side: having to live ultimately with the knowledge that I'd caved in, not just to a police chief whose overriding concern was to maintain his own perks, but to the threats of whoever out there was trying to scare me away.

Not even the see-no-evil monkey could have missed the look of contempt I gave the chief. "With pleasure," I said. I turned and walked from his office and into the darkened corridor, feeling waves of heat passing through my body.

It wasn't until I began to walk those fifty yards separating the chief's office from the one I was about to relinquish that I realized what a bone-rattling blow I'd just received. Twenty years I'd sparred with Jerry Doyle, always managing to dodge his Sunday punch. And now, at last, he'd landed it.

There are two turns between our offices, both right turns when going from the chief's office to mine. At the second corner I passed the public affairs office, currently occupied by Officer Adam Abraham, the coal-black son of semiliterates, who had never in his wildest boyhood fantasies imagined that he would one day earn his living by composing English sentences. The lights were on, and I could hear the soft, rapid clacking of his computer keyboard. I was certain that Adam, too, had been summoned into the Hall of Justice by the chief, his job to compose a release to the media announcing my relegation to the records bureau. Adam wouldn't use it, but relegation was the word; there was no way anyone familiar with police matters would take my transfer as anything other than that.

Thank God for Veterans Day, I thought as I walked into the deserted offices of the Special Investigations Division. I was totally unprepared to tell the men and women I'd worked with for a decade that we wouldn't be working together anymore. It was tough enough emptying my personal possessions from my desk and packing them into a small box. That done, I walked to the door and was about to open it when I stopped, turned and looked into the room, and was suddenly bathed in memories. I must have stood there for five minutes, recalling not so much events as feelings. To the extent I'd ever felt valid, or appreciated or trusted, I'd felt it here. We were twenty different people, but we were a community. Whenever I'd needed help, these were the men and women I'd come to. I sighed and walked from the room, certain that I'd just closed the door on a portion of my life.

In the six days since the Saturday-night attack on Maggie Winehouse, my life had been threatened, I'd nearly been killed, and my career had been derailed and potentially wrecked. As I walked down the dark corridor the only absolute certainty about my new life was that I would not stay away from Jimmy Chang—or from his Pacific Rim Bank.

As I was thinking of my first move, I remembered that with banks closed for the holiday, there was nothing I could do until Monday.

And then it hit me that Britt wouldn't be walking through my door that evening.

All in all, it wasn't shaping up as that good a weekend.

II

NOVEMBER 11 –
DECEMBER 9, 1994

10

November mornings in San Francisco are completely unpredictable. One morning the air's so crisp and clean it gives you the feeling that anything is possible. The next morning, fog, thick and damp, shrouds your spirit in its mists. This, fittingly, was one of those dispiriting mornings. As I drove through the fog, away from the Hall of Justice, the memory of my meeting with Chief Doyle still sending bad vibes through my body, I knew that the last place I wanted to be was home, alone with my thoughts and regrets. What I needed, I decided, was a cleansing. For that, I knew no better place than the Kabuki Hot Springs on Geary Boulevard in Japantown, just behind the Kabuki Theaters, and that's where I eventually went after driving around the city for half an hour to make sure that no one was following me.

First I bathed, Japanese style, seated on a stool a foot off the ground and a quarter the size of my butt, wetting myself with a spray, then soaping and scrubbing, and finally filling a pail with water and pouring it over my head. Then I soaked in a huge Jacuzzi along the north wall of the bathing room, feeling my muscles go slack. Then to the sauna off the south end of the room, followed by the steam room on the west, each of them so spacious I was scarcely aware of the dozen other men baking with me, all of them, like myself, seemingly lost in their thoughts.

Just as I was thinking that I'd cooked enough, a wiry Asian man entered the steam room and, peering through the mist, settled his eyes on me. He kept looking at me even as he took his seat, at right angles to mine. I couldn't believe that whoever was tailing me had followed me in here, but I couldn't shake the thought, either. The man, about my age, continued to stare at me. Maybe he's gay, I told myself. But it was hardly a come-on look. Between his stare and the heat, I decided I'd had enough, walked from the steam room and dunked myself in an ice-cold pool in the center of the bathing room. As I was drying off I heard my name called over the loudspeaker, informing me that it was time for the massage I'd requested on entering.

I made my way to the massage room, its light as subdued as a theater's before the film begins. Following instructions on a sign, I donned a pair of shorts. Moments later, two men and a woman, wearing whites, came through a connecting door. The men walked up to two other clients. The woman approached me. She was small, trim, brunette and young.

"You're Zack," she whispered. Not a question. She seemed to know. I figured the two other clients were regulars.

"I am," I said.

"I'm Francesca." She smiled. "Over here." As soft as it was, her voice brimmed with energy, which augured well for my massage. Francesca directed me to the first table in a row of six. I lay down on my stomach, and surrendered myself to her hands. I was right; they were strong, and seemingly inexhaustible.

The massage lasted half an hour. For the first five minutes, I was conscious only of the bliss created by a masseuse who really knew her stuff. But try as I might to stay focused on the sensations she was producing, my thoughts began to drift, and soon I was replaying my visit to the chief's office, in particular that moment when I told him I was about to go on vacation.

God knows, I'd had no plans for a vacation, even though I had time coming. But those intuitive processes that seem to guide us in moments of crisis must have told me I'd need a private period in which to investigate Jimmy before being buried in the records bureau. My sudden announcement made it sound as though my vacation had been scheduled for some time. To the chief, a veteran of more than forty years on the force, vacations are a cop's sacred right, to be canceled only in the event of a civic uprising. No matter how uncomfortable I made him, I was still a cop. I was sure he wouldn't check, or object even if he were to discover inadvertently that I'd scheduled my vacation at an instant's notice while standing in his office.

My thoughts must have tensed me up, because I was suddenly conscious of Francesca's head next to my left ear. "Relax, Zack," she whispered. I let my muscles go. "*That's* better," she said.

I tried hard to stay with Francesca by focusing on her kneading movements, but my thoughts began to drift again, and I soon found myself sorting through the ideas that had combined in that lightning moment in the chief's office into a suspicion of Jimmy Chang.

When a public person has been libeled or slandered, I told myself, especially by a deep pocket like a prosperous television station or a city government, the knee-jerk response is to hire an attorney—and not just any attorney, but a flamboyant, charismatic attorney who with one speech on the courthouse steps can strike fear into the hearts of those who have offended his client.

Jimmy Chang hadn't done that. He'd threatened suit, but hadn't sued. Instead of hiring an attorney and filing the lawsuit, he'd gone behind the scenes to plead his case with the mayor.

Why?

The simplest explanation—and how often the simplest explanation has proved to be the right one!—was that Jimmy had no case, not against KUBC, and certainly not against the SFPD. Jimmy was no dummy; if he didn't know this on his own, he'd certainly called an attorney, who had told him as much.

Jimmy loves publicity, I reminded myself, but not notoriety. What he wants is for this stench to blow away. To the extent that he's linked in any way with the attack on Maggie Winehouse, he loses face with the Chinese community. His quickest, most effective remedy, therefore, is not a legal action, which would take months to resolve, but a public demonstration of the mayor's support, one that would convince the Chinese community of his powerful links to City Hall. A public rebuke of the police official said to have cooperated with KUBC would convince the Chinese community of that, and enable Jimmy to save face.

All this time, Francesca had been working on my back and butt and the backs of my legs. Now she leaned down and whispered into my ear, "Turn over." Once I'd done so, she placed the wrist of my right arm under her right arm, pressed it firmly against her side and began to knead my right bicep. "Relax, Zack! Float!" she implored. I did, for several minutes, as she massaged my right forearm and hand and shoulder. And then Francesca was kneading my quadriceps, and I suddenly thought, a few inches higher, and this massage would be something other than advertised. A tenuous connection, perhaps, but that thought led me to wonder once again if Jimmy might not be as advertised.

Maybe he had something to hide. Maybe he *had* been mixed up in the attack on Maggie. Maybe he was the source of the threats against my life. Maybe he was some triad's front man. Maybe his bank was laundering money. Maybe there was something in his past. Whatever it was, a trial would bring it out. So a trial was to be avoided at all costs—either by going straight to the mayor or getting rid of the cop in charge of the case.

The next thing I knew, Francesca had her mouth next to my ear and was murmuring, "It was a pleasure serving you, Zack. Again, my name is Francesca. I hope you'll ask for me the next time you pay us a visit."

"I will," I whispered.

Francesca smiled, and was about to move away, when she hesitated, then, leaning close to me again, whispered, "And I hope you catch those bastards and give 'em what they deserve."

Christ! I thought. *That's* why that guy was staring at me. *Everyone* knows me. I can't make a move without being spotted.

It was a few minutes before noon when I drove from the garage under the Kabuki Theaters, my body glowing but my mind uncalmed. I turned right onto Fillmore, and headed north, intending to drive to Broadway, and then east through the Broadway Tunnel to Chinatown, where I proposed to gorge myself on dim sum. But crossing Pine Street, inspiration seized me and I made an abrupt left turn and joined the one-way traffic heading west. If it was dim sum I wanted, I could get that just as well on Clement Street. In the process of appeasing my hunger I could also appease my curiosity with a first-hand look at the Pacific Rim Bank.

At Fifth Avenue, after finding that rarest of San Francisco commodities a parking space, I began walking west on Clement. The mere thought that I was in the vicinity of the Pacific Rim Bank started the adrenaline trickling into my system. Wearing corduroy slacks, a cashmere sweater over a button-down shirt open at the neck and a leather jacket, I was theoretically indistinguishable from any white middle-class male my age. But in this crowd, all a stalker needed to do to keep me in his sights was to watch my head; there was no way I could remain inconspicuous among the parade of small-scaled people passing up and down Clement Street. I could feel my Smith & Wesson on my hip, but it gave me small comfort.

By twelve-twenty I was seated at a window table in a small, narrow restaurant, eating dim sum, drinking tea and studying the bank, which was directly across the street. It was even less prepossessing than I'd remembered from the outtakes: a white two-story building with black trim around two storefront windows and without a distinguishing feature, it was the kind of cookie-cutter structure that gets built when a contractor cons a client into believing he can do without an architect. What it had been prior to this incarnation I didn't know, but it had certainly not been a bank. It did not give me the kind of confidence I would demand before becoming a depositor, which made me wonder whether the Pacific Rim Bank really cared about getting the business of residents of the neighborhood, who, to judge by the pedestrian traffic, were predominantly Chinese.

Like the French, the Chinese buy their food fresh every day, Sundays included. There were Caucasians walking in and out of the fruit and vegetable stores, bakeries and fish markets I could see from my vantage point, but the majority were Chinese, most of them fifty or older, the women dressed against the chill in heavy wool sweaters or parkas, the men wearing short jackets. When Chinese are together they chatter incessantly and laugh frequently, but shopping to them is a serious event, requiring focused attention. I saw few smiles.

My curiosity satisfied, my hunger appeased, I was about to pay my bill when I saw a black Cadillac coupe pull up in front of the bank. A man got out, walked to the door of the bank and stood there, as though he was waiting for someone. Even from across the street I could see that he was middle-aged and prosperous-looking. A minute later he was joined by two other men. Same basic description. And then another car, this one a BMW, pulled up, and a fourth man got out and joined the other three.

And then, not half a minute later, Jimmy Chang arrived in a black top-of-the-line Mercedes, driven by a chauffeur.

As he stepped from the car and stopped momentarily, obviously reveling in the attention he was drawing, the English cut of his suit was apparent even from a distance, an announcement to those who understood such nuances that this was a man whose clothes were truly tailored. His statement made, he walked briskly up to the men, his animated round face broadcasting positive energy, a suggestion to anyone and everyone that his troubles were behind him. He shook hands emphatically with each of the men. And then he unlocked and opened the door of the bank, triggering an alarm. Seconds after he stepped inside, the alarm stopped. Then the four other men walked into the bank.

I hadn't the slightest doubt that what I'd just seen was the executive committee of the board of directors of the Pacific Rim Bank, convening for an emergency meeting.

Twenty minutes later the five men emerged, and began to walk west on Clement Street, toward Park Presidio. I took a last quick sip of tea and, my bill already paid, slipped out of the restaurant and followed them from across the street. Two blocks further on, they entered the Tong Palace, a popular restaurant specializing in dim sum. I crossed the street in time to observe them take their places at a large round table near the front window.

The sight reinforced all my doubts. What is this supposed to tell you? I asked myself. Quickly, I moved away from the window, and walked disconsolately back toward the bank, feeling stupid and vulnerable. Jimmy could have seen me. He would surely have recognized me. He would have wasted no time calling the mayor.

Jimmy's Mercedes was still in front of the bank, parked illegally in a loading zone, the chauffeur asleep at the wheel, obviously unaware of the parking ticket under the window wiper. More from habit than from hope, I noted the license number. Back in my car, I called Richmond Station. "This is Captain Tobias," I said to the officer who answered. "I'm on the street. I'd like you to run a plate for me." I gave the officer the license number, and told him I'd hold. He came back with the information in two minutes.

The black Mercedes belonged to the Golden Door Trading Company, located in the 4100 block of Geary Boulevard. I got out of the car, walked to Geary, a block south of Clement, and then to the number, two blocks east.

Well, well, I told myself, maybe we're getting somewhere.

The location of the Golden Door Trading Company was a maildrop, a Postal Instant Press establishment with Xerox machines and printing facilities and, off to the side, an alcove with perhaps two hundred postal boxes.

I continued east on Geary until I found a stationery store, bought some envelopes and addressed one of them to the Golden Door Trading Company. Then I returned to Postal Instant Press and went inside. "Can I help you?" a young Asian woman asked me. She had the serious expression and degree of alertness of someone with a financial stake in the enterprise. She was standing behind a counter. Behind her were half a dozen printing, copying and binding machines, at one of which a man her age, presumably her husband, was stacking several dozen copies of an inch-thick manuscript.

"I have a letter for one of your clients. He asked me to drop it off here." I handed her the envelope.

"Okay, I take care of it." She spoke English as though she had learned it within the last two or three years. She glanced at the envelope, then wrote a number on it. I read the number upside down: 256.

"Thanks," I said. "Incidentally, what do you charge for a box?"

She reached under the counter and brought out a rate sheet. "Depend on size of box. Read this."

"And what time do you generally have the mail sorted?"

"Eleven o'clock."

"Excellent. Thanks a lot."

"No problem," the woman said automatically, her attention already somewhere else.

I made a mental note to be back at Postal Instant Press at ten-thirty Monday morning. Then I returned to my car and drove home.

As I turned south onto Greenwich Street, my heart sank. Half a dozen cars were parked in front of my building, and at least a dozen reporters, photographers and cameramen stood on the sidewalk. I braked, put the car into reverse and backed up to Hyde Street, then drove north to Fisherman's Wharf.

The wharf is only six blocks from my home, but I couldn't remember the last time I'd been there. It's not a place where San Franciscans go, and hasn't been for years. Right now, it suited me just fine; I could mingle among the tourists without fear of being recognized.

But I couldn't stay there forever. After drinking two espressos at a coffee bar and cursing myself for maybe the tenth time for giving the chief an opportunity to derail me, I went to my car and called my voice mail to get my messages. There were a dozen—of which two were notable. The first was from Gordon. "Jesus," he said, "I'm sorry. I'm really sorry. I never dreamed . . ." He tailed off, clearly lost for words, then added, "I know this isn't any consolation, but if there's ever any way I can make it up to you, I'll do it." Again he faltered, and then said, even more abjectly, "I'm really sorry. It's just that . . . well, this whole thing is such a nightmare."

The second notable message was from my mother—notable, first, because I couldn't understand how she could have found out about my transfer, since she never listens to news reports, and second, because a call from her is such a rarity. There are jokes about Jewish mothers that end "He never calls, he never writes." In the case of Sadie Tobias, it's the other way around: I'm the dutiful son who checks in once a week. If I didn't, weeks might pass in which we wouldn't communicate, let alone see each other, even though we live scarcely five minutes apart. In fairness to Sadie, she *is* the major force behind much of the city's cultural life, everyone wants a piece of her time, and she's scheduled from 6:00 A.M., when she rises for her exercise, until dinner or curtain time, whichever is later. But the truth, the acerbic truth I've dealt with since childhood, is that I'm guaranteed Sadie's attention only when my conduct impinges on her life—this day's events being the perfect illustration. Her message was typically to the point. "My son, my son, what's happening to my son? Call me as soon as you can."

I didn't call. I drove to her house.

Somewhere in the world, there may be a more impressive collection of homes, and somewhere there may be a more beautiful urban setting, and somewhere a more dazzling view. But nowhere I've been—and I've been around—is there a more overwhelming combination of homes, setting and view than in Pacific Heights, San Francisco's premier neighborhood, the neighborhood in which I grew up.

Picture a steep hill, with streets and houses rising from the bay. The higher the street, the better the view and the more elaborate the houses, houses of every period and architectural style, most traditional, a few contemporary. The north–south streets, the ones that climb the hill, get their share of traffic, but the east–west streets, which the best homes face, are so quiet you can hear the rustle of leaves. The neighborhood is so upscale it even comes with its own special fragrance, a pungent eucalyptus scent blowing in from the Presidio.

The most desirable locations in Pacific Heights are on the north side of those streets running east and west, because the living floor of the houses can be entered from the street. Homeowners on the southern, uphill side have a good hike to their front doors. A second advantage of a northside location, one important to my father, was that the homes on the downhill side, only one or at most two of whose floors were visible from the street, did not appear to be as large as those on the uphill side, whose dimensions were entirely exposed. My father enjoyed living well, but he had nothing to prove to anyone, and he hated ostentation. Our Tudor-style home, consequently, while lovely and enviable, was far from being the biggest residence in Pacific Heights.

But it was big, no question, and as a dwelling for a single person, impractical if not preposterous. That she had chosen to remain alone all these years in a sixteen-room house, one furnished exactly as it had been when my father was alive—simply, to suit his taste—said a great deal about Sadie Tobias's indivisible ties to Ted Tobias almost a quarter century after his death.

My mother's deep, genuine love for my father compounded admiration, gratitude and intense physical attraction, the last so obvious I became precociously aware of evenings when she could scarcely wait to get him into the bedroom. Both my parents were early risers, but on Sunday mornings they never unlocked their bedroom door until almost ten o'clock, and from the day my father came storming to the door to answer my then eight-year-old sister's cries I knew better than to knock. When my father sat me down for that long-awaited birds-and-the-bees lecture, he emphasized that sex with a woman one didn't love, while pleasant, merely satisfied animal urges, whereas sex with one's beloved was the single most gratifying experience in life. I am convinced that Ted Tobias never stepped out on his Sadie. As for double-standard Sadie, she was a virgin when they married, infidelity was unimaginable, and she didn't become involved with another man until five years after my father's death.

For months after he was killed, Mother was inconsolable. She mourned him with virtually undiminished grief for several years. But as much as she had loved him, it was not just devotion to his memory that kept her single. For Sadie Singer, an insurance broker's daughter, marriage to Ted Tobias had been the defining experience of her life, elevating her from middle-class obscurity to a position of leadership and respect in the community. Although dozens of men—Jews and gentiles alike—had attempted to interest her, beginning six months to the day after my father's death, she had never remarried, preferring to remain the widow of Ted Tobias rather than become Mrs. Someone Else.

Did Mother understand that even the great passion of her life had been tempered by calculation? If she did, it would have been knowledge she would have repressed. She was, as the shrinks would say, well defended from any unlikable aspects of herself. How, then, did I know it? Because her love for me was tempered, as well. No mother could have been more diligent, but I never got the feeling that my existence had created a new love in her, focused exclusively on me. In countless ways, she demonstrated through the years that she had conceived and raised her children more to please my father than to satisfy her own maternal urges. *Everything* Sadie did while he was alive was intended to please Ted Tobias—her choice, not his demand. During my college years, when I discovered at the same time both the excitement of books and my abysmal ignorance of literature, I asked my mother whether she'd ever read to me as a child, confessing that I couldn't remember a single occasion. "Probably not," she'd replied matter-of-factly. "I was too busy taking care of your father."

"I hear you've been a bad boy," she said now as she walked across the dark wood floor of the living room to greet me. Her looks were a testimony to the benefits of diet, exercise, good taste and plastic surgery. Her straight black hair, lightly but fetchingly streaked with gray and worn shoulder-length, framed an unlined, olive-skinned face blessed with a strong chin, full lips and large brown eyes to balance a mildly prominent nose, a vestige of a long-ago Sephardic ancestor. At sixty-seven, Sadie could still make heads turn. Whoever had removed the lines in her face had drawn her skin a bit too taut, but you noticed that only if you were next to her and remembered how she'd looked before her surgery. From six feet away, my mother looked perhaps ten years older than I did, an effect enhanced by her tall, willowy figure, flatteringly displayed on this occasion by a black sheath dress topped by a single strand of pearls.

"Don't believe everything you hear," I said after I'd kissed her on the cheek and she'd pressed her cheek to mine in that don't-mess-my-lipstick manner I'd have loathed if I hadn't found it so comical. "How'd you hear about it, anyway?"

"Richard called to apologize for the public spanking he was going to have to give you." Mother could not bring herself to call her friend the mayor anything but Richard. "Would you like a drink?" she said in the same breath.

I was about to ask for tea when I suddenly thought, To hell with it. It was the weekend. I wasn't working. "A beer would be great," I said.

Sadie directed me to one of the two huge sofas, covered in a soft and muted tan fabric, that faced each other on either side of the stone fireplace, and then pressed a buzzer on an end table. In a moment a man I had never seen appeared. He was Chinese, in his forties, small and slight, and he wore a white cotton jacket. "This is my son the police captain, Sam," my mother said, her statement spiced with aspersion.

Mother spoke to her servants—invariably foreign-born and with limited command of English—as owners speak to their pets, with utter confidence that she was being understood. I was certain Sam *hadn't* understood her, but he could see by her gestures that he was being introduced. He bowed. I greeted him in Chinese. His eyes enlarged. I asked where he was from. He told me Guangdong. I asked how long he had been here. "Long time," he said quickly in heavily accented English, then directed his gaze at Mother, a movement clearly meant to convey that he hoped our conversation was over. Another illegal alien, I decided, as Mother ordered beer for me and a glass of white wine for herself.

"Did Sam come with a wife?" I asked her.

"Of course."

"I don't even want to know where you found them."

"It's better that way," Mother said, squeezing my arm. She walked to the couch opposite mine and sat carefully. "I would hate to lose them. You have no idea how hard it is to get good help these days— and they're the best I've had in years. Now, tell me what's going on."

There are people who give you the feeling as you speak to them that your concerns are, for that moment, at least, the most important issue in their lives. Sadie Tobias is not one of those people. Most of the time she's made up her mind before hearing what you have to tell her, so the feeling she gives you is that she is desperately eager to get on to something else. Her eyes drift. Her head turns. She fidgets in the manner of people with overloaded schedules who are running half an hour late. The cocktail dress she was wearing this afternoon suggested that she had a function to go to as soon as she finished with me. As accustomed as I am to her impatience and distraction, as impressed as I am with her accomplishments, and as amusing and even charming as I often find her, I am, after all, her son, so over the years I've become accustomed to leaving our encounters with an ever-deepening sense of loss. Inevitably, the number of encounters has diminished.

I believe that Sadie, without ever sitting down to figure it out, had distanced herself from me in an effort to send me a message. While she'd understood my initial motivation, she had never approved of my presence on the police force. To an extent, her disapproval was understandable and even laudable: she was certain I'd inherited my father's combativeness, which had killed him and could one day kill me. But the basic truth was that it embarrassed Sadie to have a cop for a son.

Now, it became clear, she believed that my work could threaten her social position as well, and *that* she couldn't tolerate. "Oh, Zack, this is not good, not good at all," she interrupted midway through my story, as Sam brought in our drinks, along with a bowl of macadamia nuts. "I can see why Richard's upset. There are *so* many Asians in San Francisco now that it *could* cost him the election if they decided he was anti-Asian. I would *hate* to see Harold Halderman as the mayor of this city."

"Why? Just out of curiosity."

"Because he's not one of *us*," she said softly, as though she were sharing a confidence.

I took three swallows of beer, draining half the glass. "He certainly isn't, Mother."

"I don't mean *that*. I mean he's first-*generation*." Her voice was still low, but the force with which she emphasized the last word seemed to propel it to the four walls of her ample living room.

"That's not true, Mother. His family's been in this country for at least a hundred years."

"But not in *San Francisco*," Mother said, slipping out of her shoes and tucking her feet under her on the couch. "He's first-generation *San Francisco*. He can't possibly understand the *city*. If he wins, he'll completely disrupt the way we *do* things."

"You mean he'll disrupt the way Sadie Tobias does things."

"What do you mean by *that*?"

"I mean that if Harold is elected, someone else will become the keeper of The List."

"Not necessarily."

"You're dreaming, Mother. You're not Harold's kind."

If I hadn't expected it I would have missed it: a slight narrowing of those oversized brown eyes, a tightening of those full lips. "And what do you mean by *that*?" she demanded.

"You're Jewish, Mother, whether you like it or not."

Mother reared back, and seemed to regard me in astonishment. Her right hand, bearing a single two-carat diamond in a simple setting, flew to her chest. "What kind of a statement is *that*? I'm not *ashamed* to be Jewish."

"You don't exactly proclaim it."

I couldn't recall another occasion when I'd seen her so flustered. For maybe five seconds, she simply stared at me. At last, neatly deflecting my challenge, she said, "Are you telling me that Harold Halderman is anti-Semitic?"

"Not at all. Nothing of the kind. What I'm saying is that Harold's strength is among the most conservative groups in the city, the old-time Irish and Italians who hate what's happening to San Francisco and yearn for the good old days. People like Bud Donnelly."

"Bud Donnelly's not so terrible."

I shook my head. "Bud Donnelly's a menace, Mother. He's not the man we knew."

For a moment, Mother seemed to drift. "Poor man," she murmured.

"Some Jews are as fed up as the Irish and Italians," I went on, "but the majority of Jews won't be able to discard their progressive convictions and support a right-winger like Halderman. Which means that the administration of a Mayor Halderman wouldn't have many, if any, Jews in it—unless, of course, the Jews surprise everyone by going over to his side."

Mother sat back and stared at me, her mouth ajar. "This is *not* San Francisco talk."

"A lot of things happening these days are alien to San Francisco, Mother. The question is whether we can deal with them effectively and still remain who we are."

At least one good thing could be said for my troubles: they'd at least gotten my mother's attention. She sipped her wine nervously. "So what happens to *you* now?"

"I've been transferred to records."

"That I know. What does that do to your . . . *career?*" She spoke the word as though it smelled bad, wrinkling her nose and turning away.

"It doesn't help it, Mother."

"Then, for *heaven's* sake, why don't you *quit*, Zack?" she said, her voice interlaced with exasperation and incomprehension.

It was perhaps the hundredth time she'd made that suggestion since I became a cop. I shook my head and sighed. "Mother, let's not go through that again, okay?"

"It's not as though you wouldn't have a *job*," she went on, as though I hadn't spoken. "You're *needed*, Zack."

Suddenly we'd lapsed into shorthand. Sadie might be the city's leading volunteer as well as the soul of competence but, as I've said, she was no feminist. She'd never been more comfortable than when Ted Tobias was running the family business, as she believed men were meant to do, and she was working with her charities and cultural groups in a manner designed to affirm our family's social position, as she believed women of her station were meant to do. My sister, Sari, with an MBA from Harvard, fifteen years' working experience and a lust for competition, was as qualified as anyone to run the business, but no matter how well she did—and she had done *very* well—Mother could not be shaken in her conviction that the family fortunes would fare better with a man at the helm.

"Sari's doing fine," I said for the hundredth time.

Mother put her feet down, stood, smoothed her skirt and looked at me. "There are problems you don't know about."

"Let's keep it that way, okay?"

"*Serious* problems."

This too I'd heard a hundred times. But this time the tone was a little more plaintive, the expression a little more naked. This time, I sensed, there really *might* be a wolf. I felt duty-bound to respond, yet helpless to do so. My own problems were bursting my head; I had no room left for another problem—particularly not one associated with either the business or my sister, the two subjects I loathed more than any others. One major attraction of being a cop was that it had enabled me to steer clear of both. "*Please*, Mother, not today," I said. "I'll call you first thing next week."

With that I drained my beer, hurriedly kissed her good-bye and left.

Mother had been right in suggesting that my remarks about Jews had not been "San Francisco talk." The Jews of San Francisco are deeply and comfortably enmeshed in the life of the city to a degree not found in other American cities, not even New York. Their integration into the city's mainstream goes back to the Gold Rush, when skills were at such a premium that any educated white man who could perform an economic function achieved political legitimacy, regardless of his origins. With political legitimacy came social and cultural acceptance as well. In their letters to relatives in Europe—translations of which I found at the Bancroft Library on the Berkeley campus while doing research for a paper—the Jews who had made the arduous, perilous journey to California spoke of the warm welcome they received from the pioneers, and how greatly valued they were for their urban skills, their grounding in finance and their facility with language, which helped them to communicate with the *Californios*, Mexicans who had settled the area prior to statehood. Jews helped set up San Francisco's security exchanges, and traded in the stocks of mining companies and other fledgling enterprises. Jews—among them, Levi Strauss, a manufacturer of a new, sturdy kind of pants ideal for frontier life—dominated the clothing industry. Jews such as Zachariah Tobias, my great-great-grandfather, were so important to the city's commerce that boats didn't unload on the High Holidays. The wealthiest Jews, some of whom had arrived in San Francisco with nothing, lived in big homes on Rincon Hill, next door to gentile pioneers who had also made their fortunes during the Gold Rush. Since most of the pioneers had come to California because of discontent with their existing lives, and with little if any social distinction, family history was of no consequence in San Francisco society in those days. What mattered was money. If you had it—particularly if you had made it in San Francisco during the pioneering days—you were automatically included among the city's elite, whether you were Jew or gentile.

During the 1880s, the great Pullman-Car Migration delivered thousands of Easterners and Midwesterners to California and, with them, all those historic prejudices against Jews that had largely been missing or inoperative in the frontier society. In Los Angeles, the most influential of these transplants, General Harrison Gray Otis, shamelessly used his fledgling newspaper, the *Times,* to advance his profound biases, one of them against Jews. But nothing of the sort happened in San Francisco, where the city's first newspaper publishers, recent converts to Catholicism, had been born to Jewish parents. The Jews of San Francisco were so much a part of the city's life by this point that the prejudices of the new arrivals did little to affect them, and it has remained that way ever since.

But since the mid-sixties, as social problems in the city began to intensify, so had the growling about the progressive philosophy that had dominated San Francisco life for years and, in the eyes of the city's conservative elements, invited those very problems. For "progressive philosophy," read traditional Jewish liberalism.

I stayed in on Friday night, letting myself believe that Britt might show up in a burst of sympathy for me. She did call at seven o'clock, upset by the negative spin placed on my transfer by the media, but when I invited her to dinner, she said she had other plans. I didn't have the stomach to ask what they were.

So I spent the evening alone, the alarm on and my gun at my side. By this point my fears were something like the dull ache of a muscle pull, something you get used to and are reminded of only when you move. If I stayed where I was, I was reasonably certain I wasn't going to be challenged. I read for a couple of hours, then listened to news accounts of the roundup of seven suspects in the attack on Maggie Winehouse, every one of them an Asian, every one with a criminal record—not one of them, I was certain, in any way involved.

At eight Saturday morning, as I was sitting in my aerie sipping a cup of coffee and watching a huge freighter weighted down with containers slip under the Bay Bridge on its way to Oakland, I got a call from Jim Mich.

"I was up in Oregon running a marathon," he said. "Got in late last night. What the hell's going on?"

"I'll tell you when I see you," I said.

"When will that be?"

"Don't know. I'm on vacation."

He was silent for a moment. "Well, you've left a detail of highly agitated cops, I'll tell you. I had six messages on my machine when I got home and three calls already this morning. Is there *anything* I can tell them?"

I wanted to tell him everything, but I couldn't tell him anything. "Whatever I'd tell you would only make it worse."

"You know who's replacin' you, don't you?"

By the way he asked the question I knew it was bad news, and that I was being blamed. "As a matter of fact, I don't," I said.

"Germaine."

That silenced me. If Tom Germaine, a police captain a few years younger than the chief, had been in the armed forces, he would have been passed up for promotion and cast aside long ago. He was a decent man but a so-so cop who was of no use whatever after lunch. "What can I say?" I managed at last.

"You could say a lot," Jim said. I could hear the hurt in his voice.

"Well, I can't. Look, I'm in trouble—obviously. I've got to be careful."

I heard him exhaling impatiently. "You haven't by any chance spoken to Maggie Winehouse, have you?"

I felt a rush of anger. "Why would you of all people ask me such a question?" I snapped at him. "You know I'm off the case."

"Ease off," Jim said. I could hear the shock in his voice. "We want her for the lineup." He paused for a moment. "She's disappeared."

I hesitated, surprised. "Her folks don't know where she is?"

"Unless they're lying they don't."

"You tried Gordon Lee?"

"Same answer. I believe all three of them. They're really shook."

"Are you thinking abduction?"

"We don't know what to think. What do *you* think?"

"Sorry, Jim."

"Come on, Zack," he said imploringly. "This is just for me."

I hesitated, torn. I knew Jim would never say anything directly to the chief, but he might pass my opinion along and the caution that went with it would fall by the wayside and the third or fourth person down the line might mention what I'd said to the chief. Ah, the hell with it, I thought. Anything to get rid of that hurt in Jim's voice. "I wouldn't think she's been abducted because whoever hit her has made his point," I said. "But you can't rule out the possibility."

Jim sighed. "Yeah," he said. I sensed he was already experiencing the same frustrations I had.

"Is Gordon going to use it?" I asked.

"He said he'd try to keep it quiet."

"Has the rest of the media found out?"

"Not to my knowledge. Maybe Gordon's learned his lesson."

"Don't hold your breath."

"Well," Jim said, "call me if you hear anything."

"Sure," I said, knowing that I wouldn't, lamenting that for the first time since I'd met him I hadn't been straight with my mentor—the cop I most admired on the force.

At six Saturday evening, just as I'd begun to think about dinner, the telephone rang. I grabbed it, hoping it was Britt. "Hello?" I said. The answer was silence—or, more accurately, heavy breathing. "Hello?" I said again. More of the same. I hung up.

Five minutes later the telephone rang again. Same routine.

The next time I let the answering machine take over. I sat by the machine, listening to the breathing. Enough of this, I thought. I clipped my holstered Smith & Wesson to my belt, put on my leather jacket and walked out the door. I kept the jacket unzipped, and my right hand inches from the butt of the gun.

I'd let myself believe that with my transfer now public knowledge, whoever was trying to intimidate me would let me alone. Not so.

Maybe the message I'd just been sent was "We're still watching you. Behave yourself." For the first time, it occurred to me that my split with Britt had, in one sense, been providential. With mystery men coming at me, I certainly didn't want her involved. Small consolation, though—scarcely enough to overcome my bitterness at the terrible turn my life had taken since the attack on Maggie Winehouse, exactly a week ago tonight.

I couldn't bring myself to go to the Hyde Street Bistro or any other place in the neighborhood that Britt and I had frequented on weekends. So instead of walking up the hill to Hyde Street, I started down the hill toward North Beach.

My street, Greenwich, ends in a cul-de-sac fifty feet east of my building, and resumes again on Leavenworth, just down the hill. To get to Leavenworth, you take a long flight of steps all but hidden from view by bushes and trees. If someone wanted to jump me, this was a great place to do it. I walked those steps gun in hand, feeling angry and stupid. Then I ate an unmemorable dinner in an unmemorable restaurant, which further depressed me, and returned to an empty bed, which really finished me off.

Sometime that evening, four white high school students seized an Asian girl, took her into Golden Gate Park and cut her face, an obvious retaliation for the attack on Maggie. By noon the next day, all four of the teenaged boys had been picked up. Monday morning's paper carried two sidebar stories, the first a cry for justice from the Asian community, the second a compilation of outraged calls for action from the Caucasian community following the release on Sunday morning of the seven Asian "suspects" in the attack on Maggie.

At ten-thirty Monday morning I returned to Geary Boulevard, parked a few doors from the Postal Instant Press shop, and waited. Five minutes later, a U.S. Postal Service truck drew up in front of the PIP office. The driver pulled a large white plastic basket laden with mail from the truck, carried it into the office, emerged a moment later with the basket, now empty, and drove off. I waited another fifteen minutes, figuring it would take at least that long to sort the mail, then walked into the PIP office. At the counter was the same serious young woman who had waited on me early Friday afternoon. I told her I'd decided to rent a mailbox. She gave me an application to fill out. After

I'd completed the application and paid my fee, she gave me the combination for box 274. Then I told her I wanted to order some stationery, and she gave me a catalog to look through.

"I can't make up my mind," I said with a sheepish smile when she looked my way five minutes later. Just as I was beginning to wonder how much longer I could stall her, a Chinese teenager who looked about eighteen entered the shop, walked to box 256 and removed the mail. With a regretful nod, I returned the catalog to the woman. "Maybe tomorrow," I said. Then I walked swiftly from the shop and fell in behind the teenager. He walked up Geary to Eighth Avenue, then turned right, walked to Clement Street and to the Pacific Rim Bank. I arrived at the glass doors of the bank in time to see him hand the mail to a very junior-looking bank officer.

I kept walking west, past the bank, feeling my heart accelerate. At the end of the block I crossed to the north side of the street, then abruptly turned south and walked to a bus stop across the street from the bank. There I stood, as though waiting for a bus, looking up and down Clement Street for anyone who appeared to be loitering or might be taking too long to study the contents of a store window.

A bus was approaching. Now or never, I told myself. Heart banging, limbs tingling, I crossed the street again and walked into the Pacific Rim Bank.

Imprudent? You bet. Stupid, even—particularly given the number of strangers who'd recognized me in recent days. But working by myself I had no choice. I needed the name of the bank officer to whom the mail for the Golden Door Trading Company had been delivered.

I approached his desk, hoping that his name would be displayed on a sign. It wasn't. My movement must have caught his eye, because he suddenly looked up from the mail and straight at me.

"CnIhepyou?" he said, singing the words and running them together so fast they sounded like one.

I willed myself to look back at him, lest my darting eyes give me away. "Yes, please," I said. "I've just moved into an apartment on Lake Street and I'm looking for a neighborhood bank."

"Checking or saving?"

"Both, probably. What interest do you pay on savings?"

"Interest vary."

"And do you pay interest on balances in checking accounts?"

"Interest vary. Just like other bank."

"Okay, good enough. Do you have a card?"

Was I imagining it, or did he take an extra moment to look me over before opening a drawer and retrieving a card? I took it, thanked him and strolled slowly out of the bank, mindful that I'd been the only Caucasian in it.

At home twenty minutes later, I looked again at the incorporation papers of the Pacific Rim Bank. George Chew, whose card I'd taken, was one of its three vice presidents. I got back in my car and drove straight to the State Building on Golden Gate and went to the secretary of state's office. The same amiable woman went through the same drill, and I had what I wanted in an hour.

As I'd suspected they might, the incorporation papers of the Golden Door Trading Company listed George Chew as president.

That fact established, I returned to my apartment, made myself a cup of coffee, sank into my favorite chair, and—using a little drill Jim had taught me, a way, he said, to see the trees when the forest gets too thick—asked myself and then answered a series of questions.

Why does the Golden Door Trading Company have a mail drop for an address? Because it's a shell corporation.

Why do people set up a shell corporation? Often, to make illegal transactions.

How and why does an obscure officer of a small bank on Clement Street become the president of a company set up to make illegal transactions? He's given the office to front for someone else who doesn't want his name attached. Someone like Jimmy Chang.

The answers were theories, nothing more. They would have to be proved, and other questions answered, such as what kinds of illegal transactions the Golden Door Trading Company might be facilitating, and what the connection, if any, was between the Golden Door Trading Company and the Pacific Rim Bank.

There was one man in town who could answer most, perhaps all, of those questions, provided he wanted to: Stanley Colby, special agent in charge of United States Customs in San Francisco. I was about to call him when my phone rang. It was Chief Doyle.

"What were you doing in the Pacific Rim Bank this morning?" he said without preamble.

My heart jumped. He'd caught me completely off guard. I had no response.

"I'll tell you what you were doing," the chief went on. "You were disobeying a direct order from the chief of police to stay the hell off the Maggie Winehouse case. That's insubordination, and that one brings you up on charges. So figure on a nice long vacation, Tobias, because as of this moment you are suspended from the force."

11

He had me, no question. In continuing my investigation against his direct order, I'd violated the Rules and Procedures of the San Francisco Police Department. He had two witnesses to the order he'd given me. He also had, I was certain, the testimony of George Chew, the vice president of Pacific Rim Bank, the man who had undoubtedly recognized me—pictures of me had made even the Chinese newspapers—and alerted Jimmy Chang, who had just as undoubtedly called Mayor Putnam. And if Jimmy *was* the man behind the scare attacks against me, he'd also have advised the goons who were carrying them out.

Would my tormentor, whoever he was, decide that I needed yet another scare? There wasn't much I could do about that possibility beyond staying alert and not offering the kind of target I'd given them on the bay. In any case, I was going to have my hands full trying to minimize the damage to my career with the SFPD.

It was four-thirty, too early for a drink. I made myself one anyway, not a dry martini—I'd learned *that* lesson—but a tequila gimlet on the rocks: a shot of Cuervo Gold and a splash of Rose's lime juice. I took a sip, felt the hit, then took the drink to my favorite chair, sank into it and tried to evaluate the case against me.

An investigation by the department's Internal Affairs Division would quickly establish that I was not only guilty of insubordination but of other procedural infractions as well. On two occasions, I'd gone directly to the secretary of state's office, first for a copy of the incorporation papers of the Pacific Rim Bank, and then for the papers of the Golden Door Trading Company, both times in defiance of those departmental rules obliging me to go through channels in requesting documents from other governmental agencies.

Everything exists in context, I told myself as I took another sip, and in the context of those violations of the Rules and Procedures, a board of inquiry would also find fault with my handling of Gordon Lee. I should have told him that his suppositions were ridiculous and then sent him packing, with not even an intimation that I'd do anything with his information. Instead I'd told him I'd look into the matter, thereby giving him the flimsiest basis—but still a basis—for his statement that the SFPD was investigating the possible involvement of an appointee of the mayor in the attack on Maggie Winehouse.

More context: Not once in my years as a cop had I called a reporter or courted publicity. But because of my athletic past and my family's prominence, I'd been followed by the media ever since joining the force. Inevitably, feelings of trust had developed, and over time a number of reporters had gotten into the habit of calling me for advice on police-related matters. I'd always spoken anonymously and refused even to be quoted as an SFPD source, but the chief knew of my informal contacts with the media, resented them, and could argue, now that he had a reason to, that police department protocols obliged reporters to channel their inquiries through the department's public affairs office. Reporters would laugh at the thought that Adam Abraham, who ran that office, would ever give them anything newsworthy. All Adam ever did was refer them to members of the department who had the information they were seeking—people like myself. But technically the chief was right; the Rules and Procedures obliged Gordon to start with Adam. Instead, he'd come directly to me, as reporters had been doing for years—and, as I'd done for years, I'd dealt with a reporter without worrying whether he'd been cleared by the public affairs office.

All this was bureaucratic scrap, meant to be discarded—unless someone in the department was determined to make a case against an officer, as the chief was now intent on doing. The case against me might not sit well with the media, but Doyle would happily trade some bad press—figuring he was getting so much already, a little more didn't matter—in exchange for the damage he could inflict on me. He couldn't get me kicked off the force, but he could get me suspended without pay for up to ninety days, he could put a black mark on my record and, most important, he could generate a slew of stories that would cast doubts about my judgment, thereby dimming my luster to the advocates of a police department shakeup.

It's a measure of the concern about crime, violence and unruliness in San Francisco that those advocates would be mentioning me in that connection at all, flying as it did in the face of tradition. At nineteen I could imagine myself as the chief of police; at twenty-three, after less than a year on the force, I'd concluded that for a person like me it wasn't in the cards. Up to the rank of captain in the police department, no one can stop you but yourself. Pass the civil service exams, and you advance in rank, period. Beyond captain, it's all politics. Traditionally, all mayors chose their own chief on entering office. While they could appoint anyone they pleased—man, woman, resident, nonresident, cop, noncop—politics curtailed their choices. In the old days mayors chose the chief from a list of names supplied by the Catholic Church in exchange for political support from the Church and its dominant Irish and Italian communities. Certain key departments were allocated in the same manner; a Catholic would head up vice, a Protestant traffic and so forth. In our rainbow city today, it's not that cut-and-dried—one police chief actually expressed no religious preference—but most police department spoils are still divvied up along religious lines. Past or present, no Jew on the SFPD has ever risen above the rank of captain—not something the Jewish power elite gets worked up about because it's far more interested in other political prizes. The truth is, not many Jews even try for careers with the SFPD. As one of my few Jewish colleagues on the force said to me once, "Let's face it, Zack. Being a cop is not a Jewish thing."

So, I asked myself as I made another tequila gimlet, less carefully measured than the first, why was the chief so worried about me that he would go after me on a matter that initially, given my record, deserved no more than a rebuke? To the three possibilities I already mentioned—my mother's closeness to the mayor, the media's unsolicited support for me and the willingness of those concerned about the city's increasingly intractable problems to look beyond tradition in their search for solutions—I now had to add a fourth: that someone, perhaps Jimmy Chang, perhaps Doyle, perhaps Mayor Putnam himself, had something embarrassing, even criminal, to hide.

The chief had the unilateral authority to suspend me for up to ten days. He could also order a ninety-day suspension, but that order was subject to review by the police commission. I had the right to appeal either action. As I sat in the living room, sipping what I vowed would be my last cocktail of the day and watching the last rays of daylight slanting onto the water, I went back and forth, wondering what to do. Finally, I decided: If the chief went for the ten-day suspension, I wouldn't appeal, because that was a slap on the wrist. But if he went for the ninety-day suspension, that would be an indelible mark against me, and I would have to fight it.

Or would I? Once again, I found myself peering at the two sides of surrender. What a relief it would be to be removed from the tension and frustration and peril. But could I stand myself if I didn't put up a fight? A memory flew into my mind, of *Newsweek*'s cover the week following Ross Perot's withdrawal from the 1992 presidential race. Across a picture of him were two words: "The Quitter." And I remembered thinking what a disgrace it would be to have one's life come down to that.

There was no point in worrying about it until I knew what the chief intended, and departmental regulations gave him five working days in which to decide. This was Monday, November 13; I might not know until the following Monday, the twentieth. In the meantime I had to get away. I couldn't stop the stories, but the last thing I needed was the intensified media exposure I'd get if I stayed in the city. My every move would be reported. If I holed up in my apartment to avoid attention, that would be reported too.

In addition to diminishing my exposure, I needed to talk to someone—to release some steam before the boiler burst, to try to put it all together and figure out what I should do. Getting away and talking to someone both led me to one person. For minutes I fought the urge. At last, heart thumping, I picked up the phone.

By this point I'd lived nine days and nights with Britt's accusation that I'd been a closed book. I'd hated the idea so much at the outset that I'd rejected it completely. Does anyone appreciate being told that he—or she—is aloof, withdrawn, hidden? But the more I'd thought about it, and the more the stabbing pain of our separation had settled down to a throbbing ache, the more possible it seemed. And then, I'd had that joust on the bay with the powercruiser, which had made me see the accusation in a new and glaring light. I'm not going to suggest that my life passed before my eyes in the moments out there when I thought I might die. Nothing passed before my eyes but the bay and the sky and the cruiser and the sailboard that seemed like my last fragile hold on life. But in the days since that event, I'd had to deal with the realization that if I *had* died, I would have done so without having explained myself to myself, let alone to Britt. It was suddenly, desperately important for me to do that.

Ten minutes later, I called Britt from a pay phone on Hyde Street.

She answered on the first ring. "Britt Edstrom," she said in that lilting voice I'd missed so much.

"Hi," I said. My mouth was dry.

I heard her inhale sharply. "You won't believe this," she said in awe, "but I actually had my hand on the phone, ready to pick it up and call you. I heard the news as I was driving home. This is *awful*," she said, drawing the word out. "Why are they doing this?"

"*They* aren't doing anything. It's all Chief Doyle."

"What are you going to do?"

"That's why I'm calling. I need to talk about it." I hesitated. "Will you see me?"

She seemed astonished by my question, as though I should never have doubted that she would. "Of course," she said emphatically. The unspoken message was "What do you take me for?"

"There's a catch," I said cautiously.

"Go ahead."

"I need to hide somewhere for a few days. Will you go with me?"

Her silence seemed to last forever. As I waited for her response I had never felt more alone. The reality was that there wasn't another person in town I could talk to with the same degree of trust, and no one who would be as interested. I truly didn't know what I'd do if Britt turned me down. At last she said, "Could we agree to some ground rules?"

A river of relief surged through me. "Anything you like."

"I think it would be best if we just talk and leave it at that."

"Fine with me."

"And I won't need a separate room, but I think twin beds would be best."

"No problem," I said. Anything, just to be with her.

Another small hesitation. She was obviously struggling. "You would want to leave at once?"

"Tomorrow morning. Very early."

"And what do you mean by 'a few days'?"

"Why don't we say two days?"

Another silence. At last: "I'd need to make some arrangements. . . . Where will we go?"

"It can't be Tahoe. It can't be the wine country. Someplace no one would associate with us."

About one second passed. Then Britt said, "I know the perfect place."

I listened to her description, agreed that the choice was ideal, and told her I'd pick her up at six-thirty the next morning.

For nine days now, ever since I'd received the first threat, I'd had the feeling that I was being stalked by experts. I'd turn suddenly, and see someone duck around a corner. Or I'd emerge from my flat just as a car pulled away, and find the same car on my tail a few minutes later. Each time I was tailed it was by a different car, and each time I ran a check on the plates I'd discover that the car had been reported stolen that day or the night before. By then my tail would have vanished.

I was determined that no one would follow me the next morning—and even more determined that my stalkers would not know anything about Britt's existence, let alone where she lived. Concerned by this point that my house phone might be tapped—the reason I'd called Britt from a pay phone—I used the same phone to make some arrangements. Then, buoyed by my conversation with Britt and the prospect of our trip together, I walked to the Hyde Street Bistro, hoping in the process to walk off those cocktails, and promising myself I'd have nothing to drink with dinner. Guess what?

I was in bed by ten, my alarm set for 4:30 the next morning. I didn't need it. I was up at 4:00, my mouth dry, my head throbbing, my first depressing thought of the day that I was sliding back into the drinking pattern of my rookie days. I cursed myself, vowed that I would either drink with care or not at all—the same vow I'd made countless times twenty years earlier—and dragged myself out of bed.

At 5:15, wearing jeans, a black parka and a white ski cap pulled well down on my ears, I emerged from my flat into the cold darkness with a sports bag slung from my shoulder. I hated to disturb my neighbors, but I wanted to make sure that I'd arouse any dozing sentries. So I slammed the front door, whistled as I walked the steps to my car, and then slammed the car door. Sure enough, a car pulled out from the curb moments after I turned onto Hyde Street, giving me the dubious satisfaction of knowing that I hadn't been paranoid.

Five minutes later I was on the Bayshore Freeway, heading south, my shadow at a discreet distance behind me. In twenty minutes I was in the parking structure at San Francisco Airport. I gave my shadow time to find a spot before I left my car for the terminal. Inside, I headed straight for the first men's room. The only occupant was a man my approximate size and age. His name was Willie Hyde. In our rookie days, we'd been on the beat together out of Richmond Station. Now Willie was a sergeant attached to Taravel Station, the dullest beat in town. The night before he'd been delighted with my offer of an all-expenses-paid, tell-no-one trip to Las Vegas, no questions asked. Quickly, I gave Willie my black parka in exchange for his red one, and put on the blue ski cap he gave me in exchange for my white one. We then transferred our clothes and toilet kits to each other's bags. A moment later Willie walked from the men's room, my ski cap over his ears, vigorously blowing his nose into a handkerchief that covered most of his face. I waited a minute, then walked out the door, just in time to see a slight figure, dressed in a leather jacket, following Willie to the United Airlines counter. I made my way to the arrival level and hailed an Avis shuttle bus. By six o'clock I was on my way back to San Francisco in a black Thunderbird, and at six-thirty, exactly on schedule, I picked Britt up at her house on Belgrave.

As she slid into the seat and pecked me on the cheek I had just a moment to glance at her face. Even at this hour, it seemed more luminously alive than any woman's face I had ever seen, the eyes intent and steady, the lips parted in a small, expectant smile. And yet there was a wariness to her greeting that bothered me, even though I felt it was appropriate, given the circumstances of our meeting.

The sun was just cresting the hills behind Oakland as we crossed the Bay Bridge. We drove east on 580 across the San Joaquin Valley, then took a series of back roads to Highway 4, which cut across vast stretches of undulating cattle land, climbing gradually into the Mother Lode country, its golden hills accented with scraggly Western oaks. We listened to classical music all the way, music so familiar I could hum it, yet couldn't name if my life depended on it. It was Britt who found the stations, and she played the music at a volume suggesting that it was meant to be listened to rather than serve as background. I wondered if she'd done that to eliminate the need for small talk during the ride. For my part, I was grateful. Knowing that I'd soon be unburdening myself had already relieved some of the pressure, but as the performance drew near I was getting stage fright.

Our destination was Bear Valley, a tiny ski resort near the Nevada border thirty miles due south of Lake Tahoe, which advertised itself as the best-kept secret in the Sierra. I'd heard of it, had meant to try it, but had never been there. We'd be using a cabin owned by a Swedish couple, friends of Britt's, named Sjoström. Not two months earlier, Gunilla Sjoström had told us excitedly about how the roads beyond the village center were packed rather than plowed in winter, enabling inhabitants to ski to their homes or the village from the mountain. From the village, you got to your cabin by hiking or on cross-country skis, or—in most cases—on snowmobiles. You parked your car at the transportation center, picked up your snowmobile and drove it to your cabin, pulling your suitcases and groceries on an attached sled. When Britt had called asking to borrow the cabin, Gunilla had told her that the roads were still open, most of the snow from that brief deluge nine days earlier having melted, but she'd warned that the one store in town might be thinly stocked. So we stopped for groceries in Arnold, the nearest town, and arrived in Bear Valley in the late morning, the sun now high above the trees, after climbing thirty miles through increasingly dense forests. The sky was clear, the air cold.

The sign at the edge of Bear Valley listed the altitude at 7,100 feet and the population as 150. The town—a village, really—was on the north side of the highway, nestled against a crescent of small mountains; to the south was a large meadow, laced with streams and covered with a thin layer of snow. The community seemed almost as deserted as the meadow. Only two cars, both pickups, were parked on the road leading through the village, and their drivers were nowhere in sight. The road led past a gas station, a combination firehouse and sheriff's station, an inn called the Red Dog, some low-rise condominiums and finally a lodge, a five-story structure that looked as though it had been designed by a contemporary architect with a love for the Gold Rush days. Just past the lodge, the road began to climb, curving past cabins generously spaced on either side. A mile up we came to a small lake, behind which was a mountain, its trees dusted with snow. Just past the lake was a fork in the road. We took the left fork, following directions supplied by Gunilla. Another turn, another half mile, and we were at the house, a copy of a Swiss chalet, which appeared to be the highest house in the valley. "Perfect," I said with a grateful look at Britt.

We took our bags and the groceries into the house, then walked through a rustic but comfortable-looking living room, complete with wood-burning stove, and onto a deck that hung out over a precipice. The view was awesome: a panorama of huge tamarack and Jeffrey pines, denuded aspen groves, giant granite rocks, and in the distance, perhaps twenty miles away, a mountain range. On any day, the sight would have been impressive; on this day, it all but brought me to my knees, striking me with a vivid sense of my own impermanent place in time. Had my vision of death reinforced the moment? Who knows? All I know is that I was suddenly thinking that I would be gone and all this would endure and what was I doing squandering my brief allotment of life on activities so ungratifying and ultimately meaningless and yet so life-threatening?

I suddenly felt light-headed, perhaps from the thin air, but more probably from a vision of myself waking up each morning to simplicity and natural perfection, with a woman, this woman, at my side, each of us forever rid of the complexities and threats of urban life and able to devote ourselves to each other. I turned to Britt and could see at once that she was as moved as I was.

"It's the end of the world," she said simply.

"Yes," I managed to say. I reached for the railing, giddy with the understanding that with two words—"Marry me"—I could change everything. Britt could run her gallery by fax and phone or, if she pleased, spend several days a week in town—we'd keep my place or hers, whichever she wanted. Would she want a child? Was it too late for a child of our own? If so, we could adopt one. Or several. And dogs, two dogs at least. Bear Valley was a perfect place for dogs.

A flash of terror, as swift and devastating as a lightning strike, destroyed my idyll. No matter what I felt, I was still the husband who hadn't been able to keep his wife from checking out on him—and unless it's happened to you, you'll have to take my word for what that does to your self-confidence. Besides, I didn't trust my feelings; maybe I was overreacting because I'd missed Britt. Or maybe I was doing exactly what my tormentor was hoping I'd do: backing off in the interest of self-preservation.

We changed to our hiking boots, stepped out of the cabin and walked into the woods on the other side of the road. In minutes we reached an immense slope covered with large, dead plants, their leaves spotted with snow.

"Those must be wildflowers," Britt said. "Or should I say, 'Must have been'?" She continued up the slope, her firm buttocks and lean legs accented by tight jeans. I watched her for a moment, realizing how desperately I'd missed her, understanding as never before the deep, crazy, seemingly insoluble dilemma life had produced for me, determined that before the day had ended I would explain it to her. I climbed the slope, feeling even more weight on my shoulders than I'd carried into the mountains.

By then Britt was fifty feet above me. As good condition as I was in, it was minutes before I caught up to her, and by that point my breathing was labored.

It took us half an hour to reach a plateau at the top of the mountain where the chairlifts, rising from slopes to the east, west and north, came together. The silence was so complete that we could hear the empty chairs creaking as the wind pushed them to and fro. The view to the north was completely different from the one from the cabin, but no less spectacular: a deep gorge, descending at least four thousand feet to a winding river. The far wall of the gorge was a nearly perpendicular, multicolored mountain face, its stones ranging from beige to red.

We found a huge tree whose base was matted with pine needles, sat and leaned against it, and studied the view in silence.

"So," Britt said, "I'm ready when you are."

I gave a rueful laugh. "For the moment, I'd rather just sit here and soak it in."

"Then do that."

"I wish I could." I turned to her. "I've had a lot to think about since you left."

She shook her head apologetically. "My timing wasn't the best."

"You had no way of knowing what was coming. And you did what you had to do." I faltered. "I won't pretend that it didn't shock me. Not just your leaving. Telling me I was a closed book. I'd never thought of myself that way. But you're right. I didn't volunteer anything about my childhood or my family or why I stay in this stupid job, and I sure never talked about Elaine."

The truth was that in all the months I'd known Britt, I'd mentioned Elaine's name no more than half a dozen times. As my affection for Britt had increased, my memory of Elaine had diminished, until it seemed I could have one or the other but not both. My next words were about as difficult for me as any I've ever spoken. "The more I think about it," I said shakily, "the more I realize that those subjects are all connected, which probably explains why I didn't want to talk about any of them."

The shock of the words left me silent for a moment. "So if you can stand it," I said then, "I'd like to try to piece it all together, and maybe somewhere along the way"—here I chose some innocuous stand-ins for the words I should have used—"I can come to grips with that issue you posed last Sunday."

"About us?"

"About my being a one-woman man."

"Ah! *That* issue," Britt said, trying to make light of it. She reached for my hand and squeezed it. "I came to listen. I can stand as much as you want to tell me," she said, trying to sound reassuring, but I could hear a slight trembling in her voice.

I took a breath, and stepped off the cliff.

12

"When I opted for police work, everyone thought I was crazy. They all knew how my dad had been killed, they all understood that connection, but they all believed that given my extraordinary options it was a crazy choice. What they didn't know was how desperately I'd needed to do something other than what my dad had planned for me."

With those words, the image of my father, blurred all these years by mourning, came finally into focus, and I saw him not as the myth I'd made him into but as the man he was. I suppose the shrinks would call this a breakthrough moment; for me it was more a *breakaway* moment, in which I wrenched my gaze from the prism through which I'd been viewing the world all these years and saw it with naked eyes. For seconds the vision stunned me.

"My dad was a powerhouse," I went on at last, "big, unbelievably strong, with the confidence that goes with that kind of power. Physical confidence, of course, but—more important—mental confidence about how life ought to be lived. In the process of making his choices, he inevitably created a small universe, with himself at the center. Everyone who dealt with him became part of that universe, beginning with his family. We were as connected to him as the earth to the sun."

I nodded, remembering, and looked into the distance. When I turned back to Britt, I saw that she was nodding also. "In that respect," she said, "you are describing my mother."

"Then you understand."

"Oh, yes. The circumstances are completely different, but in essence you are telling me the story of my life." There was the briefest pause, as if she, too, was having trouble with those memories, and then she added quickly, "But that's not what we're here to talk about. Go on."

I looked into her eyes and asked myself how I could have known so little of what was behind them after being intimate with this woman for so many months. I didn't like the answer, but I couldn't dwell on it now.

"When I was a kid," I said, "I was in awe of my father's self-assurance. I never questioned his judgment, first, because young boys don't question their fathers—at least I didn't—and second, because he always seemed to be right, and third, because the results were so fantastic. We lived this beautiful life on top of Pacific Heights—every room with a view, loving relatives, lots of friends, important visitors, the best schools and at least one great trip a year, not just to Europe but to Asia or Africa or South America. And automobile trips. My dad loved to drive. We'd take four- or five-day trips to Oregon or the Grand Canyon or Southern California. Whatever we did, whatever happened, we never had to worry about a thing. He took care of everything. But when I reflect now on that urge of his to arrange all our lives, I can see the damage it caused me—not my mother, who loved it, or my sister, who resisted it kicking and screaming, just me. As much as I was comforted by his concern and enjoyed what he provided, it kept me from developing confidence in my own choices. Dad would ask questions, and listen intently, but in the end he'd decide that he knew what was best for me, and lacking even the habit of making choices, let alone confidence in them, I'd figure Father knows best and go along."

By this point, Britt had taken to nodding rhythmically to my story, as though to the beat of a familiar song. I felt as energized as performers must when an audience claps in time to their music.

"By the time I was sixteen, seventeen, I'd begun to realize how much under my father's wing I'd lived, and how little thinking I'd done on my own, and how much my future was being decided by default. By that point I had a lot of misgivings about that future. Partly it was that I didn't want to be in competition with my father. I didn't want to be compared with him in any way, which almost kept me from playing football. In the end I played because, whatever problems I might have with him, I loved him to the point of worship, and this was a way I could make him proud of me—provided I succeeded, of course, which, thank God, I did."

"Weren't you an all-star, or whatever they're called?" Britt asked.

"Second team all-American. But just because I'd been as good a jock as my father didn't mean I'd be as good as he was in business. You couldn't compare a 1940 ballplayer with a 1970 ballplayer, but at work my dad would be able to measure me every day against his expectations, as well as his own abilities. I cringed at the thought."

Britt frowned.

"What's the matter?" I asked her.

"It's very difficult for me to imagine you cringing before anything."

I looked at her, upset. "Well, then I *have* been a closed book, because I did a lot of cringing growing up."

Britt rose, brushed the pine needles off the seat of her jeans, and did a little dance.

"Are you cold?" I asked.

"Stiff," she said, massaging her legs.

I took a moment to organize the chronology. "Dad wanted me in the business, no matter how I felt. Z. Tobias and Company had passed to the firstborn son for five generations. It was unthinkable to him that this continuity would be broken. There were two small problems with that. The first was that I didn't want to be the head of Z. Tobias and Company. The second was that it put me in mortal conflict with my sister, the firstborn *child,* who wanted more than anything in life to be the head of Z. Tobias and Company."

The sky had darkened as I'd been speaking, like the end of act one of some tragic opera. It was noticeably colder. Turning, I saw that a storm front was moving rapidly toward us from west to east. "We'd better get back," I said.

I stood up next to Britt and we began to retrace our steps, but the storm caught us before we were off the plateau. "Look," Britt said, grabbing my arm. We watched together as a mass of snowflakes whirled toward us. "Come on," I said, offering my hand.

"We'll do better by ourselves," Britt answered. She pulled her cap down on her head, tugged on her gloves and started off.

Descending the steep slope proved far more difficult than ascending it. The ground was soft and the footing insecure; I stumbled several times as rocks gave way. The snow quickly added to the difficulty, hiding the smaller rocks and making all of them slippery. My legs burned with the effort, but the sight of Britt below me, seemingly gliding down the slope, spurred me on. When we finally reached the upper edge of Bear Valley it was snowing so hard we had trouble spotting the cabin, and might not have recognized it if the rented T-Bird hadn't been parked outside.

I was shaking when we entered the house, as much from the effort as from the cold. I gathered paper, kindling and logs for a fire while Britt made bean soup and sandwiches. By the time she brought them to the table the stove was blasting, its flames, visible through a glass window, the only light in the increasingly dark living room. Half of Britt's face reflected the fire. The other half was in shadow.

I'd been so intent on my story that I'd had no idea how hungry I was. "Oh, that hits the spot," I said, as the hot soup warmed my stomach. For the next few minutes we concentrated on our food. "Go on with your story," she said, looking across the table at me. "You were talking about your sister."

"Don't worry. I remember."

"You've never talked to me about her."

"I try very hard not to think about her, let alone talk about her. We don't get along."

"That much I've noticed in the few times we've been together."

"Thanks for not asking about it."

Britt went to the kitchen and returned with the saucepan in which she'd heated the soup. "It wasn't because I wasn't curious," she said carefully as she ladled more steaming soup into my bowl.

"Hey, save some for yourself," I said.

She ignored me, pouring the last of the soup into my bowl. "I was sure that if and when you wanted to talk about it you would," she said as she sat back down at the table.

"I still don't want to talk about it," I said with a sigh. "But I have to."

What happened next was incredible. Even though I was only talking about Sari, had no idea where she was and was undoubtedly separated from her by hundreds of miles, I could feel the same fight-or-flight adrenaline I'd felt in confrontations with her ever since we were kids, especially during those years when she was bigger and stronger than I was and would whack me around and then threaten never to talk to me again if I told. That scared me more than the beatings, because in spite of everything I idolized her. She was a whiz in school, the unchallenged leader of her friends, and even then, she seemed as self-confident as my father. He ran all our lives, and then she ran mine.

Britt had finished eating while I recounted these details. "Your soup's getting cold," she said. "Eat." She watched me until I'd finished the soup and the rest of my sandwich. "Was there some big event that set the two of you at odds?" she asked then.

I shook my head. "It was more a series of conflicts stemming from her basically hostile attitude. Being fair to Sari, I'd have to say she was provoked. She was born in '50, a year after my parents married. For two years she was it—and then I came along. My father couldn't understand what had happened to his angelic little girl. All of a sudden, she wouldn't mind. She said no to everything. And stubborn, God, she was stubborn, with a will you couldn't believe. Imagine my dad, this powerhouse man, this center of the universe, being confronted by that. One night, at the dinner table, after he'd carved four slices off a prime rib, he put the end piece on my plate. She shrieked, 'Not fair, not fair, he had it last time.' And of course my father, who remembered everything, remembered it was Sari who had had the end piece the last time, and told her so, at which point Sari began to scream and cry."

"Just a minute," Britt said, holding up her hand. "There are two end pieces on a prime rib roast. Why didn't your father just cut the other end for Sari, and avoid the argument?"

I had my first good laugh since the night of Chief Doyle's fateful call, informing me of the attack on Maggie Winehouse.

"What's funny?" Britt said, obviously perplexed by my outburst.

"Appeasement was not Ted Tobias's thing," I said. "If he was right, he was right, and taking turns was right—in his mind, I'm sure, one more object lesson for Sari. Those lessons never took. In any case it wouldn't have done any good to give her the other end piece. She had to have the end piece he'd given *me*."

"Aha, yes, of course," Britt said, nodding. "So what happened?"

"My father ordered her to stop crying, which only provoked her more. He tried to eat, then suddenly erupted: 'You've spoiled my dinner!' He threw his napkin onto his plate, grabbed Sari's arm and pulled her, kicking and screaming, up the stairs to his bedroom. I sat there as long as I could stand it, until Sari's screams rose another notch. Then I slipped from my chair. 'Don't go!' my mother ordered, more, I'm sure, out of concern at displeasing my father than at what the sight might do to me. Normally I minded, but this time I ignored her and crept up the steps and past the bedroom door. Inside, my father had Sari over his knee and was whacking her behind with a hairbrush. Then and there I decided that the way you got through life without a beating was to be perfect."

"Oh," Britt said, rearing back, and audibly sucking air. "Oh, my."

"What?" I asked her, startled.

"The way to get through life without a beating is to be *perfect?*" She looked at me aghast, her mouth gaping, her eyes narrowed, her forehead creasing into lines. "You were how old when you decided that?"

"Five, six, seven. Can't remember. In any case, I'm sure I didn't say that to myself in so many words. What I *am* sure about is that that's the way I governed myself from that point on."

"But my God, what a burden!" she said sympathetically. "Especially for a child."

"I suppose you're right. I never thought about it."

"And did your father ever hit *you?*" she asked abruptly.

The question shocked me. I hadn't thought about that time in years. "Once," I said. "It was a Friday afternoon in the fall. I was nine, maybe ten. He'd come home early from work. I should have been in by then because we were under orders to be home before dark, and it was almost dark. So he sent Sari to look for me. She found me where I was just about every afternoon, in the Julius Kahn Playground at the edge of the Presidio, in the closing moments of a football game. 'Daddy wants you,' she announced with contempt. I told her to tell him I'd be right there, but I got caught up in a touchdown drive and I didn't get home for twenty minutes. By then, he was outside, scouring the neighborhood for me. When he returned, he was furious. I was in the kitchen, having some hot chocolate. His look drew me to my feet. I stood in front of him. 'Where were you?' he said, his voice so cold and menacing I damn near lost control of my sphincter. 'In the park,' I said. His hand came out of nowhere and smacked me across the left side of my face. One second I was standing, and the next I was on the floor. 'You're lying,' he said, standing over me. 'I'm not,' I cried. 'I was playing football in the park.' He said, 'I sent your sister to the park, and she said you weren't there.' '*She's* lying,' I cried. 'I told her to tell you I'd be right home.' My father just stood there. Didn't say a word. Then he walked away."

I sat back, surprised at how the mere telling of this long-ago story had set my heart racing. "I spent an hour alone in my room, crying, my world shattered, my jaw aching, dumbfounded by the injustice my sister had caused me, absolutely devastated by the realization that all the power in my father, this huge man, had been inflicted so unjustly on me. At dinner I wouldn't look at anyone, and answered only when spoken to. After dinner my father came to my room. 'Get your coat on,' he said—very gently. He took me for a long walk, holding my hand all the way, never saying a word, looking straight ahead, his face grim in a way I'd never seen it."

For a moment the flames visible through the window of the stove seemed to go out of focus. I shook my head to clear my vision. "That was more than thirty years ago," I went on, fighting to keep my voice steady, "and just talking about it puts me back there so vividly I can remember the pitch of the hills and the damp smell of the eucalyptus, and the feel of my father's hand, and the sense that something existed between us that had never existed before." Suddenly, my throat tightened, and for a while I couldn't speak. "When we got home," I said, my voice wavering in spite of my efforts, "we stopped outside the front door. He picked me up and held me, still not saying a word. And then he kissed me and put me down and we walked inside."

I said nothing for another minute, staring at the fire. Finally, I looked at Britt. Her eyes were soft and steady, and filled with the kind of compassion I'd seen only once before in a woman's eyes. I had to look away. "I'll tell you," I said at last, "when a parent dies young, you never get over it."

"I know," Britt said, her voice as soft as her eyes. After a moment, she stacked the dishes and carried them to the kitchen.

I opened the door of the stove and put several small logs into it. Instead of returning to the table, I moved to a couch in the living area, facing the stove. Britt came back and sank into a matching chair at right angles to the couch.

"That lie Sari told wasn't an isolated incident," I went on. "It was the norm. When it came to getting what she wanted, she was as amoral as a sociopath. The big difference between her and a sociopath is that a sociopath isn't concerned about potential consequences, whereas Sari meticulously calculated the consequences of every move she made. To her, the only consideration was whether she could get away with it. Right and wrong weren't issues. In her eyes nothing was wrong that contributed to her survival, and the older she got the more every issue seemed to her to be essential to that survival. A close cousin of ours once remarked that Sari lived as though someone early on had done her a terrible wrong, and she was bound and determined to spend her life making up for it. That sounded pretty reasonable to me, particularly since I happened to be that someone."

I sat back and sighed deeply, feeling drained, as though my confession had leached a poison from my system.

"Dear God," Britt said slowly, shaking her head in disbelief. "Do you have any feelings for her at all?"

"Only negative ones. I abhor her values and her conduct, which led, I guess, to an abhorrence of her. I feel no love, no closeness, nothing. So I'm sure you can understand how I viewed the prospect of spending a lifetime working with my sister."

"Of course," Britt said. She sank back into her seat and stared at me, as though she was seeing me for the first time. Finally, she said, "How is it that Sari never married?"

"She's the ultimate narcissist," I explained, "too good to share herself with anyone."

Britt's right hand flew to her mouth. From behind her hand came a smothered laugh. "That's terrible," she said.

"Terrible, but true. She had a ton of chances. Let's face it, she's bright and attractive, and she's loaded. A lot of good men came at her, but none of them was good enough for her."

I'd been speaking so intently that I'd been oblivious to what was happening outside. Now I glanced out the window. "My God, look at it snow!"

For the next minutes we watched the snowfall, so heavy now it completely obliterated the view to the east. "We could be snowed in," I said.

"I'd say we already are," Britt replied calmly.

"How much food do we have?" I was concerned, even if she wasn't.

"Enough for another day."

"I don't hear any plows. Maybe we should try to get out of here. I'll call the sheriff's office and see what's up."

I rose and started for the phone, but Britt held up her hand. "Don't do that, Zack. I can call Gunilla later on. I'm sure there are people in Bear Valley who make their living helping people like us. And the storm will eventually pass—as storms always do. In the meantime we can finish what we came here to do."

I noticed then that she looked upset. "Are you okay?" I said. "You seem troubled."

"Of course I'm troubled. This is all deeply disturbing."

I walked over to her and put a hand on her shoulder, wanting to touch her face, or better yet to pull her to her feet and put my arms around her, but I held myself in check, fearing that I might be breaking the ground rules. "I'm sorry," I said. "The idea wasn't to trouble or disturb you."

"There's no way you could have avoided it." Britt shook her head. "Ah, God! I wish I had known about your sister before this."

"Why would you want to know about it?" I said, sinking back onto the couch. "It's so ugly I don't even like to acknowledge it."

"Because it explains a great deal about you that I've never been able to understand."

"Such as?"

"Such as why you're not more aggressive."

I cocked my head, impressed. "That's very good," I said. "I try not to let that show."

"But it does," Britt said emphatically.

"In what ways?"

She got up from her chair and began to pace, and then turned back to me. "You don't go all out for what you want. You wait for it to come to you."

"Can you give me an example?" I tried not to sound defensive, but I have to admit I felt it.

"Being the chief of police."

"No," I said, shaking my head. "That's such a long shot it would *have* to come to me. Otherwise it will never happen. Any other examples?"

She smiled wanly, and then laughed a little. "You don't go after women. At least, not this woman. Women must come to you."

"That's something entirely different," I said. "We'll get to that, I promise. But what you've put your finger on is the fallout of growing up in competition with my sister. It wasn't enough that I shouldn't be like her. My life had to contradict hers in every way. That affected everything I did."

"Now you give me an example," she said as she returned to her seat, and swung her legs onto the armrest.

I thought for a moment. "When you play football, you're told to hit as hard as you can, not just to knock your opponent down but to make him realize what kind of punishment he's going to take the next time you hit him. I couldn't do that. I got scouted a lot my senior year, but the scouts decided I'd never make it in the pros because I didn't have that killer increment. They were right. To play the game they play you have to be willing to hurt a friend if he's on the other team. I wasn't willing to do that."

"Did it bother you not to be selected?" Britt asked.

"Not at all," I answered quickly. "By that point I'd come to hate the way the game was being played—the crowds shouting to drown out the opposing quarterback, the pass catchers pretending they'd caught the ball when they knew they'd trapped it, the win-at-any-price mentality. I preferred to lose a clean game than win a dirty one." I sighed. "Which brings me back to Z. Tobias and Company. I suppose when you want something badly enough, you can get used to making compromises. I probably could have gotten used to working with my sister if I'd really wanted what Z. Tobias and Company had to offer. But I didn't. It wasn't only because I didn't need the money. It was that making money the way they made money didn't appeal to me at all."

Britt reared back. "Why?" she said. "Were they dishonest?"

"My God, no. My dad was the soul of rectitude, absolutely scrupulous. He hated liars—that's why he hit me that time, because he thought I'd been lying. And God help anyone who got caught cheating on expenses."

"What, then?"

Now it was my turn to pace. No one had ever asked the questions Britt was asking now. I remembered what I had felt at the time, but it was a gut feeling. I'd never had to put it in words. "A salary is fine," I answered at last. "You're paid for your work. But business competition, in which you have to beat your competitors, make shrewd deals, get the best of someone, the prospect of all that made me deeply uncomfortable. I realize people have to do it, I'm sure a lot of people do it honorably, and I'm sure my father was one of those people because I never heard anything to the contrary. But if it came to the point where the only way to protect his interests was to destroy the other guy, he had the capacity to do that. I knew that I didn't."

"Sari again?" Britt asked, readjusting herself in the chair so that her feet were under her, and then leaning toward me. By this point I'd been talking for more than an hour, but she seemed more absorbed than ever.

"Yes, but not entirely," I answered, settling onto the couch again. "A lot of other things were going on. I don't know what it was like for you in the sixties, but in this country in the sixties it was a time when we chose up sides. It had happened before, but not in my lifetime. I was only ten when John Kennedy was starting to hit his stride, but my dad was a big Kennedy supporter, and talked about him a lot, so everything Kennedy was saying about duty and country sounded great to me, even if I didn't completely understand it. Forget what came later. Here was my role model: a rich guy serving his country, saying, 'Ask not what your country can do for you but what you can do for your country.' He said that at his inaugural when I wasn't quite nine, but the idea hung around for years after he was killed, and it was inevitable that I'd eventually check my own family out against that standard."

Once more I rose to poke the fire and add another log. It caught in a second. I closed the stove and went back to the sofa. "My parents did everything that was expected of them, and then some. They made big donations. They were active in all the drives. But it became increasingly apparent to me that something was missing. For all the philanthropies they engaged in, they had no contact with the objects of their charity. They were detached, in their own world, not in the trenches. My dad embraced a lot of good causes, but always as a leader. He had a serene conviction about his ability to make things happen. He believed there was such a thing as a leadership gene, and that he had it. But he wouldn't go near a slum or a poor person. My mother was the same; she wouldn't step inside a soup kitchen."

"Interesting," Britt said, casting a quizzical look my way. "You've been telling me the story of your life, but you've scarcely talked about your mother."

"What is there to talk about?" I said after a bitter little laugh. "You've been with her. You've seen how she is. If you're useful to her, she's interested. If not, sayonara."

After a moment, Britt said hesitantly, "I thought maybe that she was just that way with me."

"She's that way with everybody—to an extent even with me."

"Parents!" Britt moaned. "How do we survive them?"

"After Kennedy died, everything seemed to polarize at a much more rapid rate. All of a sudden on a lot of college campuses, it became us against them, with a lot of students seeming to be majoring in agitation. The society's screwed up, unfair, alienating, unjust. That sort of thing. The loudest voices by far were in Berkeley, which really upset my dad. He'd had his heart set on my going to college there as he had, but he started talking about sending me somewhere else. I told him I'd dreamed about playing football for Cal ever since I was a kid. That much was true. What I didn't tell him was that I was even more attracted by this point to the campus politics at Berkeley. Those activists were saying everything I was feeling by then. It had become really tough for me to be living rich in a country with millions of poor people."

I hesitated for a minute, then watched Britt carefully. "In that respect I was very much like Elaine."

Britt didn't blink.

"Is it okay to talk about Elaine?" I asked her softly.

She looked me right in the eyes, and said calmly, "I would like to know as much about her as you are willing to tell me."

It was true-confession time. I swallowed, then cleared my throat and spoke, but my voice was still unsteady. "Before anything, I want to talk about this business of my being able to love only one woman in my life. I don't think I'm that kind of man. I don't think that kind of man exists—or that kind of woman, for that matter. If the chemistry's right, if there's intellectual rapport, and the parties are caring and considerate, they usually fall in love. I'm no different. But I'd be lying if I told you that Elaine doesn't still have a hold on me."

The remark seemed to freeze Britt. She sat, immobile, waiting for me to go on.

"Elaine's father, in case I never told you, was—is—a rancher and farmer in the San Joaquin Valley. He's intensely conservative. She'd tell me about listening to his tirades against the government, how the government was socialist, how we were creating a class of professionally poor, how absolutely wrong it was for the government to give handouts to poor people, or assistance of any kind to anyone for that matter. This from a man who received millions in government subsidies each year for *not* growing crops on his lands, and who irrigated the lands he did farm with water the government delivered to him at maybe a twentieth of its cost."

"So Elaine considered her father a hypocrite?" Britt asked.

"Absolutely. The worst. They argued constantly about almost everything, beginning with human nature. 'You can't tell me that people enter this world *wanting* to be poor,' she'd tell him. 'You can't tell me that people prefer failure over success.' She was appalled at the way he treated migrant farmworkers. She reported him to Cesar Chavez's union. He damn near had a coronary."

It was harder going than I'd figured. Talking about Elaine was filling me up with her memory. I had to keep stopping to clear my throat. I'm sure Britt sensed what was happening to me, because she would look away and pretend not to notice.

"In terms of social conscience, I wasn't in Elaine's league when we met, but basically we were two rich kids embarrassed by our wealth. She wanted to save the world even more than I did. We didn't talk a lot about ourselves or our relationship. We talked about society. Whenever a new book came out about what ailed America, we'd read it immediately and either embrace its ideas or tear it to shreds. We knew what the problems were. We were looking for answers. Our vacations were study trips abroad, always looking for a social arrangement that worked.

"But while we both cared about the same things, Elaine really wanted to wear the hair shirt, and I didn't see that at all. She had no faith in our system or any system, whereas I eventually came to have faith in our system as the one with the fewest problems and the best possibilities. She felt she had to work outside the system; I thought that was a one-way ticket to oblivion. Have you ever heard the expression 'If you can't beat 'em, join 'em'?"

"Of course."

"My notion—not an original notion, but original with me, in that I figured it out for myself—was that the way you beat the establishment was to join it, and change it from within. Until I met Elaine, I'd felt disconnected. I knew there was wrong, I knew I wanted to fix it, and I'd decided that my own contribution would be through police work. My dad's murder was the catalyst, no question, but I'd also decided by that point that the top police jobs too often went by default to conservative people with dark views of humankind. Think of Daryl Gates in Los Angeles. If progressive people didn't get involved in police work they had no right to wring their hands. So I had a mission, but I didn't have a lot of conviction about my ability to carry it out. And when you don't have conviction you don't have fire. Elaine gave me that fire." I paused. "At the same time she also gave me a challenge that pretty much affected everything I did—and still do."

I told Britt then about that night in the fifth year of our marriage, sitting in the dark at our 999 Green Street apartment, when Elaine asked me the question that had enslaved me ever since: "How can you ask me to believe that what I do could change anything when you can't change anything yourself?"

"Oh!" Britt said, as though she'd been struck.

"What it came down to was that if I could prove to Elaine that I could change the world in the slightest degree, then I would somehow save her. Intellectually, I know it's untrue, but because I *didn't* change the world in the slightest degree, I feel responsible for her death." That said, I turned away and, unable to stop myself, began to shake. Maybe fifteen seconds passed. I felt Britt behind me, and then her hands on my shoulders.

"So," I said when I was finally able to speak, "I'm still trying to prove to Elaine that I can make a difference through the system. If I'm out of the system, I'm out for good, and I'll never be able to do it.

If I fail, it's as good as admitting that Elaine was right, that there are no solutions, that society is irredeemable."

I turned to Britt, and locked my eyes on hers, not easy, considering what I was about to say. "I can't put Elaine to rest until I've made that difference. And until I've put Elaine to rest, I'm not free to commit to another woman—or to go after women, as you put it earlier." I took a breath, feeling my nervousness, and then exhaled. "Ah, God," I said. "It's crazy, but that's the way it is."

"It's not crazy," Britt said, trying to sound convincing. But her eyes had suddenly gone flat, and I could hear the sadness in her voice.

I sank back against the sofa, exhausted, and stared out the window at the falling snow. The last light of day was gone. Just outside the window a curtain of flakes reflected the lights from the cabin. Beyond the curtain was blackness. I looked back just in time to see Britt take a deep breath, open her eyes wide and straighten in her chair.

"So," she said, her voice firm once again, "what are your choices?"

"The first is to roll over, take my lumps and go back to work when the suspension is over, hoping that the whole episode eventually blows away. The second is to continue to poke around, which, if I'm caught, could get me kicked off the force."

I'd come all this way, and then I'd flinched. As badly as I'd wanted to tell Britt that this choice could also cost me my life, I couldn't put that burden on her.

"And?"

Deep breath. "I've got to go for it."

"Yes," Britt said.

We rose in unison, looking at each other. I could see the fire from the stove reflected in her eyes. Although I was an arm's length from her, I'd never felt closer to Britt than I did in that moment. "Thanks for listening," I said. That scarcely conveyed the degree of my gratitude, but I was too drained to say more.

She managed a weak smile. "You're quite welcome," she said, her voice husky.

"And thanks for coming."

"Thanks for wanting me to come."

Her words seemed to drift off, and then she did too, first to the shower, then to the kitchen, where, by the time I'd returned from my shower, she was preparing dinner. As I watched, she sautéed finely chopped garlic, ginger and onions in olive oil, then added chopped artichoke hearts—obviously the beginning of a pasta sauce. After what she'd gone through today, I could only marvel that she had put her mind to something so elaborate. And then I wondered whether the complicated recipe was intended to take her mind off the sadness of what, for lack of a better word, had to be called a breakup.

I poured each of us a glass of wine and continued to watch her in silence, feeling not just talked out but drained of all energy after the long and trying day. Then I cooked the spaghetti, made a salad and set the table, taking comfort in these few simple acts. Britt said nothing all this time either, understanding, I was certain, that for the moment there was nothing more to be said.

The silence continued through dinner. I think Britt was as grateful for it as I was. We each drank two glasses of wine. I was about to pour myself a third when I suddenly remembered my promise to myself to drink carefully or not at all. I put the bottle down.

After dinner we tried the television, but the cable was out.

"Just as well," Britt said. "I'm exhausted."

"Me, too."

I'm sure we'd both been postponing this moment, not knowing what it would bring. I was two feet from her. Our eyes met. I couldn't read hers. "Will I be breaking the rules if I kiss you?"

"Not if you do it chastely."

And that's what I did, my mouth closed, my hand gently on her arm, my lips barely touching hers. Her lips felt pliant, but she kept them together. It was a chaste kiss, all right, but it still made me dizzy. After several seconds, Britt broke it off, and held me at arm's length, sadness etched into her features. Then she shook her head and sighed. "Most unfortunate," she said with a rueful smile. "A mountain cabin, a snowstorm, a fire, a beautiful man . . ."

Twenty minutes later we were asleep in separate beds.

We slept until the light woke us. It was after seven. Britt got up and looked outside. "My God!" she said, as though she'd just seen a miracle. I joined her at the window. The sky was clear. A brilliant sun shone on what appeared to be three feet of fresh snow.

After breakfast, I found a shovel, dug out the car, and put on the chains I'd providentially demanded from Avis. But they did no good. The snow was too deep. It took me an hour to raise the service station, and another hour for the tow truck to plow its way to the car. The driver looked as if he'd walked out of a Marlboro ad: tall, lean, square-jawed, deeply tanned, wearing jeans, cowboy boots and a sheep-lined jacket. He explained that the storm had caught everyone by surprise. The man in charge of snow control, who drove through the subdivision to roust the cars out before the first big dump of the winter, when they closed the roads, had driven to Stockton to celebrate his parents' fortieth wedding anniversary.

The driver towed us to the highway, and gave me an automobile-club form to sign. When I handed the form back to him, he was looking appreciatively at Britt.

Except for the most perfunctory exchanges, Britt and I drove down the mountain in silence. Only when we'd reached the floor of the valley and were moving down the back roads, past fields of denuded grapevines and fruit trees, did she finally speak. "I have something to say to you, Zack, that you may not care to hear, but I feel that I have to say it."

"Go on," I said apprehensively.

"Given everything that happened between you and your sister, I'm sure you have every reason to feel as you do. But I was awake for part of the night thinking about what you told me, and I have to say that, given the predicament Sari found herself in, I can understand her actions. Perhaps it's something a woman can understand more than a man."

"Try me," I said, my tone somewhere between defensive and belligerent.

"It's evident from what you've told me that you truly loved your father. But at the risk of hurting you, Zack, I have to tell you that as you've described him, he was a tyrant—"

"No way," I objected.

"A benevolent tyrant, perhaps," she went on without pausing, "but a tyrant all the same. *You* had trouble evolving in that environment. Imagine what it was like for Sari, a small *girl*, fighting not just that determination of your father's to run his universe and everyone in it, but the tradition of male chauvinism that so obviously permeated your family."

I turned my eyes from the road for an instant to frown at Britt. She had moved her body so that she was turned toward me, the right side of her back resting against the door.

"Why are you frowning?" she asked.

"Because I understand all that," I said, my eyes back on the road. "Everything you've just said to me I said to you yesterday."

"True, but what you also said was that only *you* were damaged by your father's urge to arrange all your lives. Just based on what you've told me, I'd say that Sari suffered as much damage as you did."

For a minute I listened to the humming of the wheels racing over the road. "I don't remember saying that, but if I said it I was wrong. I can understand how Sari was damaged."

Britt laid a hand on my arm. "There's a difference between understanding something intellectually, and understanding it compassionately."

It took me a little while to think about what Britt had said, and to compose my answer. "Sari never gave me a chance to feel compassion for her. By the time I was old enough to understand what she was going through, she'd hurt me in a hundred different ways."

I heard Britt sigh. "People do that to one another, don't they?" she said. Then she removed her hand, turned to face the road and was silent again until we'd reached the freeway and were heading due west to San Francisco. "I have one more thought," she said, an uncharacteristic flutter in her voice. "It has to do with that idea you developed as a child that the way to avoid punishment was to be perfect." Out of the corner of my eye I could see that she was looking at me, as though waiting for permission to continue.

"Go ahead," I said.

"Have you ever considered the possibility that because you think you failed Elaine, you've been punishing yourself ever since?"

Startled, I glanced sharply at her. "What do you mean?" I said. There must have been a real edge to my voice, because she became visibly uneasy.

"You weren't the perfect husband. You didn't save her. So your punishment is that you're not permitted a second chance."

"By whom?" I demanded.

"By yourself."

The thought was new and threatening. I drove at least a mile before speaking. "That sounds like something a shrink might say," I said.

"That doesn't make it invalid."

"I'll have to think about it," I said uncomfortably, then fell silent again.

Britt punched the radio button—with a shaking hand, I noted unhappily, realizing I'd undoubtedly caused that—and found a classical music station. Instantly, the interior of the car filled with the sound of lush and powerful music. As usual, I couldn't name the piece to save my life, but I knew every note of the score. More often than not my mind drifts when I listen to classical music, but this time I seized upon it like a shipwrecked man to a life preserver, and I soon found myself humming under my breath in synch with the piano and orchestra. My heart began to swell, and at the rousing yet lyrical end, I damn near cried. I'd heard the same piece a hundred times before and always been moved by it, but never to this degree. As I heard the announcer identify the piece as Rachmaninoff's Third Piano Concerto and the soloist as Santiago Rodriguez, I suddenly understood why. I'd just heard perfection.

At Britt's house I carried her bag to the door, then turned to her and put my hand on her shoulder. "There's got to be a better ending," I said.

"We'll just have to see, won't we?" she replied. But she didn't sound hopeful. Then she reached up, pecked me on the cheek and walked through her door.

I drove back to the airport, as subdued as Britt, yet feeling that, her last challenges aside, my thoughts were finally harnessed together, pulling in one direction rather than stampeding off in all directions.

At the airport, I turned in the car and reclaimed my own. Half an hour later, as I was approaching Greenwich Street, I saw an Asian man seated on the steps leading to the tennis courts in Alice Marble Park, with a perfect view of my building. He could be a stakeout. He could be a resident of the neighborhood, getting some fresh air.

I couldn't bring myself to confront him.

13

Walking into the Pacific Rim Bank had been a mistake, born of frustration and impatience. No more screwups, schmuck, I lectured myself. One more and you're not only out of business but probably permanently out of breath. Whatever I did from this point would have to be done one careful step at a time.

No question about the first step: Find Maggie. Inevitably, her disappearance had made me wonder if she'd told me all she knew. Was she afraid of another attack for reasons she hadn't disclosed? The answer to that question didn't just bear on a case—it could determine my survival.

I didn't exactly bound out of bed Thursday morning determined to take that first, careful step. To the contrary, I lay there for ten minutes, remembering the fairy-tale quality of Wednesday morning's awakening, as Britt and I looked out on a world transformed by several feet of new snow. The memory was like a blanket you're reluctant to come out from under on a cold morning. It held me snug—until I began to work backward to my protracted confession of the previous day, and to its unavoidable conclusion. Like it or not, the case of Maggie Winehouse, now eleven days old, had become the means by which I was to acquit myself to myself, exorcise Elaine's ghost and get on with my life—a life that might include Britt.

Maggie's disappearance was no longer a secret. But if the most recent story in the *Dispatch* was accurate, the police weren't looking for her. That made sense because, just as I'd warned Mike Winehouse, the case had been closed pending the development of new leads, and she was free to go where she pleased.

The Winehouses continued to profess that they didn't know where she was. To judge by Gordon's haggard look on the tube Wednesday evening, he didn't have a clue either. Even supposing he knew something, I couldn't go to Gordon. I simply couldn't trust him. For the same reason I couldn't go to Mike Winehouse.

Bess Winehouse was another matter.

The Winehouses lived in a condominium on the west slope of Russian Hill. I knew that Mike wrote at home in the mornings—he'd mentioned that fact in his column more than once—and went to his office at the *Dispatch* in the afternoon. Britt and I had returned from Bear Valley late Wednesday afternoon. I waited until one-thirty on Thursday, then telephoned the Winehouse apartment, once again using a pay phone. As I'd hoped she would, Bess answered.

"This is Zack Tobias," I said.

"Yes?" she said, her voice rising apprehensively.

"I want to help you find Maggie, but if you tell anyone, your husband included, that I so much as called, I won't be able to do that. Can you promise me you won't tell him?"

"Yes, *yes*," Bess said. The second yes convinced me.

"Good," I said. "Here's what I'd like you to do." I gave Bess some instructions, and told her where to meet me.

It was a three-minute drive from my garage to the rendezvous I'd selected, but it took me fifteen minutes to get there—five minutes to scan the street in search of a stakeout, ten minutes to drive a circuitous route to Polk and Broadway, where Bess stood waiting for me on the northwest corner. By the time I arrived I was dead certain that no one was tailing me, and I'd even begun to wonder whether, with my well-publicized suspension, my tormentors had lifted their surveillance, figuring that I was now off the case and they'd achieved their objective. On the other hand, someone had tailed me to the airport early Tuesday, the morning after the suspension had been announced, so I wasn't about to drop my guard.

Bess was wearing the same black warm-up suit and sneakers she'd worn at the hospital and carrying a Macy's shopping bag. Her hair looked as though she had scarcely put a comb through it, and the only makeup she had on was lipstick. Her lips seemed glued together. As she got into my car she gave the impression of a woman who'd had the life sucked out of her, and I would have bet that she hadn't set foot outside her apartment in days. As I drove away from the intersection, she settled the shopping bag next to her feet and placed her hands in her lap. I could see that they were shaking. Impulsively I reached over and squeezed them. She gave me a quick, grateful look, then turned her gaze back to the street.

I drove to Crissy Field, and parked at the west end. "Okay," I said, "let's see what we've got."

From the shopping bag Bess withdrew half a dozen framed photographs of Maggie as a teenager, in every one of which she was surrounded by friends. "She had a lot of friends. She was very popular," Bess explained.

"Is that Barbara Woo?" I asked, pointing to a graduation photograph of Maggie next to a Chinese girl who looked at least four inches shorter.

Bess looked over at me. "How did you know?" she asked.

"Mike wrote about her in his column."

"Right. Right."

"They were really close?"

"Closer than sisters."

"You wouldn't happen to know where Barbara Woo is, would you?"

"In Mendocino. She moved there last year when she got married." She turned toward me. I could almost see her mind working. "You think Maggie could be with Barbara?" she said, her voice trembling.

"I'd say there's a good chance. What do you know about her husband?"

"He's an artist. His name is Kaplowitz, I think. I'm sorry I don't remember his first name."

I smiled, and patted Bess's hand. "There can't be too many Kaplowitzes in Mendocino," I said.

I called information in Mendocino on my car phone. A Mark Kaplowitz was listed. There were no other Kaplowitzes. I got the address as well as the phone number. Then I started the car and turned around.

"Aren't you going to call her?" Bess said, her disappointment transparent.

"Won't do any good," I said. "I'll drive there."

"Will you call me when you get there?"

I thought for a minute. "Here's what I'll do, Bess. If Maggie's there, I'll call your house and ask for Adam. If she's not there, I'll ask for Eve. Either way, you say 'Wrong number' and hang up. Okay?"

"I won't remember which is which." Her voice was shaking.

"Then I'll write it out for you."

I drove Bess to within a block of her door. When I stopped the car, I took out a pad from my glove compartment, wrote the code down, tore off the page and handed it to her, squeezing her hand once again as I did. "I'll find her," I said, trying to sound more confident than I felt. "Just be sure you answer the phone tonight, not Mike."

Ten minutes later I was across the Golden Gate Bridge and in Marin County, driving up 101 at the speed of the fastest traffic. In an hour I passed through Santa Rosa. Thirty minutes later I turned west at Cloverdale onto State Highway 128 and raced through the Anderson Valley, passing dozens of cars. It was after six by the time I reached the coast and turned north onto Highway 1, its incomparable coves and shoreline lost in the darkness. A few minutes before seven I walked up the steps of a simple Cape Cod–style cottage, complete with porch, at the north end of Mendocino. Except for its sags and paint, it probably looked as it had a hundred years before.

A man in his late twenties, presumably Mark Kaplowitz, answered the door. "Yeah?" he demanded, staring at me from behind wire-rimmed glasses. I towered over him and outweighed him by at least sixty pounds, but he didn't seem in the least intimidated.

"I'm here to see Maggie."

"There's no Maggie here."

"I think there is."

"I don't give a fuck what the fuck you think," he said, thrusting his head toward me, his body so rigid I could see the carotid arteries on each side of his neck. "Get the fuck off my property."

"I'm a friend of Maggie's."

"I'm tellin' you, man, nobody named Maggie lives here."

"Then may I speak to Barbara?"

He hesitated for an instant. "Who the fuck *are* you?" he said.

"My name's Zack Tobias," I said, deliberately refraining from mention of the SFPD. "I drove up from San Francisco to see Maggie."

"I'm *tellin'* you, man—"

"It's okay, Mark," a voice I recognized as Maggie's called out. "Let him in."

Mark stood back reluctantly and glared at me as I entered. Behind him, to his left, stood Barbara, long, straight black hair framing a thin tan face, who seemed even more diminutive than she had in the graduation photo Bess had shown me. She was gaping at me with incomprehension, her almond-shaped eyes stretched wide, surely as dazed as she was frightened by the intrusion of an urban nightmare into what only a week before must have been a peaceful life. Behind Barbara was Maggie.

She was seated in a chair, wearing the same sweats she'd worn leaving the hospital. The bandages were off. The sight was, if anything, more devastating than what I'd seen before. Those angry red lines crisscrossing her face were now covered with thick ugly scabs. She looked gaunt. I judged that she'd lost ten pounds.

I turned to Mark and Barbara. "I need to be alone with Maggie."

"So?" Mark said, his face as pleasant as a bulldog's.

It was inevitable, I suppose, given all the frustration of the last eleven days, that someone would push me over the edge. "So," I said angrily, my eyes shooting daggers, "why don't you and Barbara go out and get us a pizza?"

"Fuck that," Mark said. "This is my home."

"And that is your friend," I said loudly, pointing to Maggie, "and I am a cop trying to help her."

"It's okay, you guys," Maggie said. "Go ahead."

Mark continued to glare at me for another five seconds. Then, ever so slowly, he turned his gaze to Maggie. "Is this the guy you told me about?" he said skeptically.

"Yes."

Seconds passed. At last he shrugged. "Okay," he said. "Come on, Barbara."

I held out a twenty-dollar bill.

"Keep your money," he sneered. Then, with a last, lingering glare at me, he ushered Barbara out the door.

I turned toward Maggie. "Thanks," I said, walking over to her. The room was so small that three steps put me next to her.

She stared at me uneasily as I approached, and tilted her head to look up at me. "I don't know why you came here," she said. "I've got nothing more to tell you." But her voice was shaking, which made me feel that she was holding out on me. One careful step at a time, I warned myself.

"You can tell me why you left San Francisco without telling your parents or your boyfriend where you were going," I asked, keeping my voice even.

"It's pretty simple. If my father or Gordon knew where I was, they'd have to tell their editors. I *had* to be alone."

I focused on her eyes, trying to link our gazes. "The only reason you came was to get away?"

"Yes," she said. But she wouldn't look at me.

"I don't believe you, Maggie," I said softly. "I think you're afraid of something."

For Maggie, the words had the effect of a sudden, unexpected shove. She fell back against her seat, her eyes wide. "Well, wouldn't you be?" she said. Then she lowered her head and began to cry.

I moved a chair close to her, sat, and put a hand on her arm. "Are you just generally afraid, or are you afraid of something specific?"

She nodded at the second thought. "Something specific?" I repeated.

She nodded again, like a child being led step by step through a confession of her fears.

I waited until she'd finished crying.

"Are you afraid of some person?"

Again she nodded, but she wouldn't look at me.

"Who?"

A cat I hadn't seen before came into the room, and rubbed against Maggie's legs.

At last Maggie turned toward me, but only partially, and when she looked at me it was out of the corner of her eyes. "If I tell you, what will you do?"

"I won't tell anyone, if that's what you're worried about."

"Will you go to this person?"

"Only if and when I find out that you've got good reason to be afraid of him. And at that point I'll arrest him. Now, tell me who it is."

Seconds passed. Maggie wouldn't or couldn't look at me. At last she took a deep breath, exhaled and turned my way. "Jimmy Chang," she said.

My spine tingled. "Aha," I said, in spite of myself. "You had dealings with Jimmy?"

She nodded. "I interviewed him while I was researching the story."

Of course she would have interviewed Jimmy, the self-appointed spokesperson for first-generation Chinese immigrants. Why hadn't I thought of that? "Was this the first time you'd interviewed him?"

"Yes," she answered weakly.

"Why him?" I asked. Even though I was sure I knew the answer, I had to let her tell the story.

Maggie still refused to look at me. "His name came up in the course of the reporting," she said, staring at the floor. "Half a dozen people said, 'Talk to Jimmy Chang.' So I called him, and he seemed really excited about seeing me. 'I give you good sound bite,' he said." She spoke the last sentence in imitation of Jimmy Chang; she had his accent dead on. At last she looked at me and, to my astonishment, she smiled. It was faint, but it was a smile.

I smiled myself, partly at the incongruity, partly to encourage her. "What exactly did you tell him you wanted to talk about?"

"I'm sure I told him that I wanted to talk about the influx of Asians into the Bay Area."

"But nothing about his bank?"

"I didn't know anything about his bank."

I believed her. Her expression and tone of voice were clear and direct. "Did the subject of dirty money come up in the course of your interview?" I asked.

"Yes," she said at once.

Again, that tingle. "Tell me."

"I don't remember exactly how it went."

"Is there a sound track? Was your camera guy shooting at the time?"

"No. I was going over with Jimmy what we'd be talking about and where we might shoot it."

In my excitement, I'd leaned closer to Maggie. Now I leaned back, hoping it would relax her. "Try to remember what you said."

"I said something about the triads bringing a lot of money into the Bay Area illegally and how they were buying up real estate and businesses, and he just seemed to get really flustered and didn't want to talk anymore."

I felt myself leaning forward again, stopped, and leaned back. "Up to that moment, he'd been cooperative?"

"I couldn't turn him off."

"Tell me exactly what happened, Maggie," I said, my voice giving my excitement away. "Try to remember exactly what he did."

She was silent for a moment. "He looked really uncomfortable, angry even. He said he had other appointments and had given us too much time. He said, 'You should have told me you wanted so much time.' And then he kicked us out."

"Just like that?"

"Just like that." She worked her back into the cushion behind her and gripped the armrests of her chair.

I chewed my lip for a second. "Have you heard from Jimmy since the attack?"

"No," she said, her voice suddenly small again. She looked away.

"Then why are you afraid of him?" I asked her, dropping my own voice.

"Because it makes sense," she said so softly I could barely hear her.

"What does?"

"What I read about. What Gordon reported." She still refused to look at me.

"About the Pacific Rim Bank, and Jimmy's involvement in it?"

"Yes. It's the only possibility." She kept looking downward.

I stared at the top of her head. "Maggie, it's really important that we don't make any more of this than we should. I know this is tough, but I want you to try to set aside what happened if you possibly can, and think back on that interview with Jimmy like the good reporter you are, and tell me exactly what he looked like when you started talking about the triads and dirty money."

"Oh, God," Maggie said. She closed her eyes. In the distance, a dog barked, then another, and another, and pretty soon it sounded like *101 Dalmatians.* She began to speak without opening her eyes, as though to isolate the scene in her mind. "He'd been smiling, and gesturing a lot. All of a sudden, he dropped his arms and looked at me like he couldn't believe what he was hearing. His eyes narrowed and his mouth got small and—what can I tell you?—I suddenly felt very unwelcome. He'd been seated behind his desk. He got up, actually he shot up, looked at his watch and started complaining that we'd taken too much of his time."

"But up to that moment you had the feeling that he wasn't under any time constraints?"

She opened her eyes and finally looked at me. "Up to that moment, I had the feeling this guy wanted to take over the story."

"Got it," I said. "Thanks a lot."

Her eyes looked heavy with apprehension. "Was that helpful?"

"Very helpful." I stood up. "Okay if I make a credit-card call?"

"Sure."

"Where's the phone?"

"In the kitchen."

A minute later, Bess was on the line. "Is Adam there?" I said.

There was a brief silence. "You've got the wrong number," she said in an unsteady voice. I could sense how desperately she wanted me to say more.

"Sorry," I said, and hung up.

In the living room, I gave Maggie a personal card. "Call me if anything happens, or even if you just want to talk."

"Okay," she said in a voice that told me I wouldn't be hearing from her.

"How long do you think you'll stay here?"

She looked away. "For the rest of my life."

"In that case, you might want to call your mother. She's pretty upset."

Maggie shook her head. "No way. If I call her, she'll tell my father, and he'll have to tell the paper."

"I don't think he'd tell the paper, and I don't think she'd tell him if you asked her not to."

She shook her head again. "I can't take that chance."

I shrugged. "Up to you. Are you going to call Gordon?"

"No way. I *know* he'd tell the station."

That I couldn't contradict. "Take care of yourself," I said, as I started for the door.

"Aren't you staying for pizza?" Maggie asked.

I smiled. "I have a feeling your friends would rather eat without me."

That evening I treated myself to a dinner of raw oysters, grilled salmon and warm chocolate cake at Café Beaujolais, the best restaurant in town, and spent the night at Glendeven, a gabled bed-and-breakfast farmhouse on Highway 1 south of town. My room, called the Briar Rose, was decorated with antique furniture and contemporary art. I sat in a wing chair in front of a fireplace and read entries in half a dozen journals made by previous occupants, unbelievably comprehensive and forthright accounts of how their stay in Briar Rose had inspired a commitment or revitalized a tired relationship.

I slept poorly.

At eight-thirty the next morning, as I was buttoning my shirt, I heard a knock at my door, and opened it to find a breakfast basket, its contents carefully wrapped in a quilted warming pad: a baked apple, hot breakfast buns and strong, aromatic coffee. Perhaps it was because I was still in the grip of Bear Valley, but as I ate the breakfast I spent some minutes thinking that there were people who ran small country inns and baked breakfast buns and lived happily ever after.

By nine o'clock I was on the road, heading back to my problems. By one o'clock, I was eating lunch in my apartment, reading another long, bitter Mike Winehouse column.

Saturday the 12th, nearly 1:00 a.m. Can't sleep. Get up, dress quietly, slip from house for a journey back in time. Destination: Pam Pam, just off Union Square. Used to go there a hundred years ago with other members of graveyard shift after we'd put the paper to bed.

Even at that hour, restaurant so crowded you had to wait half an hour if you didn't have a reservation.

Still in my twenties in those days. Younger reporters all had to pull their share of night shifts. Start at 4:30 p.m., when normal working people prepare to head home. Finish at 1:30 a.m.

Dinner hour anywhere between seven and nine, depending on the news. If there's a fire or a crime or some other breaking story, and you cover it, you might not get dinner at all.

But most nights I can count on taking my brown bag containing soup in a thermos, a sandwich and a piece of fruit into the library, where I quietly do research for one of the novels I'll never write.

Austerity and ambition are handmaidens in those days, so those early morning visits to Pam Pam with two or three other members of that night's graveyard crew are special occasions. Being bachelors with no need to save, they treat themselves to cracked crab or ground meat and spinach mixed with eggs. I nurse a glass of wine.

We talk shop, newspaper people being notoriously smitten with their lives. And we talk about our city as the only alternative to life in Paris or Rome or London, and maybe better than all of them.

Where else, we ask ourselves, could we live in excellent neighborhoods fifteen minutes from the office, and have equally easy access to operas, symphonies, ballets, plays?

Where else are the vistas so inspiring, the streets so tidy, the people so pleased about their city?

What other city blends tradition and experiment so beguilingly, and with such poise and tolerance?

Rhetorical questions. Self-evident answers.

Then.

Around 1:20 Saturday morning I park on Geary, directly across from the entrance to the Union Square Garage.

"Hello, there," a voice calls as I get out of the car. "Would you like to buy a good luck card?"

I look in the direction of the sound. A man is lying in the doorway of a shoe store. Torn shoes protrude from a blanket. He's bearded, maybe 40, 45. Dozens of cardboard cards neatly spread in front of him, with lettering I recognize as Hebrew. "They don't seem to be bringing you much luck," I say.

"You should have seen me a year ago, before I went into this business." He peers at me in the semidarkness. "You're not a druggie, are you?"

"No," I say, imagining how lousy I must look to have provoked such a question. My self-protective instinct doesn't want this conversation to continue. My curiosity wins the battle. "Why do you ask?"

"Because a lot of druggies park where you just parked this time of night."

"Why is that?"

"Because they got business across the street."

"In Union Square?" I say, pretending surprise.

"Yeah. Only druggies and drug dealers in there after midnight. The druggies are usually weirded out, and the dealers are mean m.............," he says, using an expression that wouldn't make it past the copy desk.

I pull a buck from my wallet and hand it to him.

"Thanks," he says, clearly surprised.

"All the best," I say as I walk away.

"Hey, don't you want a good luck card?"

"That's okay," I say.

I walk up Geary. Indigents in every other doorway. I cross Powell, then Geary to the north side of the street, where I run a gauntlet of pan-handlers outside the St. Francis. One tries to block my way. I step around him and walk on.

As I pass the carriage entrance of the hotel, I hear someone call my name. I turn. It's Abe Battat, the jazz pianist, whose trio plays the Com-pass Rose Room. He's wearing a trench coat over his tuxedo, his evening's work obviously ended. He comes toward me, a man in his early sixties, medium build, dark complexion, a lean face punctuated by deep-set, mournful eyes that suddenly gleam when he tells a story, usually unprintable. No gleam tonight. He takes my hand in both of his. "Man, I'm so sorry," he says in his velvet voice.

"Thanks," I say.

He shakes his head, his lips compressed. "This town, I don't know what's happening to it."

"I guess I don't either, Abe."

"I haven't seen you in ages," he says. "What are you doing out at this hour?"

"I'm going to Pam Pam," I say. "Want to join me?"

Abe's silent. I realize he's squinting at me. Seconds pass. "Mike," he says gently, "Pam Pam went out of business years ago."

I knew that. What can I say? That my mind's trying to retreat to a better time? Instead, I shrug and say, "How about David's?" mention-ing another old favorite from the past.

Abe shakes his head. "Closed."

"*David's* went out of business?"

"No, no, but it stops serving at eleven forty-five."

I think for a minute. "Tommy's Joint?" I say.

"Forget it. There's nothing open downtown. If you want a meal, try Mel's Drive-In on Lombard or the Great Eastern Cafe in Chinatown."

"What's going on?" I ask, embarrassed not only by my memory lapse but by my apparent lack of awareness of what's been happening in the heart of my own city.

"No one stays downtown anymore."

"Not even the theater crowd?"

"They go straight home. No one wants to deal with this." He gestures toward the panhandlers and shakes his head. The corners of his mouth turn down. "No one stays out late anymore, period. They're afraid to. I used to be able to play an afternoon and evening gig on the same day. Now the evening gigs start so early you can't take one in the afternoon."

"Well, you haven't changed, Abe."

"Yes, I have," he says sadly. "I don't even have a joke for you."

We stand in silence for a moment. Once again, he takes my hand in both of his. "I really feel for you."

"I appreciate that."

"See you." He turns and walks up Geary.

I jaywalk to avoid the gauntlet, pass another half-dozen panhandlers without further incident, and make it back to my car. The man with the good luck card business is still lying in the doorway, but he appears to be sleeping.

Just as I open the car door, I hear a desperate scream from Union Square, followed by cries of "Don't! Don't! Don't!" Then another scream, even more desperate than the first, then a moment of silence, and then the sound of many running footsteps, growing dimmer with each footfall. Instinctively I turn and take a step toward the square.

"I wouldn't go in there if I were you," the man in the doorway says.

"But somebody might be hurt," I say. In spite of my alarm, I'm struck by his use of the subjunctive, not a tense you'd expect from a derelict.

"From the sound of it, some guy's probably dead."

"But what if he isn't?"

"Look, if you're determined to go in there, you'd better take a good luck card. But if I were you, I'd cool it."

I stand there, divided, paralyzed. My head tells me to go, but my feet seem nailed to the ground. I know that I've gotten good advice, even if from an indigent. Yet to do nothing seems like an admission of cowardice.

Moments later my dilemma's resolved for me. A police car, sirens wailing and lights flashing, drives up. Two policemen run into the square with hands on their holsters.

As I get into the car I'm shaking. An awful thought intrudes: What if Maggie had cried out on that dark street in the Richmond and no one had responded?

And then another thought, more awful than the first: What if *I'd* been passing by, heard the cry, and not recognized Maggie's voice? Would I have responded? Or would I have stood, nailed to the ground, as I had moments before?

Abe, maybe the question isn't "What's happening to this town?" It's "What's happening to us?"

Or are the questions one and the same?

On my return to the city, I'd stopped at the Marina Safeway and bought some cracked crab, a head of romaine lettuce and a loaf of sourdough bread, eager to have lunch in the comfort and seclusion of my home. Now, cleaning the kitchen, I found myself thinking about the pain and bitterness Mike Winehouse had expressed without ever using the words, and of the several hundred thousand readers of his column who had felt his hurt and sorrow. In spite of the trouble Mike had caused me, I counted myself among them.

In twenty years I'd been involved in hundreds of cases. I couldn't think of one that, directly and indirectly, had touched the lives of so many people. Eighteen hours earlier, I'd stressed to Maggie how important it was not to make any more of her encounter with Jimmy Chang than she should. That was not just my training; it was my disposition. But it was getting harder and harder to resist the idea that Jimmy had had something to do with the events that had caused so many people such sorrow.

Guilty people almost invariably protest their innocence more than the innocent. To Jimmy's all but hysterical reaction to what could have been dismissed as a coincidence I now had to add the bum's rush he'd given Maggie when she so much as mentioned the subject of dirty money, and, more important still, his involvement in what had all the earmarks of a shell corporation.

Legend and publicity aside, who *was* this man? How did he get here, and how did he make his millions? He professed to be a citizen. But was he? It was possible that he'd entered the United States illegally, in which case his naturalization papers would be forgeries. It was possible that he had no papers at all.

Anyone serving in an official capacity must be an American citizen. The administration of Mayor Putnam would be embarrassed by the disclosure that it had unwittingly appointed a noncitizen, but that wouldn't be enough to provoke a cover-up. What the administration might *not* survive was the disclosure that Jimmy was a man with a criminal past.

I *had* to find out about that past.

My first call that afternoon was to Manny Hartman at the Immigration and Naturalization Service, a veteran civil servant who'd helped me dozens of times over the years. I came straight to the point. "Can you do me a favor?" I asked.

"Can you pay my pension if I lose mine because I helped you when I shouldn't have?"

"You think it's that risky?"

"Maybe not, but as long as you're suspended, I can't take that chance."

"Fair enough," I said.

I hung up, dismayed. Surely Manny was exaggerating the trouble I might cause him. On the other hand, that was his privilege. I had no right to ask anyone to jeopardize a career on my account, no matter how small the risk. But if I couldn't get help, I was dead in the water.

Dreading the response, I picked up the phone and, from memory, punched in the seven digits of the private line in the office of Stanley Colby, the man in charge of U.S. Customs in San Francisco.

"Sure, I'll see you, Zack," Stanley said, "but given your situation I don't know how much I can tell you. Knowing what you're involved in from all that press you've gotten, what you're going to want is privileged information, which I'm not going to be able to give you."

"Let's try it," I said.

"Lemme take a look here." He began to hum an unrecognizable tune—if it was a tune. Maybe the fight song of the University of Iowa, where he'd gone to school. Whatever it was, the way he hummed it wasn't pretty. "How's Monday at eleven?" he said finally.

"Nothing sooner?" I said, not even trying to hide my disappointment.

"Jeez, afraid not, Zack."

"Okay," I said with a sigh, "Monday at eleven."

. . .

I spent the weekend alone, scarcely budging from my apartment, preferring the solitude to the prospect of being tailed or something far worse. From time to time I scanned the streets from my window, looking for signs of a stakeout, and saw nothing suspicious. But the absence of evidence didn't totally reassure me. You don't just shake the kind of experience I'd had on the bay. I'd be reading or watching TV, and the memory would suddenly shoot into my mind with such speed and force that I'd cry out and my body would recoil as though trying to dodge the powercruiser.

In addition to dealing with my fears, I was beginning to know what it was like to feel like a pariah. Forty-two years I'd lived in San Francisco, and I couldn't think of a single person I'd grown up with, gone to school with, sported or partied with who would be happy to hear from me. They'd love to hear the dirt, for sure, but they wouldn't understand how my life had led to this moment, and they sure as hell wouldn't care. The only person I wanted to be with was Britt, and that was out of the question. In fairness to her if not to myself, I had to take care of business, clean the slate, answer all those questions.

I might have been the only person in San Francisco eager to welcome Monday. At ten o'clock, an hour before my appointment with Stanley Colby, I checked the street from my window, saw nothing and descended to my car, my gun hidden under a leather jacket. I drove yet another circuitous route, looking constantly in my rearview mirror. Only when I was satisfied that I wasn't being tailed did I drive to the U.S. Customs Office across from the Embarcadero, at the foot of Sansome Street. Even so, I was fifteen minutes early.

Colby, in his early forties like myself, had the clean but nondescript looks that suggest a small-town, church-centered upbringing. He'd gone directly from the University of Iowa into government service. He was well over six feet tall, had a flat belly, wore suspenders over a starched white shirt, its collar wings pinned together under a striped tie, and kept his hair short and neat. I would have bet money that he got a haircut every two weeks. We'd been sparring for twenty minutes in his spacious corner office and he'd never once lost his manners.

"As I told you on the phone, Zack," he said now from behind his dark mahogany government-issue desk, "what you're asking for is privileged information, and we just can't give that to you as long as you're under suspension." Directly behind Stanley were pictures of Bill Clinton and Al Gore. To his right was an American flag, hanging from a pole. Stanley lounged in an old-model cushioned desk chair, the kind that rolls and swivels and tilts back. I sat uncomfortably in a stiff, straight-backed wooden chair placed in front of the desk. Over the years, I've probably been in Stanley's office half a dozen times. We'd always sat in deep, upholstered chairs arranged around a coffee table at the side of the room. Not once had we sat as we did now, formally and physically separated. I could only wonder if the message Stanley was sending me had been consciously or unconsciously chosen.

"If you can't tell me whether you're investigating the Pacific Rim Bank, can you tell the San Francisco Police Department?" I pressed.

"Why would they want to know?"

"To establish a motive in the assault on Maggie Winehouse."

"Your thesis being that someone took offense at the juxtaposition of the bank and her remarks about dirty money?"

"Exactly."

"Is that your thesis or the SFPD's?"

"At the moment, it's mine, but it could become the SFPD's."

Stanley swung his chair to the east and looked through his big window at the cars moving along the Embarcadero, and to my annoyance began to hum that same unrecognizable song. Beyond the cars were the empty piers. "*If* we were investigating the Pacific Rim Bank," he said carefully, still looking out the window, "and *if* the SFPD called us and said they'd like to know what we have, we would tell them. But we wouldn't have volunteered the information, and it would be made clear to the SFPD that this was privileged information, which they couldn't share with a third party."

I moved restlessly in my seat. Definitely a conscious choice, I decided. He doesn't want me to be comfortable, and he doesn't want me to stay long. Well, Stanley, I said to myself, I've got a hard ass, and a dozen different approaches. Aloud, I said, "Suppose I came to you and said, 'I have proof that the Pacific Rim Bank is laundering money.' What would you do in that event?"

He turned back to me. "We would take the information and make an investigation of our own."

"And you wouldn't give me anything?"

"That's correct." He picked up a ballpoint pen and began to twirl it through his fingers.

"You wouldn't confirm or deny?"

"That's correct." He nodded his head once, as if to punctuate his refusal.

"You're tough."

Stanley laughed. "Not tough. Correct."

I sighed. "Can you tell me whether—in theory, just hypothesizing, mind you—the Pacific Rim Bank fits the *profile* of a bank that might be engaged in money laundering?"

"*Any* bank fits that profile," Stanley said, showing his first sign of unrest. "Look, I don't want to tell you things you already know. How much *do* you know about money laundering?"

I studied him, trying to gauge how much patience he had left. "I probably knew a lot at one time, but I could use a refresher. You might mention some angle I've forgotten. Would it be presuming on your hospitality if I were to ask you to assume that I don't know anything?"

"Actually, I'd prefer it."

"Shoot," I said. Anything to keep him talking.

In an instant, Stanley's comfort level seemed to soar. He dropped the pen on his desk, leaned back in his chair, and began an explanation I was certain he'd given a thousand times. "Monitoring the flow of negotiable instruments into and out of the United States is one of our most important jobs. The law is very clear about what is and isn't legal. If you carry more than ten thousand dollars in or out without reporting it, it's a violation of the law. You can carry as much as you want either way; it becomes a violation of the law only if you fail to report it. When people don't report and we find out about it, we start to look for the reason they didn't report. On a very few occasions, they may not know or understand the law, although the documents are very clear. Or they may conceivably forget. But when a great amount of undeclared money crosses the border, it's virtually one hundred percent certain that it's come from illegitimate sources."

Stanley's phone rang. He reached for it, annoyed. "Yeah?" he said abruptly. He listened for a moment. "Ten o'clock tomorrow," he said. "And no more calls." Then he put the receiver down and leaned back into the same position he'd been in.

"Money gained from illegitimate sources has to be laundered—all traces of its origins scrubbed away—before it can be used. A drug dealer with several million dollars in bills received from his clients is not a rich man until he cleans that money. Oh, he can go into a grocery store and pay cash, or buy tickets to a ball game, but if he wants to buy a nice house or luxury car he can't do it without creating a trail because real estate agents and car dealers have to fill out forms whenever such transactions occur. Once that form's filled out, it goes into the computer, and one federal agency or another is on the case. The man with illegally gotten money can't just put a vast amount of greenbacks into a bank account. Well, that's not exactly true. He can do it if the bank will accept the greenbacks, but the bank is obliged to fill out a currency transaction form, and that information gets into the computer, too. Are we still on the same page?"

"Of course." So far he hadn't told me anything I hadn't known, but his explanation was a comforting warm-up, like going back to the basics when you're reviving a foreign language.

Stanley tilted his chair even further back, put his feet on his desk and laced his fingers behind his head. "Our computer has a certain amount of artificial intelligence. It will look at data in different ways to try to kick out subjects or topics for us. For example, it will look at a person with huge cash transactions where the occupation doesn't match—an auto mechanic with a salary of twenty-five thousand dollars a year who suddenly takes a million and a half out of the country. We figure a man like that is doing something illegal."

I held my hand up.

"Question?" he said. My interruption seemed to please him.

"A request. Review some of the special ways people get money in and out."

He nodded his acknowledgment. "Getting it out isn't a big problem. You can carry it out in a purse or a suitcase. We know that people hire jets and fly the money out. We know they're crating it up and sending it out as cargo. On the manifest it's listed as washing-machine parts. Or they'll pack the money inside a compressor."

Once more I held up a hand. "How do you find out that there's money inside a compressor?"

"We get a tip from good citizens. Or from people working with us to get their sentences reduced. Or from informants who want to make money. We pay well for information."

"How much?"

"Twenty-five percent of what we capture, up to two hundred fifty thousand dollars."

"Not bad," I said.

"I'll say."

"Okay, how does the money come *in?*" I asked.

"It could come in as cargo, but almost never does. Mostly it would come in as wire transfers from a country with good bank secrecy. Usually, several transfers are involved, so that a lot of layers are created, which makes the audit trail more complex and detection more difficult."

Stanley might not be willing to name names, but he couldn't keep me from wondering if the methods he was describing were being used by the Pacific Rim Bank. "Can you give me an example?" I asked.

"Sure. Let's say you want to launder a million dollars. Your first step is to find a bank that doesn't care about the source of the money and is willing to help you launder it. You decide to do it in Hong Kong because you've heard it's easy to do there. You go to Hong Kong and talk to the bank officer—"

Up went the hand again. "Wait a minute. How do you know which bank to go to?"

He unlaced his hands from behind his head and held them out to me. "How do you know which car dealer or doctor or lawyer to go to? Word of mouth. The recommendation of business associates or friends."

"And if you don't have such a recommendation?"

"No biggie," he said, flicking his right hand as though waving off a fly. "In Hong Kong you almost don't need one. Banking and currency regulations are extremely lax there, and so favor the banks and depositors that it's a violation of the law for the authorities to look into bank records. Corporate regulation is just as lax. The public information on a Hong Kong corporation is almost nonexistent, and you can incorporate there for a thousand Hong Kong dollars, less than one fifty U.S. So once you've incorporated you open an account with the Hong Kong bank in the name of your new corporation, and into this account you deposit your dirty money. Then you have the bank initiate the laundering process. It makes a wire transfer of your million dollars, less its fee, to a bank in Vanuatu—"

"Vanuatu?" I said doubtfully.

"That's right."

"That one I've never heard of."

He smiled. "Not many people have. It's a small island nation near New Caledonia in the Pacific. Had a major U.S. naval base during World War Two. But it doesn't have to be Vanuatu. It could be any one of a dozen obscure places with lax banking regulations. Wherever the money goes first, it doesn't stay very long. The bank receiving the money transfers it, in turn, to a bank in Geneva, let's say, again holding back a fee. From Geneva the money goes to a bank in London, and from London to your account in San Francisco."

We'd come to the moment I'd been waiting for. "Would my account in San Francisco be in my name, or would I have set up a shell corporation in this country as well?"

"In all likelihood, it would be the latter."

"And," I said as casually as I could, "if I had a shell corporation in San Francisco, would I be able to keep an account in just any bank, or would I be better off keeping it in a bank whose officers might not care what business the corporation is in?"

"Obviously, the latter," Stanley said. "It makes a great difference what bank the account is in." He removed his feet from the desk, came to an upright position, then put his elbows on the armrests of his chair and laced his fingers together. "Contrary to what most Americans think, there *are* dirty bankers in this country. A dirty banker will get a wire transfer and just not report it. Or he'll fill out the form, and throw away the part that's supposed to go to the Treasury."

"At which point he's in violation?"

"Absolutely. As I said, the money transfer itself is not a violation. Failure to report it is."

"A violation by the bank as well as the recipient?"

"Right."

Go for it, I told myself. I looked him in the eye. "Is the Pacific Rim Bank a bank that doesn't care what business a corporation is in?"

Stanley laughed. "You don't give up, do you?"

My eyes didn't waver. "Is the Pacific Rim Bank a dirty bank?"

Stanley stared back. "I can't tell you."

You dumb bastard, I wanted to shout, I'm not going to give you away. We're public servants, we're supposed to do good. Give me information so I can do good. But I said, instead, "You can't tell me because you don't know? Or because you're not supposed to?"

Stanley looked down at his desk, let out his breath, then looked at me. "I'm not even going to answer that question," he said.

I inhaled deeply, trying to calm myself. But the oxygen only seemed to further inflame the fire in my belly. "Do you have kids?" I finally asked him.

Stanley frowned. "What do my kids have to do with this?"

"Then you do have kids."

His frown deepened. "Yeah. So what?"

"How would you feel if one of your kids was mutilated by some goons?"

He leaned back in his chair again, this time as if to increase the distance between us. "Do I really need to answer that?"

"You could help me a great deal by answering a single question."

Stanley stared at me in silence. "What's the question?"

"The question is 'Am I getting warm?' "

He shook his head and waited for at least ten seconds before speaking. "I'm sorry, Zack. I can't answer that. For what it's worth, I wish to hell I could."

14

I n the end, Chief Doyle went for the ninety-day suspension, and I decided not to fight it.

Three reasons went into my decision. First, I figured it would be fruitless to argue. Second, the simpler the charge against me, the better off I'd be; if I rolled over on the insubordination charge, there'd be no investigation of my other breaches of departmental regulations. The third reason would have been sufficient all by itself: I was so convinced by this point that the chief was protecting Jimmy Chang—as a means of protecting the mayor—that I wanted to work on my own, no matter how much more difficult that would make it. If the black mark on my record kept me from achieving my long-term ambitions, so be it; given the significance I'd attached to this case, its solution meant more to me by far than becoming the chief of police.

The hearing, held on Tuesday morning, November 22, in Room 551 at the Hall of Justice, was cut-and-dried. I'd disobeyed a direct order from Chief Doyle. The Police Commission duly noted that it could not lightly pass over such conduct, least discipline on the force break down. The vote of the commissioners was unanimous.

After the hearing, Bud Donnelly, the most senior of the commissioners, whom I'd last seen in Mayor Putnam's office railing at his childhood friend, caught me in the hallway, grabbed my upper arm in his huge hand and walked me to the elevator, just down the hall from my old office. "I hated to vote the suspension, Zack, but without a defense you left me no choice. May your sainted father forgive me—and may you forgive me as well."

I halfheartedly patted his hand. "It's okay, Bud. I understand."

At the elevator, he released my arm, turned and stood a foot from me. I smelled coffee on his breath. Usually, it was alcohol. "I'll say somethin' between us, though, if that's all right," he said, his voice barely above a whisper.

"Sure," I said, uncomfortable and a little dubious.

Although no one else was waiting for the elevator, he leaned even closer, until his mouth was next to my right ear. "I think yer on to somethin'."

The elevator arrived before I could ask what he meant. Two cops were already aboard. They averted their eyes when they saw me. By the time we reached the lobby the elevator was full. There Bud nodded, waved and walked briskly away—to Zuka's, I was certain, the watering hole of choice among most cops and DAs—leaving me to wonder what he could possibly know that I didn't.

In addition to unburdening myself to Britt, my getaway with her had relieved the pressure in other ways. For the better part of two days I'd not had to deal with telephones, or the media, or the constant need to determine whether I was being tailed. Now, with Thanksgiving two days off, I decided that the best thing I could do was to leave San Francisco until my suspension had become old news. Out of sight, out of mind—or so I hoped. By the time I returned perhaps my adversaries would truly have decided that I was no longer in the picture and would drop their surveillance.

The thought of being alone on Thanksgiving saddened me, but I'd long since learned that it was better than being with my mother and my sister.

When my father was alive, Thanksgiving had been my favorite holiday, mostly because it was his favorite, and he reacted to it with such gusto. Each year, rain or shine, the day would begin with a long, fast walk through the Presidio to the beach. Mother and Sari were always invited, but they never came. I was glad; I felt possessive about that time alone with my father. We talked about serious matters, as befitted men of the world, even if one of them had to run at times to keep up with the other. We'd return about one o'clock, and my father would invade the kitchen, ostensibly to make sure that everything was on schedule, but in reality to sample the uncooked platter of extra stuffing, or lick the pumpkin pie filling from the mixing bowls or scavenge anything else he could find, because he never ate lunch on Thanksgiving and by this point was ravenous. At two o'clock he'd take me to his wine cellar, where after inspecting a dozen different candidates, he would choose several vintage bottles, usually from Bordeaux. As he decanted them he would explain why the years in which they'd been bottled had been so exceptional. Then a bonding moment if there ever was one: Each of us would taste the wine. First, swirl it in the glass. Then, drop your nose into the glass and inhale. Finally, sip and aerate the wine before swallowing. We'd smack our lips, reflect, then look at each other. "What'd you think?" my father would say. "Not bad," I'd say, at which point my father would invariably throw his head back and roar with laughter. I found out why only after his death, when my mother asked me to inventory his cellar. To buy a bottle of wine today equivalent to those special ones he'd served at Thanksgiving would cost about three hundred dollars.

At three o'clock my father would be at the front door, heartily greeting his parents—my mother's parents had retired to Palm Springs and seldom came north—and other guests. There were always other guests. He loved inviting "strays," as he called them, unattached people who found themselves in San Francisco over the holiday with no place to go. Between three and four, he served a dry sherry to his adult guests—no hard drinks permitted before a dinner in which a great wine would be poured—and a fruit-juice punch to the minors. At four we sat down to dinner. No matter that the cook could do as good a job, my father carved the turkey. He also poured the wine. Everyone but Mother took second helpings. When dinner ended, my father made his one speech of the year, which, in addition to giving thanks for our bounty, managed to incorporate everyone at the table. When he finished, he called in our cook for a round of applause, and then led a final one for Mother.

A tough act to follow. Each year after his death, Thanksgiving had become that much more painful, Mother, Sari and I all wishing we were anywhere else. My marriage to Elaine only compounded the problem. Mother had never warmed to Elaine; she felt I should have made a "better" marriage—in other words, to a daughter of a front-rank San Francisco family. Sari considered Elaine a traitor to the wealthy class. As for Elaine, she divided people into two categories, listeners and talkers. Listeners ask questions of others in order to learn about them. Talkers never ask questions of others; they're either too self-absorbed or too insecure—often both. Listeners begin to lose interest in talkers when they realize the talkers have no interest in them. Elaine, a listener, remained interested in Mother through two visits; she lost interest in Sari the first time they met.

As a result, each year of our marriage, Elaine and I had gone skiing over the Thanksgiving holiday, and I'd continued the habit after her death. My destination depended on the snow reports, which were carried in the sports section of the *Dispatch.* I would wait until the Thursday before Thanksgiving, and reserve a room at the resort with the deepest snowpack.

This year the choice was Vail, Colorado, which—my troubles aside—didn't exactly please me. Anyone who's skied around knows that for the quality of its snow and the amplitude of its runs, Vail is hard to beat. That, in turn, is Vail's problem. On any winter day, thousands of skiers—many from Europe and South America—line up for the high-speed lifts that whiz them to the mountaintop. Evenings the skiers crowd the restaurants, making it difficult to reserve a table at a convenient hour. Lodgings can also be hard to come by; Vail is mostly a condo town and few good hotels exist. A final drawback: the town, charming as it is, is smack up against an interstate highway; each time you've just about convinced yourself that you've been miraculously transported to a Bavarian village, a convoy of trucks barreling down I-70 destroys the illusion.

But the same edition of the *Dispatch* that listed the favorable snow report from Vail carried an ad for the Hyatt Regency Beaver Creek, a year-round resort community eleven miles to the west. Walk out our door, the hotel's ad said, and you are on the slopes. On an impulse, I called and, with no trouble, booked a room for four nights beginning the following night. The next morning, Wednesday, my Smith &

Wesson clipped to my belt, I scanned the street, saw no one, threw my skis into my 4Runner, and drove to San Francisco Airport, reasonably certain that I hadn't been followed. I would have liked to have carried the gun with me, but as a suspended cop I had no right to do so. So I left it in the 4Runner, flew to Denver and rented a car. Two and a half hours later, I turned off I-70 and onto a road that wound its way up a canyon for several miles. No trucks this time, I told myself with satisfaction.

For three days I skied down manicured, uncrowded slopes as wide as the Champs-Élysées, hearing nothing but the crunch of my skis as they carved up the snow, seeing nothing at the base of the mountain but a village, styled in the spirit if not on the scale of a French Pyrenees village, and set so carefully into the landscape that no single structure obtruded. When I wasn't skiing, I walked on walkways heated by underground pipes to melt away the snow, past buildings designed down to their doors and windows to carry through the Alpine theme. The hotel seemed like the jewel in the crown. It looked right, its mansard-roofed façade accented by gables and clustered chimneys. Its capacious public rooms reminded me of the Palace in St. Moritz. The slopes, visible through the seventeen-foot-high windows of the hotel's pine-paneled, 3,200-square-foot lobby—I know these numbers because I asked—were, indeed, just outside the door. God forbid you should have to carry your skis; there were ski valets to take them from the ski check room to the snow at the beginning of the day, and back inside after your last run. After skiing I had my choice of several Jacuzzis circling a heated pool on the terrace, just beyond the lobby, and when I'd tired of the Jacuzzi and pool, I could swim under a glass wall and into a well-equipped health club. Each day I took breakfast and dinner beneath the vaulted ceiling of the Patina Grill, which served from an innovative, first-class kitchen. One dinner of medallions of elk was as good as any I'd ever eaten. After dinner I could read alongside a fireplace in a cozy library just off the lobby, the kind of space you could live in for the rest of your life. My room was generously sized, warmly furnished and extremely comfortable, with a view of the mountain. Never, in short, had I experienced such a combination of elegance, amenities, service and superb skiing. And never had I had a worse time.

The fault was not, God knows, the hotel's, and not Beaver Creek's.

It was all mine. I refused to let myself have a good time, almost as if enjoying myself would be a sin. Given my separation from Britt, I was under no constraints of fidelity, and given how long it had been since we'd broken off, my sexual appetite was strong, yet I avoided the gaze of women whose smiles suggested they'd like to get acquainted. In my mood, even Britt's presence might not have made a difference. The simple truth was that there was only one thing I wanted to do, and that was to follow the trail of Jimmy Chang in the hope of discovering what secrets he might be hiding—chief among them who had assaulted Maggie Winehouse, and who was toying with my life.

The only thing that kept me in Beaver Creek through the weekend was the knowledge that there was nothing I could do in San Francisco during those days to further my cause.

If you've ever felt your life sinking into a deep hole, you'll probably recall how each time you're sure you've hit bottom you slide down a little further. But you keep trying to climb out of the hole, certain that the most recent slide had to have been the last one.

Down to my last option, I called Jim Mich at home on Sunday evening as soon as I walked in the door from the airport. "I'm not going to kid you," I said. "I need help, but helping me could get you into trouble, so feel free to turn me down."

"Try me."

"First off, I need a copy of Jimmy Chang's driver's license application."

"No problem."

"Don't be too sure. Jimmy's a household name these days. Some DMV clerk could figure reporting the inquiry would be worth a promotion."

"I said, 'No problem,' " Jim said serenely. "I have a niece in the DMV. Helped her get the job. I can have that copy first thing in the morning. Anything else?"

"All the press clippings you can find on the mayor's trade mission two months ago to Japan and Hong Kong. I think it was in early September."

"Piece of cake. I'll have those by noon."

In my vulnerable state, Jim's positive response was like a formal declaration of support. "You got anything tomorrow afternoon?"

"Not unless something goes down between now and then."

"Then meet me at two o'clock at 176 Belgrave. Stanyan dead-ends at Belgrave. Turn left. The house is in the middle of the block, on the downhill side."

The address I'd given him was Britt's. I'd used her home before for private meetings, and had a standing offer to do so whenever the need arose. I certainly needed it now. If I was still under surveillance, it would be disastrous for Jim as well as myself to have him spotted walking into my building. And then there was the need to make calls from a secure phone. Since the night I'd received the package with the cleaver inside, I hadn't made a call without wondering whether my phone was tapped. I had no reason to believe that it was. I'd heard no static while making calls. At my request, Pacific Bell had checked the line and found it clear. I'd even checked the telephone lines in my basement and found no connections. Still, surveillance equipment being so highly developed, you never know. It would be far less inhibiting to work out of Britt's house than my own—provided, of course, that I didn't inadvertently lead my stalkers to her house.

Even though I had that standing offer from Britt, and my own key to her house, the circumstances gave me a good excuse to call her, which I hadn't done since our return from Bear Valley. I told her where I'd spent Thanksgiving weekend.

"How was it?" she asked.

"Lonely," I said.

"I'm sorry," she answered, sounding as though she genuinely meant it. That, I thought, was class. Part of me wanted to know what *she'd* done over the long weekend, but the other part of me figured it was better that I didn't know.

She seemed surprised that I'd ask if I could use her house for a meeting. "Of course it's all right," she said. "You know that."

"I thought I should at least alert you."

"Consider me alerted." Her voice sounded friendly enough, but there was nothing in it to suggest that she was waiting for an invitation.

"Speaking of being alerted," I said, at least in part to fill the awkward silence, "you haven't by any chance put that alarm system in, have you?"

"I'm sorry. I haven't had the time."

"Britt!"

"You're right, you're right. I'll do it."

"If you like, I'll do it for you. I've got lots of time these days."

"No, no, I'll do it."

"Promise?"

"Promise."

You'd have to hear a Swedish woman pronounce that word to understand the effect it had on me. It sounds like two words, with the stress on the first, each "word" slowly and carefully pronounced, as though the speaker truly means what she's saying. No big deal, I suppose, unless it reminds you what a singular person the speaker is, and how much you've missed her voice.

"Thanks again for your shoulder," I said after a painful pause.

"Thanks for sharing all that," Britt said. She, too, had hesitated, as though she couldn't quite think of how to respond.

"Did it make sense?" I asked.

"Oh, it made sense," Britt said, a tinge of irony in her voice. "I'm not sure it makes for a happy ending."

A second passed, then five, then ten. I could hear her breathing. "I miss you," I said.

Another silence, hers to break. "That helps. I guess."

I spent Sunday evening at home, wishing mightily for Britt and not doing much else.

On Monday morning my phone rang half a dozen times, a welcome sound because it signaled the end of the long and lonely holiday weekend, but equally unwelcome because it reminded me how unprepared I was to deal with the outside world. I listened to the callers on the speaker without picking up the phone. Once again, there were two noteworthy calls, and once again from the same people. The first, from my mother, sounded ominous. "I *must* talk to you about that business matter," she said. "There's a problem we *must* discuss. You and I. *Not* Sari. On the odd chance that you might speak to her, please say *nothing* about this call."

Mother almost never spoke to me about Sari. It saddened her that her two children didn't get along, but I sensed that having witnessed the deterioration of our relationship, she understood my discomfort and even sympathized with me. To whatever antipathy she herself might feel for Sari, you had to add her uneasiness about having a woman in charge of Z. Tobias and Company, in which virtually all of her worth was invested. It didn't matter that Sari had done spectacularly well with the firm from the day she arrived from Harvard with her MBA under her arm; as I explained earlier, for Mother it simply wasn't the way things should be done.

I couldn't imagine what possible difficulty the firm had encountered that would be prompting Mother to make her clandestine call. Whatever it was, I had no time for it, but it did leave me with an uncomfortable feeling that some problem was out there, unaddressed.

The second noteworthy call was from Gordon Lee. I hadn't heard from him since his abject apology. "I told you I'd make it up to you," he said. "I've got some hot information. I'm beggin' you to call me. I'm at home until eleven, at the station after that. Call me there if you have to, but it would be better if you called me at home." He left his number.

Given my predicament, I couldn't pass up a potential lead. I called. He started to apologize all over again. "Skip the preamble, Gordon," I said, not even trying to be pleasant.

It didn't faze him. "Jimmy Chang owns a shell corporation," he said breathlessly. "It's called the Golden Door Trading Company. He could be using it to launder money through the Pacific Rim Bank."

For a moment I was too stunned to speak. "Where'd you get that?" I said, trying to keep my voice even.

"That I can't tell you."

"Okay. Fair enough. Are you going to use it?"

"We've learned our lesson, Zack." There was no mistaking the subtext of that statement; it was a plea for forgiveness.

I wasn't ready to forgive. "Good," I said. "Thanks for the call." I hung up before he had a chance to say more.

Gordon was no reporter. How on earth had he tumbled onto the Golden Door Trading Company? If he exposed it, another lead would be blown. Despite his assurances, I had no confidence that he'd keep the information to himself.

Anyone following me to Britt's house that day would have had his work cut out for him. I left home at 10:45 and, instead of driving, took a cable car to Powell and California, where I transferred to the

California cable line. By 11:30, I was seated at the counter of Tadich Grill—having just beaten the daily crowd—eating a plate of rex sole meunière. Then I strolled through the financial district and over to Macy's on Union Square, window-shopping as I went, ostensibly a cop on suspension with nothing to do. Once inside, I raced up the escalators to the eighth floor, then darted through the furniture department until I found a stairway, which I took to the ground floor. For good measure, I walked over to Market and Montgomery, and took BART—the Bay Area Rapid Transit system—one stop to Powell before transferring to the N Judah trolley. I rode the trolley to Stanyan, then climbed the steep hill, as certain as a human can be that no one had followed me. Overkill, I suppose, but I would have never forgiven myself had I led the wrong people to Britt's house.

The house was on a steep slope leading to Twin Peaks, nestled among trees. With its stone walls and pitched roof and mullioned windows, it seemed to have been transplanted from the English countryside. The inside, which she'd extensively remodeled, was a stunning counterpoint. By knocking out a wall between the living and dining rooms, she'd created an unusually large living space for a home of that size. Track lights hung from wood beams illuminated huge paintings hung on white walls. In the center of the room two soft, oversized contemporary couches faced each other across a large square glass coffee table and on either side of a fireplace with a hearth built of river stones. An oak floor, deeply and richly stained, was accented with several small Oriental rugs. The view, through picture windows, was due north to the bay and Marin County. The peaks of the Golden Gate Bridge were visible to the northwest.

I'd calculated my arrival for 1:45 P.M., to be sure I'd be there to greet Jim. I got there at 1:50. He arrived promptly at 2:00. Even though we'd talked several times on the phone, I hadn't seen him for two weeks.

"Hello, old buddy," he said when I opened the door. That Picasso face of his was a pretty sight. As we shook hands I pulled him to me and gave him a hug, feeling his marathoner's leanness even through his jacket. He hugged back. "You'll get through this, Zack," he said.

"I'm glad one of us thinks so," I said, leading him into the living room.

He stopped in his tracks. "Wow," he said. "What a place. Who's the owner?"

"A friend of mine."

He threw me a disapproving look, which, given his expressive face, was pretty hard to miss. "Hey, that really tells me a lot. Male? Female?"

"Female."

"Friend friend, or romantic friend?"

"Boy, you're nosy," I said, laughing.

"I'm paid to be nosy. Answer the question."

I hesitated so long he began to look concerned. "What's the matter?" he asked.

"It's not an easy answer. At the moment, we're between the two categories."

He turned full circle, staring at the art and the views, shaking his head in admiration. "Better nab her."

"Because she's got a nice house?" I scoffed.

"No, you jerk," he said, giving me a stiff poke on the bicep. "Because anybody who can create an environment like this has to be a gem."

"I'll tell her you said so," I said, suddenly impatient. "Got anything for me?"

Jim handed me a manila envelope without a comment. I motioned him into one of the couches and sat on the other. "No problems?"

"Nah." He fixed me with those wide eyes that never seemed to miss a thing. "You gonna tell me what it's for?"

I was tempted. God, I was tempted. Of all the people I might tell, Jim was the one I *should* tell. "You don't want to know," I said reluctantly.

"Oh, I want to know, all right," he said firmly.

"But if I'm caught," I insisted, "you want to be able to say that you had no idea what I wanted with the material."

"I'll take my chances."

The remark ambushed me. We'd done stakeouts together, been each other's backup, and on a couple of occasions probably kept each other from getting hurt, maybe even killed. But all that was expected, part of the job. This was different—a man offering to risk his job to help me. I had to swallow a couple of times before speaking. "I've got all the burdens I can handle, Jim," I managed finally. "Getting you into trouble would finish me off."

He scrutinized me for a minute, as if to assure himself that I really meant it. "Suit yourself," he said. Then he stood.

I walked him to the door. "Just remember," he said as we shook hands, "I'm there if you need me."

"Got it," I said, not trusting myself to say more.

He punched my arm again. "And nab that girl," he said.

As soon as Jim left, I ripped open the envelope and found the copy of Jimmy Chang's driver's license application. "Damn," I said aloud. To check Jimmy out with law enforcement or immigration authorities in the U.S., Canada or Hong Kong—especially Hong Kong—I would need to know his Chinese name. Many first-generation Chinese immigrants use their full names at birth as second names on their applications. Jimmy hadn't done that. A huge disappointment, its significance magnified ten times by the story that unfolded from the clips.

It was as I'd remembered it. Ten weeks earlier, on the morning of September 7, Mayor Putnam and half a dozen members of his administration had flown from San Francisco Airport on the first leg of a trade mission to Japan and Hong Kong. A picture of the mayor, his group and three kimono-clad stewardesses, taken at the terminal, accompanied the article.

Jimmy was not in the picture.

No one belonged on that trade mission more than the chairman of the San Francisco Port Commission. Why wasn't Jimmy there? A paragraph buried far down in the story explained it. Jimmy, it said, had had urgent business in Vancouver. He had flown there a few days earlier, and would join the mission in Tokyo.

A follow-up story had Jimmy in the thick of things in Tokyo.

A third story noted that Jimmy hadn't flown on to Hong Kong with the delegation. He'd been felled by a stomach virus in Tokyo. By the time he recovered, the mission was all but over, so he'd returned independently to San Francisco.

That story reeked of deception.

Vancouver is a two-hour flight from San Francisco. If Jimmy had had business there, he could have gone at any time. Why fly to Tokyo via Vancouver at your own expense, losing not only money but the opportunity for media exposure as well as the camaraderie and red-carpet treatment that characterize every trade mission?

The most likely explanation was that Jimmy Chang didn't have a U.S. passport, and didn't want his traveling companions to discover that. He finessed that problem by flying via Vancouver on a phony passport, probably from Hong Kong, but maybe from somewhere else. The passport might even be legitimate; there were at least a dozen emerging countries where you could become a citizen for a price.

Why didn't Jimmy have a U.S. passport? I asked myself. There could be only one explanation: because he's not a U.S. citizen.

And why didn't he go on to Hong Kong, where his foreign passport—phony or legit—would have gained him admittance? Once again, it could have been because he didn't want his traveling companions to see that he didn't have a U.S. passport. But I was sure that Jimmy Chang, the publicity hound, could have found some way to finesse that problem—and he would have risen from his deathbed in order to return triumphantly to the city he'd left as a pauper. The media would have found the story irresistible, and a Jimmy Chang with nothing to hide would have made certain they found it.

I figured that if Jimmy didn't make it to Hong Kong, it was because he was afraid to go. The only logical conclusion, it seemed to me, was that Jimmy Chang had something to hide. And the question that followed from that conclusion was whether Jimmy Chang had planned to leave Hong Kong more than twenty years ago—or whether he'd fled.

I went into Britt's kitchen—newly redone with black granite counters, cabinets with glass doors framed in natural wood, a chrome sink and a Wolf range—made myself an espresso, then picked up the telephone and called Bob Bein, the best, most amiable Immigration and Naturalization Service agent I'd ever worked with. Bob had been transferred from San Francisco to Reno a year before to head up the agency's office there.

"Well, well, fancy hearing from you, Zack," he said. "I can't imagine what you're calling about."

"How's life in Reno?" I asked him, wanting to warm him up before asking my favor.

"You mean aside from being too hot in the summer, too cold in the winter and dull, dull, dull?"

"Aside from that."

"It isn't pretty, the restaurants are lousy, the dry air makes the wife's skin itch, the kids hate the schools, and I don't gamble. What can I do for you? As if I didn't know."

"I need to check out Jimmy Chang."

"What a surprise! And they won't help you in San Francisco. Pity."

I let him have his fun, knowing he'd help me if he could, because he believed, as I did, that if you followed regulations to the letter nothing would ever get done. "How about it?" I said.

"Do you know Jimmy's Chinese name?"

"No."

"Then you might as well forget it," he said with finality.

"Is it possible that he used Jimmy Chang on his naturalization application? He used it on his driver's license."

"Oh, yeah, it's possible," Bob said as though he was about to deliver the punch line of a joke. "About a million to one. He'd have to show us a birth certificate."

"The birth certificate could be counterfeit."

He laughed. "Hey, Zack, we've done this a few times. We'd suspect that if we saw the name Jimmy Chang on it."

"Okay, so we rule that out," I said, feeling not just frustrated but foolish. "You've got to forgive me. I'm racking my brain here." I thought for a minute. "What about a court order changing his name? Is that too far out?"

"No," Bob said. "He could have gotten one of those."

"Would you have honored that?"

"Sure. If Jimmy Chang's his legal name, no problem."

"So could you check it out?"

"For you, sure. But don't hold your breath." I was in the process of exhaling with relief when he offered the advice.

"And while you're at it," I said quickly, "could you also do a lane check for me?" If Jimmy had entered the United States from Japan, and he was not a U.S. citizen, he would have had to list his country of citizenship on his entry form; a lane check—jargon for the computer trail travelers leave as they enter the U.S.—would produce that information.

Bob laughed again. "A lane check of the name Jimmy Chang would explode the computer. We'd have thousands of declarations for Jimmy Changs through the years. You'd have to narrow it down to a port of entry and a date."

"The port of entry would be San Francisco, and the date would be sometime between September fifteenth and September thirtieth."

"This year?"

"Right."

"Yeah, I could probably handle that," Bob said. "What's your number?"

I looked quickly at my watch. It was now three-thirty. It occurred to me that if I stretched out my work, I'd still be at Britt's when she returned from her gallery. That temptation lasted less than a second: not fair. "How long do you think you'll be?"

"Give me till five."

I gave him Britt's number, and then my own, in case he couldn't get back to me before day's end.

He called back in an hour. "INS has no file for a Jimmy Chang. And a Jimmy Chang did not enter the United States through San Francisco between September 15 and September 30, 1994."

"Not as Jimmy Chang, in any case."

"Correct. That doesn't mean he doesn't have a U.S. passport in his Chinese name."

"I realize that."

"And it doesn't mean there's no file under his Chinese name."

"I understand," I said.

I must have sounded as discouraged as I felt, because Bob said consolingly, "I told you it was a long shot."

"I know, but you always hope."

"Anything else I can do for you?" He sounded as though he hoped there was.

"Just check me out on something."

"Shoot," he said eagerly.

"When was that last legislation on aliens?"

"In '86."

"As I recall, it said if you're an alien, and if you were here before '82 and could prove it, you could come into a legalization office and get a work authorization."

"That's correct."

"The applicant would get fingerprinted at that time?"

Bob chuckled. "You better believe it."

"And you'd check the applicant's country of origin for a criminal record?"

He chuckled again. "That one you can take to the bank."

"So if a guy like Jimmy has a criminal record somewhere, he's not about to take advantage of that opportunity, particularly since he's already established himself without legal papers."

"Give the man a cee-gar."

"Is there anything I haven't thought of?" I finally asked him, my voice surely betraying my weariness.

Bob must have picked it up. "Maybe you're making this too hard for yourself, old buddy," he answered, suddenly serious again. "If Jimmy has naturalization papers, there's a number in red in the upper right-hand corner. That's the number of his file. If you could get me that number, I could tell you in a heartbeat if this guy is kosher."

"Yeah, right," I said. "What am I supposed to do, break into Jimmy's office?"

"Or his home, if it's not hanging in his office."

"Got any other great ideas?"

"For once, I'm not kidding, Zack. Don't you have any informants who could go to Jimmy's office on some pretext?"

"If I were in the clear, that's an approach I might consider. As things stand, it's out of the question."

"Okay," Bob said, dragging the word out, probably to give himself time to think. "There's one other possibility. The U.S. District Court keeps records of all naturalizations. You could go to 450 Golden Gate and go through their stacks."

"Are you telling me they're not computerized?" I said, thinking of the almost impossible task if they weren't.

"Not for the years that would interest you. But they keep an index with biographical information on all the applicants, and a list of all the people who attend each naturalization ceremony."

I couldn't imagine how I could handle that task on my own, and I couldn't think of anyone other than Jim Mich I could ask to help me—and I wondered if it was fair to ask him. But I didn't tell Bob any of this. "I'll give it a try," I said instead. "Thanks, Bob. Much obliged."

"That's okay, Zack." He hesitated for about a second, then said, "Sorry about your troubles." The words were plain, but they did the job.

"Thanks," I said, meaning it.

"You gonna be okay?"

"We'll see. In the meanwhile, it would help if you could keep this conversation to yourself."

"What'd you say your name was?" He chuckled and hung up.

It was my impression, based on our Friday nights together, that Britt generally returned from the gallery by six. But I'd never actually been there to greet her, so I couldn't be sure. It was now five o'clock; not wanting to abuse my privileges, I left, albeit reluctantly, and made my next call from my car. It was to Ernie Beyl, the affable San Francisco public relations man who, during a forty-year career, had represented scores of clients, several of them charities in which my parents had been active. I'd run into Ernie at countless functions, and knew he was well regarded. More to the point, I knew he'd handled PR for various airlines, and would almost certainly be able to answer my next question.

"Do you know who does PR for Cathay Pacific?" I asked him.

"Before I answer that, can you tell me why you want to know?" Ernie said, surprising me with his guardedness.

"I need a small favor from someone who can be trusted not to say anything about it. Am I asking too much?" I added uncertainly.

"Depends on the favor."

I hesitated. "Why are you being coy, Ernie?"

"What's the favor, Zack?" Ernie insisted. He wasn't being hostile, but he was sure being firm.

"I need to check the passenger lists from Tokyo to Vancouver from September 15 to October first."

"You're looking for a name, but you don't want your own name involved?"

"Exactly."

"I think I know someone who could help you."

"Who is he?"

"Me."

I laughed in disbelief. "*You* handle Cathay Pacific?"

"I did till they moved to LA."

I laughed again. "Wise guy," I said.

"Careful guy. I've gotta protect an ex-client. I had to know what you wanted. What's the name?"

At six that evening, as I sipped a Sierra Pale Ale in my living room, and stared at the downtown skyline and beyond it the Bay Bridge, Ernie called me with the answer. Jimmy Chang had flown Cathay Pacific from Tokyo to Vancouver on September 23, and then connected to a Delta flight to San Francisco.

Several airlines fly nonstop from Tokyo to San Francisco. The only justification for returning to San Francisco via Vancouver would be if the round-trip fare cost less. In the case of Jimmy, a busy multimillionaire, the savings would not have justified the longer flight.

One more reason to believe that Jimmy Chang didn't have a U.S. passport.

If I'd been in the clear, I could have contacted half a dozen people at this point who might have helped me reconstruct Jimmy Chang's life—or that portion of it, at least, that he'd spent in San Francisco. Under the circumstances I felt there was only one man I could trust.

Hiram Leung was the closest thing to a patriarch in Chinatown. He was in his eighties, the father of three, grandfather of ten, great-grandfather of nearly thirty. In addition, a brother and sister he'd resettled in San Francisco had each spawned large families. When the Leung family and its offshoots met to celebrate Chinese New Year, it filled the largest of Hiram's four Chinatown restaurants. The restaurants were only a sideline; since his arrival from China in the late thirties, Hiram's time and effort had been invested primarily in what had become the two biggest Chinese-language newspapers in San Francisco.

I'd known Hiram for twelve years. We'd started badly. One of his reporters had totally mucked up a story, attributing a Chinatown homicide to a Vietnamese gang that had had nothing to do with it. The gang had threatened to retaliate. I'd called the reporter to ask for a retraction. The reporter had refused—he couldn't bear the loss of face—so I'd stormed over to the newspaper's office and confronted Hiram.

I didn't know it at the time, but confrontation is not the Chinese way. You almost never get anywhere by trying to bang straight in.

The Chinese won't talk to you with any seriousness until they know who you are. To a degree unmatched in our culture, they prefer to get acquainted over a table. In this instance there was no time for niceties, let alone a meal. Vengeful young men were preparing for war. In spite of my bad Western manners, I somehow got my point across. Hiram printed the retraction and fired the reporter, but he wasn't pleased. He'd lost face as well.

I called him twice, but he didn't respond. So I called a Chinese reporter on the *Dispatch* and told him what had happened, emphasizing that Hiram's statesmanlike response had probably averted a gang war. That prompted a glowing profile, which didn't help Hiram much in Chinatown, where almost no one reads the *Dispatch*, but provided him with some overdue acknowledgment from the city fathers. Hiram knew where the story had come from and recognized my gesture. A few months later he called me. One of his grandsons had gotten involved with a gang. Hiram wanted me to impress him. The boy and I spent a morning at San Quentin. That took care of it.

Over the years, as the gang problem escalated, we kept in close contact. In the process, I'd managed to gain Hiram's respect, which was saying something. Despite his more than fifty years in San Francisco, he maintained the classic view of traditional Chinese toward non-Chinese: white, black, brown, Christian, Jew, Muslim and other Asians as well, they are all barbarians, progeny of inferior cultures.

Hiram's English was abysmal, so when we sat down to dinner that evening at a table in the back of the Door of Happiness, his smallest restaurant, we spoke Chinese. Having long since learned to proceed at a measured pace in such situations, I waited an hour before asking the question that had brought me to his table—a table that was, alas, not the best in Chinatown, a fact Hiram compounded by insisting on ordering his idea of what would please a barbarian's palate: egg rolls, egg drop soup, sweet and sour pork, chicken chow mein and egg foo yung. When the waiter had finally cleared our plates, I asked, "How did Jimmy become the chairman of the San Francisco Port Commission?"

Hiram was not an enemy of Jimmy Chang's, but he held him in contempt for his assimilationist views. Before answering, he looked around at the neighboring tables, all of them filled with Chinese-speaking Chinese. Then he turned back to me and regarded me through his small eyes. In the artificial light of the restaurant, his skin looked waxen. "Only one way," he said, switching suddenly to English and speaking in a low voice. "Give money to mayor."

It was the way he said it even more than what he said that made me jump. It wasn't conjecture, it was knowledge—or, at least, that's the way it sounded.

"How much?" I asked, keeping my own voice low.

"Lotta money."

"He's allowed to contribute only five hundred dollars."

Hiram smiled faintly, and studied me almost patronizingly from behind his thick bifocal lenses, as if to say, "Ah, young man, how little you know of the ways of the world."

"Was it more than five hundred dollars?" I asked him.

Hiram said nothing, but he nodded his head a fraction.

"How much more?"

Once more he checked the other tables. Then, apparently satisfied that no one was eavesdropping, he said, sticking with English, "Many thousand more."

"How many?"

"Maybe fifty. Maybe hundred."

I sat back and stared at Hiram. This wasn't making sense. Richard Putnam was not simply an honest man, he played everything by the rules. He would no more violate the laws governing contributions to political campaigns than he would take a bribe. It just didn't figure that he'd have taken a huge contribution from a single donor. Nor did it figure that Jimmy would make a hundred-thousand-dollar contribution to a political campaign, legal or illegal. That was a big number even for extremely wealthy people. Jimmy had money, but not *that* kind of money, unless I was badly mistaken.

"What for?" I asked. "What can he gain?"

"Face."

"A hundred thousand dollars' worth of face?" I said as quietly as I could but not even trying to hide my surprise.

Hiram nodded. "Make big picture."

For a moment, I was confused. "You mean a big impression?"

Hiram laughed at himself. "Yeah. Big impression."

For a moment, I didn't know what to ask next. Finally, I said, "Is Jimmy so rich that he can give away that kind of money?"

"Not all his money."

"Oh, I know that," I said quickly, "I know Jimmy's got a lot more than a hundred thousand dollars."

Hiram shook his head, then leaned close and whispered in my ear, speaking Chinese.

"Ah, ha!" I said, realizing my mistake, and suddenly understanding everything Hiram had been saying. "Jimmy didn't just *contribute* money. He *raised* money."

Hiram looked nervously at the other diners, then back at me. "You get it," he said, speaking English again.

"Who were the contributors?"

Hiram shook his head, and smiled once more. "That your job find out." This time, the smile seemed frozen. I knew this conversation had ended.

Our waiter seemed to know it, too. He appeared at the table bearing hot tea and a plate of fresh litchis, which were delicious. As we ate them Hiram lapsed into Chinese, telling me, among other things, that his grandson, the one I'd taken on a tour of San Quentin, had graduated in the spring from Stanford Law School.

It didn't take a detective to discover who had contributed money to Mayor Putnam's campaign fund. All contributions of one hundred dollars or more must be reported to the registrar of voters, and are matters of public record, available for inspection at City Hall.

But which of the hundreds of contributors had Jimmy solicited? And what would their identities tell me, even if I knew? With no real hope of a payoff, I laboriously wrote down the names, addresses and occupations of all Chinese donors of five hundred dollars. There were more than two hundred. That evening, having decided that I could never do the job alone, I called Jim Mich at home from a pay phone and told him I wanted to take him up on his offer of help.

"About time," he said emphatically.

At home ten minutes later I faxed him the list of names.

The next morning—Wednesday, November 30—we went to work. We'd agreed that it would be impossible to check the entire list of donors, and to focus, instead, on every fifth name. Using his office computer, Jim checked for criminal and Department of Motor Vehicles histories. I checked with the post office, Pacific Gas & Electric and

Pacific Bell. We both searched the telephone directory, and Jim also utilized the reverse telephone directory, which lists addresses first, then the names. For good measure we went to a number of the addresses, rang doorbells and talked to apartment-house managers.

One must always hope.

By late Friday we knew that only three of the forty donors we'd checked out were legitimate. The other thirty-seven were straw men. Some were dead, most were fictitious.

The money Jimmy had "raised" for Mayor Putnam's campaign had been his money, meaning triad money, laundered in some manner through the Golden Door Trading Company and the Pacific Rim Bank.

It had to be. It just had to be.

15

That weekend, home alone, I tried to give some meaning to what I'd learned.

Assuming I was right, and the contributions Jimmy Chang had raised for Richard Putnam's mayoral campaign had been paid with tainted money, it didn't necessarily follow that Putnam had been aware of it. Everything I knew about him suggested the contrary. It was highly possible, however, that *Mayor* Putnam had subsequently found out—perhaps when Jimmy was lobbying for an appointment— and was frightened that the deception would become known. No one could blame him for what Jimmy had done. But his appointment of a man who would engage in such dishonesty could be politically damaging, at the very least casting doubts on the mayor's ability to judge character. Even more to the point, because Jimmy was a first-generation Chinese immigrant, the issue could be exploited by Harold Halderman, the mayor's xenophobic opponent in the forthcoming election.

In such a situation, Chief Doyle's marching orders would be simple: Circle the wagons. Protect the mayor.

Was I right? I was so exhausted from the week's work that I didn't even want to think of what else I'd have to do to make sure—or even where the information would then lead me. All I wanted to do was sit in my favorite living-room chair, listen to that tape I'd made of the second movements of my favorite concertos, and read.

It was in this mode that I finally got around that weekend to the pile of newspapers that had accumulated during my trip to Beaver Creek, and found Mike Winehouse's follow-up article to the one describing his early-morning visit to Union Square. It was the latest in what was evolving into a series of devastating portraits of the city, and it had run on Thanksgiving Day. Like the first two he'd written since the attack on Maggie, this one defied categorization—too long for a column, too subjective for a feature. What it demonstrated incontestably was that since the attack on his daughter, Mike Winehouse was writing with a broken heart about the city he'd loved all his life. The only resemblance to the Mike Winehouse I'd grown up with was his trademark elliptical style.

> Two a.m. Drive up Lombard to Mel's Drive-In. Desperate for refuge and sustenance. After postmidnight visit to Union Square, need to remind myself can have either anytime I want them.
>
> The street's practically deserted. Eerie feeling, as if everyone's fled the city.
>
> Almost everyone. Those remaining are all in Mel's Drive-In.
>
> Visit to Mel's is a trip back to 50s. Chrome, vinyl, linoleum. Jukebox selectors at every booth. Walls covered with blowups of 50s teenagers served by 50s waitresses as they sit in 50s cars parked in front of Mel's.
>
> Waitress arrives. Out of central casting. Fifty-five, peroxide, overweight, looks like her feet hurt. Peruse menu for healthy meal. What the hell; life's a bitch, and then you die. Order Lumberjack's Special—ham steak, three eggs, potatoes, pancakes.
>
> "Good choice," waitress says.
>
> Look around. A dozen customers, each one alone. They eat or read or stare out window, avoid one another's gaze. Reminded of a letter from a reader complaining about Muni buses. Graffiti. Unpredictable, eccentric drivers. Passengers afraid to look at one another.
>
> Mind suddenly awhirl with Muni stories collected over last year from readers. Grab a pen from wallet pocket of coat. Feel for notebook. Always carry a notebook. Tonight no notebook. Signal frantically to waitress.

She walks quickly to table. "Yes, doll? Feeling guilty? Want to change the order?"

"I need something to write on."

"A paper napkin won't do?"

"It's not the best."

"How about one a these?" She pulls an order pad from a pocket, and hands it to me.

"Perfect," I say.

Start writing notes for stories:

* Muni driver stops bus in rush-hour traffic, walks down aisle, demands passengers keep feet out of aisle. Cars honking. Passengers shouting. Driver adamant. Won't move on until all passengers have feet under seat in front of them.

* Muni driver crawling along. Passengers frowning, wondering what gives. Suddenly, driver stops bus. "When you gotta go, you gotta go," she announces. Runs into restaurant, presumably to bathroom. Returns five minutes later, looking manic. Races bus through streets.

* Muni driver with four green lights ahead of him stops in midblock when light five blocks away turns red.

* Young passenger, male, stands at front of bus, shows purchases to other passengers, demands to know how they like them. "Pay attention!" he demands of passenger who turns away.

* Middle-aged passenger, female, boards bus, looks for seat, sees one at window, next to scruffy man in aisle seat, takes it, settles in. Older female, standing in aisle, leans over, whispers in seated woman's ear. Seated woman screams, and pushes past man into aisle. Driver slams on brakes. Standing passengers pitch forward. Some fall to floor. What had older woman said to younger woman? "Don't sit by window. Perverts can trap you."

Food comes. Eat greedily. Waitress clears. "Okay if I sit here awhile?" I say.

"As far as I'm concerned, doll, you've bought the table for the evening."

Memory floodgates open. Random snippets of city life:

* San Franciscans who decline invitations to dinner in Sausalito or Berkeley because traffic on bridges so hopeless.

* Public garage in North Beach that stinks of urine and excrement.

* Young man who carries a package under his arm as he walks through downtown each day, stopping every so often to put package on sidewalk and scold it. "You've been naughty again. Didn't I tell you not to do that?"

* Woman walking down Post Street in midafternoon, suddenly attacked by unkempt man, who beats her on head with wooden coat hanger. Hundreds of pedestrians witness attack, but no one stops man, and after he's gone, no one assists victim.

* Two women, lunching in Cole Street Cafe, comparing notes on how they'd been mugged.

* Three down-and-out men, probably in forties but hard to tell, seated on Golden Gate Park bench, a few feet from Stanyan Street, sharing slices from a package of bread. It's an early December morning, 1992. Behind them, scores of human forms, faintly illuminated by streetlights, some covered by blankets, others in sleeping bags. Even money they're holdovers from Haight-Ashbury hippie heyday, brains so far gone they're no longer able to measure their degradation. Last of three men crumples bread package, now empty, and drops it to ground, two feet from trash can.

I write on and on, retrieving stories that had been used once and then filed away—random events revealing no larger truth. Each story crammed onto single piece of paper. Together, they cover the table.

What do they all add up to, these pictures of San Francisco? That the city everyone loves to visit is, in fact, a metaphor of national malaise.

One day the city's wonderful, and the next day it isn't, and the difference begins with the homeless and the indigents.

The homeless population of San Francisco is large precisely because of the city's reputation for compassion. They come from everywhere, knowing that the morning after they arrive, they become eligible for $341 a month in benefits.

Our city's general assistance fund is welfare program of last resort for any resident of city, no matter how long, tapped out of federal and state programs. Among those receiving $341 a month are ex-servicemen who never applied for veterans' benefits, and older people who never filed for Social Security benefits. Nearly half the men on general assistance are under 30 and able-bodied.

Our city's public health service costs us $500 million a year. Hefty chunk goes to support victims of AIDS. Laudable expense. But our city maintains 122 mental health programs and 38 drug abuse centers at 81 sites in a 43-square-mile area, an oversupply so profound that the staffs at many of these sites go searching for clients to justify their existence.

Our city's expenses increasing twice as fast as revenues. More people working for the city than it can afford. Thousands of city employees—

those ditsy Muni drivers prominent among them—diminishing the public coffers still further with unnecessary overtime.

Want to do business or build in our city? You're at the mercy of officials who make their living off your frustration and confusion, and codes so complex that no one, not even those who administer them, understands all of them.

Our city's government stultified by encrusted bureaucracies intent, above all, on self-perpetuation, incapable of rousing itself to stanch the criminal encroachments of intruders such as those who ruined Maggie Winehouse's life.

But, hey, who's the government if not you and me? I am at fault for having placed wish above fact. The wish was for my city to remain what it had been through the years, a civilized alternative to an increasingly crass society. The fact is that my city—our city—supposedly so impregnable, so good-spirited and progressive, has been undermined by the weakness and overrun by the detritus of a society gone to hell.

Nearly five a.m. when I pile the pieces of paper into a stack and signal for my check. "Here's for the rent on your table," I tell the waitress, handing her ten dollars.

"What a sport," she says. "What do you do for a living, anyway?"

"I sometimes wonder," I say.

Those of you who have not spent your lives in San Francisco may not entirely understand what a downer that Mike Winehouse column was. For nearly thirty years he'd been the city's watchdog and its conscience, the man we read before deciding how we felt about issues and events, the transplant turned zealot who insisted that we were the Chosen City—his term, not mine.

God, he could make us feel good! In all America, he told us, we were the ones who'd best learned to assimilate differences; we were progressive, humanistic, accepting, temperate and balanced, as thrilled by a great opera as by a 49ers blowout; even our establishment's taste in clothes, traditional and understated, earned his admiration. We soaked it up.

But Mike was no simple cheerleader. He had done his homework, thought it all through and constructed an elaborate argument to defend his views. This is how it went:

There are mean cities and gentle cities, the difference being determined primarily by size. The bigger the size, the meaner the city, first, because difficulties exist in direct proportion to size, difficulties that boil tempers and promote survival tactics, and second, because bigness attracts power-loving, ends-justify-the-means people. Although power-grabbing happens wherever there are people, it happens less in San Francisco principally because the city's finite shape—it's surrounded on three sides by water—keeps its population at around 750,000. Those who chose to make a life in San Francisco had automatically opted for power's minor leagues, meaning that their *need* for power was not as great as it was among those who decided to duke it out in bigger cities like New York or Chicago or Los Angeles, or smaller cities at the center of power like Washington and even Sacramento. As much as our generations of lawyers and bankers and stockbrokers and politicians might have chafed at San Francisco's professional and financial limitations, they accepted them in exchange for the stimulus of life in a beautiful and accessible metropolis. Like salt and sourdough starter to our famous bread, Mike concluded, these elements of history and geography made San Francisco what it is: a gentle city, the most gentle of them all.

Who knows when his disenchantment began? I guessed it had happened to him gradually. Clearly, he'd been nearing the edge when the assault on his daughter pushed him over. But as I remembered the pride and optimism of his message in those days and compared them with the anger and dejection of his last three columns, I knew I wasn't just reading a portrait of a devastated man but the story, as well, of what had happened to his Chosen City.

16

That Mike Winehouse column was like a lighted firecracker tossed at my feet. You've got to bust this case, I told myself, if only to save your own butt, and to do that you've got to stop trying to operate in a town where every second person knows you on sight, where almost no one who could help you is willing to, where the city administration's against you, where someone's determined to spook you, if not kill you, and where you've already done everything you can do. You've got to get moving—to Vancouver and Hong Kong, and wherever else the trail of Jimmy Chang might lead you.

On Monday morning, first thing, I called my travel agent and booked a flight to Vancouver for the next morning on Delta, and another two days later on Cathay Pacific from Vancouver to Hong Kong. I wasn't sure I'd be any luckier in either place, but at least I'd be doing something.

And I wouldn't be going empty-handed. During the uproar over the Pacific Rim Bank, the *Dispatch* had run several photographs of Jimmy. I'd had the clips photographed and had new prints made from the negatives. I'd also managed to squeeze in some hours at the San

Francisco Public Library, poring through microfilms of back issues of the *Dispatch* until I'd found half a dozen photographs of Jimmy dating back to 1979. I'd copied these too. The pictures weren't as good as actual photographs, but they'd do. If the authorities in both cities were willing to cooperate—a big if, the way things were going in my life—they could try to match my pictures with the photographs of criminals in their files. I had contacts in both places. I knew they'd have a harder time saying no to me in person than over the telephone.

My desire to get moving was reinforced Monday afternoon when Jim Mich reported in on his check of the Superior Court naturalization rolls. To the surprise of neither of us, there was no record of a Jimmy Chang.

Jim did have a surprise, though, and an ugly one. "Remember those high school kids who cut that Chinese girl?" he asked.

"Of course," I said, meaning, "How could I forget something like that?"

"Turned out they all had records."

"It figures."

"Listen to this," Jim said, excited by what he was about to tell me, but clearly bothered as well. "One of the kids finally broke this morning. He told us some guy had paid 'em a thousand dollars to cut the girl."

"Oh, Jesus," I said, feeling suddenly sick. "Oh, my God. Did he identify the guy?"

"Didn't know him, or so he said. I have a feeling he's telling the truth."

"No description, nothing?"

"Pretty vague. Nothing to go on."

I took a deep breath, and let it out slowly. "I'm out of here," I said.

"To Hong Kong?" Jim demanded.

I would have preferred he hadn't asked, but having called on him for help, there was no way I couldn't tell him.

"First Vancouver. Then Hong Kong." I hesitated. "Between us, okay?" The moment I said it I knew I'd made a mistake. I could hear Jim expel a lungful of air. "Need you ask?" he said, clearly exasperated.

"Sorry, Jim. I guess all these leaks have gotten to me."

Jim has a quality I wish I had. When something's over, it's over. "Okay," he said, his voice back to normal. "Good luck."

That evening I called my mother to say good-bye. Big mistake.

"You can't leave," she cried the minute I told her. "You absolutely can't. I absolutely forbid it."

She hadn't used language like that with me since my high school years. "Mother," I said, puzzled, "I'm forty-two years old. You can't order me to do anything."

"Oh, Zachary, please. Haven't I got enough to worry about?"

There was a tone in her voice I'd never heard before. Bear in mind that this is one collected woman, who does not rattle easily. And what I heard was panic. "Look, start over, okay?" I tried to sound calm. "What's the problem with my leaving? I'll be back in a week."

"There are two problems with your leaving. The first is that you'll miss the Christmas party—"

"What I have to do is far more important than your Christmas party."

"Oh no, it's not," she said with the kind of certainty that makes her sound right even when she's wrong. "If you're not there, people are going to think that this terrible business with that disgusting police chief has come between us, and I will not have that."

I had better explain here that my mother's annual Christmas party, scheduled for Wednesday evening—two days later—was the first, the biggest and usually the best party of each holiday season. It was her signature event, the one that reaffirmed her each year as the city's social leader. Everyone who was anyone in San Francisco was invited, and almost everyone came. At Mother's request, I always served as host. She was right: for me not to show at the party would cause speculation of a schism within the Tobias family due to my recent misfortunes—not something I wanted any more than she did. I've said some heavy things about my mother; let me say something positive for a change: She is maniacally loyal. Her brood is her brood; you attack it at great risk. And she never takes family problems public. No one outside our family ever knew how thoroughly she disapproved of my choice of career.

"What's the second reason, Mother?" I said, sensing I was losing.

"The second reason is our talk about the business. It absolutely can't wait any longer."

I squeezed my eyes and hit my head with the heel of my hand. I hadn't answered her Don't-tell-Sari call of the week before. A shrink could get three hours out of that one. "Then let's deal with it right now," I said.

"I'm too tired right now."

"Tomorrow morning, then. First thing."

"I'm booked tomorrow morning from seven o'clock."

She didn't even wait for me to concede. "I want you at the party an hour early," she said. The strain in her voice was palpable. She was always nervous before the party. This was different.

"Mother, what is it about the business?"

"I don't want to talk about it on the phone."

"Give me a hint."

"Come at five-thirty."

"Have we lost some money?" I persisted, a note of disbelief in my voice. Except for two years of the Great Depression, Z. Tobias and Company had always been in the black. It was only a question of how much profit there would be.

"It's worse than that," Mother said.

"What?"

"Come at five-thirty."

"Mother!"

But she was gone.

The next morning, Tuesday, hating what I had to do, I canceled my flight and booked a new flight for Thursday. For the next thirty-six hours, I did little but chafe, fret and feel sorry for myself. The last thing I needed was to worry about being followed, so with no need to go out, I stayed home until late Wednesday afternoon. As I had when flying to Denver, I carried my gun with me when I left my apartment, but left it in my 4Runner when I arrived at Mother's house. You couldn't hide a Smith & Wesson under a tailored suit, and I wasn't about to alarm Mother's guests.

Two trucks were in front of the house. One belonged to Dan McCall, Mother's favorite caterer. The other belonged to Stanlee Gatti, the city's most popular party designer, who I supposed had come to do the flowers, as well as to decorate the perfectly shaped sixteen-foot Christmas tree, now laden with lights and ornaments, that filled the stairwell.

Mother was in the living room, wearing a dressing gown and a scarf over her hair, directing a parade of people. "Not now," she snapped when she saw me, before I'd had a chance to say hello.

I'd never been to a party of this magnitude an hour before it was to begin. Out of curiosity, I drifted into the kitchen, from which waiters and waitresses were streaming, bearing glasses, dishes, cutlery and plates of food. Several years before, in an act suggesting that she had finally come to terms with my father's death, Mother had gutted the old kitchen and produced a contemporary masterpiece. The pièce de résistance was an addition, a spacious breakfast room cantilevered over the hillside and enclosed on three sides by greenhouse windows. In my father's day, Mother had rigorously supervised the preparation of meals, often cooking the main dishes herself, but as far as I know, she'd never cooked in the new kitchen. Unless she was giving a dinner party, she seldom ate at home, and her only concern when she did was that the meals be nutritious and slimming. Her Christmas party was probably the one occasion of the year when the marvels of her kitchen were utilized to their fullest.

As I glanced around the kitchen, filled with chefs, waiters and waitresses swiftly and deftly performing their tasks, I noticed Sam, Mother's new servant, standing against a wall, looking lost and threatened. I supposed it was because his alien's sanctuary had been breached by all these strangers, any one of whom could give him away. Next to Sam was a small, frail Chinese woman with a sharp chin, obviously his wife, who stood as close to him as she could, watching the activity through eyes compressed to slits and appearing even more menaced than her husband. I walked over to them. "Don't worry," I said in Chinese, trying to sound reassuring. "This happens only once a year."

Sam made no reply.

"Is this your wife?" I asked. He nodded, but didn't introduce me. I turned to her and said, "I am Mrs. Tobias's son." She refused to look at me. Perhaps Sam had told his wife that their employer's son was a policeman. What a nightmare, I thought, having to live your life in fear and trembling. Ten days before, I could never have empathized with them to the degree I did now. As I watched them I could only wonder at the dangers and discomforts to which they'd exposed themselves to get here, and the enormous debt they must now have hanging over them. I suddenly remembered Clarence Ho, the slumlord, and his Sunset Travel Services Limited, and wondered if Sam and his wife might have conceivably been his clients. But that operation, with its forged permits and flights to El Salvador via Hong Kong and mysterious entries into the United States, seemed too elaborate and daunting for the humble and frightened couple before me. At the other end of the smuggling scale were those nightmarish freighters trying to slip their cargoes of wasted, seasick Chinese past the Coast Guard on both coasts. One such freighter had even made it into the Golden Gate and was discharging its cargo before being discovered. But Sam didn't seem young enough or hardy enough for such a voyage, and, besides, I'd never heard of a woman being on one of those ships. However they'd come, they were here; cop or no cop, I wouldn't have had the heart to turn them in even if I'd found them in someone else's home. With a nod of my head and a smile, I left them alone and returned to the living room.

By then, the helter-skelter activity had subsided, and almost everything was in place. The florists had departed, leaving only the caterer's staff. But now Mother had vanished. I went upstairs and knocked on her door. "Who is it?" she said testily.

"Your son," I said. "Remember me?"

"Not *now*, I'm dressing."

"Mother," I said, letting her hear my exasperation, "you asked me to be here an hour early to talk about this problem of yours."

"Problem of *ours*, problem of *ours*."

"Please, Mother, I don't enjoy talking through doors."

There was a silence, and then the sound of footsteps. Finally, Mother opened the door, turned and marched back to her dressing table.

It had been years since I'd been inside Mother's bedroom. It was as though I'd just stepped inside her mind. The ordered, systematic, fastidious woman the world knew was nowhere visible. Instead, there was full-blown chaos: every surface covered with papers, every corner filled with file folders and envelopes. Over the years, the bedroom had obviously evolved into her command post, from which she ran the many organizations in which she was involved. The small desks Sari and I had used as children—I was astounded to see them—had been moved into the room, and each of these was covered with papers as well. I could only wonder why, with so many empty rooms at her disposal, Mother had chosen to sequester herself in her bedroom. The only reason I could think of was that this was the room in which she had felt her truest passions and greatest comfort, and being here kept her close to those memories.

"I'm sorry, Zachary," Mother said, "I know what I told you, but I hadn't counted on last-minute problems and I've fallen behind, as you see, and I just can't concentrate on what I'm doing and talk to you at the same time. It will have to be after the party."

"Just answer yes or no," I said, trying to sound calm. "Is theft involved?"

"No."

"Is *any* sort of crime involved?"

"Not to my knowledge." She faltered. "But maybe. Now please leave me, Zachary, please!"

I returned to the living room, feeling, if not alarmed, damned uneasy, and more exasperated with myself than with her. I knew from experience that she'd be incapable of a conversation before her Christmas party, no matter how important it was, and still I'd agreed to her request.

Twenty minutes later—exactly ten minutes before the guests were scheduled to arrive—her door opened, she stepped onto the landing, pausing for a moment just above the Christmas tree, and then walked down the curved staircase, the force emanating from her so powerful that it was some time before I noticed her costume. Mike Winehouse would have approved; it was, as always, beautifully understated: a simple silver cocktail dress, a silk sheath and matching jacket, complemented by a modest sapphire necklace and matching earrings. More points for Sadie; it was last year's dress. Mother enjoyed living well, but her middle-class upbringing had taught her not to waste money. Other women in her position would have had a hairdresser like Mr. Lee come to their home two hours before a party; Mother had always done her own. Like my father, she never flaunted her wealth. An ample house, not a huge one. No expensive foreign cars. And no jewelry that's so valuable it has to be kept in a bank vault. At this moment, her face glowed more radiantly than any diamond she might have worn; as she walked through the foyer and into the living room, casting a pleased gaze on the perfection of the arrangements, she seemed nothing less than a queen entering her throne room, in full control of her destiny.

What happened next had neither the force nor importance of an epiphany, but given our less than gratifying mother-son relationship all these years, it was halfway there. For the first time I saw my mother as the woman she'd willed herself into being in the years since my father's death. She never would have made it without my father's money, because society is organized around philanthropy and you have to pay to join. But all the rest had been Sadie's doing. When he was alive she'd been involved in charities because she knew it was expected of her as the wife of Ted Tobias. After he was killed she wanted to be so overburdened she would have no time to think of him. She volunteered for everything. Within a year the charities had become her life. Given her drive, her rise to the top was inevitable.

Mother's Christmas party was an opportunity for her to say thank you to all the people who had helped her get there and stay there. But it had a secondary purpose, as well. Mother liked to say that she wanted nothing to do with politics, but the hidden agenda of the party was peace, if not on earth at least in San Francisco. Year after year she attempted to get all of the city's contending elements under one tent, and she almost always succeeded. This year, for the first time, I was one of the contenders.

At six-thirty exactly the guests began to arrive, the women in cocktail dresses, the men in dark suits or blazers with gray flannel pants. Mother and I stood side by side in the foyer, next to the Christmas tree, greeting each of them. It was not quite the same crowd that would have been there ten or even five years before. As in other cities, old families and old money were the heart of San Francisco society, and those people were, as usual, well represented. But not as well as in years past. No fault of Mother's. Over the years, many descendants of those first families had either lost interest in the social whirl or no longer had the discretionary income to dispense to charities to the degree their parents and grandparents had been able to. During the last few decades, as a consequence, San Francisco society had opened up to people with new money—not all people with new money, mind you, only those with the good sense not to wear ruffled shirts and gold chains—who were willing to contribute quantities of it in support of the city's cultural and social institutions, and these people were out in force tonight.

By seven o'clock, 90 percent of the guests were present, even though the party was scheduled to run until nine, and usually ran an hour longer. It always happened that way. Mother interpreted this early rush as a tribute; I suspected it was at least as great a tribute to her timing. Her Christmas party, held every year on the first Wednesday in December, was the first opportunity of the holiday season for the cream of San Francisco to find all their friends in one place. No slow, awkward start to this affair; the decibels were rising even before the guests had finished their first drink.

Among those guests, perhaps two hundred in all, were some sixty members of San Francisco's Jewish elite, every one of them known to me, most of them either old friends or the parents of friends. All of them had kind words and squeezes for me. Maybe it was my imagination, but there seemed to be a subtext to their condolences: "You were schmuck enough to become a cop, you got what you deserved."

At seven-fifteen, Mayor Putnam and Harold Halderman arrived almost simultaneously, shook hands with each other, chatted quietly, then parted, and were immediately surrounded by supporters. Two minutes later the mayor separated himself from his group and walked over to me. He grabbed my arm, and led me aside. "I *had* to support the chief, Zack," he said.

"I understand."

"I tried to talk him out of the ninety-day suspension, but he was adamant. Said he had to make an example of you."

"I understand."

"I want *you* to understand how much I think of you in spite of what's happened."

I nodded, but said nothing.

"And I want you to know that as long as I'm the mayor of this city, you've got a big future." He locked his eyes on mine as he said it, to emphasize that these were words with meaning behind them. "Just keep your powder dry." He squeezed my arm, then moved off.

His subtext was unmistakable: Behave yourself in the future and good things will happen. I found it extraordinary that the mayor of a great city would suck up to a mere police captain. I didn't have the slightest doubt that he'd just tried to neutralize me. He wanted no further embarrassments. Was it unfair of me to conclude even more firmly that the material for such embarrassments existed?

And then, suddenly, all these speculations vanished, as Britt came through the door. A small charge shot through me. I'd had no idea she was coming. She hadn't been to last year's party, and Mother had said nothing about inviting her to this one. On the other hand, Britt had earned an invitation. She was the talk of San Francisco's art world. Nominally, that world was closed and self-protective, taking care of its own and building walls against intruders. But Britt's original approach—offering the works of artists from underdeveloped countries at a fraction of the price of comparable works by American artists—had caught the fancy of the *Dispatch*'s art critic, and other critics had quickly taken up the cry. Not only had the Britt Gallery become too important to ignore, it had made collectors out of people who would never otherwise have become interested. For this, the other gallery owners had to be grateful, and so it came to pass one day that they opened the gate and let Britt in. From that moment on, Britt had been thrust into the rarefied social life of San Francisco's art world—and someone on Mother's staff had obviously put her on the invitation list.

As she gave her coat to a maid, I received a second shock. In all the months we'd dated I'd seen Britt mostly in jeans, sweats and shorts. When we'd gone out, she'd worn sweaters or blouses and slacks. For the theater or a concert, she'd usually worn a suit. I'd never seen her in a cocktail dress. Hers was black silk and looked as though it had been cut to fit her body. She wore a single strand of small pearls and a single matching pearl on each ear. She'd pulled her long, light-colored hair back and up, accenting her high cheekbones and graceful neck. There is nothing quite like the sight of a well-conditioned woman athlete making an all-out acknowledgment of her femininity, and I could see at once that I wasn't alone in my admiration. Women as well as men turned her way, but she looked right past them, and as she did she suddenly frowned. I turned in the direction of her gaze and realized that she could only be staring at the Christmas tree. A minute later she looked my way, saw me, smiled, and then walked directly over to Mother, who was still standing at my side.

"So nice to see you," Mother said, a greeting she used whenever she couldn't place someone. I wasn't surprised; it had been six months since I'd brought Britt to meet Mother. Britt hadn't taken to Mother any more than Elaine had, so after the second dinner party I'd stopped bringing her.

"Britt Edström," Britt said, sensing Mother's lapse.

"I *know* who you are, my dear. I'm *so* happy you could come."

"Mother," I said, taking Britt's arm, "can you hold the fort for a few minutes? I want to get Britt a drink."

"It's time we both circulated," Mother said. "Everyone should be here by now."

The moment we were alone Britt turned to me with concern. "I should have called you to ask if it was all right for me to come."

"Nonsense," I said. "I'm delighted you came."

That didn't seem to satisfy her. "I received the invitation three weeks ago. I didn't say anything because of our situation. I wasn't going to come but then I decided that life goes on and that, crass *commerçante* that I am, I really ought to be here."

"Britt, it's okay," I said as emphatically as I could. "Tell me what you were frowning about a minute ago," I said, trying to redirect the conversation. "Is something wrong with the Christmas tree?"

"It's a beautiful tree. It's just that I was surprised to see it because you never told me your mother wasn't Jewish."

"She *is* Jewish."

"Then," said Britt, gesturing toward the tree, "I don't understand."

It was a typical Britt remark, as direct as a child's, and ingenuous as well, one that could have been made only by someone unfamiliar with our ways. Even so, it caught me off guard. I couldn't come up with a response, let alone an answer. "You know what?" I said to her at last. "Neither do I."

"Have you always had Christmas trees?"

"Since I was six or seven."

"But why?" she insisted.

"I suppose I'm partly to blame. All the kids I knew had Christmas trees and got presents at Christmas, so that's what I wanted. My sister felt the same way."

"Didn't you know any Jewish kids?"

"They *were* Jewish kids."

Britt reared back and looked at me closely. "You're joking. You must be joking."

I smiled. "Only partly. Sari had gentile classmates at Hamlin, and I had gentile classmates at Town, and they had Christmas trees, which probably gave all the Jewish kids ideas. But our closest friends were Jewish, and they all had Christmas trees, so we could argue that if they had them, we should have them."

Britt shook her head, and continued to look skeptical. "How did your parents feel about it?"

"My mother was all for it. My father wasn't. I remember his telling my mother that he didn't want to commemorate a man in whose name so much suffering had befallen the Jews."

Britt nodded, as if she found my father's position completely reasonable. "What did she say?" she asked in a way that suggested Mother had no proper response.

"That she didn't want her children growing up feeling left out and different," I said, the words calling up the memory of that long-ago argument conducted in front of Sari and myself. "The truth was that *she* didn't want to feel left out and different. My dad was the exception. Most Jews have a great need to belong. They don't like to be left out. If there's one day a year when everybody in the country is doing one thing and they're doing another, they don't feel very comfortable about it."

"Is that how you feel?"

In my state of mind, I had no time for an identity crisis. I held up a hand. "I'll have to think about that," I said, managing a smile. "Now, how about that drink?"

"Sounds good."

"Mother serves a special punch at Christmas. Will you try it?"

"Lovely."

I looked around for a cocktail waiter, but they all seemed to be passing hors d'oeuvres. "I'll be right back," I said. It took me a minute to make my way through the crowd to the bar set up in the dining room, and I waited another two minutes for my turn. By the time I got back to her Britt was engaged in a spirited conversation with two couples. Clients, I thought, frankly relieved, having no desire to return to Britt's question. I gave her her drink, introduced myself to the couples, promised I'd be right back and went looking for Mother. Before I could find her, I was hailed by Harold Halderman, who was standing with Bud Donnelly, the police commissioner.

Bud, my father's long-ago football teammate, had been to our house at least three times a year until his death, and Mother had included him in the Christmas party from the first year she'd given one. This was Halderman's first visit to the Tobias family home. Mother was right; nothing about him seemed prototypically San Franciscan, not his clippered haircut or aviator glasses or white shirt with starched collar or striped suit with its characterless cut. He looked exactly like who he was, a big-eared, fair-skinned homicide prosecutor with a stunning run of convictions, an us-against-them battler who in his run for mayor had pitted himself against the city's well-organized radical coalition and won the hearts, in the process, of the Chamber of Commerce, the Downtown Association and executives of the utilities and banks.

"Jesus, but you look like yer old man," Bud said after I'd shaken both their hands.

"So they tell me."

"God, he was a great one, Harold," Bud said to Halderman. "Best goddamn Jew I ever knew."

"Funny you should say that," I said. "Just before he died Dad told me you were the best goddamn Irishman he ever knew."

The two men laughed. Bud turned to Harold. "Fuckin' crime, the way that man died. Coupla nigger kids where they didn't belong." He turned back to me. "How old was he, fifty?"

"Fifty-two," I said uncomfortably, wishing I could escape.

"Terrible," Halderman said emphatically. "Got to put an end to that kind of thing."

"How would you do that?" I asked him, irked by his remark. I didn't like having the murder of my father described as "that kind of thing."

Harold answered so quickly it was as though he had expected the question and had memorized his response. "The first thing I'd do is get a new chief of police, someone who backs up his officers when they investigate the possible commission of a crime, and doesn't throw them to the wolves the minute the wolves start howling."

"Amen," Bud said heartily.

"What happened to you is a terrible example for the police department," Harold went on. "It sends a message to every cop: Don't rock the boat. I say a crime is a crime, whether it's committed by John Doe or an appointee of the mayor."

Whoa, I thought. With no knowledge of the case other than what he'd read or heard, Halderman has already convicted Jimmy Chang. There wasn't another man or woman I knew in the district attorney's office who would have gone that far. *I* hadn't done that, even though, God knows, I had more reason to than anyone. No wonder Jimmy was upset. "I have to tell you, Harold," I said, "that there's no evidence linking Jimmy Chang to the assault on Maggie Winehouse."

"Who else would have done it?" Bud interjected angrily.

Halderman didn't pick up on Bud's assertion. "In another thirty years," he pressed on, "San Francisco's going to be the first city in North America in which Asians constitute the largest segment of the population. It's crazy, just crazy for the chief of police to neutralize the one non-Asian on the force best qualified to create a liaison with that community."

This, I thought, is a political animal. He is making a speech to an audience of one. He talked on and on, punctuating his sentences with a Kennedy-like stab of his finger, although there was nothing Kennedy-like about his message. As Harold spoke, Bud nodded his head metronomically in agreement with everything he said. "And I want you to know, Zack," Harold concluded, "that when I'm elected, your phone is gonna ring, and we're gonna have a long talk, you and I, and if I like what I hear, you're gonna be sittin' in a new chair."

"Sounds exciting," I offered, for lack of anything else to say. "Excuse me, I've got to play host."

What *could* I have said? The man had just made a blatant effort to gain my political support and, through me, my mother's. An hour earlier the mayor had effectively done the same. The mayor would have Mother's support in any case, but having just disciplined her son, he had no way of knowing that.

As I moved through the crowd its sounds told me that the party would be well remembered. A hundred different conversations were under way, people all but shouting to be heard. Every few seconds laughter erupted from a different part of the living or dining room. Year after year, the scene was as lively as ever, due in no small part to Mother's—actually Trader Vic's—Fish House Punch: quantities of rum and brandy flavored with brown sugar, lemon juice and a small amount of peach brandy, as delicious as it was powerful.

It took several minutes, but I finally located Mother. She was working the room, talking, listening, laughing, touching a hand or an arm of each of her guests, then moving on. Watching, I saw her join Jodie Stevenson, the society editor of the *Dispatch*, who would have fit right in with the crowd if she hadn't been scribbling into a notebook. They stood by the windows in the living room, the lights of the city behind them, Mother talking, Jodie listening, and jotting notes every now and then. In Friday morning's *Dispatch*, Jodie would reassert Mother's position at the top of the city's social hierarchy. Several photographs would accompany the article, Mother having agreed to permit a *Dispatch* photographer to cover the party in order to give herself leverage with the newspaper when she next wanted coverage of one of her benefits.

"Hello, Zacky," an assured voice behind me said.

I felt a tingle of apprehension all the way to my calves. Turning, I did my best to smile. "Hello, Sari," I said.

I'd spotted her half an hour earlier as she'd entered the living room from the foyer. She'd gone up immediately to Bud Donnelly, a sort of father figure to her since the days when he'd come so close to being her father-in-law. He'd led her to a corner, where they'd stood with their heads close together and had an earnest chat—about what I couldn't imagine. I'd spent from then until now planning my moves so as to postpone the inevitable.

She was an hour and a half late for the party, as she was every year, and the reason, as always, was visible in her face. It was perfectly made up. I am no authority on how women apply their makeup, but I have seen the results on hundreds of women, and been on enough movie sets to know what actresses do. Sari's efforts fall exactly in between, as technically good as a makeup artist's, but toned down for public use. This may be a brother's wary observation, but I have seen her without her makeup, and I know what a difference the makeup makes. Sari is an attractive woman, I'll give her that, but she is not the beautiful woman she imagines herself to be. Character does eventually invade a face; she is too tough to be beautiful. Am I being unkind? Has my antipathy for Sari made me incapable of seeing the reality? Could be. Men have always flocked to her, drawn, I suppose, by her commanding stature—she's almost six feet, a genetic gift from our father—as well as by the willowy figure, olive-skinned Sephardic face, and long, thick, glistening black hair she inherited from her mother.

Perhaps I'm giving myself credit after the fact, but I believe I could see even then, in the calm before the storm, that Sari had brought an other-than-normal aura to the party. The normal one was an in-your-face assertiveness that dared anyone to dispute her. Tonight, she seemed laid-back, content, even serene, as though she had finally reached port at the end of a dangerous voyage.

"Don't I get a kiss?" she asked.

I leaned over to kiss her cheek. She kissed the air, squeezed me and issued a grunt of what was meant to sound like pleasure. She was forever telling people how much she loved me, and how proud she was of me. I think Sari had convinced herself that she loved me, but the pride she always coupled with her affection in speaking of me was an out-and-out lie. She'd been ecstatic that I hadn't entered the family business but disgusted by my career choice.

In kissing Sari, I'd placed a hand on her arm, and felt a strange tension in her body. When I stepped back, I saw that the glass in her hand was shaking.

"How are you?" I asked.

"I'm fine. Just—*fine.*"

She certainly looked fine. She was wearing a burgundy satin cocktail suit, the jacket loose and long-sleeved, the tight skirt reaching her calves. But she didn't look comfortable. She never did in party clothes—something I'd considered for a long time before figuring out why. It wasn't the clothes, I'd concluded, so much as the context they put her in, that of a woman at a party, where she was expected to act like other women and, worse yet, mingle with them. She disliked the company of women. She enjoyed the company of men. This wasn't a matter of preference; it was an absolute. I've seen it a hundred times: Sari, entering a party divided into groups of men and women, walking up to join the men. You'd think that she'd want to use every means at a woman's disposal to attract men. Not so. She wouldn't use sex. Sari was determined to be accepted as the brains-and-guts equal of the best man in the room.

Thinking of her in this way, I suddenly recalled how Britt had asked me, as we drove home from Bear Valley, to imagine Sari as a small girl fighting to evolve in a household so totally dominated by my father, and as part of a tradition that passes the right to lead the family firm to the firstborn son. And I felt a welling of regret for what that trial had surely turned Sari into, and then, to my amazement, a rush of love spilling over the barricade I'd erected against her. Stunned by this second mini-epiphany of the evening, I must have gaped at her, because she narrowed her eyes.

"What's the matter?" she asked suspiciously.

"Nothing, nothing," I said quickly. "How about you? Everything going well?"

"Everything is absolutely *splendid.*" And then a sudden change in tone, to overt animosity: "Unless you're planning more surprises for us."

It was vintage Sari: pointed, acerbic, judgmental. I remembered my reply to Britt, that by the time I was old enough to understand what Sari was going through, she'd hurt me in a hundred different ways. Forty years of training went into my response. "None that I know of, Sari," I said, trying to sound calm, fighting my anger down.

"I hope not. It's not good for the business to have a Tobias on the front page in such a negative context."

I have to admit to a certain elation over a remark like that. It persuades me that it's not just me, that I'm not making it all up, that regardless of what caused it my sister really *is* the shit I believe her to be. I stared at her for a minute in disbelief, then said, fighting to control every word, "Is the negative context you're speaking of my suspension or a young woman mutilated by criminals?"

Sari didn't hesitate. "You know what I'm talking about, Zacky," she said sternly.

Just as I was wondering how I could escape, Sari spotted someone she knew, patted my face—in case anyone was watching, I suppose—and moved on. I stood there for some time, finding it hard to believe that another human being could get to me the way Sari did.

It was after eight-thirty when I saw Bud Donnelly again. He was in a corner with Mayor Putnam. They were standing close together as though they didn't want others to hear their conversation, which, judging from the way their heads were bobbing, looked pretty heated. But each held the other's arm with one hand while gesturing with the other, a reminder to me that while they might be at odds politically they still had a lifelong bond. As I watched, Putnam abruptly gave Bud a bear hug, then detached himself and walked away. Bud turned, looked about in a daze for a moment, then saw me and immediately walked my way. I saw now that he was tanked. "Zack," he said, throwing his arms around me. "My God, I might as well be huggin' yer father. God, how I loved that man. Best goddamn Jew I ever knew."

Maybe it was like what happens to metal when it fatigues, because right then the iron tie that had existed between myself and Bud for as far back as I could remember suddenly buckled. "Did you *know* any other Jews, Bud?" I asked him simply.

Bud drew back and looked at me in bewilderment. Suddenly he guffawed, and just as suddenly was serious again. He put his face close to mine. The smell of whiskey was overpowering; he obviously hadn't been drinking the punch. "I'm no bigot, fer Chrissake, but this town, fer Chrissake, this goddamn town is gettin' killed, just killed, Zack. First the faggots and then the slopes and then the homeless. And they keep comin'." He backed off and regarded me, as if to see what effect his pronouncement had made. "Where does it end, man? I'll tell ya where it ends, it ends with us down the bloody tube." His face screwed up as though he was going to cry. "When I think of that beautiful young girl . . ." He turned and drifted off in midsentence.

By nine the crowd had thinned, but not appreciably. Britt came up to me. Her skin was rosy. She looked relaxed. "I should be going," she said. "I had a lovely time."

"Sell any paintings?"

She smiled. "I met some interesting people."

"I'll walk you to your car."

Britt shook her head at once, and put a hand on my arm. "You don't have to do that," she said uncomfortably.

"I know I don't. I want to. Give me your ticket."

"I didn't use valet parking. I found a spot while I was driving here."

"How far away?"

"Three blocks."

My father had been murdered three blocks from our house. "In that case," I said, "I'll definitely walk you to your car."

She got her coat. At the door she paused, looked once more at the Christmas tree, then at me—this time with a little smile added—just as she had on entering the house. At her car, she reached up and kissed me lightly on the cheek, started to say something, seemed to think better of it, then slipped behind the wheel and drove away.

I wasn't in the best of moods when I returned. Seeing Britt had stirred me up. Her remarks had really gotten to me. Her final question—Was I a Jew who didn't like to feel left out?—had ambushed me. I wanted to leave too so that I could finish packing and get a good night's rest for my flight the next morning. But I was obliged to stay until all the guests had gone and then—at last, I hoped—find out what was happening at Z. Tobias and Company that had gotten Mother so upset.

By the time the guests had all left, Mother had once again disappeared. Not finding her in the living room, dining room or kitchen, I went upstairs to her bedroom. This time I didn't have to knock. The door was open. Mother was seated at her desk, her left hand propping up her head. Her eyes were red, her face was puffy and her makeup was ruined. She'd obviously been crying for some time. I hadn't seen her so unhappy since the year my father died.

To the side of the desk was Sari, seated comfortably in a lounge chair, her skirt smooth and carefully arranged, looking grim but satisfied, as if she had just settled an old score.

Mother looked at me with reproach. "You're too late," she said. Then she turned to Sari, and stared at her with an anger soaked in a lifetime of failed attempts to understand her daughter. "You *had* to ruin the party, didn't you?" she said bitterly. "You just couldn't wait until morning."

17

Mother's accusation seemed to hang in the air. Sari did nothing to acknowledge it. She just sat there, unmoved—or so it appeared—by Mother's words or tears. At least ten seconds of silence passed as I looked from Sari to Mother and then back to Sari again, and then insisted, "Will someone please tell me what's going on?"

"Go ahead," Mother said to Sari. "I'm sure it will please you to ruin your brother's life, too."

"Nobody's ruining anybody's life, Mother," Sari said calmly. "If you had the slightest comprehension of what business is all about, you'd understand that."

"Well, if you don't mind, I'd like my life just the way it was before you ruined it, thank you."

"Please!" I implored, frantic by this point.

Mother glared at Sari. "Tell him!" she said contemptuously. Then she turned away, as though, knowing what was coming, she couldn't bear to watch.

Sari remained untroubled, her eyes fixed and calm. The only giveaway to the excitement that must have been raging within her was the tint of her skin, olive like Mother's, darkened still more in this moment by the accumulation of blood just beneath its surface. Before she spoke she smiled.

"On Monday morning Z. Tobias and Company will announce three acquisitions that will double the size of the parent company."

I drew a sharp, involuntary breath. Never, to my knowledge, had Z. Tobias and Company acquired another enterprise, because acquisitions meant borrowing money and, aside from rare occasions when it needed short-term working capital, the firm had never done that. The rule was simple: If you couldn't afford it, you didn't buy it. So fanatical had my father been about maintaining control of the family fortune that over the years he had bought out every minority stockholder, relatives every one, until he owned 100 percent of the stock. He, his firm and his immediate family were impregnable, exactly as he wanted it. And now Sari had just undone everything he'd accomplished.

"How much?" I asked. She knew what I meant: How much had she borrowed?

Sari waited a few seconds before speaking, not, I am certain, out of any apprehension, but to savor her moment, and as she did I had a fleeting memory of that long-ago day when my father had her over his knee in this very room. I would have bet anything that she had thought of it too. "A billion dollars," she said slowly, practically masticating the statement, as though it were some unimaginably delicious delicacy.

"Oh, my God," Mother moaned. She put her elbows on the desk and covered her face with both hands.

Shock strangled whatever response I might have made. Somehow, at the first mention of the acquisitions, the figure of a hundred million dollars had leaped into my head. The reality was ten times worse, but it seemed a hundred times worse, given the impossible hole it put us in. I sank down on Mother's bed. "You're crazy," I finally managed.

"Like a fox," Sari said, still smiling. "I bought each company for twenty-five cents on the dollar."

"And put us in a position to be wiped out if anything goes wrong."

"Did I tell you?" Mother said, raising her red eyes to me, and wringing her hands.

"That's not going to happen," Sari snapped back at me, ignoring Mother.

"You know that, do you?" I said, not even trying to hide my scorn.

"Yes, I know that, Zacky," Sari said. "It's what I do." Since I'd entered the room, she'd remained in the same relaxed position in the lounge chair, seemingly serene. Now suddenly, she moved to the edge of the chair, and thrust her head forward. "In case you haven't noticed, the net worth of Z. Tobias and Company has quadrupled since I took over. Two years from now, with these acquisitions, the company will be worth five times what it is today. Four times five is twenty, in case you've forgotten your multiplication tables—meaning that in two years, each of your shares will be worth *twenty* times what they were when I started."

"Assuming we're not wiped out."

"We're not going to be wiped out," Sari said sharply. "That's an absolutely stupid thing to say."

I leaned back on the pillows piled against Mother's headboard. "Why did you do it, Sari?" I said. It was all I could say.

"Why did I do it?" she asked incredulously, her voice rising. "What kind of a question is that? I just told you why I did it."

"But what's the point?" I said, reaching my hands out to her. "Assuming you make all this money, what are you going to do with it that you can't already do with the money you have? How much money do you need? How rich do you have to be? How many pairs of shoes can you wear at one time? How many cars can you drive?"

Sari looked at me as though I had confirmed for all time that she was by far the brighter of the two of us. "You don't get it, Zacky. It's survival-of-the-fittest time. This isn't the Gold Rush, when our peddler ancestors could sell anything they could get their hands on. It's a global economy. Anyone can go anywhere and undercut anyone, I don't care how long they've dominated the market. It's not like we sell one-of-a-kind products that people *have* to buy from us or do without. We sell food, we sell clothing, we sell shelter. Guess what? So do our ten thousand competitors. With these companies, we can institute economies of size, lower our price and knock off the competition."

Silence in the room, except for Mother's sniffling.

"That's it, that's why you did it, to knock off the competition?"

"That's it, Zacky."

"It's not possible to coexist with the competition?"

Sari shook her head so slowly it scarcely moved her long, thick hair. "Can't take that chance."

"You're that certain that the competition is going to knock you off if you don't knock it off?"

"Name of the game."

"So as long as there's competition, you're at war?"

"You're catching on," she said with such a patronizing tone I wanted to wring her neck.

"Oh, God, oh, God," Mother moaned, rocking now in her chair.

Sari's last remark had gone down about as easily as a horse pill. "It didn't occur to you to consult with Mother and me before committing to something that could wipe us out?" I asked, fighting to control my voice.

"Look, let's cut the crap," Sari said. In a second, whatever prettiness there was in her face had disappeared. "I'm as much at risk as you are and I don't engage in ventures that are going to wipe me out. And, Mother, stop that sniveling."

It was utter turnabout: the child as parent, the parent as child. For Mother, it appeared to be the ultimate affront. Summoning some reserve of resistance, she suddenly stiffened, glared at Sari, then, squaring her shoulders, drew her head back and turned to me. "We can outvote her!" she said triumphantly.

My heart sank. "We *can't,* Mother," I said, trying not to sound impatient.

"Of course we can. We're two thirds to her one third."

I sighed. "Mother, I've explained this a dozen times. You refuse to remember it. Daddy left a third to each of us, but he provided that the head of the company would have absolute authority. It's what he had, and he wanted his successor to have it."

"Because he believed his successor would be you," Sari said with bittersweet satisfaction.

Desperate to contain my anger, I got off the bed and began to pace. "Would you mind telling us what you bought for a billion dollars?" I asked. Just saying the figure out loud made me ill.

"Would either one of you know what I was talking about if I did?" she said. It amazed me how much she enjoyed demonstrating her disdain.

"Try us," I said.

"One's a food company, one's a clothing company, one's a shelter company."

That, at least, fit the business profile created by my father, who had sold off or shut down all incidental divisions in order to concentrate on the three most basic human needs. Not an original strategy, but a shrewd one nonetheless.

"What kind of shape are they in?" I asked.

"They're all good companies, earning excellent revenues."

"Then how is it you were able to buy them for twenty-five cents on the dollar?"

"Because they all got overextended, and took on too much debt," Sari said with satisfaction.

I laughed derisively. "A lesson obviously lost on you."

"Oh, *can* it, Zacky," Sari said angrily, her expression suddenly so scornful that I had to look away.

"Where did you get the money?" I said finally, looking at her again.

I thought I saw Sari stiffen. "The name would mean nothing to you," she said, a little too quickly.

"Try me."

"You'll know soon enough."

I took a step toward her. "By God, Sari, Mother and I have a right to know."

She smiled up at me. "Are you going to hit me, Zacky?" she said.

I took a few slow breaths through my nostrils. "If you don't tell us the name of that firm, Sari, I'm calling *The Wall Street Journal* tomorrow morning."

She stared at me for a long time, but kept her smile plastered in place. Only then did I start to realize what pleasure she was getting out of jerking my chain. "Kirschner, Metzger," she said at last. "They're investment bankers out of Los Angeles."

"And where did *they* get the money?" I persisted.

"From a private source in Hong Kong."

I sucked air. Circles were closing. "What do you know about the lenders?"

Sari had resumed her original position in the chair. Now she leaned back against the cushions. "That they have billions," she said contentedly.

"What's the source of those billions?"

That, I believe, was the moment Sari remembered she was talking not just to her brother but to a cop. "Money's money," she said impatiently and—unless I was imagining it—rather uncomfortably.

"What if it's dirty money, Sari?"

"Meaning?"

"Triad money. Money from drugs, prostitution, extortion, illegal gambling—"

"Oh, come on, Zachary," Sari exploded, cutting me off. She stayed where she was, but thrust her head forward. "Life isn't all cops and robbers. These are responsible people. They've been in business for a hundred years."

"The Mafia's been in business a lot longer than that."

If looks could kill, as they say, I'd be a dead man. "I've checked them out six ways from Sunday," Sari said, pulling her head back. She kicked off her shoes and drew her legs up under her. "They're legitimate, and clean."

"Then I'm sure you won't mind giving me their name."

"In good time."

"I want it now, Sari."

Her voice was icy. "There's nothing you can do, Zachary. It's a done deal."

The night my father died I felt alone, unmoored, powerless. That's close to the state I was in as I drove away from Mother's house. But on this night there was an extra ingredient: shame.

One of the first coming-of-age lessons my father taught me was that every Jew had a responsibility to all other Jews to live a moral life, so that no single Jew could make life tougher for other Jews by giving the community at large something to point its finger at. The greed of the late-nineteenth-century robber barons of American industry, gentiles every one, never provoked a blanket denunciation of Christians. The greed of the junk-bond wizards of the 1980s, Michael Milken, Ivan Boesky, Martin Siegal and Dennis Levine, Jews every one, provoked knowing nods among non-Jews everywhere— even in San Francisco.

Milken, Boesky, Siegal, Levine. I cringe at the names. Maybe I'm old-fashioned—the Alan Dershowitzes of the world believe that Jews have as much right as gentiles to be robbers, pimps or embezzlers—

but I have a feeling that most Jews are like me, convinced that the disgrace of any Jew is almost as mortifying as a disgrace in one's own family.

I've told you about the great good fortune of the Jews of San Francisco, who may live more comfortably among their neighbors than any Jews of the Diaspora. They are the beneficiaries of the legacy of the great Jewish families of San Francisco—the Hellers, Ehrmans, Slosses, Fleishhackers, Haases, Schwabachers, Lilienthals, Sterns and, yes, the Tobiases—who helped put the city on the map not only economically but culturally. Without their generosity there would be no opera or symphony or ballet of the quality we enjoy today. The same for our parks and museums and zoo. The non-Jews who care about such things know this and are grateful for the contributions of their Jewish peers to the life of the city. Jews and gentiles serve side by side on the boards of the opera, symphony, ballet and museums, as well as the city's many charities, and come together at benefits for all such organizations, and at times on a more intimate level. For all that, integration at the top levels of San Francisco life has always been more economic than social. The old-time Jews created the Concordia and the Argonaut not simply because they wanted clubs for themselves but because they were not welcomed in the clubs of the gentiles. It's only in my time that our august Pacific Union Club, athletic Olympic Club and notorious, much coveted Bohemian Club have accepted Jewish members in significant numbers. Before World War II, Jews were not listed in the Social Register and Jewish girls didn't make the debutante lists.

For generations, my family had been the Jewish paradigm: well established, well and fondly regarded, able to live exactly as we wished. In those comfortable circumstances, Jewish identity had become an afterthought for Mother, and Sari had taken it a step further: she no longer thought of herself as Jewish. But let a wisp of scandal foul the air, and each would instantly be reminded of who and what they were. Unlike the Jews charged with insider trading, Sari had done nothing illegal. To the contrary, she would be applauded by her peers for the brilliance and audacity of her action—provided, of course, her judgment proved to be sound. If it didn't, our family's reputation and position in the community would be destroyed.

It wasn't the potential loss of my share of the business that distressed me, because the million dollars my paternal grandparents had bequeathed me at birth had grown to more than thirty million dollars. What shamed me was that Sari had acted out of the same uncontrolled greed that had inspired Messrs. Milken, Boesky, Siegal, Levine and their cohorts—and I, as an owner of the family firm, was associated with her actions.

The only good thing I can say for what happened next was that it kept me from dwelling on my disgust and anger at Sari.

It was after eleven when I pulled into my garage. Ever since the arrival of that warning package, I'd looked for stakeouts whenever I'd driven away from or back to Greenwich Street. I don't recall doing it this time; I was too dispirited and exhausted by the emotions of the family quarrel. But a minute after entering my apartment I was listening to a telephone message from Britt that snapped me back to the present: "Please call me right away, no matter what time you get in." She seemed to be trying to keep any sense of alarm out of her voice, but she hadn't succeeded.

I dialed her number at once. She answered on the first ring. "What's up?" I said.

"I was followed on the way home."

You know that ping you feel when you hear shocking news? I felt it. "You're sure?" I asked, my own shock putting a warble in my voice.

"No question." It was a level response; even if I'd never spoken to Britt before, I would have known that I wasn't dealing with an hysteric.

"Where did he pick you up?"

"Sorry?"

A stupid time for copspeak. "I'm sorry," I muttered. "When did you first notice the car?"

"Three or four blocks after I drove away."

"You're sure it was the same car all the way?"

"Absolutely."

Hearing such certainty from a witness is usually music to a cop. Hearing it from someone you love—and there is nothing like knowing such a person might be in danger to clarify your thoughts on that score—was another matter. "What kind of a car was it?" I asked, forcing myself to run through the standard questions.

"A Mercedes."

"What color?"

"Black."

Jimmy Chang, I thought. For sure.

"Is the car outside now?" I asked.

"I don't know." The fear in her voice was unmistakable now.

I thought for about half a second. "You didn't by any chance put that alarm system in, did you?"

She took a second, perhaps to swallow. "No," she said with a sigh.

"Pack a bag. I'll be there in ten minutes."

"I don't want to overreact, Zack," she said, but I could hear her relief.

"Where are you now?" I asked, disregarding her comment.

"In the bedroom."

"Good. Stay there." Her bedroom was on the second floor. "Lock the door and stay away from the windows. If you have to pass a window, crawl. Anyone rings the bell, ignore it. I'll let myself in."

"Zack?"

"Yes?"

"Be careful."

"You bet."

Fifteen seconds later I bolted from my apartment, my Smith & Wesson on my belt.

Normally it's a ten-minute drive from my flat to Britt's house. I drove it in seven, no siren, just speed, weaving through traffic, running red lights, trembling from the rush of adrenaline, devastated by the realization that in spite of all my precautions, I'd exposed Britt. I didn't have the slightest doubt that whoever was stalking me had decided to turn his attention to her as a means of intimidating me.

The last block of Stanyan is one of the steepest streets in the city. I drove it without lights, crept onto Belgrave and drove the half block to Britt's house at five miles an hour, searching for a black Mercedes. I passed Britt's house, went to the end of the block, made a U-turn and parked in front of her building. No black Mercedes, and no one sitting in other cars. As quietly as I could, I got out of my car and walked the perimeter of the house with my coat unbuttoned and my hand near the butt of the gun. Only when I was satisfied that no one was outside did I enter the house. I checked the first floor, then went upstairs.

Britt was seated on her bed, looking apprehensive but not rattled. She had been transformed, Cinderella-like, from the vision in black who'd earned a hundred stares at my mother's party into the familiar homebody in jeans, work shirt and sneakers in whose presence I'd found such comfort. Her hair was tied behind her neck, as it had been at the party, but instead of being piled atop her head, it flowed down her back. She greeted me with a nervous smile. I'd carried ten tons of guilt into the room; seeing her unharmed lightened my burden by a ton.

I sat on the edge of the bed and took her hand. "I'll tell you what," I said, "I don't think anyone's out there, but I can't be sure, so let's stay here until daylight. You get some sleep."

"What about you?"

"I'll sit here," I said, indicating a chaise longue positioned near a window. I crawled over to it and pulled it into the center of the room.

"That's silly," she said. "You can sleep in the bed."

"I won't be sleeping," I said, as I sank onto the chaise.

She regarded me in silence. Her eyes didn't waver. "Maybe you'd better tell me what's going on."

"I'd say someone's trying to scare me by scaring someone I care for. It wasn't an accident that you noticed the Mercedes. They wanted you to know that you were being followed, because they knew you'd call me."

"Why are they trying to scare you, Zack?"

"That I *can't* talk about."

"No!" Britt said sharply. As I watched, her upper body seemed to grow two inches. "If I'm involved I have a right to know."

She was right. I knew it at once, but it took a few more seconds to surrender. Call me what you want, I'm constitutionally opposed to dumping that kind of a burden on any woman, let alone a woman I care for. Once I began, though, I held nothing back. I told her about the cleaver used to cut Maggie Winehouse and the cleaver and T-shirt I'd been sent. I told her about all the times I'd been followed, and about my deadly game of windsurf tag on the bay. It felt so good to share the burden that when she asked me for the reason behind it all,

I told her about the triads and the Pacific Rim Bank and the Golden Door Trading Company and, as a further act of trust, even confided my suspicions about Jimmy Chang. "Now try to sleep," I said when I'd finished.

Britt had said nothing while I'd spoken. She hadn't so much as nodded. She greeted my suggestion with a cynical snicker. "Oh, yes, of course," she said dryly. But she took off her sneakers and lay down on the bed in her jeans and work shirt and pulled a comforter over her.

I watched her in silence, excoriating myself again for getting her involved, impatient for the daylight that would enable us to get the hell out of there. It was after two when I finally heard her deep, even breathing. By that point I'd long since decided to postpone my trip to Vancouver and Hong Kong until I'd made some security arrangements. The first would be to install Britt in my apartment, with its excellent alarm system. The second would be to set up an around-the-clock bodyguard service for her. For that, I knew right where to go.

Almost every cop on the force has a second job, life being all but impossible to afford on a policeman's salary. It's no surprise that many of these jobs are security-related. Two SFPD officers have set up lucrative security services, employing off-duty policemen. One of the two entrepreneurs, paradoxically, is Joseph Pendola, the man I caused to be transferred from the Gang Task Force when I took command of the Asian detail. The other is Tony Garibaldi, a sergeant like Pendola, who provides security for some of the richest people in town, the Gettys among them. At least twenty cops, some of them captains and lieutenants, are working for Tony at some point during any given week. Approximately the same number work for Joe Pendola. Many of the same cops work for both men.

No surprise: Tony was my choice. Before I could make an arrangement with him, I would, of course, have to get Britt to agree to it. I was sure that wouldn't be easy. It wasn't. Daylight brought a resurgence of courage.

She awakened at seven, shook her head and looked at me. "Did you sleep at all?" she asked, obviously concerned.

"I'd like to think that I didn't," I answered with a little smile, "but judging from the flannel in my mouth, I'm sure I dozed on and off."

"Good," Britt said. She started to slip from the bed.

"Hang on," I said.

I made another search of the house, hand on my gun, and then returned to the bedroom and gave a thumbs-up to Britt.

She shook her head again, sighed heavily and, without another word, went into the bathroom. Within minutes, I heard the shower running.

"How is it going to look to my clients if I've got some big thug standing next to me while I'm showing them a painting?" she said impatiently as we drank coffee in her kitchen. Wearing a beige wool skirt and a matching cashmere sweater, she looked like the consummate professional woman eager to be off to work. Only her bloodshot eyes testified to the tense night she'd spent.

"That's not how they work," I said, trying to calm her. "They're not thugs, they're cops, and they're very discreet. After a few days you won't even notice them."

"Yes, certainly," she said with a voice that could rust iron.

"Please, Britt. I can't leave unless I know you're safe."

She'd been on her way to the sink to empty her coffee cup. She abruptly turned back to me, the sunlight streaming in through an east-facing window backlighting her head. "It's not me they're after. You said yourself that the purpose of following me was to scare you. Well, they've obviously done that, so they've no further use for me. I love you for your concern, Zack, but I don't want a bodyguard."

I knew better than to try to force her. I was also too tired and strung out to try. "Will you at least stay at my place until you get your security system installed?"

She sighed. "If it will make you happy."

"It will make me happier."

"All right. I will. Let me pack a bigger bag."

While Britt packed I called Delta and changed my flight to the following day. Twenty minutes later I carried Britt's bag to the garage and put it in her car. She met me in the foyer. "Thank you again for your concern," she said, embracing me. "I do appreciate it."

Her touch caught me by surprise and left me momentarily breathless. If anything happened to her, I knew I'd have not one but two lives to account for, each a woman I loved profoundly. I wanted to tell her how bad I felt, but I didn't dare, not because I was afraid to express my feelings but because I was sure it would shake her up even more. "Before you leave," I said instead, "just let me look around outside."

Britt nodded. "Be careful," she said.

I got no further than the front door.

During one of my dozing spells I'd been awakened by what sounded like a sharp knock on the front door. Hearing nothing more, I'd dismissed the noise and eventually dozed off again. Now I saw what had caused it.

The front point of the cleaver had been embedded into the oak door so deeply that the weapon hung suspended like an ornament.

It killed me to do it, but I had no choice. I called Britt to the door and gestured toward the cleaver. Her eyes enlarged, her brow shot up, and she stood, frozen, as though in a trance. I moved behind her, put my arms around her and squeezed. "I'm sorry," I whispered. "I'm sorry."

An hour later, Dan Coltrain, an off-duty cop employed by Tony Garibaldi, drove her to her gallery. At six o'clock, Sam Bartlett, another off-duty cop, drove her to my apartment and we all settled in for the evening. Half an hour later, a delivery man brought a six-course Chinese dinner.

After dinner, my cupboard being bare in expectation of my trip, I set out for the Marina Safeway to buy breakfast food for my unexpected overnight guests. Before leaving, I'd checked for stakeouts and seen none, and no car had followed me. Or so I'd thought. Just as I entered the intersection of Hyde and Lombard streets, I felt a slight bump. I looked into my rearview mirror, and what I saw sent a charge of fear through my body. A huge car, one of those oversized station wagons, had crept up behind me with its lights out, and engaged my rear bumper. The next second, it was pushing me forward through the intersection so powerfully the force overrode my brakes. As we hit the crest of the hill my car was going at twice the prudent speed, and my heart rate must have doubled. For two seconds the cars were separated, and in that time I managed to check my rearview again. I could see two men in the cabin of the big car. I had no time to process the details, but I could see they were Asians. And then—bang—their car hit mine again, pushing it faster and faster down the hill. I turned my wheels frantically, first to the left, then to the right, trying to lose them, but the big car managed to stay right on my bumper, smacking back into mine whenever we parted, pushing me to such a speed that any sudden turn of my steering wheel would have rolled the car. I narrowly missed one car coming up the hill, then another, and finally a cable car, causing its conductor to clang his bell frantically in alarm. I was sure I was going to die. With a final burst of power, the big car sent me, horn blaring, brakes screeching and heart and lungs bursting, hurtling into the intersection of Bay and Hyde. "Look out!" I screamed, although no one could have heard me.

Only one thing saved me: a green light. I flew through the intersection and came to a screeching, skidding stop just as the big wagon—a Suburban, I saw now—careened onto Bay and headed west. By the time I got my own car turned around, the Suburban was out of sight. But I raced back to Hyde, turned on two wheels, floored the accelerator, lowered my window, grabbed for my red light, put it on the roof, then picked up my Icom radio, intent on reporting the incident.

And then, just as I started to key the radio, I froze. Where's this going to get you? I asked myself. Report it, and you're grounded indefinitely while an investigation cranks up.

My foot eased on the accelerator. I turned off the radio and pulled in the light from the roof. You're all alone on this one, pal, I told myself.

I drove on to Safeway, watching my rearview mirror, then waited in the car for five minutes until my racing heart had calmed down and I could take an even breath. Then I stepped warily from the car, and, hand on my gun, walked through the parking lot to the supermarket.

Back in the car, I began to shake, just as I had after my joust on the bay. I drove home at twenty miles an hour.

In my garage I took a look at the rear end of my 4Runner. It looked like something out of a scrapyard.

Sam had set himself up on a living-room sofa with a full view of the front door and was watching TV, his gun at his side. Britt was in my bedroom, which I'd told her to use since she'd be using it while I was away. Thank God for small favors—she was asleep.

I slept in the guest room. Tried to, that is. I had probably never been more tired, but each time I closed my eyes it was as though I were in a movie theater, watching a film of those maniacs pushing me down the hill. Their faces would almost become clear, then suddenly get fuzzy again.

When I woke up at six, it was as though my unconscious had edited the film, because the faces were fixed in my mind, as clear as a sharply focused snapshot. The driver was in his mid-forties and overweight, the man beside him lean and no more than twenty-five.

At eight o'clock I made arrangements to have my car fixed. At nine I took a cab to the airport. Just before boarding my flight to Vancouver, I called Jim Mich and told him I had reason to believe that the men who'd attacked Maggie Winehouse had either returned to San Francisco or had never left.

III

DECEMBER 9, 1994– FEBRUARY 22, 1995

18

"In 1973 Canada offered an amnesty program. We invited practically everyone under the sun to apply. We advertised in the newspapers. We said if you were in Canada by November 30, 1972, and have remained here ever since, whether as a visitor or without legal status, we're going to give you until midnight, October 15, 1973, to make our country your country. The ads didn't even mention that you had to be of good character or healthy."

Dick Osborne, a veteran of Canada's Department of Citizenship and Immigration, was speaking. We were seated in a small, plant-filled café six blocks from the center of the city, eating fish that, to judge by its taste, had been feeding itself at daybreak. Thirty feet from our table, beams of sunlight, a rare sight in Vancouver in December, bounced off False Creek, and small ferryboats plied between a dock just beyond the café and Granville Island, so near you could see the shoppers at the island's vast public market, its stalls laden with the generous yields of the rich lands and waters of the Pacific Northwest.

Osborne shook his head, incongruously covered with thick sandy hair despite his sixty years. "The people came out of the woodwork. I don't remember how many applied, but fifty thousand qualified. We were so inundated with applicants we were unable to check them out. The man you know as Jimmy Chang could have obtained his papers under an alias, using an invented story."

"Such as?"

"Such as damn near anything, frankly. He jumped ship. He paid to get smuggled in. He came in on phony papers, got scared and threw them away. He had a counterfeit passport. Whatever story he gave us would have worked at that time."

"You wouldn't have asked if he had a criminal record?"

"Of course we would have asked. We *did* ask. But the chances are a hundred percent he'd have said no."

"You didn't check fingerprints?"

"No."

"Chancy, wasn't it?"

"This country needs people, Zack," Dick said, spreading his arms, as though to emphasize the self-evident. We'd spoken a dozen times on the phone over the years, but this was the first time we'd met. I'd imagined him to be a big man, perhaps because of his hearty voice, but he turned out to be slight and wiry. I certainly hadn't envisioned that amazing head of hair. "I'll give you a thirty-second version of The Speech," he went on. "We're as big as the United States with a tenth the population. Twenty-nine million people, the annual birthrate of India. Our fertility rate is zero. We're probably the most underpopulated developed nation in the world. We need people to work and make money and spend money and pay taxes that pay for all the damn services we give them—because if we don't we're gonna go broke. The idea at that time was that all the good people we'd get would make up for the few bad ones we'd get, and we'd take care of the bad ones in due course."

It was my fourth and last day in Vancouver, an experience that had frustrated me, humbled me, and, at the moment when I was least able to handle it, brought the ghost of Elaine surging back into my thoughts.

I'd wanted to spend no more than a day in Vancouver. I'd flown in early Friday afternoon, December 9, now four days behind schedule, hoping nonetheless to finish my business that day and the following morning so that I could fly on to Hong Kong on Saturday afternoon.

Crossing the international dateline, I'd arrive in Hong Kong on Sunday evening, which meant that I could hit the ground running as the week began, and return to San Francisco by the weekend to deal with my multitudinous problems.

Of all of those problems, the one involving Britt distressed me the most. It was one thing for me to be a target; that came with the territory. The possibility that she might be harmed as a consequence of my actions had absolutely undone me—undoubtedly what whoever was orchestrating this aggression had counted on. Based on what I knew, I had to surmise that that person was Jimmy Chang. Who else had a stake in the matter? Who else stood to gain by scaring me off the case? Since Britt's call I'd racked my brain for another answer, but it always came up Jimmy. Yet I had no proof that Jimmy was involved. I could surmise that the black Mercedes that had followed Britt home had been Jimmy's but you couldn't tell a jury that it was his. I could surmise that Jimmy had sent me the cleaver and the T-shirt, hired someone to capsize my sailboard and send my car careening down the Hyde Street hill, but I had absolutely no proof. All I had were my jangled nerves.

Under normal circumstances, I would have called ahead to set up my Vancouver appointments, but so many people had turned their backs on me by this point that I didn't want to give my Canadian contacts, who had constant and vital business with the SFPD, time to think about the propriety or practical effect of dealing with a suspended SFPD cop. Since the people I'd be seeing were all civil servants, I'd assumed that they'd all be at their posts until the end of the business day. My taxi driver gave me my first inkling that I might have made a mistake.

He'd been silent during the first portion of our ride in from the airport, perhaps sensing that I was preoccupied. He was right. I'd brought my troubles with me, and they were flying around in my head. After making security arrangements for Britt, I'd spent the rest of the previous day trying to learn more about Sari's secretive, unprecedented expansion deal. It had taken some coaxing, but I'd finally gotten Mother to identify the person who had alerted her to the possibility that Sari might be pulling something funny. It was a woman named Anna Primi, a veteran Z. Tobias employee who had worshiped my father and mourned his death almost as much as

Mother had. At the time, Anna had been a bookkeeper; she was now the chief accountant. She'd known me since I was four. I'd learned the alphabet seated on her lap, pecking on her typewriter.

"Your mother promised me she wouldn't tell!" she whispered in dismay into the telephone.

"Blame me, Anna," I said, trying to soothe her. "I made her tell me. Now tell me what you know."

"I don't know anything else," she insisted.

"Come on, Anna, this is Zack you're talking to."

"And this is dead meat you're talkin' to if Sari finds out."

"Sari isn't going to touch you."

Anna laughed derisively. "She finds out, she not only fires me, she cancels my pension."

"Anna," I said, "if Sari fires you I will hire a lawyer to get you reinstated. If that fails I will find you a job, and if I can't find you a job I will pay you myself. *Talk* to me."

She sighed. "What do you want to know?" she said at last, in a voice so small I could hardly hear her.

"How did she get a billion-dollar loan, particularly on such short notice?"

A long silence. "You gotta understand something. Sari did this deal entirely on her own. No one at Z. Tobias knew about it until it was finished. Not even me. So whatever I'd tell you I'd be guessing."

"Go ahead and guess."

Another silence. "She probably paid a premium."

"How much of a premium?" I insisted.

"A point to the investment banker, and another point to the lender."

"A point being the same as a real estate point?"

"That's right."

"So that's ten million to the investment banker and ten million to the lender?" I said, making a question out of it instead of a statement, I suppose, because I didn't want to recognize the truth.

"That's right."

Chicken feed to such investors, but unimaginable sums to me in terms of the services rendered. "What rate did she pay?" I asked.

That small, reluctant voice again. "I'd be guessing."

"I understand."

"Probably two points over prime."

"What's prime?"

"When she made the deal in October, it was seven and three quarters. But the loan rate floats with the prime rate, which went up to eight and a half in mid-November."

"So, two points over eight and a half is ten and a half, which means she's paying more than a hundred million dollars a year in interest." My throat constricted as I said it. "Is that right?"

"She's not paying it. The company's paying it." Anna was one of those old-fashioned people for whom employment was tantamount to a marriage; I could hear the pain in her voice.

"How on earth does she expect to make a profit?" I said, my tone clearly betraying my conviction that there was no way she could.

"Synergy," Anna said at once. "Combining the four companies into one company." About three seconds passed before she added bitterly, "You save tons that way."

"I'll just bet," I said, wondering suddenly whether part of Anna's motivation in calling Mother was the realization that in any merger older, higher-salaried persons like herself are the first to lose their jobs. "Next question," I went on. "How could she get a billion-dollar loan when the assets of Z. Tobias are eight hundred million?"

"Because the market value of Z. Tobias is more than twice that."

"How's that?" I said, feeling embarrassed by my ignorance as well as upset with myself for my stubborn refusal all these years to educate myself about business.

"Market value's figured at ten to twelve times pretax profits. Last year, pretax profits were one hundred eighty million, meaning that you could sell Z. Tobias for two billion, give or take."

My God, I said to myself, my God, my God, my God. I owned a third of *that*? I'd had no idea. When I finally had my voice back, I said, "How could she possibly arrange a deal this big so quickly, particularly in this market?"

Anna gave a little laugh. "You know Sari," she said, and immediately shifted into a dead-on imitation of my sister's deep, brusque business voice. " 'You want to do this deal, don't give me five thousand pages. We can put it on a napkin. I want it finished in a week.' Etcetera."

In another context, I might have laughed at Anna's performance. "That's her, all right." I sighed. "Who put up the money, Anna?"

"I don't know."

"Anna!"

"I honest to God don't know," she said so convincingly that I was sure she wasn't lying.

"Then you haven't seen the documents?"

"No one but Sari's seen them."

"Not even our attorneys?" As independent as Sari was, I couldn't believe she would do this deal without at least consulting the firm's attorneys.

"Remember, she doesn't want five thousand pages. At the last minute, she'll present the attorneys with a fait accompli."

"But she *will* show them the papers before she signs, won't she?" I asked her desperately, only now beginning to realize the degree of power-hunger Sari had displayed in doing this crazy deal herself. If it went through, Sari could have more assets at her command than any woman in America. No wonder she didn't want anyone interfering.

"How do *I* know?" Anna said, betraying her own desperation. "We've never had a situation like this."

My next call was to my attorney, Paul Stengler, a teammate at Cal. He listened silently while I explained the situation, until I got to the billion dollars. Then he grunted as though I'd punched him in the stomach. "You've got some kind of sister," he muttered.

"Tell me something I don't know. What can I do to stop her?"

"You alone? Not you and your mother?" The way he asked the question foreshadowed what was coming.

"In the crunch, I don't know what Mother would do," I admitted. "Let's hope she'd go along, but let's not assume that."

Paul's response was immediate and emphatic. "If she doesn't go along, you might as well forget it."

I quickly calculated the selling job I'd have to do on Sadie to make her take our problems public *and* go after one of her children. It would take some doing, but I thought I could swing it. "Okay," I said, "assume she goes along. What can we do?"

"You can sue Sari for control of the company. But you'd have to prove she was incompetent. With the kind of numbers she's racked up, that would be tough. You'd have to prove that this acquisition was imprudent to a point that it could bankrupt the company." His voice didn't ring with confidence. "I'm not gonna kid you, Zack," he said after a pause. "It's damn near impossible to prove something like that."

"Could we at least get a restraining order while we look into it?"

"Doubt it. Same reason. The acquisitions come down to a matter of judgment, and with those numbers, no judge would fault hers."

I didn't need a crystal ball to predict the future. Sari would perform her synergistic magic, and thousands of good people, people who had given their professional lives to their firms, would disappear from the payrolls. Because of three acquisitions whose underlying purpose, regardless of the competitive threat that Sari had alleged, was to create a financial empire with her as its head. Sari hadn't created the mentality that had put the greed of the few above the welfare of the many; she had simply taken advantage of it. That subtle detail would be lost on those whose lives would be ruined. The finger would point at their executioner: Z. Tobias and Company—of which I was a one-third owner.

I'd landed during the tail end of a storm, and driven through a drizzle toward downtown Vancouver. Now the sun appeared, so suddenly and brilliantly it was as though someone had snapped up a shade in a darkened room. Only then did I register the beauty of the scene unfolding before me.

We were crossing a bridge. Directly ahead of me was the center of the city, looking as though it had just been scrubbed. The air was as clear as polished glass. In the distance, mountains thick with evergreens and crowned with snow rose directly out of the water, which shimmered in the sun.

It's impossible for me to exaggerate what happened next. Perhaps, in the interval, I have jumbled time and space and invested that moment with later sights and soundings. Whatever the truth, I was seized by a feeling that the earthly paradise I'd been seeking all my adult life lay dead ahead.

At this point, you would have every reason to wonder why a man with my means would be looking for an earthly paradise. You've probably calculated what a one-third share of two billion dollars would be. You may have even calculated the tax. The remainder, when added to my trust fund, put my net worth at a shade under $500 million, a number that had stupefied me when I'd calculated it myself. But all that money had not bought me a safe and clean environment, a clear conscience or peace of mind. Until my recent troubles, I'd been relatively secure in my aerie and able to move unmolested about my city along carefully chosen routes. But let me venture onto its downtown streets or into its parks or travel to its opera house or symphony hall, and I would be overwhelmed by the evidence of a society deteriorating around me.

So it was that everything I would see and hear in Vancouver in the next few days would be compared with my own reality. Like most San Franciscans, I had lived my life on the assumption that my city, for all its problems, was the finest in the world. I would leave Vancouver not at all sure.

"First time in Vancouver?" the taxi driver asked as we approached the city. He was thin, looked to be in his early thirties, wore a neatly trimmed beard and heavy wool camper's clothes, and regarded me with the same placid smile with which he'd greeted me at the airport as he stowed my bag in his trunk.

"How could you tell?"

"The way you're lookin' around." A friendly voice complemented his relaxed manner.

"This city's something to look at."

"It's that, all right. I never get tired of lookin' at it. It's why I drive a cab instead of workin' in an office. Where you from?"

"San Francisco."

"Well, *that's* pretty nice to look at."

"That's for sure," I agreed.

We entered the downtown area. For a Friday afternoon the traffic seemed to be moving easily. Well-dressed pedestrians, bundled against the breeze, moved in and out of stores. I saw no vagrants, no papers on the streets. At each intersection, I looked left or right and got a glimpse of the sparkling harbor.

"Here on vacation?" the driver asked amiably.

"On business."

He gazed at me for a moment in his rearview mirror, one eyebrow cocked. "You're comin' here to do business on a Friday afternoon?" The way he said it, the question sounded rhetorical.

"Something wrong with that?" I asked, puzzled.

"Not many Vancouverites in their offices on Friday afternoons. They're all headin' out somewhere, drivin' to Whistler Mountain to go skiin' or on their boats headin' for Vancouver Island."

"On their boats in *December?*"

The driver smiled. "Oh, yeah. We're a hardy bunch up here. Besides, it almost never gets too cold."

"What do their bosses say to their taking off like that?"

He laughed, and looked at me again in his mirror, as though the joke was on me. "The bosses are generally the first ones out the door. Half of 'em turned down promotions to Toronto in order to stay in Vancouver."

"The living's that good, is it?"

"There's nothin' that beats it," he said emphatically. "It's got everything a big city has to offer without a lot of the problems. I'm a native, but I took off for two years after university to see the world— partly to see if I could find a better place. I found nothin' out there I liked nearly as much, not even San Francisco."

I hesitated for a minute, knowing what I wanted to ask him but wondering if I should. "You finished college, did you?"

He looked into the mirror yet again, his smile widening. "Surprised that a university graduate would be drivin' a cab?"

"A little," I admitted, embarrassed that I'd given myself away so readily.

The driver must have sensed my reaction. "People here don't measure success by how much money you make," he said quickly. "It's the quality of your existence. I do fine drivin' as much as I need to. My wife's a teacher, so we can go hikin' or fishin' or skiin' whenever school's not in session. If I had a job, I couldn't do that."

I should have dropped it, but I was suddenly, intensely interested in this life story. "No kids yet?" I asked.

"One in the oven."

"Do you plan to have a big family?"

"Two, maybe three kids, depending on how the wife likes working and raising the baby."

"If you don't mind my asking, are you and your wife going to be able to pay for your children's education on your combined incomes?"

"Government pays for that." He smiled again, anticipating my next question. "Pays for the baby, too. Havin' her costs us nothin'. Well, sure it does. We pay the taxes. But our medical costs are completely covered. So's our retirement, pretty much."

"So you figure you're getting your money's worth?" I said with another look around at what had to be the most well-ordered city I could ever remember seeing.

"Oh, yeah, absolutely," the driver said. It took him about four seconds to pronounce the last word. "A lot of people grumble, and say they want lower taxes, but if you ask them whether they'd be willin' to give up the benefits, they say no, we want the benefits *and* lower taxes. I figure you get what you pay for, and we get a lot. How can you put a price on peace of mind?"

If the scenes of the city passing before me could be likened to scenes in a movie, the driver's comments were like the musical score. "You seem very much at peace," I said. "Is that what accounts for it?"

"It's a big, big part of it. It also comes from knowin' I'm livin' in the best city I could possibly be livin' in."

I couldn't remember the last time I'd heard such an unequivocal statement. "What's the one thing that makes Vancouver so special in your opinion?" I asked, wild with curiosity by this point.

"The one thing?" He laughed. "That's tough. The city's so beautiful and life's so easy."

"Which is it? The beauty? The easy life? The peace of mind?"

He thought for a minute. "All of them, really." He thought some more. "I guess the most important thing is that we live in a cultural situation where people don't shout at each other."

How many trips had Elaine and I made in search of our earthly Paradise? At least half a dozen. And we'd never thought to visit Vancouver, through whose immaculate streets I was now passing.

With her in my thoughts.

What might have happened if I'd brought her here? Would she have decided that something worked, after all? Would she have been inspired to check it out? Would the evidence she found have immunized her against despair? Would she be alive today?

"What's your name?" I asked the driver.

"Jeff Nelson."

"I'm Zack Tobias."

"Nice to meet you, Mr. Tobias."

"Call me Zack." An impulse seized me. "What are you doing for the rest of the day?"

"Just drivin' my cab."

"If you're right and I can't get hold of the people I need to see, how'd you like to show me what a great place Vancouver is?"

He was driving thirty-five miles an hour in traffic on a downtown street, but he turned in his seat and grinned. "You're on," he said.

Jeff had been right. My contacts weren't in their offices. No one said they'd gone skiing or sailing. I was simply told that I could reach them first thing Monday morning. I thought about leaving my name and hotel number, thought better of it, accepted my fate and put myself in Jeff's hands for the rest of the afternoon and the next day as well.

He proved as creative as he was indefatigable, taking me first to a vacant apartment on a high floor of a just-completed building in the West End, Vancouver's premier neighborhood. "This'll help you put yourself in the picture," he said with a grin.

"What made you think I could afford something like this?" I asked.

"First of all, you took a cab from the airport. Second, you gave me a big tip. Third, your Hartman luggage. Fourth, your choice of hotels. People of moderate means don't stay at the Meridien. Fifth, you've got a certain air about you, like a guy who's used to money."

"What'd you study in college?" I asked.

"Business administration."

"You should have been a detective."

He laughed. "That's the *last* thing I should have been."

"Why's that?"

"My whole life's structured around *avoiding* problems and complications."

"Is that just you, or is it typical for this place?"

He laughed again. "In that regard, I'm Mr. Vancouver." He waved me into the apartment. "Have a look."

The apartment—priced well below what a comparable property would sell for in San Francisco—occupied the entire floor, with drop-dead views in all directions. Jeff identified the downtown landmarks, most less than a mile away, the Strait of Georgia, English Bay, the Lions Gate Bridge—under which a freighter was slipping en route, I supposed, to some Pacific Rim port—and beyond the harbors, the homes of North and West Vancouver edging up the slopes of the mountains. Below us was Stanley Park, which we visited next, one thousand acres of stately redwoods, Jeff informed me, and lawns like deep-pile carpets, a rose garden with flowers in the summer as big as soccer balls, lily ponds and streams that slithered through miniature rain forests covered with ferns, wildflowers and moss. For amusement, Jeff boasted, there was tennis, swimming, separate seven-mile cycling and jogging paths around the park's perimeter, a number of hiking trails, an aquarium, a teahouse serving serious food, and for the children a miniature railroad.

All this just outside your door. As we toured the city it became quickly evident that proximity to both essentials and luxuries was even more of a virtue in Vancouver than it was in San Francisco. Residents of the West End could walk to their place of business, as well as to department stores, museums, theaters, concert halls and the city's best restaurants. Summers, they could walk to the beach, or the ferries to Granville Island, or to any one of a dozen marinas where their boats could be docked at half the rental they'd pay in San Francisco. Nothing in Vancouver—not parks or Gastown, with its restored turn-of-the-century red-brick buildings and sidewalks, or Chinatown, the second biggest in North America, or the airport, not even, for God's sake, a ski lift—proved to be more than a short drive from anything else.

Try as I might, I couldn't make Jeff acknowledge any significant imperfections in his city or the life it gave him. Yes, Vancouver had a traffic problem, he conceded as we crossed a bridge linking downtown to North Vancouver, but that was only during rush hour; at all other times, the traffic flow would make a visitor from New York or Chicago or Los Angeles or even San Francisco wonder what Vancouverites were complaining about. Yes, it rained a lot, he granted, fifty to sixty inches a year, but rain was as necessary to the city's beauty as aging was to experience. Yes, there was unemployment, he allowed, but Canada, unlike the United States, had a safety net designed to catch the most unfortunate—and soothe one's conscience in the process. There were no slums in Vancouver, and, compared with the States, few homeless people. Yes, there was crime and even murder, he said as he drove me back to my hotel late Saturday afternoon, but the rate of assaults involving firearms was seven times higher in Seattle than it was in Vancouver. Yes, there was the occasional mugging, but again it couldn't be compared with what happened in the States.

Anyone strolling through the city at night, even Stanley Park, could almost certainly do so without being bothered, let alone attacked. "Vancouver is a terribly safe place to be. I wouldn't caution you about walking anywhere."

His words were like puffs from a bellows, heating the coals of my envy. "Come on, Jeff," I said, "it can't be that perfect. There's got to be *something* wrong."

"Okay," Jeff said after a pause, "we've had an increase in gang activity in the last few years, mostly Asian kids. And that's disturbing. But mostly they fight among themselves. It doesn't bother us." He thought again. "Aside from a few environmental problems—a bit of smog, and some water pollution—that's pretty much it."

I reached for my wallet to pay for my tour. "Look," I said, transported by my discovery of a truly happy man, caught up in the euphoria he radiated, not wanting it to end after all these days of sadness, tension and danger, "if you and your wife aren't doing anything this evening, why don't you join me for dinner?"

Jeff tilted his head in surprise. "That's very nice," he said. "That's a first. We'd love to."

"You don't want to check with her and call me?"

He laughed. "I don't have to ask my wife if she'd like to go out for dinner. What time would you like to meet and where would you like to go?"

"Let's say seven-thirty. Do you have a favorite place?"

"How much do you want to spend?"

"Sky's the limit."

Jeff's eyebrows lifted and his eyes enlarged, as though he'd just learned that he'd won something. "There's a restaurant called Bishop's that we're always readin' about—best this, and best that. Never been there."

"Bishop's it is, then."

"Could be really expensive."

"I can handle it."

"So I was right," Jeff said with a grin. "You *are* rich."

I grinned back. "The truth would spoil your dinner."

"Try me," Jeff laughed encouragingly.

"Trust me," I said, unwilling to take it any further. "I'll have the concierge make a reservation."

"And I'll pick you up at seven-fifteen."

"Tell me something," I said as I handed Jeff his money. "How did you happen to know that the number of crimes involving firearms was seven times higher in Seattle than in Vancouver? That's an odd fact for the lay person to know."

"It is, I suppose," Jeff agreed. "Of all the cities I looked at, Seattle was the most tempting alternative, probably because it's got a lot of the same amenities Vancouver has, and the people have pretty much the same outlook. So I did some library work, and came up with a bunch of quality-of-life comparisons. Seattle didn't measure up to Vancouver in a lot of categories. Crime was the worst."

I shook my head. "Two cities, almost across the border from each other, with many of the same natural endowments, and one has an armed crime rate seven times higher than the other. How do you explain it?"

"In Canada, self-defense isn't considered a valid or legal reason to buy a handgun," Jeff answered without hesitation. "To me, that alone was reason enough to choose Vancouver."

Bishop's, on West Fourth Avenue in Kitsilino, the neighborhood just south of downtown, was a small, attractive bistro decorated with contemporary paintings done by local artists. The food—not as expensive as in comparable San Francisco restaurants—measured well against those citadels of California cuisine. The owner, John Bishop, a thin, genial man of fifty, personalized the experience by join-ing us for a glass of wine. Sharon Nelson, Jeff's wife, a petite but sturdy redhead who reinforced my conviction that women are never more beautiful than when pregnant, seconded her husband on every-thing he'd told me. She anticipated a long, fruitful, comfortable and secure life in Vancouver. "If Jeff had decided to settle elsewhere," she said merrily, "he would have had to find himself another wife." She looked as though she was only half joking.

It all seemed so perfect—the handsome setting, the contented cou-ple, their tangible pride in their paragon of a city—that I did what I had to do with the utmost reluctance. "I hate to spoil the evening," I said over coffee, "but in all this talk about how trouble-free Vancou-ver is, how come neither one of you has said a word about all the bad feelings toward the Hong Kong Chinese?"

The restaurant lights were dim, so I couldn't be sure, but it seemed that both Jeff and Sharon blushed. They both dropped their eyes. "You know about that, do you?" Jeff said sheepishly.

"I do."

"How come?" he asked.

"It's my business to know," I answered simply.

"You never did tell me what your business was."

"Food, clothing and shelter," I said, because the other truth would have been too complicated.

"So you've heard about 'Hongcouver,' " Jeff said, again looking sheepish. He chewed the inside of his mouth. "Yeah, well, we're not very proud of that," he said after thinking for a moment, "so you don't talk about what you're not proud of." He sipped on his wine. "Maybe another reason I didn't mention it is that the problem was a lot worse five years ago than it is today. And I'm not sure it was resentment of the Hong Kong Chinese so much as it was resentment against immigration in general, mostly in the affluent white communities. But you know how people are, they eventually get used to just about anything, and a lot of that stuff has faded away."

"But there still *are* bad feelings against the Hong Kong Chinese?" I pressed.

"Oh, sure," Jeff said. "There sure are."

Once more I was struck by his apparent honesty and straightforwardness. "So, could you talk about it now?"

They exchanged uneasy glances. "You do it," Sharon said to Jeff. "I wouldn't know where to begin."

"Where you begin," Jeff said, squirming in his seat, then sitting back, as though in resignation, "is that we'd be up the creek just like the rest of Canada if it weren't for all the Hong Kong money that's come in here. Everywhere else there's recession and unemployment, and here it's boom time, and the main reason is that all the millionaires in Hong Kong are moving money to Canada in anticipation of '97, and their favorite Canadian city by far is Vancouver, maybe because it's so beautiful or the winters aren't nearly as cold as the rest of Canada or because the harbor reminds them of Hong Kong or just because it's closer to home. Whatever the reason, they've put a ton of money into Vancouver. The irony is that we've been working for years trying to encourage exactly this kind of investment. It's going to put us on the map. It's going to change our perception of what's possible here, because people from Hong Kong don't understand when you say to them, 'It can't be done.' "

Listening to Jeff, I'd been aware of a low hum in the room, that special sound people used to pleasure make when they're wining and dining well. Earlier, I'd noticed that every table was taken, and that the occupants were all well dressed. The streets were filled with late-model cars; I couldn't remember seeing an old one. The evening before, on a stroll along crowded downtown sidewalks, I'd seen shops and restaurants filled with people. Jeff was right: to judge by Vancouver, you would never know that Canada was experiencing economic troubles. If the Hong Kong Chinese had made the difference, they ought to be beloved.

"So what's the problem?" I asked.

"It's not one problem, it's a lot of problems. There's still a feeling that these people aren't like us, that they don't blend into society here. And then a lot of people are angry because the Asians are taking up too many slots at the universities, and businessmen are angry because they feel that the Chinese have the inside track on money at Chinese banks—they have a big bank here now, the Hong Kong Bank, and they bought the Bank of British Columbia. But mostly it's what they've done to the housing market. That's what's got everyone upset." By the look of him, he was part of that group. The placid smile that had seemed a permanent part of his features had disappeared, replaced by a grimace. He shifted nervously in his chair. "They can buy all the hotels and office buildings they want and nobody would care, but when they turn the housing market upside down it affects everybody." I could see him struggle with this thought for a minute. At one point he glanced hurriedly at Sharon, who encouraged him with a quick nod. It must have worked, because there was more starch in his voice when he continued. "I'll admit it," he said. "I'm pissed off. Now that we're gonna have a family, we'd like to have a house with a yard and a basement. Forget it. The Chinese have priced us out of the market."

"You've been looking?"

"Hell, yes, we've been looking. We must have looked at thirty places since Sharon got pregnant. Twenty-eight were owned by people from Hong Kong. Most of the owners had bought for speculation. They weren't even living there."

"I remember '89," Sharon said. "That's when it was the worst. They'd fly in here for a week on Cathay Pacific charter flights. They'd tour the neighborhoods on buses, gawking at us out of the windows. They'd troop through the houses and apartment buildings. And they'd buy, boy, did they buy. One zillionaire saw ten condos, couldn't decide which one he wanted, so he bought all ten."

I drew my head back. "You know that for a fact?" I challenged.

"Well, we only heard the story," Sharon admitted. "But I'm sure it's true."

"Everything all right?"

I looked up. It was John Bishop.

"Fine," I said.

"You all look quite serious. I hope it wasn't something you ate."

"No, no, I assure you," I said, doing my best to look cheerful. "The food was wonderful."

"If you need anything, let us know," he said, and moved off to say good night to some departing guests. I turned back to Jeff and Sharon.

"Whether that particular story Sharon told you was in fact true or not, it was true in spirit," Jeff said doggedly. "And it's still goin' on. A lot of the condo developers don't even wait for the people to come. They put ads in the Hong Kong papers announcing their visit, then fly there, set up exhibits in some hotel and sell condos to buyers sight unseen. It's just incredible." He shook his head. "All that demand has pushed prices through the roof. And *that's* a fact."

Shades of Maggie Winehouse.

Thinking of her, I suddenly remembered Jimmy Chang, protesting so vehemently at the meeting in the mayor's office that Chinese immigrants were being blamed entirely for a problem they'd only partially caused. Whatever subsequent suspicions I'd developed about Jimmy, what he'd said at the time had sounded reasonable. "Are you sure it's just the Chinese?" I asked. "Couldn't the increase in demand have something to do with baby boomers coming of age, or couples with double incomes, or people moving to British Columbia from other parts of Canada?"

Jeff flicked his hand, as though to brush away my questions. "Yeah, I've heard all that stuff. I don't put much stock in it. As far as people coming from other parts of Canada, a lot of *them* are Hong Kong Chinese who immigrated to other provinces first and then decided they'd rather live in BC." He took a deep breath. "I'm tellin' you, this real estate market is driven by the Hong Kong Chinese. To them, our prices are peanuts."

"And then there's reassessment," Sharon said, as upset as though she were a homeowner. "People who love their homes and don't want to move have been forced to sell because of tremendous increases in their property taxes."

"Wait a minute, wait a minute. These people supposedly sell their homes to rich Asian immigrants, right?"

"So?"

"So they must be getting twenty, thirty, forty times what they paid for those homes. They can't be all that unhappy."

"And then these rich Asian immigrants come in, tear the old homes down and put up these monster homes," Jeff said, ignoring my remark, his argument really in gear now. This wasn't my placid, pleasant tour guide any longer; this was an angry man. "Eight thousand square feet," he went on, drumming on the table in rhythm with his words, "with high, thick, concrete walls around them. They cut down the trees and pave over the lawns. Changes the whole character of the neighborhood."

"And then the kids come to school in limousines," Sharon added fervently.

"Oh, come on," I said.

"Not all of them, but some of them. If it's not a limousine, it's a Mercedes or some other ritzy foreign car, as often as not chauffeur-driven. These are rich kids. They keep to themselves. They don't even try to make friends with the Canadian kids." Then she laughed. It was not a merry laugh. It was bitter and rueful. "And *then*," she said, "they win all the academic prizes."

Her remark was like a rock hurled against glass, shattering the Happy Couple image I had conjured for them, and I saw them, suddenly and sadly, as just as human as the rest of us. It wasn't the rise in the cost of housing that concerned them so much as it was the introduction of a mentality completely at odds with their own—the mentality of people with limitless ambition and limitless energy to achieve it. What would happen when that mentality intruded itself into a community of people who valued the balanced life above all else, who turned down promotions to maintain it, whose lives were structured around the avoidance of problems and complications, who left their offices early on Friday to head for their sailboats and the ski slopes? It was a variation of the "intolerable competitors" story I'd told Mike Winehouse at lunch at Yuet Lee: the natives' discomfort with gifted, hardworking newcomers. It happened wherever such newcomers landed in search of greener pastures, but somehow, given the bountiful and beautiful conditions in which Vancouverites lived, it seemed a little more wrong here than in other places, as incongruous as a pimple on a pretty face.

As absorbed as I'd been by my tour of Vancouver, I'd thought of Britt and the danger I'd put her in at least once every fifteen minutes. I called her first thing Sunday.

"I see it now. It never would have worked," she said lightly. "You would have wanted to keep your flat, and I would have been unable to give up my house."

"You sound reasonably cheerful."

"As cheerful as any woman can be who's been dispossessed." Only then did I pick up on the tightness in her voice. "How long do I have to stay here?"

"Until I get back and can get a handle on the situation."

I counted two deep breaths, loud and clear through the phone line. "This isn't some devilish plot on your part to send me running back into your arms, is it?"

"I'm not that clever."

"When *will* you be back?"

"End of the week. I hope."

"Hurry, please. I miss my house."

It was the way she said it, that all but imperceptible emphasis on the last word. "You really know how to hurt a guy," I said, knowing I had no ground to stand on, yet wishing somehow that in all the uncertainty swirling around me, Britt at least would remain a fixed point.

"I learned from an expert."

I winced, shut my eyes and, pulling the phone away so that Britt couldn't hear, moaned softly. This was more than banter, and not in character. I could only imagine the strain she was under, and the resentment she had to be feeling at having been drawn so ominously into a battle that wasn't hers. In these circumstances, the weapon nearest at hand was denial, and she had obviously grabbed it. "Are Tony Garibaldi's men treating you okay?" I asked her, hoping to change the tone.

"Each one's better than the last one." The remark was as suggestive as it was bitter.

"Britt, please," I pleaded, really squirming now. "Don't make me feel any worse about this than I do."

"Yes, of course," she said after a pause. "I apologize. But you have to understand, I've never been in jail before."

"It's hardly jail," I protested.

"Detention, then. Same thing."

She wasn't going to relent. "One thing you *can* do," I said desperately, "is get that security system set up at your place."

"They're going on Tuesday to look it over."

"Good."

"But they can't do the installation for three weeks."

"Maybe I could talk to them," I said, desperate to be helpful. "Who are you using?"

"I don't remember. Tony arranged it."

"He can lean on them."

"He already has. They originally said five weeks."

The more she spoke, the more irritation I heard in her voice and the more upset I became. There was no use continuing. "For what it's worth, I apologize again," I said. "The best thing I can do for all of us is to get to the bottom of this. And that's what I'm going to do."

Brave words, with nothing to back them. Hanging up, I repeated to myself what had become my mantra of frustration: No clues, no leads, no suspects other than Jimmy Chang, and only circumstantial reasons to suspect even him.

Monday began with a soft knock on my hotel-room door. I was on the floor in yesterday's underwear, doing some stretches. I got up and put on my traveling robe. As I walked to the door I looked at the radio alarm. It was a few minutes after seven. "Who is it?" I asked. The answer was another soft knock. "Who is it?" I demanded again.

"Open up, Zack," a voice whispered. It sounded familiar. I made sure the chain latch was on, then unlocked the door and opened it a crack, my shoulder against it in case I needed to force it closed. Outside, in the softly lit, carpeted hall, stood Brian Lampert, the head of Vancouver's Asian Crime Squad, a cautionary finger at his lips stifling my cry of surprise. He slipped a folded piece of paper through the door. The instant I had it he turned for the elevators.

I closed the door, my head filling with questions his note didn't answer. "Meet me as quickly as you can on the hotel loading dock," it said. "Use the service elevator and walk through the kitchen."

I'd known Brian Lampert for eight years, if one can be said to know someone with whom almost every conversation has been by telephone. We'd talked at least half a dozen times a year, more when criminal activity warranted it. We'd met, at last, three years earlier, in Honolulu at a conference on Asian gangs attended by representatives of every Pacific Rim country. Big men begin with a lot of shared understanding, and Brian was almost as big as I was. Even though he was twenty years older, we got along as well in person as we had on the phone.

"What the hell's going on?" I said five minutes after he'd knocked on my door, as we walked rapidly away from the hotel.

"I was hoping you could tell me," Brian said. Except for his height, he seemed, in the faint morning light, indistinguishable from other early risers walking to their offices in downtown Vancouver, the collar of his tan raincoat turned up against the chill, a white shirt and dark tie visible beneath the coat.

"How did you know I was in Vancouver?"

"The chief got a fax from your chief, advising him you were heading this way. It said you'd been suspended, and that we shouldn't give you any help."

Oh, Christ, I thought. Chief Doyle tracking me! I could only wonder how he knew I was heading to Vancouver. I didn't wonder how Brian had found me at the Meridien. That was a couple of phone calls. "Did you see the fax, or did your chief tell you about it?" I said.

"There was a copy on my desk this morning," Brian said. "It was dated Friday. I would have called you right away, but I'd taken Friday off to have a long weekend. Lucky I got in early this morning before you called anybody. You might have got your ass in a wringer."

Brian steered me into a coffee shop and put me into the last booth, with my back to the street. From his seat, facing me, he could watch the traffic. I'd taken the same precaution countless times over the years with witnesses and sources—even, out of habit, with Mike Winehouse at Yuet Lee a month before. It didn't reassure me that Brian felt I needed to be protected. "So tell me your story," he said.

I told him everything I knew, finishing just as we finished breakfast.

"Jimmy Chang means nothing," he said. "The story means nothing. Brings absolutely no one to mind."

"I figured it wouldn't, but I have some photographs."

The corners of his mouth turned down. For the first time I noticed how tired and older he looked compared with the last time I'd seen him. His hairline was higher, the remaining hair thinner and grayer. There were liver spots on his hands, and his skin looked dry and flaky.

"No way," he said. "Our chief needs your chief more than your chief needs our chief. At least he thinks he does. I'm not sure it's true, but as long as he believes it, we have to proceed as though it is. He sent a note along with the fax. It said, 'If this man shows up, I want to know about it. No exceptions.' That last part was for me. He knows we're buddies. So pardon the James Bond shit, but I figured it was best for both of us." He took a deep breath and then shook his head. "There's no way we can help you, Zack."

That did it. I slumped against the banquette, feeling the fight draining out of me. "I'm fucked," I said. "Utterly, totally fucked."

The next hour was the closest I can remember coming to throwing in the towel. If Chief Doyle had asked the Vancouver police to shut me out, he'd certainly made the same request of the Royal Hong Kong Police. But that seed of suspicion in my gut was now the size of a baseball. The chief was spooked, no question, and I just couldn't shake my conviction that whatever had spooked him involved Jimmy Chang. He knew Jimmy's legend as well as I did; he knew that Jimmy had come to San Francisco from Vancouver. How the chief had known I'd gone to Vancouver I hadn't the faintest idea, but *why* I'd gone wouldn't have puzzled him for a second. It figured that if he was trying to stop me from working in Vancouver, he was trying to stop me from learning about Jimmy's past. There was no other explanation.

I worked my anger off in the Meridien's gym. At ten o'clock, back in my room, I called Cathay Pacific and booked a first-class seat on the 2:00 P.M. flight to Hong Kong. Then I played the only card I had left. I called Dick Osborne at Citizenship and Immigration, praying that his department had received no faxes from Chief Doyle. I knew at once by his delighted greeting that it hadn't. "You're in town. Lovely," he said. "Do I get to buy you lunch?"

"It'll have to be early. My flight's at two."

He laughed. "I'm always hungry," he said.

And so it was that I found myself at that plant-filled café, just across False Creek from Granville Island, having my first face-to-face encounter with yet another man I'd gotten to know by telephone. Other than the forthcoming manner in which he had entered into our exchanges over the years, I knew nothing about him. I liked his handshake, surprisingly strong for a man of his small size, as well as his steady gaze and natural smile, but I wasn't ready to confide in him until I'd felt him out. So I asked a lot of questions during the first half of our lunch, learning in the process how thousands of wealthy Hong Kong residents had already secured Canadian passports by investing $250,000 in a business in Canada and establishing residency for three years, how the requirement had been increased in 1993 to $350,000 and five years—and how in any case, he said with a grin, the average investment of Hong Kong Chinese settling in Vancouver was $2 million. Right now, he said, the government had declared a moratorium on the program, to figure out how to monitor it better.

"Is that because it's so popular?" I asked.

"Ottawa runs the program, so I don't really know, but I'd say that's a pretty good guess."

I told Dick about my conversation on Saturday evening with Jeff and Sharon. "They're right and they're wrong," he said with a shake of his head. "Of the seventy thousand people moving into British Columbia's lower mainland between 1990 and 1994, fifty-six thousand were foreign-born, so that should tell you where the demand is coming from. But while a lot of those people were from Hong Kong, not all of them were by a long shot." He sighed. "Those big homes are being built all over the city by all ethnic groups these days, but they're still called 'Chinese monster homes.' "

Then I'd explained my interest in Jimmy Chang. It felt good to be talking, at least, but Dick's replies, so far, had given me nothing to go on.

"Supposing Jimmy Chang registered under the amnesty program," I went on. "What would that have entitled him to?"

"You mean papers?" Dick said, stopping a piece of salmon inches from his mouth.

"Right."

"He would have received a landed immigrant's card."

"Could he travel on that card?"

Dick nodded as he chewed his fish, then swallowed and said, "As far as we're concerned, he could have. But I doubt that he'd have tried to leave the country unless he actually had some kind of passport."

I thought for a moment, taking a last bite of my tuna. "There was no way he could have had a Canadian passport by that point, was there?" I asked then.

"Not a legal passport," Dick said, "unless he'd become a citizen." He sat back, finished with his meal, and smiled pleasantly again, his steady eyes regarding me from beneath sandy eyebrows. "But he could have had a fraudulent one. If he was playing that game, it would more likely have been a counterfeit Hong Kong passport or a passport from some other Asian country. Actually, in those days you could buy citizenship in some of those countries for ten thousand dollars."

"You still can, can't you?"

"I'm sure."

A busboy came to our table. He was dark-skinned, in his early twenties, with black hair. "Have you finished?" he asked with a thick accent. We nodded that we were.

"Pakistani?" I asked when he'd left.

"Probably," Dick said. "But I can't always tell. We're getting them from all over these days."

"Unless I'm mistaken," I said, returning to my subject, "ten thousand dollars would have been a lot of money to a Jimmy Chang in those days. Chances are he wouldn't have had a passport." I thought for a minute. "What were the popular ways of slipping into the United States in the early seventies? Assuming Jimmy went in illegally, how would he most likely have done it?"

"Exactly the same way he'd do it today. He could have entered on a tourist visa and never left. He could have been put ashore in Washington by small craft. Or he could have crossed the border on foot—we've got fifty inspection stations along thirty-six hundred miles of border. We've got thousands of miles of unpatrolled scrubland and farmland. When you think about illegals entering the States from Canada, you can't think about a border. Effectively, it doesn't exist. The illegals heading south sure as hell don't recognize the border. To them, LA, San Francisco and Vancouver are all the same."

I nodded. "In any case, they wouldn't leave much of a trail, would they?" I said, discouraged.

"If there's any trail at all, it begins in Hong Kong." He regarded me for a moment from beneath those sandy brows. "That's where you're going, is it?"

I hesitated before answering, asking myself again what good it would do. "Yeah," I said. "That's where I'm going."

When Jeff dropped me off at the hotel after our Saturday-night dinner, he'd made me promise to contact him through his dispatcher as soon as I knew when I was leaving Vancouver so that he could drive me to the airport. His treat, he'd said. I broke my promise. The vibes hadn't been that good after our discussions about the Hong Kong Chinese, and given everything else on my mind I just couldn't bring myself to confront him.

As the taxi drove me away from the city, I could see a new weather front moving in. I thought about the sunny beginning to my visit. Sunny beginning, stormy ending—your basic courtship. My euphoria about the city hadn't evaporated, but it had certainly diminished. I could only wonder how I'd feel if I were in Vancouver for a month.

I had gone through immigration and was sitting in the international passengers' lounge reading the *Vancouver Sun* when a Canadian Pacific flight en route to Hong Kong arrived from San Francisco. A few minutes later the passengers began filing into the terminal and walking along a corridor separated from the outbound passengers by a glass wall. Watching them idly, I suddenly raised my newspaper in front of my face.

One of the passengers was Gordon Lee.

19

The flight to Hong Kong was as agreeable as long plane trips can be: an on-time departure, then zealous, almost worshipful attention from two delicately beautiful young Chinese women, food as good as any I'd tasted in the skies and wines to match the food. But the headwinds had surpassed two hundred miles an hour, forcing an unscheduled stop in Taipei to refuel, and arrival in Hong Kong was three hours behind schedule. My body, bound to a seat—even a first-class seat—for eighteen hours, ached with fatigue.

At least a dozen times in my life I've dreamed that a jumbo jet on which I was a passenger was flying over the downtown area of a major city, just above street level, its wings all but touching the buildings on either side. I'd puzzled over the dream, wondering if it meant I was intruding on spaces where I didn't belong. Awaking just before our early-evening landing in Hong Kong, I thought for an instant that I was having that dream again. Every light in the city seemed to be on. We were so close to the buildings that I could see people in their apartments.

Inside the terminal I jogged down one of those seemingly endless corridors, hoping the activity would revive me. But I still felt achy ten minutes later when I passed through customs and into the greeting hall, and then walked fifty feet to a door marked HOTEL TRANSPORTA- TION. I gave my name to a dispatcher, who looked on his list and immediately spoke into a two-way radio. Within half a minute a vin- tage Rolls-Royce Phantom was at the curb. The chauffeur, a moon- faced man, unusually portly for a Chinese, wearing a black cap with a visor and a gray suit, got out. "Welcome to Hong Kong," he said in a manner suggesting they were probably the only English words he knew. He opened the back door, smiled and bowed and even held me by the elbow as I got into the car. As I settled into the backseat, I won- dered why the driver had made me so immediately uncomfortable. It wasn't until we cleared the terminal building that I had it figured out. The Asian man driving the car in which Maggie Winehouse had been abducted had, by her description, been overweight. The Asian man driving the car that had pushed me down Hyde Street had been over- weight. A heavy Chinese man stands out. Guilt by association.

On my last trip to Hong Kong in the mid-eighties, there'd been a huge billboard just outside Kai Tak Airport, at least sixty feet high, featuring a Marlboro man in an immense Stetson, blowing smoke rings. As we cleared the airport I saw that the sign was still there. See- ing it made me think about that mountain man in Bear Valley who'd towed Britt and me to the highway after we'd been marooned. And that made me think—and feel guilty and worried all over again— about Britt and the trouble I'd caused her. Whoever my antagonist was, he knew exactly how to play me. After three threats against me, I was still hanging in there, but a single threat against a loved one had made me want to turn and run.

A loved one. Yes. Absolutely. No question on that score any longer. Her absence alone had clarified that even before the threat. Whatever ingredients add up to love—attraction, admiration, compatibility, comfort—I felt them all. More than that, I ached without her. Imag- ine being deprived forever of the simple presence of the person you cherish most, and that's the feeling I'd carried with me to Hong Kong. Britt belonged in my life. I wanted her in my life. But the obligation I'd explained to her in Bear Valley was ironclad: the need to make a dif- ference in order to put Elaine to rest.

One break, I told myself, I need one break.

Once the Rolls reached the other side of the open space around Kai Tak, the city became a blur of buildings that seemed no more than an arm's length from the winding and dipping elevated freeways on which we sped in the darkness. At some point I dozed off, awaking only after the car had stopped and the chauffeur was standing beside the open door, beckoning me with a smile.

Next to the chauffeur stood a young Caucasian, no more than twenty-seven, wearing a morning coat and striped pants, summoned, no doubt, from behind the reception desk by a call from the Rolls. "Welcome to the Mandarin Oriental, Mr. Tobias," he said. He had the fair skin and accent of a Swiss German. He led me through a lobby whose harmonious decor, restful colors, cool marble and sense of order exactly fit my needs, and into an elevator. By the time I'd answered his questions about my trip, we were on the fourteenth floor, where he led me down an empty corridor. In another minute we were inside a small corner suite with a view of Victoria Harbor, its surface twinkling with the lights of countless ships, and beyond the harbor, Kowloon. A dozen yellow roses, a bottle of white wine chilling in a bucket and a tray of small pastries sat on a coffee table. I signed the registration card, and then the young man was gone. No registration lines for the wealthy, a fact I'd almost forgotten. Without bothering to open my bag, I took off my clothes, got under the covers of a king-sized bed and, twenty-seven hours after waking up in Vancouver, fell asleep at once.

Eight hours later, at nine Wednesday morning Hong Kong time—I'd lost Tuesday crossing the international dateline—my phone rang. "Good morning, Captain Tobias," a young woman's voice said. "Welcome to Hong Kong and the Mandarin Oriental. This is Angela Smith, the hotel's public relations director."

"Good morning," I said, my voice fuzzy with sleep, but my mind clearing quickly enough to wonder what the hotel's public relations director wanted with me, and how she knew my rank, since I'd deliberately avoided any mention of it in making my reservations.

"Oh, dear, have I *awakened* you?" she said, stressing the next to last word, as I'd so often heard Londoners do. Her inflection suggested that Angela Smith had gone to English schools but was not herself English, and that she had spoken another language, probably Chinese, all her life.

"It's okay," I said. "I'm glad you did. What can I do for you?"

"The question is, what can I do for *you?*"

Even with two cups of coffee in me, I would have found this conversation puzzling. "I'm sorry," I said, "but you've got me at a disadvantage. I don't quite understand why you'd want to look after me."

She laughed merrily. "That's part of my job, Captain, to look after famous guests."

"I'm hardly a famous guest."

"Maybe not elsewhere, but in Hong Kong you are famous, I assure you."

What now? I asked myself. "I haven't the vaguest idea why," I said.

"Then let me explain it to you," she said, that same cheerful lilt in her voice. "How about a cup of coffee in, say, half an hour? Will that give you enough time?"

"Half an hour's fine."

"Good," she said. "I'll have it sent up."

Was *everyone* tracking my whereabouts? I wondered as I showered.

Angela Smith, who obviously did not wait on invitations, arrived as the coffee did, exactly half an hour later, during which time I'd noted that the bottle of wine, an expensive Meursault, had come from her. She was the kind of woman whose entry would drop the noise level in the bar of the Hong Kong Club across Statue Square from my hotel. Her face was classically oval: a large brow under short, shining, jet-black hair, the characteristic almond eyes of a Chinese woman, high cheeks, a small nose, full lips and a lean jaw. It wasn't any single feature, or even all of her features in combination, that made her so instantly memorable. It was her expression, intense and quizzical and yet empathic, the eyes enlarged, the eyebrows raised, as though she couldn't quite get over the perpetual surprises life provided. Her lustrous ivory skin was set off by a white silk blouse under a double-breasted blue blazer. A short, tight gray flannel skirt and gray high-heeled shoes completed the striking picture. Over the next several days I would find her a disturbing woman, as deceptive and changeable as a volcano, dormant one minute, exploding the next. She exuded competence and professionalism, and seemed more than capable of holding her own in this far more chauvinistic world than the one I came from, imperfect though it still was. Yet when we shook hands, she laid hers in mine so softly it was as though a butterfly had landed on my palm.

Angela had ordered not just coffee but juice, breads and scrambled eggs and bacon, which I attacked with gusto, surprised that I was so hungry after the array of rich food on the flight. The waiter poured coffee for Angela but offered her nothing else; I surmised that he'd been in this situation many times before and was accustomed to her habits. Without being bidden to, he handed her the check, which she quickly signed. "So what makes me so famous?" I asked as soon as he'd left.

"This is Hong Kong, Captain, where we've all been compelled to think about emigrating by 1997. I'm sure I don't have to tell you that every second resident has at least thought of relocating to San Francisco. Many of us already have relatives there. So anything that happens in San Francisco that relates to the Asian community is big news in Hong Kong. That terrible story about the TV reporter was very disturbing to us, particularly since her attackers were Asians. And then that business about the bank and your suspension—"

"*That* made the news here?"

"Oh, yes. Jimmy Chang came from Hong Kong."

"You'd heard of Jimmy Chang?" I said, amazed.

"We hadn't. But we have now."

"And that's how you heard of me?"

"Small world, isn't it?" she said, her eyes fastened on my face, the power of her concern more than making up for whatever small imperfections in her features kept her from being truly beautiful.

"Well, well." I couldn't have been told worse news. "Tell me about Angela Smith," I said, making conversation to cover my distress.

Suddenly, Angela's lips parted into a devastating smile. "As in what's a full-blooded Chinese woman doing with the name Smith? And where did my English accent come from?"

I doubt that there's a man alive who wouldn't have been stirred by that smile. I laughed, in spite of my mood. "As in those things."

"My parents were Hong Kong Chinese. My father was killed in an automobile accident when I was two. A year later my mother married an Englishman named Smith, who adopted me. I was educated in English-language schools here, and spent two years at school in London." She paused just long enough to smile again. "Is there anything else you'd like to know?"

It was a challenge, no mistaking. I was being teased. And that smile seemed, if not an invitation, at least an introduction. But I couldn't think about that now. "There is," I said. "Are you going to tell any of your friends in the media that I'm in Hong Kong?"

The smile disappeared. She was instantly all business. "Not if you don't want me to."

"It would be the last thing I'd want you to do."

"I understand." To judge by her serious look, she seemed to. I could only hope that she did.

She left a few minutes later, after putting her hand in mine in that same light-as-a-butterfly manner.

The next days were as discouraging as any I've ever experienced. I'd counted heavily on my personal relationship with Inspector Dennis Hampton of the RHKP, the man I'd contacted for information on Clarence Ho, to break through the bureaucratic barriers. An Englishman my age with a well-developed palate, Dennis had been to San Francisco several times since we'd met at that big conference in Honolulu on Asian crime, and I'd wined and dined him. But it was clear from the moment we shook hands that all those dinners weren't going to get me what I wanted now.

Dennis confirmed what I'd most feared, that his boss had received a fax from Chief Doyle, requesting that I not be assisted "in the interest of future interdepartmental harmony." His boss had issued explicit instructions that the request was to be honored. "Nothing I can do, old man," Dennis said apologetically.

In the next two days I tried every member of the RHKP with whom I'd had any dealings, no matter how slight, hoping that one of them was out of the loop and hadn't heard. Everyone I contacted was willing to see me but not one of them was willing to help me. They wouldn't so much as look at the photographs of Jimmy Chang I'd brought to our meetings. "It'd be my ass if I got caught," one of them told me.

After being rebuffed by the RHKP, I tried an end run, contacting a doughty official of the crime commission set up in the mid-seventies following disclosures of massive corruption within the RHKP. "I'll be happy to listen to anything you have to tell me," he said, "but I can't open any doors for you. Couldn't if I wanted to. It's the law." The same speech I'd heard in San Francisco, just a different accent.

When an American police official makes an investigation in a foreign country, protocol obliges him to inform the U.S. embassy or consulate. Since I wasn't representing the San Francisco Police Department, I obviously couldn't do that. I managed to talk the Immigration and Naturalization man at the consulate into having lunch with me on Friday, but he offered friendly advice and no more. To fill the awkward silence, he gave me a statistical picture of the flight from Hong Kong that had already begun in anticipation of the takeover of the colony by the People's Republic of China in 1997. "There's an exodus," he said, "and anyone who says there isn't is lying. It was twenty thousand a year in the mid-eighties. By '90 it was more than fifty thousand a year. Last year it was fifty-four thousand. Between now and '97, they could lose another six hundred thousand of the finest people they've got, most of them middle-class, upwardly mobile, professional and moneyed. What society can survive that?"

Interesting, but not information I'd come for.

By four o'clock on Friday afternoon, my third full day in Hong Kong, I'd run out of ideas. I must have looked as discouraged as I felt, because Angela Smith came up to me as I walked through the lobby on my way to the elevators. She took one look at me, frowned deeply and said with typical directness, "You look positively wretched."

"Then, in this case, looks aren't deceiving."

"How can I help?"

My first thought was that she couldn't. My second thought made me reach out and touch her arm. "I'd like to talk about that. Can I buy you a drink?"

"You can't buy it, but I'll have a drink with you."

We walked up a flight of stairs to the Clipper Lounge, on a mezzanine overlooking the lobby, and took a table by the railing, not far from the top part of an immense Christmas tree that stretched from the floor of the lobby to the ceiling. It was as heavily and ornately decorated as any tree I've ever seen. I had a blip of a memory of Mother's party, and Britt's reaction to her tree, but pushed it away. "That tree is worthy of Rockefeller Center," I said.

"We're actually quite proud of it," Angela replied. "It's a forty-foot fir, shipped from Norway. We contract with the same people every year."

A waiter appeared. I ordered a Tsing Tao beer, Angela a glass of white wine. "You were right about my being famous," I said. "It's the wrong kind of fame. It's closed all doors. I'm going to have to take some chances. If you know any journalists who specialize in crime and would be willing to set me up with them, you'd be helping me a great deal."

"I'd be more than willing to if I knew any. I don't." She thought for a moment. "But if you want a well-connected journalist, someone who might lead you to someone, there's no one better than George Golden, the Hong Kong manager of Associated Press. He's been here forever."

"Is he discreet?"

"Totally. Would you like me to set up a meeting?"

"As soon as possible."

"I'll just be a minute," she said. She returned in five. "He'll be at the FCC in an hour. Says he'll be happy to help you." She reached for my hand and made another butterfly landing. "Now, do me a favor, will you?" she said, her intent, quizzical, empathic gaze turned full on.

"Tell me," I said.

"Breathe deeply."

I've had some unusual requests from women, but that one was right up there. I spent a few seconds taking in Angela, and decided she was even prettier than I'd thought. She was also a knockout dresser; today's costume was a tan gabardine double-breasted suit with a long jacket and short skirt. "I look pretty uptight, do I?" I said.

She flashed that devastating smile. "I'll stick with 'wretched.' "

I closed my eyes, and took several slow, deep breaths. Only as I felt my muscles relax did I realize how tight I'd been. When I opened my eyes, Angela was staring at me, looking pleased.

George Golden appeared to be in his fifties but looked as though he might expire of a heart attack at any moment. He was standing at the huge oval bar of the Foreign Correspondents Club, just inside the entrance, exactly where Angela had told me he'd be. "Look for the reddest face under the whitest hair in the place," she'd said. "He'll be wearing a tan gabardine suit and a blue shirt and a regimental striped tie, and wiping a very wet brow with a pale blue handkerchief." She'd been right on every detail.

"Ah, you're Tobias," Golden said as I walked up to him, the envelope containing the photographs of Jimmy Chang in my left hand. He was American, but years of living among the English had tinged his accent. "Been reading about you. Have a drink." As he signaled the bartender I looked around. The bar was in the center of a long, rectangular room, its walls of thick concrete; I'd read somewhere that the building, two stories high and dwarfed by skyscrapers, had once been a dairy company's icehouse. The bar was jammed, the patrons, mostly men, standing two and three deep, speaking loudly to one another in order to be heard above the din they themselves were creating. Golden's was not the only reddened face in the room. These were practiced drinkers.

"Noisy, eh?" Golden said, grinning, leaning close to my ear.

"Is it always this busy?"

"Only on Friday nights. Everyone starts the weekend here. If you think it's crowded now, wait an hour. You'll hardly be able to move. That's why the fights almost never end in a knockdown—no place to fall."

"You have a lot of fights?"

"It wouldn't be Friday at the FCC without one."

"I've never seen so many journalists in one place."

"Oh, they're not all journalists," Golden said quickly. "The journalists are the ones at this end, along with the PR people. The other end's lawyers and RHKP inspectors."

"And on the sides?"

"Riffraff—stockbrokers and corporate VPs." Golden laughed at his remark.

"But they're all members?"

"Oh, yes. We couldn't stay open otherwise."

The bartender came at last. As I had at the Mandarin I ordered a Tsing Tao beer. Golden ordered a Scotch and water even though the one he was drinking was still half full. "So you're a friend of Angela's?"

"Not a friend. We just met. I'm staying at the Mandarin."

"Best PR person I've ever known. Absolutely no bullshit. Tells it like it is. Knows everyone in Hong Kong and everything that's going on. She can be very helpful if she likes you, and it sounded as though she likes you." He nodded for emphasis, a not very subtle suggestion that there was more to what he was saying than the words themselves conveyed.

Our drinks arrived. Golden emptied his old drink in two swallows, then picked up the new one. "Good luck," he said.

"Good luck," I repeated, raising my glass to his.

"So what can I do for you?"

"That depends on whether you're going to feel the need to file a story about my presence in Hong Kong."

"You're not a story just because you're here, old man, not until you do something. I'll take that back. You'd be a story if you were agreeable to an interview. But I gather from Angela that that's the last thing you want."

"Right. I'm hoping we can keep this conversation to ourselves."

"You have my word."

A stranger's word means virtually nothing, a heavy-drinking stranger's word even less. I had only Angela's appraisal to go on— the word of another stranger. A terrible position to be in, but I had no alternative. "The people I've dealt with over the years aren't able to help me," I said, trying to keep it simple, hoping that would do.

"Too sticky, eh?" Golden said. He seemed to be satisfied.

"Exactly."

"So you need someone who's off the beaten path, someone you haven't dealt with before."

"Right. Someone who's not only willing to help me but is in a position to be able to."

Golden nodded his understanding, then looked away from me and toward the other end of the bar. His eyes narrowed. "Ah!" he said with sudden energy. "We can fix you up right here. Come on." He motioned for me to follow, setting off through the crowd. A minute later we were standing in front of a husky man my age, maybe a few years older, just over six feet tall, whose flushed face was almost as red as Golden's. "This is Detective Inspector Dirk Richards of the RHKP," Golden said to me. "A good Aussie." To Richards, he said, "And this is that chap from San Francisco we've all been reading about. Zachary Tobias. *Captain* Zachary Tobias."

"Ah, yes," Richards said, extending his hand and shaking mine with good strength. "Sorry about your problems. Know a little about that sort of thing myself."

"The captain needs some help, Dirk," Golden said. "Your chaps haven't been very helpful."

"A bit leery, are they?" Richards said, grinning. "Happy to help if I can. You Yanks are the world's most generous people. Gave me a free education."

"How's that?" I asked.

"Did a bit of running as a lad. University of Oregon gave me a track scholarship."

Somehow, I wasn't surprised. Despite his apparent love of drink, Richards had the setup of an athlete and radiated an athlete's energy and self-confidence. "What'd you run?" I asked.

"Quarter mile."

"You know, I think I remember you."

"Really? You did track and field, did you?"

"No, played football. But I followed track. Went to all the meets. Didn't you win the Pac-10 one year?"

"I did," Richards said, greatly pleased. "In '71. Who'd you play for?"

"Cal."

He peered at me. "Tobias, Tobias. You know, I think I remember *you.*"

We laughed together. I was immediately comforted.

We turned as one to Golden. "Well, I'll leave you two jocks to swap lies," he said, and headed back to the other end of the bar.

I turned back to Richards, and, with no hesitation, spent the next few minutes telling him everything I could about Jimmy Chang. "Unfortunately," I wound up, "I don't know his Chinese name." I held up the envelope. "All I have are some photographs."

Richards shrugged. "That's mighty slim, but we can at least have a go at it. Unofficially, mind you."

"I understand," I said, feeling instantly better than I had in days. But in the same moment I also felt a twinge of guilt. "I'm not getting you in trouble, am I?" I asked.

Richards smiled, and patted my arm. "Not as long as that directive about you hasn't reached our station, and it hadn't as of an hour ago."

"That's great," I said, exhaling with relief. "Where's your station, anyway?"

"Shatin. It's in the boonies north of Kowloon. Nice, quiet satellite town, filled with commuters, many of them Hong Kong–style yuppies."

I handed Richards the envelope. "I appreciate this."

"Haven't done anything yet," he said. "I assume you have copies."

"Oh, yes."

"Right, then." He put the envelope on the bar.

"Can I buy you a drink?"

"With pleasure," Richards said, beaming, his suddenly visible teeth showing the stains of tea or nicotine or both.

"What are you drinking?" I asked.

He laughed. "Just point to me. The bartender knows."

It took me two minutes to catch the bartender's eye. I pointed to Richards, and held up my own drink as well. The bartender nodded. Then I turned back to Richards.

"I could be wrong," he said, "but I think somebody at the other end of the bar is trying to get your attention."

I turned in the direction of his gaze. There was Gordon, waving and smiling.

The last time I'd heard from Gordon had been on the tape of my answering machine. His voice had been filled with contrition, and he'd sounded at an absolute loss. One minute with him in Hong Kong persuaded me that while he was still contrite, his hangdog manner had completely disappeared. He was once again the urbane, self-assured young anchorman on the rise he projected so successfully on the tube.

"Look," he said earnestly as our taxi drove us away from the FCC, "I meant what I said when I told you I'd make it up to you. We're both here for the same reason, and I'm in a position to help you. Why not throw in together?"

"*You're* in a position to help *me*?" I just laughed. The guy's self-confidence was off the chart.

"That's right." His voice was as composed as the look on his face.

But my mind was filled with angry memories of my run-in with Gordon at his studio, and the misery he'd caused me. Nothing he'd done since then had given me any reason to believe that he wouldn't make another misstep. In the meantime, the stakes had risen. A mistake at this point could be fatal.

"What makes you so sure I need your help, Gordon?" I asked, watching him closely.

"I have it on good authority that no one's willing to help you chase down Jimmy Chang as long as you're on suspension."

I wasn't a good enough actor to cover my surprise. I waited a few seconds, until I was sure I could keep my voice steady. "Who's your 'good authority'?"

"Can't say." He turned in his seat until he was facing me, and looked at me beseechingly. "Trust me, Zack. *Please.*"

The taxi had reached the downtown area. I stared at the store windows, filled with high-fashion clothing and the latest in sportswear. Then I turned to Gordon, who was waiting expectantly. "What makes you think you can help me?" I said, recognizing as I did that even my question was an acknowledgment of how weak my position was.

"I found out about the Golden Door Trading Company, didn't I?"

"What'd you find out in Vancouver?" I asked him abruptly.

He didn't miss a beat. "More than you did."

I had thought to surprise him with my knowledge of his trip to Vancouver. Instead, I was the one who blinked.

"How did you know I was in Vancouver?" I had to ask.

"Same source."

"And you're not going to tell me who it is?"

"I'll tell you if you agree to work together."

"Why do you want me to work with you if you're so sure you're getting more stuff than I am?"

Gordon leaned back against the seat of the taxi. "Because I don't know the big picture. Even if I get what I'm after, I may not be able to put two and two together." For about a second, I had a glimpse of the vulnerable young man who'd come to my apartment for help. And then a confident smile enveloped his face. "Plus, we're not competitors—and for the moment, you're not even a cop."

It was a measure of how desperate I was by this point that I was even listening to Gordon's argument. By himself, he was of no value, but someone good was helping him, and that person might be able to help me provided he was someone I could trust. "Before I'd even consider working with you, Gordon," I said with a sigh, "you'd *have* to tell me who your source is."

Gordon shook his well-tended head. "Sorry," he said. "It'll have to be the other way around."

The taxi had wound its way into downtown Hong Kong. I told the driver to let me off. "Have a nice weekend," I said to Gordon as I prepared to step out of the cab.

"If you're getting out here because you don't want me to know you're staying at the Mandarin Oriental, you're wasting your time," Gordon said impatiently, clearly miffed.

"Be careful," I said as I shut the door.

I could not imagine where Gordon was getting his information. I could only worry about who besides him knew my every move.

F or the second time that day I met Angela as I passed through the
hotel lobby. This time, I suspected, it wasn't a coincidence. It probably
hadn't been the first time, either. I began to think that George
Golden's appraisal of the situation had been right on; she did seem to
like me—and, as I'd already learned, she didn't wait on invitations.

"How did it go?" she asked, coming so close to me she had to tilt
her head to talk. For the early evening she'd added an orange silk
scarf around her neck, which she'd tucked into her tan gabardine
jacket. The color contrasted wonderfully with her black hair.

"Your Mr. Golden was very helpful," I said.

"Good. I'm glad. Are you through working for the day?"

The question had the music of a prelude in it. Her wide-open eyes,
gazing steadily into my own, and her slightly raised eyebrows further encouraged an affirmative answer. "I guess I am," I couldn't
help saying.

"Do you have plans for dinner?"

"I don't," I admitted, knowing where this was going, not certain
that I should go with it.

"Then would you like to have dinner with me?"

It was suddenly, giddily tempting. It had been years since I'd been in Hong Kong. I had no desire to be alone in a city I scarcely knew. Angela was bright, attentive, beguiling. "Could we make it my party?" I said. "I'd like to reciprocate your kindness."

"Whatever pleases you." It struck me that she wasn't just being polite; her steady look and earnest tone told me that she meant it.

"I'll tell you what would really please me," I said after thinking a minute, "I'd like to get on the Star Ferry and go to Kowloon and have dinner at Spring Deer."

Angela uttered a little shriek. "Perfect."

"It's still there?"

"Of course. I'm surprised that you know it."

"I had an epic meal there seven years ago. But I remember it as being tremendously popular. Do you think we can get in?"

"I'll take care of it. Wait here." She returned in two minutes. "All set," she said. "The headwaiter said we'd have to be there in thirty minutes. Do you need to go upstairs?"

"I'm fine."

"Then," she said with that sudden, explosive smile, "let's go."

From the Mandarin it's a three-minute walk through a tunnel to the Star Ferry, which connects downtown Hong Kong to Kowloon on the other side of Victoria Harbor. We sat on the first-class deck. As we edged away from the protection of the terminal, a cool wind began to whip through the open sides of the ferry. In another few minutes we were in the center of the harbor, which even at this hour teemed with boat traffic. I turned to look back at Hong Kong Island, and was instantly struck by the splendor that night conveys on the city. By day the skyline is a jumble of contrasting shapes and sizes pressed hard against one another; by night it's like a mountain range strung with Christmas lights. Somewhere up there, obscured in the dark, was Victoria Peak, where I'd stood for an hour one day in 1987, two years after Elaine's death, looking down at the city and the harbor, ready to give away years of my own life if I could have had her next to me again.

Seven minutes after leaving central Hong Kong, the ferry reached the Ocean Terminal in Kowloon. A taxi took us to Spring Deer. It was exactly as I remembered it, up a narrow, uninviting flight of steps and into a long, brightly lit, narrow room bereft of decor and filled with huge tables occupied by animated, contented-looking Chinese. At first glance, it appeared that I was the only Caucasian in the room. Angela spoke to the headwaiter in Chinese—the first time I'd heard her use the language. The headwaiter denied that we had a reservation, and said they were fully booked. That, too, was exactly as I'd remembered it. While his back was turned, Angela rolled her eyes at me, and translated what he'd said. "Don't worry," she added, "I know this game." When the headwaiter turned back, she insisted she not only had made a reservation thirty minutes earlier but had spoken to him personally. He denied it. She told him that, as the public relations director of the Mandarin Oriental, she would have to counsel the hotel's concierge not to send guests to a restaurant that did not honor reservations. The headwaiter said that would be fine. She told him we refused to leave. He said that, too, would be fine, just stand out of the way.

"It's always the same," she said to me while he was seating another party. "I'll wear him down."

A minute later the headwaiter was back. While Angela wasn't looking, I slipped twenty Hong Kong dollars—about $2.50 U.S.—into his hand. A minute after that we were seated at a table for two squeezed between two massive round tables, each packed with extended Chinese families.

"What did I tell you?" Angela said triumphantly.

"Terrific," I said.

"Shall I order?"

"My party," I said, raising a hand. A moment later a waiter arrived. I asked him in Chinese what three dishes he would order if he knew he could have only one meal in his life at Spring Deer. He proposed Peking duck, shrimp with chili sauce and scallops with deep-fried vegetables. I nodded my agreement, then turned to Angela, who, mouth agape, regarded me with astonished eyes.

"What other tricks do you do?" she asked.

"That's about it."

"I'll bet it's not."

It's possible that my desires were affecting my interpretation, but the remark seemed sexually charged. So did the rest of the evening. Dinner—every bit as good as I remembered it—was a subdued version of the famous eating scene in the film *Tom Jones*. Angela would lock her eyes onto mine as she was about to put food into her mouth, then continue to stare at me as she chewed, smiling with unalloyed pleasure. Her actions aroused me; I stared back as I ate, but I didn't smile. I was too confused. My groin was telling me one thing, my head and heart another.

After dinner we walked to the Regent Hotel and sat in the capacious lobby bar, its wraparound window boasting the best view of Victoria Harbor and Hong Kong Island in all Kowloon. The music was soft, the light muted. Angela slipped her soft hand into mine. Butterflies again. "Have you ever been with an Asian woman, Zack?" she said.

"No," I answered.

"Once you have, you'll never go back."

"Why is that?" I asked, as startled by her boldness as I was curious.

"It's not something I can explain. It has to be experienced." She didn't lower her eyes as she said this. She looked straight into mine.

As I've described Angela's actions she sounds like a predator. That's not the way it was. My eyes and expressions and body language had to have been sending her encouraging signals because it was impossible not to respond to her. But the thought of Britt held me back, and Angela, I'm sure, had sensed the reticence I was feeling, despite my potent attraction to her, and was too honest to be coy. I appreciated that. I must have taken thirty seconds to reply. "Assuming that was an invitation, it's as tempting and flattering as any I've ever had. I don't want to seem ungrateful—"

"But there's someone else."

"Yes."

"Tell me."

"That would be tacky."

"If you'd volunteered it, it would have been. I asked."

So I told her about Britt, haltingly at first, then with increasing confidence as I recognized how genuine her interest was. To explain Britt, I had to talk about Elaine. With Britt, who had a stake in the outcome, it had been torture to do that; with Angela, who didn't, it was therapy. It was ten minutes before I'd finished. "So now you know more than you ever wanted to know about Zack Tobias," I said.

"No. That's not true. I know there's more, and I want to know it.

I'll tell you what. Whatever you're doing here, I'm sure you can't do anything about it on a Saturday. Have you ever been to Macao?"

"Never."

"Then why don't we go?"

"I don't gamble."

"Nor do I. But it's a nice trip by hydrofoil, and there's a beautiful place for lunch. We'll be back in time for dinner, in case you have plans."

She was right. There was nothing I could do tomorrow, or, in fact, anytime after that, until I heard from Dirk Richards. It was not a reality I wished to dwell upon—which I'd undoubtedly do if left to myself. "You're on," I said.

Everything was as advertised: a swift, smooth hydrofoil ride, an hour in length, across a coral sea and between countless small, rocky islands; a lunch of bacalhau ao forno, a Portuguese codfish and potato dish, accompanied by a cold, biting Chablis, on the tree-shaded terrace of the Pousada de São Tiago, a traditional Portuguese inn built atop the foundations of a seventeenth-century fortress; and a prolonged sexual encounter that added a whole new dimension to my experience.

It was Angela who orchestrated that experience, but the invitation to it had been mine. From the moment we'd met late on Saturday morning at the hydrofoil port, I sensed she'd decided that if anything of the kind was to happen, it would be at my initiative. She was casually dressed in a soft black leather jacket, a pink shirt and designer jeans, and her mood seemed as laid-back. She let me buy the tickets. On the hydrofoil she sat silently next to me. I'd once read an astute, if simple, definition of Zen as "the art of doing what you're doing." Halfway through the hydrofoil ride it occurred to me that Angela was doing exactly that, focusing on the moment, not diluting it by reading or speaking.

I'll say this much for having your life threatened: it gives you a taste for the present. Suddenly, the moment clicked in for me as well. Accident had given me an opportunity for an intimate encounter with a splendid woman made up of many complex layers, of whose existence I had been unaware only four days before, and I wasn't going to let it pass.

I willed my cares from my mind. And I willed Britt from my mind along with them—Britt, who, not two weeks earlier, had told me that I didn't go after women, making them come to me instead. That characterization had made me uncomfortable; for all I know, what happened with Angela was partly a consequence of a desire to prove Britt wrong. Put all that aside, and you come to the most important factor, that urge building in my groin. I'd had no sex for a month. I had no idea when another opportunity would arise—or, given the way things were going, whether another one ever would. I hadn't asked Britt to abstain, and didn't expect her to. I don't believe she had any such expectations of me.

Throughout lunch I was as alert to Angela's presence as she was to mine. Once again, eating became a restrained form of foreplay. I'm certain she sensed what was building in me, because when I signed the restaurant check with a room number, took our wine bottle and led her up a flight of interior stairs, she didn't seem surprised.

I'd arranged for the room during lunch, after excusing myself on the pretext of going to the men's room. "You are in luck, sir," the receptionist had said. "We had a cancellation. Normally, we are completely booked every weekend." The room, he'd told me, was the best in the house. Furnished with heavy, dark rosewood pieces, it was directly over a swimming pool two floors below, set in natural rocks, beyond which was the West River Delta.

From the moment we entered the room, I took my cues from Angela. She undressed me, and I her. Her body surprised me. Given her vigor and forthright nature, I'd expected it to be compact, even hard. But it was as delicate as her touch. She gave me a moment to admire her, then drew me into the shower, where we soaped and rinsed each other with infinite care. After we had dried each other, she drew me to the bed, produced a small bottle of perfumed oil from her purse and massaged me, first my temples and the back of the neck, then every part of me save my genitals, down to my toes. Gone was the butterfly touch; in its stead were the firm, sure strokes of a practiced masseuse. When it was my turn, I tried to emulate her deftness. I doubt that I did, but I wouldn't have known it from her murmurs of appreciation. When I finished, I began to mount her, but she gently held me back, then sat up, crossed her legs, and bade me do the same.

"Breathe deeply," she said, just as she had in the Clipper Lounge of the Mandarin. Only this time she whispered, adding, "Fill your belly with air." And that is what we did, for minutes on end, until I felt a sense of peace I had never experienced during sex. Angela seemed to know what I was feeling, because she smiled and nodded, then whispered another instruction. "Squeeze your crotch," she said. Seconds passed. "Again," she said. I could tell by the contractions in her lower belly that she was doing it too. We did it in unison, any number of times, until I felt I had struck some untapped pool of desire. At that point, I wanted desperately to take her in my arms, to kiss every part of her, and then to go inside her, but she held me off yet again. At some point she'd brought the wine and two glasses within arm's reach. Now she poured it and handed me a glass. We drank together.

At last, she lay back on the bed. I stood over her, thinking that no body ever need be more beautiful. She beckoned me to kneel astride her, just above her hips. When I'd done that, she took my right hand and placed it first over her heart, then onto her head and forehead and throat. Grasping my other hand, she pulled both of them to her ears, and then to her breasts, where she guided my fingers around her dark, erect nipples, moving them in a clockwise motion. A gentle push from Angela was my cue to move to her right side. Once I had done so, she guided my hands to her stomach, and then to her legs and down past her knees to her feet, rising from the pillow as she did. At last, she placed my hands on her inner thighs, then opened her legs and put my right hand on her genitals. By this point, an hour had passed, and I had totally absorbed her rhythms. I parted the lips of her vulva, and in the same slow, methodical manner I'd been using, stroked her until she smiled, then bent to appease my hunger.

For the third time I tried to enter her, and for the third time she held me off and then, to my astonishment, rose from the bed, placed me where she had been and repeated every caress on my body she had guided me through, ending with her lips softly around my cock.

By this point, I had lost all sense of time, and urgency, as well. My erection had never flagged but I no longer felt the need to culminate. It was then, at last, that she mounted me and put me inside her, and lay on top of me, twining her fingers with mine, placing her face so close to mine that our breath mingled, as she caressed me with her eyes. When I began to move beneath her, she bore down on me, smiled and shook her head, an unmistakable set of signals that I was to lie still. Feeling her vagina close around me, I moved my hands to her buttocks and pressed her against me.

And then her contractions began, powerful, rhythmic contractions that enveloped me as never before. It was all happening in there, without strain or external movement. After minutes that seemed like hours, we rolled onto our sides, still linked, our fingers still intertwined, our eyes locked together.

And then the heat began, first in the genitals, then spreading slowly down my legs and through my torso and into my arms and head. The intensity built and built until lightning suddenly burst within me. Angela's cries assured me that her experience had matched mine.

We slept for an hour. When I awoke, her mouth was around my cock. I lifted her until she was straddling my head, then feasted on her genitals. When we coupled, it was once again with that same timeless rhythm.

Never have I been the lover I was in those hours. Every few minutes Angela would moan and shudder, then, after a brief rest, change positions and resume her movements. Emptied of anxiety, I felt I could have continued forever. There came a point when she no longer wanted me to. She rode me to a climax that had me screaming.

We had dinner in our room, and began our lovemaking again as soon as the trays were removed. Through the night, we slept and loved.

The next morning we returned to Hong Kong, sitting close, not speaking, our arms touching, our hands linked. I had no way of knowing whether Angela was typical of Asian women. I was certain only that I had spent the night with a sexual genius who brought to the bed a singular attitude to match her special knowledge, one that exalted her smallness, her tenderness and her power to give to a man what he could never get alone.

For all that, I knew that my father had been right: Sex with a woman one didn't love, even the incomparable sex proffered by an Angela, could only satisfy one's urges. Sex with one's beloved, on the other hand, was the most gratifying experience in life. The only sex I'd had like that since Elaine had been with Britt. To have it again, I would have to commit to her. To commit to her, I would have to exorcise Elaine's ghost. To exorcise Elaine's ghost, I would have to change the world. Exposing a conspiracy to move millions—perhaps billions of dollars in illegal triad assets—from Hong Kong to San Francisco would qualify.

Piece of cake.

21

On Monday morning Gordon called and insisted he had to see me. He would not be denied. "You can't afford not to see me," he said. "I told you I'd make it up to you, and now I'm in a position to come through." His voice rang with conviction. I was still waiting for that one break that would gain me entry into the inner mysteries of this case. It sounded as though Gordon was already inside. I couldn't imagine how a newsman with no knowledge of investigatory reporting had managed that. But Gordon's double negative was right on; I couldn't afford not to see him. "There's a restaurant in Central called Heaven's Gate," I said. "Can you meet me there at noon?"

"I'll be there," he said in an instant.

"Just a minute. Don't you want directions?"

"I'll find it," he said. "Gotta go."

He arrived half an hour late, and I could see him in the entry, looking impatiently and despairingly into the vast dining room, its five hundred seats occupied by Chinese, mostly men, whose collective noise approached the decibel level of a George Lucas sound track. I stood and waved my arms, instantly drawing the attention of a fifth of the patrons.

"Sorry," Gordon said when he reached the table, but he didn't look it. "I got lost, and I couldn't find anyone who spoke English who also knew where Heaven's Gate was."

I couldn't resist the dig. "How does it make you feel to realize that I speak more Chinese than you do?" I said as I pulled out a chair for him.

"How's your Hebrew?" he countered as we sat.

I laughed in spite of myself. "*Touché,*" I said. "Do you speak any Chinese at all?"

"Hey, I'm third-generation American," he said with a shrug. "My *parents* hardly speak Chinese."

"But doesn't it feel strange to be in a country populated by your own people and not speak its language?" I said, determined to make my point.

"No stranger than you being in Israel and not speaking Hebrew," he insisted, obviously just as determined as I was.

I felt suddenly uneasy, but before I could figure out why, a waiter arrived with a pot of tea and hovered over us, waiting to take our order. He was tall and thin, and appeared to be in his fifties, and there were tiny craters in his face, as though he had once suffered from acne or had had a terrible bout of chicken pox. I wouldn't have noticed these details except that he seemed so impatient. "There's a dish I had here seven years ago and never forgot," I said to Gordon. "It's made with eel, mushrooms and a ton of minced garlic. How does that sound?"

"Terrible," Gordon said, wrinkling his nose, and squinting. "You want to know the truth? I don't like Chinese food that much. I'm strictly meat and potatoes. Order whatever you want. I may not eat anything. I'm too excited."

If I was about to find out that Gordon had accomplished what I hadn't been able to, I would need to console myself. I ordered the eel, and diced chicken with cashews, garlic and red chili.

The waiter had seemed to stiffen when I'd addressed him in Chinese. He'd drawn his head back, and looked at me in astonishment, as though this was the first time he'd ever heard a round eye speak Chinese—odd for Hong Kong. "No soup?" he mumbled. "Soup good. Hot and sour. Best in Hong Kong." He fidgeted as he spoke, and kept looking over his shoulder.

"Okay," I said, "a cup of hot and sour soup."

With that, the waiter bolted, not even taking the time to collect our menus.

I started to pour some tea into Gordon's cup, but he waved me off. "Never touch the stuff," he said.

I laughed. "What kind of Chinaman are you, Gordon?" I said as I poured some for myself.

"Before I get to the main subject, I've got some news," Gordon said, ignoring my remark. "Maggie's back in San Francisco. She'd been hiding out in Mendocino at the home of her best friend. You'd have thought the police could have figured that out."

Before answering, I took a sip of tea. It seemed unusually strong, even for black tea, and had an unfamiliar taste. "The police weren't trying to figure it out," I said. "She hadn't been reported missing, so they weren't looking for her."

"Her parents should have figured it out, then. Or I should have."

"You can't think of everything, Gordon," I said with a tinge of sarcasm—not enough to register, apparently, because Gordon continued his report without a pause.

"The bad news is that she's getting a runaround from the station. The day she got back, she told them she wanted to do a series on Asians in the Bay Area. They said great, but guess what? When she tried to get a camera crew, they told her they couldn't spare one for a non-breaking story. Which is bullshit. The truth is they don't want her on camera anymore, which just fucking upsets me, man. I mean, they owe her more than they could ever pay her." He inhaled through clenched teeth. "If those bastards don't put her on camera, we will fucking sue them."

This was not the craven man who'd shown up, distraught and disheveled, at my apartment just a month before. "Wouldn't that put your network aspirations in jeopardy?" I asked, genuinely curious about Gordon's welfare for the first time since the broadcast that had led to my suspension.

Before Gordon could answer, the waiter arrived with my soup, scarcely breaking stride as he set it down, then hurrying off in the direction of the kitchen. One sip aroused my doubts that it was the best hot and sour soup in Hong Kong, but it did have a distinctive taste, one I couldn't place.

"Network's the last thing on my mind these days," Gordon said. "All I care about right now is finding the bastards who did this to Maggie." His voice rang with conviction. I could only wonder what had come over him.

"You sound like you might be making progress."

He smiled tightly. "Before the day's over, I'm going to know a lot about Jimmy Chang."

"Good for you," I said halfheartedly. I still couldn't quite bring myself to believe him.

"Throw in with me, Zack," Gordon said, pleading even more urgently than he had four days earlier, "and the information's yours."

I ate several more spoonfuls of soup before replying. "I haven't exactly been idle, Gordon. I may have the information myself before the day's over." I hoped I sounded more convincing than I felt.

"And then again, you may not," Gordon said. "But you will for sure if we're working together."

I finished the soup, then turned my head to look for our waiter. I was suddenly, unaccountably ravenous. Far from appeasing my hunger, the soup had seemed to reinforce it. My limbs had begun to tingle, and I was starting to feel dizzy, as though I was experiencing a sugar withdrawal. But I wanted the food for another reason. I needed a distraction. Gordon was getting to me. I could feel my resolve weakening.

A small army of waiters was hurrying through the tables, but I didn't see ours. I called out to a man who looked like a headwaiter, but my voice was lost in the din. After a minute, I gave up, and turned reluctantly back to Gordon. "Will you just tell me where you're getting your information?" I asked him for the umpteenth time.

Gordon shook his head. "Can't do it." There wasn't a trace of give in his voice.

"Then I'm telling you what I've already told you. I won't pool with you until and unless I know your source."

Gordon exhaled in exasperation. "Why is that so important as long as the information's good?"

A wave of weariness engulfed me. Too much uncertainty, too little action, I told myself. "Gordon," I said, speaking slowly not simply for emphasis but because along with my sudden torpor I was feeling a little thick-tongued, "I would love to know what you know, I really would. But unless I know your source, I have no way of knowing that the information's good."

"Can't do it," Gordon said. His features were so immobile they might have been cast in bronze.

"Then I can't even consider helping you."

Gordon reared back. "Hey, Zack, *I'm* offering to help *you.*"

I shook my head, as much to clear it as to express my disbelief. For a second, Gordon had gone out of focus. I had to force myself to keep my eyes open. "You amaze me, Gordon," I said with considerable effort. "Two weeks ago, *you* were begging me to help *you.* I'm really curious about how you turned things around."

"There's only one way to find out," Gordon said with finality.

"No sale." I reached for the teapot, thinking the tea might revive me, and poured myself another cup.

Gordon sighed. "It's your funeral."

I squinted at him from beneath heavy eyelids. "Let me give you some friendly advice," I said, my voice cold. "If you stay this cocky, it could be yours, and that's not a figure of speech. This isn't a game, Gordon. It's dangerous work. Be discreet. Be cautious. And don't wander off anywhere." I sat back, exhausted by the effort.

"Nothing to worry about," Gordon said serenely. "That's just not a problem." Now it was his turn to squint at me. "You okay?" he said. His tone suggested that he didn't think I was.

"Why?" I said.

"You look like you're falling asleep."

I shook my head again. "I must be having a sugar fit."

"It's more than that," Gordon said, leaning forward as I dropped my head. "You look like you need a doctor."

My breathing was heavy. I couldn't keep my eyes open. I heard myself mutter, "I'll be okay as soon as the food comes."

It was then that the realization materialized, as slowly as a freighter emerging through a fog: The soup. The tea. The fidgety waiter.

Getting to my feet was like coming up from a deep squat with four hundred pounds on my shoulders. I looked around the room. As before, dozens of waiters were moving through it, but our waiter wasn't one of them.

And then I saw him. He was at the far end of the restaurant, standing against a wall. He'd obviously been watching me, because seeing me rise, he bolted. "You son of a bitch," I muttered. I staggered into the aisle, bumping diners at the next table, and began weaving toward him. In my condition, I shouldn't have been able to catch him, but I had the angle on him, the same way I'd sometimes get it on scrambling quarterbacks, and each step either of us took closed the gap between us. I moved from table to table, reaching out for support, knocking over unsuspecting diners, chairs, food and finally a table. As I lurched after the waiter, I was dimly aware of a commotion behind me, growing louder and louder, and of Gordon's voice shouting, "Zack! Zack!"

Near the kitchen, I lunged for the waiter, missed him, then followed him through the swinging doors. He raced down the crowded kitchen aisles toward an exit. I stumbled after him, knocking over dishes and pushing cooks and waiters aside. He had half a dozen paces on me, but the exit door swung in and I caught up just as he opened it. I slammed into him so hard he was stunned, then I grabbed his arm, pulled it behind him and forced it up until he screamed. "What did you put in the soup?"

"I don't know," the waiter cried. "Man pay me to do it. Say he playing joke. Say you fall asleep."

"Who was he?"

"I don't know. Never saw before."

I put more pressure on his arm. He screamed again. "Was he Chinese?"

"Please! Please!" he cried.

"Was he?"

"Yes!"

I let go of his arm, took one look at the audience of dumbfounded cooks and waiters behind me, then staggered through the kitchen door and into an alley, convinced that I had to keep moving. My legs felt like logs. I must have looked like a crazy man, because crowds parted for me, and stared at me in silence. I ran on, running, I was sure, for my life, back to the hotel, where I believed I'd be safe. I should have been running to a hospital, because at the door of the hotel I collapsed.

They told me later that an ambulance raced me to Tang Shiu Kin Hospital in Wanchai, not far from Central, that my stomach was pumped, that I was out for three hours, that the doctors repeatedly tried to arouse me by pressing a knuckle into my sternum or a finger behind my ear, that each time they did I'd move away from the pain but wouldn't awake.

The first sight I remember is the face of a Chinese nurse. "How you feeling?" she said in English. I must have nodded off again, because I felt her patting me gently on the face. "Come on, wake up, someone need to see you."

It was Dirk Richards, the RHKP detective, displaying not a trace of the joviality of the man I'd drunk with at the bar of the Foreign Correspondents Club. His face was grim and his voice sounded constrained, even stiff. "Well," he said as he drew a chair up next to the bed, "you've given us a bit of a scare."

My first conscious thought was of yet another problem to worry about. "I got you into trouble, didn't I?" I said morosely.

He waved his hand, as though to banish the subject. "Not serious trouble," he said. "Rap on the knuckles. Nothing compared to the trouble you've apparently gotten yourself into."

"You got caught?" I insisted, pushing myself up in the bed, aware for the first time that I was wearing one of those skimpy hospital gowns, the kind that open at the back.

His mouth tightened for a minute. "Actually, what happened to you obliged me to bring my betters into it. Under the circumstances, it seemed like the right thing to do."

"I'm sure you're right," I said, relieved that he had. "Did you talk to the waiter?"

"Oh, yes. Indeed."

"Get anything?"

"Said a man paid him five hundred Hong Kong to slip a vial of liquid into your soup and your tea. Said the man told him it wouldn't hurt you, just make you so sleepy your head would fall into your soup. Just a joke, he said."

I sighed. "Yeah, that's pretty much what he told me. Did you get a description on the guy?"

Richards shrugged. "Chinese. Forties. Medium height. That narrows it down to a few hundred thousand suspects." He paused for a second. "Now I have a question for you." His bloodshot eyes, two feet from mine, widened slightly. "Why would someone go to the trouble of drugging you without trying to kill you?"

I squinted. "What are you talking about?"

"The poison was chloral hydrate, which as I'm sure you know is fatal only at very high doses. And this dose, while considerable, wasn't in the fatal range." Richards sat back, and watched me for a reaction.

I turned away from his gaze to isolate my thoughts. I thought about the package I'd received containing the cleaver and the T-shirt with its "You can't be first but you can be next" message. I thought about my narrow escape on San Francisco Bay, and my even narrower escape on Russian Hill, and I thought about the black Mercedes that had followed Britt home, and the cleaver in her door, and now this nonfatal drugging, and all I could conclude was that someone was enjoying himself at my expense. The message he was sending me was that he could kill me at any time. "I don't have a clue," I said, turning back to Richards.

"Maybe this will give you one," he said, producing a large manila envelope. He rose from his chair, and flipped a wall switch. A light came on over my bed. Then he opened the envelope and withdrew a large glossy photograph, which he handed to me.

It was a picture of a couple seated at a nightclub table. Instead of focusing on them, the photographer had focused on two young men seated behind them.

"Surveillance photo," Richards said, anticipating my question. "That your man?" he asked, putting his finger on the man on the right.

My heart banged so hard it seemed to have been jolted out of position.

It was Jimmy Chang, no question. Twenty years younger and fifteen pounds lighter, but the same round face and the same lively expression. He had scarcely aged in the interval. "Sure looks like a younger Jimmy Chang," I said. My voice shook with excitement. "Who is he?"

"Name's Li Ching. Walked out of China in the early sixties with the other fellow. They were buddies in the Red Guard."

"Wait a minute. *Walked* out of China?"

"The Chinese have been doing it for years. They strap planks on their feet and walk through the duck farm marshes at Sha Tau Kok, at the northeast corner of the New Territories, just south of the Chinese border. Once they were in Hong Kong, Li—your Jimmy—got involved in petty crimes, came to our attention as an enforcer for one of the triads, was eventually picked up and questioned in regard to a murder. Not long after this photo was taken, he dropped out of sight. But the other fellow stayed on, and today he's the man we'd most love to put away. Runs a perfectly enormous drug operation, and deals in a dozen other forms of contraband."

"Name?" I said, my torpor totally vanished, so impatient by this point I wanted to shake the information out of him.

But Richards was obviously not going to be rushed. He seemed determined to do this at his own pace, in his own way. He paused, perhaps to impress me with the importance of what he was about to say. He needn't have bothered; nothing could have impressed me more than his answer, or surprised me more either. "The name, old man, is Ying Shen."

I could only stare at him, rendered momentarily mute by the information. It was almost too enormous to fathom: Jimmy Chang not just a criminal but a onetime buddy—and maybe still a buddy—of one of the most powerful gangsters in Hong Kong.

To understand Ying Shen's importance, you have to know that the really big hitters in Hong Kong's criminal world operate on their own. They may be members of a triad, make use of other triad members, and make contributions to the triad from time to time, but the triad has no hold on them and doesn't sanction their activities. There is no Chinese equivalent of the Mafia's family. Ying Shen probably accounted for more big-time criminal enterprise than any single triad. At that moment, I was ready to bet anything that a check of Jimmy's phone bills would show dozens of calls to this man.

What a lonely and dangerous trip it had been, but what a payoff! Under any other circumstances, I would have been elated. But how could I be elated, or anything this side of despairing, knowing that this very same payoff had pitted me against as vicious an opponent as existed in all of Asia.

Dirk's thoughts must have been traveling along the same line, because when he walked out of the room a minute later, I noticed that an RHKP guard had been posted at the door. I turned off the overhead light, sank against my pillow, put my hands to my head, and worked my fingers into my forehead, as though the action might somehow dislodge the awful reality my brain was processing.

• • •

Gordon arrived a few minutes after Dirk left, as excited as he was shaken.

"Man, what a scare you gave me," he said.

"Don't say I didn't warn you."

He exhaled. "Yeah, you sure made your point. How you feelin'?"

"A little weak, but glad to be alive."

Gordon nodded, but I could tell that he'd only half listened to my response. His thoughts were obviously elsewhere. "You found out about Jimmy, didn't you?" I asked.

He nodded.

I waited for a few seconds, then said, "So did I."

Now I had his attention. He stared at me, doubt in his eyes. I had my own doubts. "There's a way to be sure we're talking about the same guy," I said. "You say his first name. I'll say his second name. Deal?"

"Deal," he said reluctantly.

I looked in the direction of the doorway. The policeman was still outside. "Close the door," I said. After he'd done that, I turned on the TV set from my bedside control. The set was tuned to a Chinese language station. I turned the volume as high as I could. I was probably overreacting, but I had to proceed on the assumption that Dirk had installed a bug. Then I motioned for Gordon to pull a chair close to the bed. "Go," I said softly.

He had the unconvinced look of a neophyte making his first dive off a high platform. "Li," he said at last.

"Ching," I said at once.

Gordon's brows lifted in surprise. "Nice goin'," he said with what sounded like grudging admiration. "The way they had the deck stacked against you, I didn't think you'd be able to pull it off."

After regaining consciousness, I hadn't even thought to ask what time it was. But since Dirk Richards' arrival, the last, weak rays of sunlight outside the window of my room had disappeared, replaced by an unrelieved blackness. Other than a light in the bathroom, the only illumination was from the TV screen. It played now on Gordon's troubled face.

"There's more, isn't there?" I said.

His eyes shifted uneasily. "You tell me," he said.

My gorge rose. "Someone poisoned me, Gordon. Stop playing games. Did you, or didn't you, find out about Jimmy's friend?"

Gordon swallowed. If I hadn't known better, I would have sworn he was covering up a crime. "*You* say the first name. I'll say the second," he said.

"Ying," I said quickly.

The air went out of his chest. "Shen," he said dejectedly. "How the hell did you do it?"

"That's not important. What's important is who poisoned me, and might poison you. Have you told *anyone* about what you've found?"

"Christ, no," he said, his voice rising. I put a warning finger to my lips. "Are you kidding?" he said, dropping his voice. "I'm green, but not that green."

"Did you even hint to anyone?"

He shook his head emphatically. "No way. Who would I talk to? I don't know anyone in Hong Kong other than my source."

"It's time you told me who he is."

Gordon squirmed. His eyes darted. "Sorry, Zack. I just can't."

His answer was like a torch igniting a tinderbox. I went up in flames. "For Christ's sake, Gordon," I said, "I could have been killed!" I pulled off the blanket, lowered my bare legs, sat upright and then stood. Or tried to. A second later I was reeling, and had to grab a night table to steady myself.

"Careful!" Gordon said, leaping out of his chair.

"I'm okay, I'm okay," I said, sitting back on the bed, but it took half a minute and several deep breaths before I could continue. "Whoever poisoned me could try the same thing on you," I said, my fury mounting again. "Now, goddammit, I want to know where you've been getting your stuff, and what exactly you've learned!"

Gordon looked away. He swallowed several times. The TV program blared on. Finally, he looked back at me, a plea for pity in his eyes, and leaned closer. "I told you I didn't know the first thing about crime reporting, right?"

"Right."

"Well, I hired someone who did."

"You *hired* someone to do your reporting?"

"I suppose you could put it that way," Gordon said glumly.

"Was this person a reporter?"

He hesitated before answering. "It wasn't a person."

That stopped me. "What do you mean, it wasn't a person?"

I've seen criminals confess to their crimes with less reluctance than Gordon displayed in relinquishing his secret. He sighed. "It was a firm of private investigators."

Maggie had been mutilated. Britt had been threatened. I'd been suspended from the SFPD, my reputation had been ruined, and on three occasions I'd come close to being killed. I burst out laughing.

Gordon looked at me, stricken.

"I'm sorry," I apologized when I'd finally gained control of myself, then burst out laughing again. He watched me, chagrined, then, fighting it all the way, broke into a grin. "Pretty smart, eh?"

"Diabolical, Gordon. Which firm?"

"The Morris Group."

I nodded in appreciation. "Well, I must say, you've got good taste. They're the class of the corporate investigators. How'd you get the idea to go to them?"

And suddenly he began to talk easily, as people do once they've gotten past the toughest part of a confession. "There was a day when the pressure got so bad I couldn't stand it, so I left the office to get a haircut, and happened to pick up *Fortune* as I got into the barber's chair. There was this rave story on the Morris Group. I'm trying to find out about the Pacific Rim Bank, I figured they gotta be able to help me. An hour later I was in their San Francisco office, and an hour after that I was their client."

I nodded, relieved to have at least this small mystery resolved. "They must be costing an arm and a leg."

"I think of it as a career investment," Gordon said. He didn't sound like he was joking.

"They're the ones who kept track of my whereabouts?" I was really thinking out loud, because I was virtually certain of the answer.

"Among other things," Gordon said, shifting in his chair, unable to repress a satisfied little smile.

"They have an office here?"

"Yeah. A guy named Steve Crown runs it. He's the one who got me the skinny on Jimmy Chang." Gordon rolled his eyes. "Can you beat it? What a story. I can't wait to break it."

I threw my head back, stared at the ceiling, then looked despairingly at Gordon. "You're doing it *again.* You can't do that!" I said sharply. I had the feeling I was scolding a child. "All we know now is that Jimmy has a past. We *don't* know what he's doing with it. If you blow the whistle now, we'll never make those connections—and he'll still be out there, doing God knows what, including slicing up young women."

Again, Gordon squirmed. He looked away, as though he was suddenly embarrassed. "I know you're right, but I've gone as far as I can. I've gotten all I'm gonna get, and I've got a duty to do this story."

"Jesus, Gordon," I exploded, standing suddenly and hovering over him. For about one second I thought I was going to wind up in his lap. Then I grabbed the bedside table again. "At a minimum, you've got a duty to save your own ass, if nobody else's matters." I stood there, panting from the effort. The skimpy hospital gown didn't exactly reinforce my sense of confidence and well-being. "How do you know you've gotten all you're going to get?" I demanded.

"Because they dropped me," Gordon answered flatly.

My eyebrows must have touched my hairline. "The Morris Group *dropped* you?"

"Just like that."

"Did they give you a reason?"

"Nope."

"You were willing to keep paying?"

Gordon nodded vigorously. "Absolutely."

A moment's thought led me to the only possible conclusion. "Then they found out something they don't want you to know." I sat on the edge of the bed again, and leaned toward him. "You've got to go back and make them want to tell you."

There was no fight in his face. "I've tried, believe me. I've been on my knees."

"Begging doesn't help," I said, exasperated. "The only reason people tell you what you want to know is when you've persuaded them that it would serve their interests."

Gordon shook his head. "I've tried that, too. Didn't work."

I leaned back and stared at Gordon. "Then I'm going to try."

Gordon waved a hand, as though dismissing my suggestion. "Steve Crown won't see you. He's an old FBI man. Hates cops."

I nodded, unimpressed. "FBI men generally do. Do you have a home number for him?"

Gordon looked uneasily at me. Then his eyes began to wander, settling at last on the television set. "He told me not to give it out," he said finally.

"He's not working for you anymore," I retorted.

"But I gave him my word, and I might need to go back to him for something."

I would not like to be on the receiving end of the baleful look I gave him. I moved close to him, conscious that I was shaking. When I spoke, my molars were touching. "I don't give a flying fuck what you might need, Gordon, or what you promised Steve Crown. When you gave him your word, lives weren't at stake. You may not care about yours but I care about mine, and I care even more about the life of a lady who shouldn't be involved but is."

Gordon's eyes weren't wandering now. They were big and filled with apprehension, exactly as I wanted them to be.

"You said you owed me, Gordon," I went on, my face still close to his. "Now's the time to pay up. I want that goddamn number, and I want your promise that you'll play dumb until I tell you you can talk. Anybody calls you, you know nothing more about Jimmy Chang. If you fuck me again and I get through this alive, I'm going to destroy you when my suspension is up."

For about ten seconds he continued to stare at me, taking short, rapid breaths through his slightly open mouth, pushing back against his chair in an attempt to increase the distance between us. When he spoke his voice was quivering. "I'll give you the number, but I'm not gonna let you or anybody tell me when I can or can't do a story. If I cross that line, I might as well hang it up."

He reached for his wallet, looked through it, and extracted Steve Crown's card. When he handed it to me his hand was trembling. Without another word, he rose from his chair and headed for the door.

I was right, but so was Gordon. As he walked through the doorway, I watched him, feeling like a bully, sick with the knowledge that this case was turning me into someone I didn't want to be.

22

As soon as Gordon left, I rang for the nurse. "CnIhepyou?" she said on the intercom. I damn near levitated. It was the *exact* singsong intonation of George Chew, the young vice president of the Pacific Rim Bank, and president of the Golden Door Trading Company—the man who'd blown the whistle on me. I could have been talking to his sister.

"When can I leave?" I asked after a deep breath.

"Maybe in a few hours."

"What do you mean, 'maybe'?" I said, exasperated. "I feel fine now. Come on in and see for yourself."

"Not up to me," the nurse said.

"Then get a doctor."

"Not up to doctor. Up to RHKP."

So that was it. My guard was there not only to keep the wrong people out, but to keep me in.

I walked to the door and looked at him. He was seated in a chair directly across from my door, a silent, expressionless Chinese cop in his late twenties, his uniform flawless, his shoes gleaming. He looked at me impassively, as though what I had done to merit his protection was of no concern to him. That led me to wonder what, if anything, *did* concern him, and whether his generation of police officers was any less cynical and susceptible to bribes than previous generations, and what would happen to him when the Communists took over in 1997.

All that took about a minute. I spent the next hour going nuts.

I wanted desperately to call Steve Crown, but I was afraid to. He'd want to know where I was calling from, and once he knew, he'd be furious. His first thought, like mine, would be that the telephone was bugged. It wasn't in his interest to have the RHKP know that he was involved. And it wasn't in my interest to upset him; he certainly wouldn't talk to me if I did.

At 6:30 the Chinese language news came on. As I'd figured it might be, my poisoning was the lead story. The newscaster stated as fact that I was in Hong Kong pursuing those responsible for the attack on Maggie Winehouse, and speculated that the attempt to poison me meant that I'd found the culprits.

It was sixteen hours earlier in San Francisco, just past 2:30 A.M. I wondered if the story had arrived there in time to make the late-evening newscasts or the final edition of the *Dispatch.* Even if it had arrived in time, most San Franciscans wouldn't learn about it until the next morning.

At 7:30 a doctor came in, took my vital signs and walked out without a word.

At 8:30 Dirk Richards finally arrived. He had the harried look of someone whose daily cocktail hour had been seriously delayed. "I'll take you to your hotel," he said brusquely. He refused to look at me.

"Thank God," I said. I got dressed in three minutes.

Three more policemen were waiting in the hall. With my guard, they surrounded me and led me down the corridor and out the hospital entrance, where another several cops were waiting, along with a small army of media. Half of the cops formed a wedge that pushed through the reporters and cameramen and soundmen, with me at the center, to a dark blue RHKP car. The other cops served as lookouts. The instant the car door slammed shut, the driver, a uniformed policeman, shot away. "Use the siren, Charlie," Richards told him. On came the siren, clearly more respected in Hong Kong than at home. The cars ahead of us veered to the side as though the road had suddenly been tilted.

"Jesus," I said. "With all those people following me, how in hell am I going to work?"

"You're not going to work, old man," Dirk said. "You're on a plane to San Francisco tomorrow afternoon."

My heart hit my gut. "Please don't do that, Dirk," I pleaded.

"Not up to me, old man," Dirk said. He still wouldn't look at me. "My betters don't want a dead American policeman on their hands, and I can't say that I blame them."

"Then let me talk to them."

Dirk shook his head. "They won't talk to you."

"I'm begging you, Dirk. I've got to break this case. It means everything to me. I've got a lead, someone I've got to see. But I don't know if he'll see me tonight."

"Sorry," Dirk said. He sounded like he was. "One other thing. You're to be confined to your hotel room until your flight. I hope that's not too great a hardship."

I sagged. "Do I have a choice?" I asked caustically.

He didn't miss the dig. "The other choice," he said slowly, "is for us to lock you up."

Another young uniformed policeman, the clone of my hospital guard, was seated at the door to my suite when we arrived. He stood as soon as he saw us. The second we were inside, Dirk excused himself and began to search everywhere a bomb might have been planted. "Can I buy you a drink?" I said when he'd finished.

He cast me an "I thought you'd never ask" look. "That would be lovely," he said. It was the first time that evening I'd seen him smile. "A straight whiskey would be grand."

There was a small mirrored bar in an alcove off the living room leading to the second bath. I found some premium Scotch in the refrigerator, poured Dirk a double, and one for myself.

"Cheers," Dirk said when we touched glasses.

"Cheers," I said with no cheer at all.

"I understand how you're feeling," he said as we sank into facing chairs. "But you would understand how *we're* feeling if you knew more about Ying Shen."

"I thought I knew a lot about him."

Dirk took a full swallow of his whiskey. "Ah!" he sighed with deep contentment. Physiologically, the alcohol couldn't have done anything for him yet, but its impact was instantly visible. The lines in his face loosened. His body sagged against the cushions. That engaging manner of the previous Friday was once again on display. "I'm sure you know all about Ying's criminal activity. You may not know about the man himself."

"Then tell me about him," I said.

Dirk took another long pull on his drink, already half gone. "A very bright man, bright as they come. He could have been anything—doctor, lawyer, corporate head." He uttered a small, ironic laugh. "He's that in a way, isn't he? Runs one of the biggest bloody corporations in Asia, without benefit of incorporation papers." Another swallow. "He puts on this immaculate front—charities, community activities, cultural stuff, the works. But he's as dangerous as they come. Go up against him and you're a dead man, and from everything we've heard, by the time he's done with you, dying's your most fervent wish. That's why we've never been able to move against him—he's got everyone so petrified that we can't get an informer in there." One more sip and his whiskey was gone.

I promptly rose to get him another. "I've thought about the drugging," he said when I'd returned and handed him his glass. "It's very much in character."

By this point I was listening with decidedly mixed emotions, fascinated by the portrait that was emerging, but not all that comfortable learning about the habits of my potential executioner. "In what way?" I said, doing my best to sound merely curious.

"Ying loves to toy with his opponents. Gratifies his considerable ego. Keeps him amused, too, because by this point he's got so much money that making more money can't be all that interesting. For him, the game's the thing—how to score one more against the authorities. Could be you're his latest game. Drugging you but not killing you is his little warning to you. 'I can kill you anytime I wish,' he's saying, 'so you'd best back off.' "

That much I'd figured out myself. But a theoretical conclusion was one thing; it was quite another thing to have a known quantity attached. "He likes being the master puppeteer, is that it?"

"Exactly." Dirk took another large swallow. He didn't even blink.

"Gives him more pleasure to pull people about than to actually destroy them. Once they're gone, they're not amusing anymore. And, incidentally," he said without skipping a beat, "the preparation of your meals will be supervised by one of our people, so you can have full confidence on that score."

The more I thought as I ate my poison-proof dinner, the more convinced I became that I was just one piece shy of having the picture together. Many pieces were already in place.

Jimmy Chang alone was a pipsqueak. But Jimmy Chang allied with Ying Shen was a giant. I had no proof that they were in contact. But Dirk Richards had said they'd been "buddies" who'd sneaked out of China together, a bonding experience if ever there was one. Several years later, they're both triad enforcers, out on the town together. That certainly suggested they'd remained good friends. Then Jimmy gets into trouble, flees to Vancouver and then San Francisco, where he quickly prospers. Now I had a plausible answer to my question of where he'd gotten the money to set himself up. From Ying Shen, of course, whose own career was blossoming back in Hong Kong.

Call it experience or call it a hunch, I was ready to bet the farm that Gordon's helper, Steve Crown of the Morris Group, held the missing piece to the picture—or else knew where it was. It sounded as though he'd freaked when he discovered where the case was leading. I had to know why. I had to get to Crown, and then try to convince him it was in his interest to tell me what he knew.

A call from my suite was as out of the question as a call from the hospital. The line would surely be tapped. I thought about calling Angela and asking her to carry a message to Crown. But I was sure the RHKP would either follow her, in which case Crown would be compromised, or intercept her, find my note and make her talk. A bad experience all around, with no winners.

How desperate was I? For a couple of minutes I even entertained the idea of bribing the cop at the door to let me go to the lobby to make the call. I figured a hundred U.S. dollars would do it, but I couldn't bring myself to try because I was afraid he'd accept—and I couldn't have lived with myself if I'd corrupted a cop.

There was, finally, only one possibility.

It was a few minutes before 11:00 P.M. in Hong Kong, just before

7:00 A.M. in San Francisco. For five minutes I sat, staring at the phone, trying to talk myself into doing what I knew had to be done. Okay, I told myself, the man is bullheaded, biased, poorly educated, ill-informed, cruel and selfish. He is probably capable of small dishonest acts, and he would certainly push the boundaries to keep his job. But he hates criminals and would never ever protect one, no matter what the consequences. Whatever he might have thought he was doing to protect Mayor Putnam from scandal, he could not possibly have known what I've learned today. Remember what he said in his office the first day we discussed Jimmy Chang? "The guy's a fucking angel." Right. The important thing is that he believed it.

At last I reached for the phone and called Jerry Doyle.

"What the fuck do *you* want?" he said, his voice hoarse.

"Among other things, I want to save your ass," I said. I didn't apologize for waking him, which I was sure I had.

Seconds passed. "Are you drunk?" he said angrily.

"Haven't had a drop."

"Where the fuck *are* you?" He sounded totally puzzled.

"You know where I am," I said bitterly.

"How the fuck would I know where you are?" He was shouting now. "I don't have time to keep tabs on suspended cops. I've got a police department to run."

For a few seconds I couldn't imagine what he was up to. "You really don't know where I am?"

"Get to it, Tobias. You woke me up."

"You didn't know I was in Hong Kong?" Now *I* was the totally puzzled one.

"No, I didn't know you were in Hong Kong," he said impatiently. He was so angry I figured he couldn't be lying. "If you've been out there looking into Jimmy Chang, you might as well start looking for a new career. Now what the fuck is this about?"

I let him have it and, God, but it felt good. "It's about a possible criminal conspiracy that could cost the mayor the election and you your job, and yes, it involves Jimmy Chang. I know who he is, and he isn't Jimmy Chang."

Since everything I knew was already known to the RHKP, I decided I could speak without restraint. I told the chief what I'd learned about Jimmy's triad past, and his friendship with Ying Shen. I gave him the highlights of Ying's criminal career. I described everything that had happened to me. I told him that I'd done what I could to stop Gordon Lee from broadcasting the story prematurely, but that once he returned to San Francisco the pressures on him would be unbelievable. I told him that, as matters stood, I had only twelve hours to break the case.

"Why twelve hours?" the chief asked. They were the first words he'd uttered in five minutes.

"Because the RHKP doesn't want any more trouble. They've got me under house arrest, and they're putting me on a flight tomorrow afternoon."

When the chief spoke next I could barely hear him. "The RHKP is absolutely certain that the guy with Ying Shen in the photo is Li Ching?"

"That's right."

"And you're absolutely certain that Li Ching is Jimmy?"

"I'd bet my life on it," I said, immediately struck by the irony of my words.

I can only imagine what went through the chief's head in the next couple of minutes. Thick walls of deeply embedded hostility were being penetrated by undeniable facts. "What do you need?" he said at last. For the chief, it was a capitulation.

"The cooperation of the RHKP, which I can't get because of the fax you sent them."

"What fax? I didn't send them no fax."

That stopped me. "You didn't send them a fax requesting that they turn me away if I came to them for help?"

"Hell, no," he said indignantly. "What the fuck are you talking about?"

Every nerve in my body seemed to fire at once. "You didn't fax the same request to the Vancouver police?"

"Hell, no. They told you I did?" By this point, his voice had risen an octave.

I took a breath, and spoke slowly. "Both departments received a fax from your office, in your name, requesting that they shut me out."

Ten seconds of silence passed. When the chief broke it, he sounded as rattled as I felt. "What do you make of it?"

"It sounds to me like Jimmy Chang has a friend in the department. Someone with access to your office."

The chief didn't go so far as to agree with me, but his next words said as much. "What do you want me to do?"

"Call the RHKP right now," I said, thinking it through as I spoke, "and ask them to patch you through to Commissioner Wong. If he's not available, get the highest ranking officer you can. Tell him you didn't send that fax. Tell him I need time, and the freedom to work by myself. I won't get anywhere with an RHKP escort."

Twenty minutes later Dirk Richards called me. "You're in the clear, old man. I just hope you know what you're doing."

Moments before midnight on Monday, December 19, 1994, one of the longest days of my life, I called Steve Crown from a pay phone.

He was not pleased to hear from me. "I know who you are," he interrupted impatiently as I began to identify myself. "What do you want?"

"I want to help you."

"How can *you* help *me*?" he scoffed. Gordon had been right; like most FBI agents, present and past, Crown obviously had a low regard for cops.

I gambled everything on a guess. "By doing something for you that you can't do for yourself because it will compromise your client."

By his silence I figured I'd guessed right. "Where are you calling from?" he asked at last.

"From a pay phone in the Mandarin," I said, grateful that I'd taken the precaution. "I just got on. There's no way it's tapped."

"I'm listening," he said after several seconds. There was a "Show me" tone to his voice, but it was no longer abrasive.

"You dumped Gordon because working for him produced a conflict of interest."

"Go on," he said.

I knew I wasn't guessing anymore. "Someone you represent is involved with Ying Shen."

Another silence. "Not because he wants to be."

"And he's afraid to take him on," I said confidently.

"He can't afford to take him on." Crown's voice was matter-of-fact.

I would have given anything to be talking face-to-face, but I was sure Crown wouldn't see me unless I could convince him that I could help him. "What if *we* took him on—and kept your client out of it?"

"Who's 'we,' the San Francisco Police Department?" Crown said, doubt creeping back into his voice.

"Gordon and I."

The longest pause yet. "What do you have in mind?"

I was ready. "Our basic interest, as I'm sure he explained, is in finding out who ordered the attack on Maggie Winehouse. Does your client have information that could help us determine that?"

"You'd have to be the judge of that, based on what my client might tell you. But he'd never talk to you."

"Unless we can prove to him that we can help him," I said quickly.

"You'd have to prove that to me first." It wasn't the "Show me" challenge of a minute ago; to the contrary, it was an implied invitation.

Again, I was ready, this time with the only possibility that made sense, given the facts as I knew them. "How about a media exposé of Ying Shen's efforts to move his assets illegally from Hong Kong to the States with the help of Li Ching—or Jimmy Chang, as he now calls himself?"

"You could do that?" His voice contained a new ingredient: respect.

"If your client has the missing pieces," I said with assurance. "Moving assets has got to be what this is about."

The silence on the other end was so protracted I began to wonder if we'd been disconnected. "Let me make a call," Crown said at last. "If I learn anything, I'll call you."

"Better I call you," I said quickly.

"Right, right," Crown agreed. "Call me in twenty minutes."

They were a long twenty minutes. I decided to get some air, started toward the hotel entrance, thought better of it and returned to the sanctuary of the lobby and the comfort of numbers. It was now well past midnight but several clusters of people were still in the lobby, seated near that massive Christmas tree, and a dozen others were having drinks in the Clipper Lounge on the mezzanine.

I sat on a couch and tried to inspect some of the gilded wooden carvings of ancient temples that decorated the walls. That lasted about a minute. Then I walked back to the reception area, and began pacing the marble floors, getting several strange looks in the process.

At first I couldn't figure out why. Then it dawned on me: television. I was the man whose poisoning had led the newscasts earlier that evening and now here I was, just hours later, prowling the lobby of the Mandarin Oriental. It made me wonder what kind of reaction I'd provoked in San Francisco, where everyone was now awake and had heard the morning news.

Oh, shit, I thought in the next instant, and bolted for the pay phone in the arcade behind the concierge's desk.

First, I called Britt, then my mother. Neither one answered. I left messages for both of them: Don't worry, I'm fine, it wasn't as bad as it sounds, I'll be back in a few days. Gray lies. I was glad I'd thought to call, and relieved that I hadn't had to talk to them.

One break, I kept telling myself. I need one break.

Exactly twenty minutes after we'd spoken, I called Steve Crown again. "My client has agreed to see you at five o'clock tomorrow afternoon," he said. "Be at my office at four o'clock."

"That's great," I said. "Do you want to call Gordon, or shall I do it?"

"Gordon's not involved," he said flatly.

"Wait a minute," I said. "How do you get your media exposé of Ying Shen if Gordon's not involved?"

"Out of the question for now, until we see how it goes. Those are the terms. Yes or no?"

"Yes," I said. I felt I was breaking faith with Gordon, but I had no choice.

At seven the next morning, after a night of almost no sleep, I called Dirk Richards at home. "I may be on to something," I said, "but I need another favor."

"Go ahead," he said without enthusiasm. He spoke carefully, like a man who didn't want to excite his head.

"Gordon Lee knows as much as I do at this point about Jimmy Chang and Ying Shen. He's edgy and inexperienced, a real loose cannon. I'm worried he could get in trouble."

"And you'd like us to detain him," Richards said, a trace of sarcasm in his voice. He sounded as if he was hurting. I could only imagine how much more drinking he'd done after he left my hotel room.

"For his own good."

"On what pretext?"

"He was a witness to my poisoning, the only one."

"We've already questioned him at length."

Patience, Zachary, patience, I lectured myself. "Look, it's not just his safety I'm concerned about. You said you'd love to nail Ying Shen. I'm working on something that might do that. But if Gordon gets back to San Francisco before I do and broadcasts a story about Jimmy and Ying, I'm dead in the water. Is there some way you could make sure he doesn't leave before I do?"

"That's tough," Dirk said after a moment. "Let me see what I can do."

He called back fifteen minutes later, sounding a little healthier. I guessed he'd had time for a cup of coffee. "We'll pick him up and bring him in for questioning, and keep him occupied until today's flights to the States have left. That do it?"

I'd gained a day—but also a deadline. Deep breath, I told myself, deep breath. "It'll have to, won't it?"

As soon as Dirk hung up, I called Angela's office. She picked up the phone. A minute later she was in my suite, and in my arms. "How horrible," she said, over and over.

After a minute I led her to a sofa. We sat side by side, holding hands. "I had no idea," she said finally.

"It's done with," I said. "Now I've got some work to do. Can you help me?"

"Anything."

"Are there any media people downstairs?"

"They're everywhere."

"I've got to get out of the hotel this afternoon without being seen."

At once her face took on that intense, quizzical, yet empathic expression that had so struck me in our first moments together—eyes stretched wide, eyebrows raised and lips slightly parted—and I could almost feel the formidable energy she seemed to be applying to my problem. "Let me see what I can do," she said simply.

When Angela left I called a telephone operator and asked her to hold all my calls, no exceptions. Then I went back to bed and slept for three hours. At one o'clock, I went up to the Health Club, had a work-out, a sauna and a swim. At 2:30, I had lunch in my room—or, more accurately, I picked at the lunch I'd ordered. My stomach was healthy again, but I was too nervous to eat.

Angela came for me at 3:40.

"Media still here?" I asked.

"An army," she replied calmly.

She took me down a service elevator to the ground floor. We stepped out into a large corridor that seemed to be a combination employees' entrance and delivery area. On the other side of a door-less entry was a covered alley, and in the alley were three of the hotel's four 1963 Phantom Rolls-Royces, used mostly to ferry guests between the hotel and the airport. One of the cars was directly opposite the entry, its back door held open by a driver. I grabbed Angela's hand and gave her a quick, discreet squeeze, then dived into the well between the front and rear seats of the Rolls. Seconds later the car pulled out of the alley and into downtown Hong Kong.

At exactly four, I walked into Steve Crown's plush, contemporary office high above downtown Hong Kong and got a pleasant surprise. Based on our phone call, I'd visualized a dour, driven man. I was wrong on both counts. Crown was affable, in advanced middle age, slightly overweight, with a cards-on-the-table manner. "I don't hate cops," he said with an engaging laugh after commiserating with me about the poisoning. "I just think most of them do a lousy job and half of them are dishonest."

"Which makes you a typical FBI agent."

"Former FBI agent," he stressed. He'd joined the Morris Group four years earlier, he told me, after thirty years with the bureau. He likened the experience to back surgery, which he'd had two years ago. He'd kept postponing it because he'd been scared of it; after he'd had it, his relief was so great that he'd only wished he'd done it sooner. He'd arrived in Hong Kong the year before, after three years in the Morris Group's Washington office. His immediate impression was that he'd died and gone to heaven: an apartment with spectacular views five minutes from the office; a live-in cook and maid, which had made his wife deliriously happy; Chinese food three times a day if he wanted it; a car and driver; and a level of challenge and intrigue to his work that had made him feel young again. Oh, yes, he'd just ordered half a dozen custom-made suits, a blazer and a sportcoat, and I'd be doing myself a favor by squeezing in a visit to his tailor.

All this in our first fifteen minutes together, at the end of which time he glanced out his window, saw a helicopter approaching and, putting on his coat, said, "Let's go."

An elevator whisked us to the roof. The helicopter was landing as we arrived. In another minute we were airborne, and half a minute after that we were over the harbor, where at least a hundred ships of all dimensions lay at anchor and an equal number moved slowly through the water, which shimmered in the slanted, late-afternoon light. The day was so clear I thought I could see Macao, where, just three days before, Angela had guided me so tenderly and patiently onto a new plateau of sex. For a fleeting moment I let myself dwell on those memories. Then I turned to Steve. "Want to tell me where we're going?" I shouted over the din.

"To the New Territories, to meet a man named Kurt Muller. Ever heard of him?"

"No."

Steve smiled. "Doesn't surprise me. He keeps a low profile. Quite a guy. German Jew. Got out in 1937 with the help of a conscience-stricken Japanese diplomat and some well-placed bribes. He was twenty at the time. Begged his parents to go with him, but they didn't want to leave Germany. His father had been decorated in World War One. Considered himself more German than Hitler. Said Hitler would never last. Muller went to Lithuania, then Russia, then Manchuria, finally Japan. Found out after the war that his parents had died in Auschwitz. Came here in 1946 with nothing more than a small sack of diamonds. Today he owns a majority interest in the China Coast Group."

"*That* I've heard of," I said. "Shipping, isn't it?"

"Mainly shipping. But textiles, gems and a dozen other things."

"Any trade with China?"

"None."

"Why is that?"

"He'll tell you about it."

We were across the harbor by this point, and flying over Kowloon, and for the first time I could appreciate how densely this sprawling commercial and residential district north of Hong Kong Island had been developed. Minutes later we were over the New Territories, green and wet with rice fields. In another minute we descended into a walled compound on a hill surrounded by fields, its grounds covered with tropical plants and trees. We landed on a helicopter pad and walked toward a house that looked as though it had been built by a Chinese contractor for a wealthy Englishman in the final years of the reign of Queen Victoria. The building defied architectural categorization, its roof and façade an acknowledgment of the Orient, its sturdy shape and grand dimension a statement of Empire.

As we approached the door it opened. A Chinese servant in black silk tunic and trousers stood to the side, his feet in slippers. The moment we walked inside I saw a tall, pale, gaunt-looking man—in his late seventies, I guessed—emerge through a doorway on the left side of a long hall, its paneled walls covered with contemporary paintings. He was wearing a brown double-breasted business suit and tie. His head was bowed, his shoulders were rounded and he seemed to be in pain. He waited for us at the doorway; when we reached him he extended his right arm. He held my hand, but didn't shake it. "This is Captain Tobias of the San Francisco Police Department," Steve said to him. Then Steve turned to me. "And this is Mr. Muller."

"You were kind to come all this way," Muller said in a tired voice. "I am only sorry it has caused you such difficulty." He spoke English with an accent that gave away his German ancestry. Up close, he had the haunted, intense, angry look of an eagle, his features so sharp they seemed sculpted. His dark, recessed eyes, separated by a long, thin nose, were riveted on mine.

I wondered if Muller believed I'd come to Hong Kong just to see him, but I let it pass. "You were kind to meet with me, sir," I said as he beckoned us to follow him.

We entered a study spacious enough to serve as the library of a club. The ceiling was low, the walls paneled, and the furniture darkened by age and polish. Muted lights highlighted several large contemporary paintings and vases of exquisite jade filled with fresh tropical flowers. Rows of books rose to the ceiling between the paintings. On the mantel of a wide and deep fireplace stood a large pewter menorah, the candelabrum used in Jewish worship, especially at Hanukkah, the eight-day holiday commemorating the recapture of the Temple of Jerusalem from the Syrians. Each of its nine stems was twisted, perhaps to suggest the struggles of the Jewish people. As loaded as my mind was, it nonetheless found room to register surprise at finding a Jew who had lived a long and fruitful life in Hong Kong.

Muller gestured us into comfortable armchairs. He chose a high, straight chair for himself, the kind you normally find at the end of formal dining tables. He then looked expectantly at Steve. "Gentlemen," Steve said, "my job was to bring the two of you together. It's up to you to find out whether you can help one another. I'm here to help you if you need me, but otherwise I'm just going to sit here and listen."

Muller turned to me. I don't think I have ever seen so much pain in another man's face, held in check by such forbearance. "I know why you are here," he said, "so let me begin." Very carefully he placed the fingertips of his hands together. "The story goes back to 1983, when it became apparent to me that Britain was going to turn over control of Hong Kong to the People's Republic. At that time I decided it was important to begin to move some assets out of Hong Kong to more stable areas, and I began to do so. Nothing major, just enough personal funds placed in banks abroad to which I could have ready access in case events got out of hand and I was compelled to move my family. I'd had the experience once in my life of being unprepared for adversity, and I was determined not to repeat it."

"I understand," I said, but I wondered if anyone could understand who hadn't been through the experience. It was easy enough sixty years after the fact to say that all the German Jews should have seen what was happening and fled. But what about those who loved their country, and didn't want to start over in a strange land?

"As you well know," Muller went on, speaking so coherently and precisely he might have been using notes, "the basic agreement to transfer authority to the PRC in 1997 was reached in 1984, and took effect in 1985. As a consequence, I kept augmenting my resources abroad. Still nothing exceptional, however. Then, three years ago, I decided that it was time to undertake some major shifts in corporate assets. As I'm also sure you're aware, you can double your money in Hong Kong every three to four years. Many of my business colleagues, consequently, are waiting until the last moment to move their assets. Given my history, as well as my age and my responsibilities to my now considerable family, which looks to me for leadership, I was not content to do that."

"Perfectly understandable."

"About two years ago," Muller went on, "I received a visit from a gentleman named Li Kwan. Have you ever heard of this man?"

"No, sir," I said, completely puzzled by this point as to where this narrative was taking us and what its pertinence was.

"He is from the People's Republic of China," Muller continued in his precise, German-tinged English. "His father is a very well-placed member of their ruling body. He came to Hong Kong two years ago ostensibly to run a commercial research company, but it is well known that he is here to be the Hong Kong station chief of the PRC's Ministry of State Security." Muller paused. "Do you understand what this ministry does?" he asked me.

"Yes, sir," I said immediately. "What our CIA does."

"That is correct."

"So what did Li Kwan want with you?"

"He told me that he had become aware, through friends in the banking world, that I had begun to move assets out of the country in a rather significant way."

I still didn't know where the story was taking us, but I was so caught up by this point I was content to go along. "Any idea how he might have learned this?" I asked.

"Just a general idea. Someone at my bank has to be on his payroll."

"Or was sent in from China by the Ministry of State Security to get a job at your bank?"

"Either one," Muller said, suggesting with a shrug that it really didn't matter how the information had been passed.

"How were you moving the assets, if I may ask?" I said, stealing a look at Steve as I did, wondering if I'd overstepped the bounds. But he seemed completely absorbed, and not in the least alarmed by the course the conversation was taking.

"You may ask anything you wish," Muller said, undisturbed as well. "I will tell you what I can."

"Good," I said, letting myself sink back for the first time against my armchair's heavy cushion.

"It's really very simple. I borrow against our corporate equities, then transfer the money abroad."

It might be simple, but I hadn't thought of it. "Specifically?"

"To British Columbia, primarily. California, as well."

"And what do you do with the money?"

"Most of it has been used to buy real estate. The rest is in short-term paper."

Could this conceivably be the man who had loaned money to Z. Tobias and Company? I was burning to know, but didn't ask, afraid that it might disrupt the interview. "Okay, I've got the picture. Go ahead."

"Li told me that Muller was an important name in Hong Kong," Muller continued. As he shifted position in his upright chair he seemed to wince, and I wondered if he'd avoided a more comfortable chair because of a back problem. "The disclosure that Kurt Muller was moving assets out of Hong Kong in anticipation of the changeover would be a blow to public confidence, he said. Therefore, his government was respectfully requesting that I stop—and as an incentive, was prepared to discuss some special arrangements whereby business with the PRC would be thrown my way."

"And what did you say to that?"

Muller smiled grimly. "I told him I would think about it."

"And did you?"

"Not for a moment," he said quickly, his German accent suddenly more noticeable. "One experience in a lifetime under a totalitarian regime is enough for anyone. I would no more do business with China than I would have done with Nazi Germany."

So much for the question I'd asked Steve in the helicopter about whether Kurt Muller traded with China. "You continued to export assets?" I asked.

"To an even greater degree."

"And then?"

"And then the troubles began." Muller inhaled and exhaled audibly and rubbed his eyes with his left hand—the first signs of strain he had shown during the entire narrative.

"Please go on," I said softly.

"At first it was just China Coast Lines."

"Your shipping company."

"Correct."

"What kind of trouble?"

"Initially, with the dockworkers. We couldn't get manpower to load or unload our ships."

I glanced at Steve. He was looking at me. He raised his eyebrows once, as if to say, "Here it comes." I turned back to Muller. "Don't the triads control the docks?"

"Yes."

"Had you had problems before with the triads?"

"Nothing out of the ordinary. The triads are a fact of life in Hong Kong. You deal with them as best you can."

Something wasn't being said that ought to be said, if it was true. "Is it your feeling, Mr. Muller, that the triads were put up to this by Li Kwan?"

"It is," he answered simply.

Wherever this narrative was headed, I sensed we were getting closer. "Can you prove it?" I asked, surprised by my quavering voice.

"Not at all."

I hadn't expected that he could. His answer didn't diminish my excitement. "Anything else?" I said.

"Oh, that was just the beginning," Muller said, smiling for the first time, however ruefully. "After the problems in Hong Kong we began to experience problems at every port our ships called on, not just problems on the docks but far more serious problems. You know that everything today is shipped in containers, which almost all shipping lines rent. Suddenly we couldn't get them when we needed them, and if we did manage to get them we couldn't get rid of them when we were finished with them. Each day that we held them the rent on them continued. The cost was staggering. Three years ago, China Coast Lines was a profitable company. Its losses became horrendous, requiring a tremendous infusion of capital to keep the ships afloat. In normal times even that problem might have been surmounted, but suddenly, out of the blue, China Coast Group, the parent company, became the target of an unfriendly takeover bid, forcing me to buy my own shares on the open market at inflated prices, and putting a serious drain on my capital resources."

"Thus compelling you to return the money you've removed from Hong Kong back to Hong Kong?"

"Much of the money."

"Clever."

"Indeed."

I was sure we were almost there, even if I still didn't know where we were going. "Who's making the takeover bid?"

"The names are of no consequence," Muller said with a dismissive wave. "They haven't the wherewithal to take over one of these hamburger franchises. They have to be stand-ins for someone, and it's my very great hunch that that someone is the People's Republic."

It was too much to process. I'd completely lost my bearings, like a hiker in a snowstorm. Somehow all these facts had to tie together, but I still couldn't see how. "Where do matters stand now?" I asked, for lack of a better question.

"Do you mean, am I in serious jeopardy?"

"Yes."

The lines in Muller's face deepened before my eyes. "I am desperately short of cash and in danger of losing everything."

"Everything, that is, but what remains abroad."

Muller slowly shook his head from side to side, at the same time pulling down the corners of his mouth, as though to deprecate what I'd just said. "What remains abroad is perhaps fifteen percent of what's here," he said. "I could live on that, of course, but I am not particularly eager to lose most of what I've labored for fifty years to build up. Nor, on the other hand, do I wish to be blackmailed by the PRC." Muller sighed deeply. "Unfortunately, my wishes do not count for much in this situation."

Four months ago, Muller went on, he'd received an offer to purchase the shipping company at 20 percent of its book value. He'd been obliged to accept it.

And suddenly there it was—the destination, the harbor, the connection. "Is there any link between the problems of the shipping line and the offer to purchase?" I asked.

Muller turned to Steve. "Would you like to answer that, Mr. Crown?"

"Gladly," Steve said. He turned to me. "The man who wrecked the operations of the shipping line at the behest of the PRC is the same man who bought the shipping line, using stand-ins."

"And would this man by any chance be Ying Shen?" I asked, my heart pounding.

Steve looked at Muller, who nodded. Then he turned back to me. "He would."

23

"I don't get it," Gordon said, plainly vexed.

It was 8:00 P.M. I'd come directly to the Regent Hotel after our return by helicopter from Kurt Muller's estate. Gordon had spent the first ten minutes fuming about how he'd missed his flight to San Francisco because the RHKP had insisted on questioning him all over again about our lunch together. I'd heard him out, offering silent thanks to Dirk Richards for a job well done.

As upset as Gordon was about the delay, it was nothing compared with the frustration he was feeling at having had to play dumb in the twenty-six hours since I'd warned him to keep his mouth shut. The story of my poisoning was on the front page of all the Bay Area's newspapers, and was the lead on all the local newscasts. As a witness to the poisoning, Gordon had figured in all those stories. Our presence together in Hong Kong had aroused intense speculation as to whether we were jointly on the trail of Maggie Winehouse's assailants, but in deference to me—not in *fear* of me, he emphasized— he'd rebuffed all inquiries, even those from his own station. On reflection, he'd decided that I was at least partly right; for the moment, it was more important to delay the story in the interest of getting the goods on the man he was convinced had ordered the attack on Maggie.

Journalism, like nature, abhors a vacuum; in the absence of fact, conjecture had filled the void. Every story, Gordon's boss, Jim Smith, had told him, had additionally speculated that we were both in Hong Kong to look more closely into the financial dealings of San Francisco's Pacific Rim Bank and its major stockholder, Jimmy Chang, the mayor's appointee to the Port Commission. The attempt on my life, the news reports all suggested in varying degrees, indicated that I was about to break a case so scandalous it could bring down the mayor— and that Gordon had the inside track on the story. Jimmy Chang was once again crying foul, and threatening to sue every media outlet in the Bay Area for libel, and Gordon and KUBC for harassment as well.

Whether I liked it or not, Gordon and I had become partners in this enterprise. To appease and reassure him, I'd come to his hotel to give him a report on my meeting with Muller.

"Muller can't take on Ying Shen," I explained from the upholstered chair I'd sunk into as soon as I entered his room, "because he would have to accuse the PRC of hiring a criminal to deep-six his shipping line. He can't do that because the PRC has him by the short hairs."

The minute I finished speaking, Gordon stood abruptly and paced up and down the room like a caged animal seeking an escape route. Then he abruptly sat down again. "I still don't get it," he said. "Something's missing."

I was drained from the excitement, hungry for some dinner and eager to get back to the Mandarin, but I willed myself to be patient. "Okay, let's go back a couple of steps. Ying Shen is brought in by the PRC to wreck the shipping line as a means of bringing Muller to heel. Ying, thinking ahead to '97, sees an opportunity to create a permanent conduit for the shipment of drugs and other contraband to the United States. The port of entry for his new fleet of ships would be San Francisco—where Jimmy Chang, the mayor's appointee to the Port Commission, makes all arrangements for a hospitable reception. The business is conducted with the Golden Door Trading Company, and the money eventually winds up at the Pacific Rim Bank."

Gordon slapped his head. "Of course!" he said. "It all ties in!"

"When Maggie did her broadcast in front of the bank," I went on,

"Jimmy not only became nervous, he figured he'd lost face, because even though Maggie didn't intend it, the implication to those in the know was that the bank was the laundry for the dirty money, and they knew that Jimmy owned a big share of the bank. The old-timers in Chinatown may know better than to fuck with the press, but Jimmy's a short-timer. More than that, once a triad enforcer, always a triad enforcer, and triad enforcers don't let such things pass. Jimmy can't do the job himself, so he calls Ying Shen and asks him to send in some hit men. For Ying, attacking Maggie as a means of intimidating the media would be business as usual."

"Sounds right," Gordon said excitedly. "Now, how do we prove it?"

I leaned across and put a hand on his shoulder. "At the risk of hurting your feelings, Gordon, *we* don't. I do. Or try to."

Gordon scowled. "After everything that's happened you expect me to go back to San Francisco, tell the station I got zip in Hong Kong, and hope that you come up with something? That's asking a lot, Zack."

I nodded. "I figured you'd say that. Here's what I'm prepared to do. Do you have a camcorder with you?"

"No, but I can buy one."

"Good. At ten tomorrow morning, bring the camcorder to the Mandarin. I'll make a full statement—Jimmy Chang's true identity, how he came out of China, how he got in with the triads, how he had to leave Hong Kong, his prior association with Ying Shen, Ying's record, the works. I'll hold up the surveillance photo showing the two of them together. When I'm finished with my statement, you can ask me questions. I'd say that would make a pretty good exclusive, and I'd say that's worth waiting for."

Gordon had been listening to me with increasing agitation. "Why is it worth waiting for?" he exploded when I'd finished. "I know all that stuff already."

"Three reasons. The first is, you can't identify your sources, which means that you're not going to be believed, whereas your audience will believe the captain of the SFPD's Special Investigations Division—"

"Just a minute," Gordon interjected, springing to his feet again. "You're not in charge of the Special Investigations Division anymore."

"I will be again, very soon," I said. He started to ask about that, but I cut him off. "That's all I can say right now on that score. The second reason you should wait is that if you do the story without a source to hang it on, you're going to get your ass sued, whereas if you hang the story on me you haven't got a legal problem." I paused to be sure I had his attention. "The third reason is you'll run the tape when and if I'm killed."

His head jerked back, as though to slip a punch. He lost color, and sat down. "What are you planning to do?" he asked, his voice subdued.

"I can't tell you that."

"Will you tell me when it's over?"

"If I'm alive to tell it, Gordon, you get the exclusive story. But no story until I give the green light, unless I'm killed—in which case you have the tape. That's the deal."

He watched me for another minute. "Who keeps the tape?" he said then.

"You do. But put it in a bank vault."

I could almost see the wheels turning. "How long do you think this will take you?"

"Not long, either way."

Suddenly Gordon closed his eyes. For half a minute he sat silently. I could see his Adam's apple working up and down, and hear him breathing unevenly through his nostrils. At last he opened his eyes, and when he spoke his voice shook. "Do you know what just happened to me?" he asked. "I had about two seconds there—maybe not even two seconds, maybe only a second, but even a second is bad enough—in which it flashed through me how much better a story it would be if you were killed. I mean, it would make me famous, wouldn't it? It'd shoot me right up to network, wouldn't it? *Jesus!*" He dropped his face into the palm of his right hand, kept it there for a couple of seconds, then raised his head and shook it. "I can't *believe* what's happening to me," he said. "I don't know how much more I can take."

I watched him for a minute more, then put a hand on his shoulder again. "I know what you're feeling, Gordon," I said softly. "It's getting to me, too." I hesitated. "Do we have a deal?"

He looked up at me. "Yeah," he said miserably. "We have a deal."

• • •

Getting back into the Mandarin was no problem. As I approached the hotel I could see that the photographers and cameramen who'd been waiting at the entry were no longer there. Apparently they'd given up for the day. Just to be on the safe side, I had the taxi driver continue around the block and let me off at the alleyway on the Queen's Road. I walked into the hotel through the employees' entrance.

I'd like to think that what I did next reflected grace under pressure, Hemingway's measure of courage. The more likely truth is that, knowing someone was out there who could kill me at his pleasure, the last thing I wanted was to be alone with my apprehensions. I needed someone who could remind me that life goes on. I needed Angela.

It was well past nine o'clock, too late, I was certain, to find her in her office. Although she scarcely seemed like the kind of person who would embarrass easily, she did work for the hotel, so asking the concierge to run her down was hardly appropriate. Which meant that I wouldn't see her again, because I intended to leave the next day.

Quite apart from wanting her to help me quiet my fears, I'd wanted to be with her again. I was grateful for what had happened, not so much for the sexual memory as for the manner in which she'd unwittingly helped me clarify my life. I couldn't thank her specifically for that, but by asking her to be with me on my last night in Hong Kong I could let her know that our time together had meant more than a memorable roll in the hay.

I had another reason for wanting to be with her. Three recent episodes had converged in my mind, like rivulets of water coursing down a mountainside that merge into a stream. The first had been Britt's bewilderment at finding a Christmas tree in a Jewish home. The second had been Gordon's "How's your Hebrew?" riposte at lunch two days before when I'd ribbed him for not knowing Chinese. The third had been my meeting, just a few hours earlier, with Kurt Muller.

Why it should have surprised me to encounter a Jew in Hong Kong I didn't know. The spread of Jews throughout the world is not only a fact of Jewish life but a foundation of Diaspora humor. My father loved to tell the joke about the American Jew who finds himself in Shanghai on the evening of Rosh Hashanah, the Jewish New Year. Walking the streets, alone and disconsolate, he hears the faint sounds of familiar liturgical music. The further he walks the louder and more unmistakable the music. In another minute he is standing in front of what looks for all the world like a synagogue. Entering, he finds, to his astonishment, a congregation of Chinese Jews in the midst of worship, led by an elderly Chinese rabbi. He sits, enthralled, through the service. When it's over, he rushes up to the rabbi. "Rabbi," he says, "I can't tell you how moved I was by your service. It was as beautiful as any I've ever attended." The rabbi looks quizzically at the American. "Are you Jewish?" he asks. "Why, yes," the American replies. "That's funny," the rabbi says. "You don't look Jewish."

In all my stocktaking over the years, the major theme had been whether my life would matter to anyone but myself. Identity had never been my problem. I'd thought I'd at least known who I was. Now, suddenly, I wasn't sure. How could I berate Gordon for living without regard to his ancestry when I had so little regard for my own?

Surely, not many Jews could be living in Hong Kong, I thought, and yet, if his menorah was any sign, here was Kurt Muller, remote from the Jewish mainstream, maintaining a Jewish identity. George Golden, the Associated Press man, had told me that Angela knew everyone in Hong Kong. I was suddenly, intensely curious about what life was like in Hong Kong for a Jew like Kurt Muller, and I had hoped she could tell me. But now it was too late.

I should have known better. There was a message from Angela waiting for me. I was to call her at home as soon as I returned, no matter what the hour.

"Are you all right?" she asked the instant she heard my voice.

"I'm fine," I said. "Have you had dinner yet?"

She laughed. "You took the words out of my mouth. My party this time. Would you prefer the Pierrot on the roof, with a harbor view, or the Grill?"

"Your party, you choose," I said, hoping she'd choose the Grill, a dark, comfortable restaurant on the ground floor of the hotel, with the feeling of a dining room in a private club. During the day the Grill was *the* place for Hong Kong's version of the power lunch. In the evening, however, it was relaxed and less crowded. I wasn't in the mood for a rich French dinner or the formal setting of the Pierrot.

"The Grill's cozier and the food's simpler," Angela said, reading my mind. "I'll see you there in twenty minutes."

She greeted me with a handshake that was like an embrace. No butterfly landings this time. She squeezed my hand with astounding strength. A look poured from her eyes that sent vibrations all the way to my feet. It was a look not of love but of regard. It said, "I care about you. I'm glad you're alive."

The maître d'hôtel led us past an extravagant display of meats and seafood to a table about twenty feet from the open kitchen. As he seated Angela in a soft slipcovered armchair, I had a moment to look at her. It seemed hard to believe that this small, composed, almost China-doll-like woman, with near-perfect features framed by dense, black hair, dressed so carefully in a long, high-collared silk dress, its black color a striking contrast to her pale skin, was the same woman who had led me through such an explosive, prolonged and physically memorable bout of sex. I fought back those memories, knowing what would happen if I let them surface. I didn't want that; it would muddle the clarity I'd gained from the experience.

Knowing how direct Angela was, I'd worried that she'd ask me to tell her what our weekend together had meant to me. I needn't have. She seemed completely comfortable, as though she'd expected nothing more from the experience than the experience itself. She didn't so much as allude to our weekend, asking instead for assurances about my health, and—once I'd satisfied her on that score—whether I'd made any progress in my work. To the extent that I could, I let her know that I'd achieved my objectives in Hong Kong, and I thanked her again for her help. "I couldn't have done it without you," I said.

"Just doing my job," she said, but I could tell she was pleased.

Moments later, the maître d' arrived to take our order. "May I?" Angela asked me with a smile. "No offense, but you look as if one more decision would break you."

It was the perfect observation, perfectly timed. I leaned back, feeling each part of my body relax. "By all means," I said with an answering smile.

"Anything you don't eat?"

"No."

"But your preference is fish and seafood."

"As a rule."

"Because it's healthier." The way she said it, it sounded like a description of my character more than a statement of fact.

I grinned. "Yes, as a matter of fact."

Angela turned to the maître d' and spoke softly to him in Chinese without consulting the menu, so softly that I could have overheard only by leaning nearer. Instead, I looked around at the splendor of the room, its intimate brown, tan and green decor, a hybrid of European and Asian taste, reinforced by a low, slatted ceiling and strategic, minimal lighting.

When the maître d' left, Angela turned expectantly to me, waiting, it seemed, for me to take this evening wherever I wished it to go.

"I met an extraordinary man today," I said.

"Who was that?"

"Kurt Muller."

She beamed. "One of the kindest, most generous men in Hong Kong."

"You know him?"

"Not personally. He's used the hotel in connection with some of his charities. I've had dealings with him perhaps half a dozen times. He's very zealous about his charitable work. Doesn't just make a donation. He really runs the show."

Shades of my father, who, had he lived, would be just a few years younger than Muller. "Are there many people like that in Hong Kong?" I said.

"Kind and generous people?" Angela gave a quick shake of her head. "Not to that degree. This is a money-driven culture. The objective here is to acquire money, not give it away. Money's your ticket to the upper class."

"What I meant, actually, was, are there many Jews in Hong Kong?" I asked, surprised at what a difficult time I was having saying what was on my mind.

"I've heard estimates as high as three thousand," Angela said without reflection. "The ones I know are very high quality."

"High quality meaning rich?"

She shook her head again. "They're all well-to-do, but that's not what I meant. They live exemplary lives, are active in city affairs, charities, all the good things."

What a good feeling that gave me. Under the circumstances, my next question sounded almost crass, but it was something I felt I should know. "Is Kurt Muller the richest Jew in Hong Kong?"

"Oh, no. Not even close. That would be the Kadoories. They have billions. You know of them, of course?"

I shook my head, embarrassed. "Actually, I've never heard of them. What's the source of *their* wealth?"

"Flip a light switch and they're making money."

"They own the power company?"

"They own four power companies. Also banks, textile mills, construction companies, trading companies and all sorts of other things."

A sommelier had approached the table as we were speaking, and stood silently and patiently, waiting to be noticed.

"Ah!" Angela said as she saw him. She beckoned him with her right index finger. He bent close to her. She whispered in his ear. Whatever she said provoked a respectful smile. He straightened, took a step back, bowed, then walked away.

"You *do* seem to have an in here," I said.

Angela smiled. "Now, you were asking about the Kadoories."

"Do they identify as Jews?"

"Oh, very much so. Pillars of the Jewish community."

"How long have they lived here?"

"Since the late 1800s. The founding father was Elly Kadoorie. He became a lord. So did his sons."

"British subjects, then?"

"Oh, most definitely."

"Do Jews have any special problems here?" I asked carefully.

Maybe it was because I was looking for a reaction, but Angela seemed to hesitate before answering and regard me quizzically. "You'd have to ask them," she said, "but I would very much doubt it. Chinese people have no special brief against Jews. To them, they're no better than any other white person. Among foreigners, the usual biases prevail, but the Jews are fully integrated into Hong Kong society. They belong to all the best clubs."

"Do the Jews have a synagogue?"

"Ohel Leah Synagogue." A shadow crossed Angela's face and she drew back suddenly. "Why are you asking all these questions? You're not Jewish, are you?"

It was one of those exquisitely timed moments that you couldn't plan if you tried. As I was about to answer that I was, our waiter arrived with a huge platter of oysters, clams, shrimp and lobster claws. A month before, I would have laughed; now I felt a sudden melancholy. "I'm not sure," I said.

Angela drew back a little further. "What do mean by *that?*"

"What I mean," I said, composing my thought as I spoke, "is that yes, I'm Jewish, but no, I'm not, because absolutely nothing I do in my life has anything to do with my being Jewish other than openly identifying as a Jew." I nodded toward the food platter. "The man who brought my father's side of our family to America would be spinning in his grave if he knew what I was about to eat, because Orthodox Jews eat nothing from the sea that doesn't have scales. I'm so far removed from that ancestor that I don't really know what I am."

The sommelier returned with a bottle of Dom Pérignon. As he opened and then poured the champagne, Angela watched me so closely I had the feeling she could see inside me. "You sound sad," she said after we'd touched glasses.

I wasn't going to deny it. "I'm not sure 'sad' is the right word. 'Regretful' might be more accurate." I hesitated, as a new thought took shape in my mind. "I'm beginning to wonder if there may be something about the American experience that grinds away the edges of everyone who goes there. I suppose it's inevitable that people who move from one culture to another wind up being something they wouldn't have been had they remained where they were. But I'm not sure it's such a good thing."

"Why not?"

"It breaks people down. Devalues what they were. They spend their lives trying to become the kind of people they believe the new society values. Those who can't do it fall through the cracks. They're the ones I see."

Angela had been nibbling as we talked, but so far, I hadn't touched the seafood. "Would you like to order something else?" she asked softly.

"No way! I just hope this is dinner because I'm going to stuff myself."

"It's not dinner, but stuff yourself anyway. You've earned it."

I dug in. It was heaven. "Is there really something after this?" I asked.

Angela smiled. "Something you'd never order for yourself—the best steak in the house, accompanied by French fries."

It was exactly what I'd wanted. And she was right, I never would have ordered it. I shook my head and laughed. "You're scary," I said. "Three meetings, and you know me better than I know myself."

The sommelier reappeared, this time with a velvety Burgundy. I suppose that what happened next was a measure of how much I'd been softened up in the past month, combined with that reference to my ancestor, but as I put my nose to the glass, I was engulfed in memory, back in my father's wine cellar. We were going through our tasting ritual together and I knew he was watching me out of the corner of his eye, and in a moment he'd ask me what I thought of the wine and I'd say, "Not bad," and he'd throw back his head and laugh. Now, thirty years later, on the other side of the world, I was suddenly paralyzed, my nose stuck in a wineglass.

"Is something wrong?"

I squeezed my eyes and cleared my throat and only then lifted my head. "I got caught up in a thought," I said.

We finished dinner with small talk. I had nothing more to give.

"Let's take a walk," Angela said.

"That's not a good idea," I said. "What about the Harlequin Bar?"

She smiled. "Lovely," she said.

The bar, on the twenty-fifth floor, was even more dimly lit than the Grill, probably to emphasize the dazzling city and harbor views framed in its huge windows. It was well past eleven, but ferries, junks and small cargo ships were on the move, their lights playing on the water. As I turned and looked at the countless apartment buildings that climbed up the slopes, almost every light seemed to be on. "The Kadoories are making money," I said.

Angela smiled. "You don't have to worry about the Kadoories."

We settled into soft chairs in a corner of the room, and ordered espressos. "I wonder what will happen to the Kadoories when the People's Republic takes over," I said when the waiter left. Then, suddenly, I touched her arm. "Never mind the Kadoories. What will happen to *you?*"

She raised her eyebrows and smiled with an effort. "Well, we'll just have to see, won't we?"

"Will you leave?"

She studied her hands, then looked up at me. "I don't think so," she said. "This is my home. I love it. I love my job. I have family and friends. If the Communists are smart, they'll leave us alone and let us continue to do what we do well. If they're not smart, and they make life unpleasant, then I'll leave."

We all have our battles, I thought. "I'm sure you know that I wish you well," I said. It seemed so inadequate. "If there's ever any way I can help you, promise you'll let me know."

Her eyes fastened onto mine. "That's very kind," she said softly. A pause. "And you? You'll be leaving tomorrow?"

"If I can get a flight."

She frowned. "Four days before Christmas—that could be a problem. Let me work on it straightaway in the morning. First class?"

"If possible, but I'll take anything I can get."

"Consider it done." Her frown disappeared, replaced by a gentle smile. She put a hand on my face. That butterfly touch once again. "You are leaving me with a memory I will carry all my life." By the softness in her eyes I knew it was a good one.

I covered her hand with mine. "The same to you."

Our coffees came. We sipped in silence. In the elevator a few minutes later, I kissed her good-bye. At the ground floor, she squeezed my hand and walked quickly through the lobby to the entry and got into a cab.

I'd sincerely meant my offer of help, but having experienced Angela's independence, I had a feeling that we wouldn't meet again.

The next morning, early, I called Dirk Richards and told him I needed a copy of the photograph of Jimmy Chang with Ying Shen as soon as possible. It was delivered to my suite as I was eating breakfast in the living room.

At nine-fifteen, Angela called, all business. "You're on United at one-forty-five. I got you the last seat in coach, and you're top of the list for a cancellation in both first class and business."

"You're marvelous," I said.

"No. I'm corrupt. Promises were made."

I laughed.

"We'll get you out of the hotel the same way as yesterday. You'll want to leave by eleven-thirty. At the airport the driver will take you directly to the VIP lounge, so you won't have to go through the terminal. From the lounge you walk directly to your plane. So I shouldn't think you'd be bothered." The slightest pause. "I *was* right, wasn't I? You prefer not to be bothered?"

I laughed again. "It will help me a ton to slip out of town. I'm very grateful."

"Good luck, then," she said, her voice as cheery as the morning I'd first heard it. And then she was gone.

I sat for a minute, dealing with this small new void in my life. Then I went into the bedroom to pack. At ten o'clock Gordon arrived with his camcorder, and we proceeded with the interview.

Gordon was once again the consummate professional, smooth and urbane. But there were moments when he acted as though he were interviewing a dead man. In those moments, his voice sounded heavy, and he faltered when asking his questions. "Cheer up," I said when we finished, "this interview's my insurance policy."

Gordon's face darkened. "What do you mean by that?" he asked anxiously.

"Let's leave it at that. Just be sure you put the cassette in a bank vault. Come to think of it, make arrangements with the bank to have it delivered to KUBC in the event something happens to you."

Gordon looked sharply at me. "You think I'm still in danger?"

I shrugged my shoulders. I just didn't know. "Until I settle this, neither one of us is safe." I paused. "I know what the pressure's going to be like when you get home. *You* know what happened when you caved in the last time. If you cave in again, it could cost me my life."

He regarded me solemnly. "I'm going to have to say something."

"Just be sure it doesn't involve me in any way, not even by implication."

He exhaled slowly and audibly, shook his head several times, and sat heavily on a couch. After a minute he looked at me imploringly, as though asking for understanding. "I'll tell you something," he said, "nothing's going to be the same for me after this. When you broadcast, you sit there reading those screens and looking into the lens and acting like you know everything that's going on in the world. What this experience has taught me is that I don't know *anything* about what's going on in the world. I'm not sure I want to spend my life pretending that I do."

"Does that mean you've changed your mind about moving up to network?"

He rolled his eyes. "Network's the last thing on my mind. It means that I've got serious doubts about living a life in which getting a story takes precedence over life itself. It wasn't just that moment with you yesterday. It's this whole goddamn thing. The woman I love gets cut up by scumbags, but I'm not even given time to grieve. The pressures to get the story are so unrelenting there are times when I actually forget about her. That's not right. That's just not right." He sat in silence, bent at the waist, elbows on his thighs, his head hanging down.

I watched him for a while, wondering if Gordon was really a changed man, or whether he'd forget all about it once he was back at work. "Be careful," I said as we walked to the door.

"Hey, *you* be careful," he said, his voice heavy again. "Don't make me use that tape."

The moment Gordon left I telephoned Steve Crown at the Morris Group office. "Didn't expect to hear from you," he said affably. "Had a call from Kurt Muller this morning. He liked you. He's a little scared, but he believes you'll do the right thing."

"*If* I break this case, I *will* do the right thing," I said.

"I believe you," Steve said.

"You tell him what I said, okay?"

"With pleasure. Keep me posted."

"Don't worry." I hesitated. "Actually, this is a personal call. I need your help on a business matter, for which I'll be happy to pay you." I told him about the loan my sister had arranged for Z. Tobias and Company, and asked if he could conceivably find out who had made it.

"Well, I'll be damned. Of course. Zack Tobias. Z. Tobias and Company. Never made the association. What the hell are you doing playing cop? Why aren't you on the Riviera?"

I had to laugh at his bluntness. "I sometimes wonder. What do you think? Can you run that down?"

"Not easy," he said, "but I'll see what I can do."

I thanked him and gave him my telephone number in San Francisco. Then I checked out by phone, took the service elevator to the ground floor and once again slipped from the hotel in the well of a 1963 Phantom Rolls.

In the VIP lounge at Kai Tak Airport I made one more call—to Chief Doyle. I'd waited this long so that I could call him at home—it was now 8:00 P.M. on Tuesday in San Francisco—rather than at his office. I didn't want whoever had faxed those messages in his name to Vancouver and Hong Kong to intercept my call.

For the first time in all the years I'd worked for him, the chief sounded glad to hear from me. "Relieved" is probably the right word. He listened in silence as I laid out the theory of the case, much as I had for Gordon.

"Sounds right," he said when I'd finished. He paused, then said, "Shit! Jimmy Chang!" Then a strange noise bounced off the satellite and into my ear. It took me a moment to identify it. It was exactly like the sound you make when you spit out a cherry pit. "What happens now?" the chief said.

"I pay a call on Jimmy Chang."

The chief was silent for a few seconds. "You should take a partner," he finally said.

"I don't think so, Chief. Until we find out who's helping Jimmy inside the department I'm better off working alone."

I could hear Doyle sigh. "Yeah, you're right," he said. "Is there *anything* I can do?"

"You bet," I said at once. "You can lift my suspension."

He was silent for so long that I began to wonder if he was still on the line. At last he said, "It's not that simple. There'd have to be a hearing."

"I don't have time for that," I said.

Another deep breath bounced off the satellite. "Let me work on it first thing tomorrow," the chief said.

"Do you and I have an understanding that my suspension is lifted?" I pressed.

"We do." No waffling in his voice. "Anything else?"

"Yeah. When this is over, I want my job back."

"That's a promise," he answered at once. "Is that it?"

"One more thing. Call Stanley Colby at customs and tell him I'm arriving on United 806 at nine-thirty tomorrow morning. Tell him I could use some special handling getting off the plane. Tell him if he can help me I might have a nice present for him."

The flight from Hong Kong took just under twelve hours. Miraculously, a first-class seat had become available, no doubt thanks to Angela and her "promises." Cocktails came shortly after takeoff, and then lunch. Dinner was served six hours later. Both meals were excellent, but not in the same league with those on Cathay Pacific. Nor was the service, as good as it was, a match for that gentle, unobtrusive attention Asians give that suggests they consider their work a high calling and not a compromise.

The moment the lights were dimmed after dinner, I fell asleep. When I awakened the cabin was dark. Immediately I started thinking about Jimmy Chang.

I had no illusions about how tough it was going to be to expose him. Dirk Richards had told me how certain the RHKP was that Ying Shen was a major drug dealer, smuggler and a murderer. Yet they hadn't been able to put him away. How was *I* to nail Jimmy, who hadn't committed any crimes that I knew of, let alone could prove? Changing your name isn't a crime.

The one thing I did have was information that could ruin Jimmy.

I tried to sleep again, but couldn't. Soon, daylight began to seep into the cabin, and before long, the cabin attendants were serving a breakfast snack.

When we landed in San Francisco, Stanley Colby came aboard with a man from the Immigration and Naturalization Service the moment the door opened. I shook hands with both of them, then shouldered my Hartman bag.

"Do you have any more luggage?" Stanley said.

"No. That's it," I said.

"That sure simplifies it."

They led me out a door of the ramp and down a flight of steps to a car. As we drove off the field I gave the man from immigration my landing card.

"So where's my present?" Stanley said as we arrived at the Avis lot.

"I have to wrap it first," I said. "But count on it." I got out of the car and leaned back inside to shake Colby's hand. "Thanks for this," I said, nodding as well to the man from immigration.

He waved. "Happy to help," Stanley said.

We both laughed.

My best chance, I figured, was to confront Jimmy at his home. That meant I'd have to wait until evening. I would have given anything to wait out the hours in my apartment, but I was afraid to take the chance. Whoever was helping Jimmy might have continued to stake out the building in anticipation of my return. If Britt was there, her bodyguard would be there as well, and he might mention my presence to the wrong people. I didn't even take a chance on calling her. Instead, after renting a Ford at Avis, I checked in at the Courtyard on Bayhill Drive in San Bruno, and—it being the middle of the night in Hong Kong—easily slept through the day.

Jimmy lived at 221 Edgewood Avenue, just below Twin Peaks, a short street paved with bricks and lined with fruit trees. I'd always thought of it as the prettiest street in the city. The trees were bare now, their leaves lost until the spring, but even in the dim light from the streetlamps, the naked limbs gave a starkly beautiful frame to the street. On either side of it were two- and three-story homes, nearly touching one another on one side, separated on the other by a narrow passageway. If you wanted to live on Edgewood Avenue, I calculated, it would cost you at least a million dollars. Not bad for a triad enforcer who'd left Hong Kong penniless twenty years before.

I found a parking spot and studied Jimmy's house through a windshield speckled by a cold December drizzle that had begun just as I'd driven up. Two stories were visible from the street. The main floor was at street level. Bedrooms would be on the upper level. A lower floor had been dug into the hillside. The exterior of the house was wood shingle, the wood darkened so deeply it appeared to be almost black. From what I'd learned in shopping for my own building, I judged this one to be sixty years old, but it seemed so settled into the landscape it might have been there forever. It was on the east side of the street, which meant an unimpaired view of San Francisco Bay and the Bay Bridge. The best homes in Hong Kong overlook the city and the harbor; perhaps it was the view that had sold Jimmy on the house.

Just before seven, Jimmy's black Mercedes turned onto Edgewood.

Half a minute later he emerged from the backseat. His chauffeur—and almost certainly his bodyguard as well—waited until Jimmy had entered the house, then drove away. That's a break, I told myself. I waited five minutes, then walked to the door, which was decorated with a large Christmas wreath of fresh boughs held together by a red ribbon. I rang the bell.

Jimmy answered.

"Hello, Li Ching," I said.

24

I suppose my doubts had begun even before I'd walked to Jimmy's door. A onetime triad enforcer didn't belong in such a setting; it was too establishment, too sedate, too refined. But at the instant of our encounter the doubts were mere ripples in my brain, repressed by the sight of a man—or, more accurately, his façade—disintegrating before my eyes.

I have no recollection of Jimmy's mouth opening or jaw dropping or eyes bulging, or any of the other physiological responses we associate with shock. What I remember is the life force seeming to drain from his face, and his features hardening as they do in the moment of death. In those first seconds after my greeting, only his eyes showed life. He stared at me as though I were the Devil come to claim him, and then he looked into the street, his gaze blank and unfocused. I'd worried that he might rush for a weapon. I needn't have. In that moment, Jimmy Chang, alias Li Ching, was utterly incapable of defending himself.

He turned slowly and walked unsteadily through the foyer to the library, at one point reaching out a hand to brace himself. He hadn't signaled me to follow him, but I sensed that that was what he expected me to do. Walking behind him, I became aware of an interior that seemed interchangeable with countless San Francisco homes: overstuffed Victorian furniture on dark hardwood floors covered in places with Persian rugs, a brass screen in front of a beige-and-white marble fireplace, a baby grand piano, a floor-to-ceiling bookcase, its clusters of books interspersed with photographs, white walls broken up here and there by paintings in the style of the Impressionists. A six-foot-high Christmas tree, ablaze with lights and laden with ornaments, had been wedged into a corner of the living room. There was not a single Asian artifact to remind one that the occupants of the house were first-generation Chinese immigrants. Edges ground away.

Jimmy walked behind his antique desk, planted his hands on its well-polished surface and sank slowly into a chair, his gaze still vague and distant. Finally he looked at me, gestured for me to close the door and then to sit in a chair across from his desk.

Minutes passed. Instinct told me to remain silent, and instinct was all I had to go on, because never before, neither as a cop nor as a civilian, had I seen anyone break down as instantly and completely as Jimmy had. I had no option but to wait for him and not force the issue.

At last Jimmy closed his eyes, squeezing tears from them. And then he began to cry. He cried for several minutes, his body shaking and heaving. He cried for the most part in silence; only an occasional moan issued from his constricted throat.

There was a loud knock on his door, and a woman, certainly his wife, shouted in Chinese, "What's going on?"

"Go away," Jimmy shouted back in a choked voice, also in Chinese. A brief silence, and then I heard her retreating steps.

A few more minutes passed. He stopped crying, mopped his cheeks with a handkerchief, took several deep breaths and looked at me. His sorrow was so great I could scarcely bear to look at him. His eyes were puffy, his round face seemed to have elongated, as though it were being squeezed in a vise. "What you want?" he said. It was not a demand. It was a statement of surrender.

"Before we talk," I said, "you should know that everything I've learned is on a tape that will be aired on television if anything happens to me."

"Tell me what you learn," Jimmy said submissively.

For the first few minutes he listened as though paralyzed. Then he began shaking his head from side to side, as if to refute everything I was saying.

"First part true. Rest not true," he said when I'd finished. "Name Li Ching. Ying Shen best friend. Walk out of China." As he spoke, his eyes took on a far-off look and his voice seemed to slow and deepen, as though it were coming from a record on an old Victrola that was winding down. "Cross duck farms, like you say. Hong Kong very hard, very hard. No one help. Steal to eat. Sleep in parks. No way keep clean. One day cops catch us, lock us up. Big luck." Now, suddenly, the pitch of his voice rose, as though the Victrola had been cranked up, and he began to make small jabbing motions with his hands. "We get shower, clean clothes, food. In jail, meet triad guy. Say he help us when get out. That how get with triad. Do little jobs. Look-see. Driver. Messenger. Collections. Don't hurt nobody. Nobody."

He was looking straight at me now, his eyes as fixed as rivets. "No kill nobody." He leaned forward, and slammed a palm on the desktop. "No—kill—nobody!" he said as emphatically as I've ever heard anyone say anything. "Cops ask about killing. I scared. No alibi. Who believe me, anyway, kid from China? I sure they get me, I spend life in prison. I ask triad help. They run seamen's union. They get me ship to Vancouver."

Jimmy sat back, and his hands settled into his lap. The memories seemed to soften his eyes. "In Vancouver, jump ship. Stay one year. Then 1973, big—how you say?—miracle. Canada make amnesty. Get papers. Right away, go San Francisco. In Chinatown, meet triad guy from Hong Kong. He tell me Ying rich now. Write for loan. Ying send me ten time what I ask. He say invest for me, we split profit. I do great. Make plenty money. All honest. No crime." He leaned even closer to me, his gaze now as imploring and unwavering as a dog's at dinnertime. "*No crime.* I clean. Hundred percent clean."

"So you want me to believe that you're absolutely legitimate?" I said.

"You bet. Hundred percent," he said pugnaciously, shoving his head forward.

"If that's true, Jimmy," I said softly, "why do you need the Golden Door Trading Company?"

His reaction this time was like the aftershock of an earthquake, similar in characteristics to the main event, merely less intense. He closed his eyes, drew several deep breaths, then sank back into his chair. When he opened his eyes again, I saw the same look of resignation I have seen a hundred times in men and women confronted with their fate. "I tell you truth, Ying Shen kill me," he said. It was a statement, not a plea.

"If you tell me the truth, I may be able to help you. If you don't tell me the truth, your life in this city is over."

He stared at me, then turned away, closed his eyes and again began to shake his head from side to side. It went on for a minute. At last he turned to me. "Life here over anyway," he said. His voice was unutterably sad. He took a nervous breath, then resumed his narrative. "By 1980 I rich man. Want nothing with Ying. I try pay him. He say not now. Maybe later. All time try. Same answer. Not now. One day Ying call. Say I owe him million dollar. I say no way. He say forget money, he don't want money, he want favor. He say take money and open bank. So I open bank. Put up five hundred thousand dollar. Then he say open trading company. So I open trading company. Then business start."

Jimmy was nodding now, affirming the truth of his story. The pitch of his voice had risen along with the volume. "I find out running Chinese laundry. I tell Ying no way, I quitting. He say you quit, I tell RHKP, they get you for murder. I say I not do murder. He say you run away, they not believe you." Jimmy shrugged. "What can I do?" He raised his hands, palms up, the universal sign of resignation. "Year pass. One day, Ying call. He say, one more favor. I own ships now. You head of port for city. You fix it so no problem when ships come San Francisco."

He winced as he said it, and then his eyes enlarged. Either he was the greatest amateur actor I had ever seen, or what I was witnessing was a man reexperiencing the pain of a friend's betrayal.

"What did he mean, no problem?" I asked.

"No problem get stuff off ship."

"No problem with customs?"

"Right."

"He asked you to bribe U.S. Customs?" My voice gave away my surprise.

"Yes, right."

"What did you tell him?"

"I tell him he crazy. Not like Asia."

"And?"

"And he tell me I fix right away or he tell RHKP."

"How long ago was this?" I asked.

"About ship?"

"Yes."

"He call first time three month, maybe four month. Last time call five, maybe six week."

"What did you do?"

Jimmy laughed scornfully. "Do nothing. Shit hit fan. Everybody watch bank. I tell Ying, Ying back off."

Since the moment I'd entered Jimmy's home, that ripple of doubt I'd felt as I'd sat in my car, waiting for his return, had slowly built into a giant swell, engulfing not the story he was telling—which stood, for the moment at least, on the high and dry ground of logic—but the mind-set I'd brought to this case. All my professional life I had fought against making judgments on the basis of random clues. I knew, because I'd seen it happen so many times, that by selectively choosing clues you could make almost any case you wanted. Since there was invariably a "clue" for almost any thesis imaginable, almost any thesis could appear to hold up. Add to this the tendency of cops who, despite the best intentions, unconsciously gravitate toward the "clues" that appear to confirm the theories they bring to the job, and you can see how possible it is to cobble together a case that may not mirror reality.

The process of mental editing I've just described is not exclusive to cops. Prosecutors are guilty of it. So are judges, politicians, lawyers, journalists, doctors, stockbrokers, executives—anyone, in fact, with the slightest leanings or stake in an outcome. Society is guilty, as well. For years now, I'd sensed that my city, by selectively choosing its clues, was turning slowly but surely toward a new and terrible perception: that because Asian gangsters and their dirty money were moving into the city, it followed that the influx of Asians was, if only indirectly, contributing to the decline of the city.

I had fought that perception every chance I had, most recently in front of Mike Winehouse. And yet from the moment I'd discovered the triad imprint on the crime against his daughter, every judgment I'd made had been skewed by that same bias against Asian criminals. Maggie had broadcast a five-part series on the impact of Asian immigration to the Bay Area. The series had concluded with an evaluation of the criminal elements attached to that immigration. A week later she'd been attacked by Asians. Cause and effect had seemed pretty clear.

To my credit, I'd resisted the attempt to hang the blame for Maggie's assault on Jimmy—at least initially. Yet even I had ultimately been softened up by the series of disclosures that had seemed to incriminate him. But each "clue" had led me closer and closer to the wrong conclusion—or so it now appeared.

I had one more surprise in my arsenal. "Why did you order the hit on Maggie Winehouse?" I asked.

Jimmy's eyes bulged. He gagged and rushed from the library. Seconds later I heard him retching and flushing a toilet. Then I heard him running through a corridor, away from the library. Another ten seconds passed. Then I heard his footsteps once again, this time coming my way. Had he gone for a gun? I was unarmed; I'd left my gun at home on the assumption that a suspended cop might have some explaining to do if he brought a gun to Hong Kong. At the moment, it seemed like a foolish decision. I rose and moved to a wall next to the door, intent on hurling myself at Jimmy, if need be, the moment he returned. I heard other footsteps. Moments later the door opened, and Jimmy's three daughters filed through the door, propelled from behind by their father. The oldest looked about fourteen, the youngest around eight. All three had long gleaming black hair, smooth skin and almond eyes, and a look of deference that suggested they lived in awe of authority. All three were dressed in parochial-school uniforms. They all looked like their mother, a handsome, slender, carefully dressed woman of about forty, who stood behind Jimmy, as anxious and bewildered as her daughters. Jimmy was shaking. "How I could do that?" he said to me. "How I could do that?"

For the next few seconds the only sound was Jimmy's panting. Then he gently turned his daughters, patently the treasures of his life, and led them from the room. Jimmy's wife, having obviously figured out who I was by this point, cast me a withering look, then followed her daughters.

Nothing I'd ever learned as a cop helped me to decide in that moment that Jimmy's story was true. I simply knew it. I sat, diminished, ashamed, and crushed by the realization that after all this time and effort I had no idea who had attacked Maggie Winehouse—or who had threatened me. If Jimmy wasn't involved, then Ying Shen wasn't involved; unless Jimmy had complained about Maggie to Ying, Ying would never have known about her—or me.

Jimmy returned a minute later, looking drained and ashen-faced, sat back down in his desk chair and waited for me to speak.

"I believe you," I said, "but no one else will, as matters stand. The only way you're ever going to be in the clear is if we find out who's behind this. Will you help me?"

He stared at me for a long time, as though he was trying to decide whether to believe me. "What you need?" he demanded at last.

"I need to find the two men who attacked Maggie Winehouse."

"How I do that?" he scoffed. "I tell you, I know nothing."

"Maybe you know someone who knows something."

Jimmy's eyes flitted from me to the walls of his library, every inch covered with plaques and photographs of himself with celebrities— no framed citizenship papers, I noted—then back to me again. "I help you, I dead man."

"I'm asking, Jimmy. The decision's yours."

He looked away again, and began to grind his teeth. Audibly. "You no say nothing?"

"Not even to my chief."

"How I know that?"

I sighed. "Because I'm ashamed, Jimmy. Do you understand that word? I was wrong about you. I caused you grief. I want to make it up to you." The words didn't begin to convey what I was feeling. I'd made mistakes before, but none remotely as serious as this one. I was shaken to my marrow at the thought of how close I'd come to causing an awful injustice.

Jimmy regarded me intently, his eyes not blinking, as if he might somehow suck out my spirit through my eyes and hold it up for inspection. Finally, he reached for the telephone.

In the next ten minutes, he made four calls. He made them in Chi-

nese, speaking rapidly, obviously assuming that I couldn't under-
stand him. But I could follow every call. The first two were fruitless.
The third produced a lead, the name of someone who might know
someone who might know something about the attack on Maggie.
"This is Jimmy Chang," he said to the next person. "You remember
that television girl who got her face cut?" There was a short silence.
"Right. Right. Do you know who hit her?" Another brief silence.
"Someone giving me trouble," he went on. "I want to scare him good.
Maybe these guys could help me." He listened, made some notes,
thanked his party—whom he had not identified by name—and hung
up. "You lucky," he said. "Two guys come from Hong Kong, do job,
like San Francisco so much they stay here."

So, I'd been right, in all likelihood. The men in the car pushing
mine down Hyde Street were probably the same ones who'd hit Maggie. "You have their names?"

He handed me the piece of paper. Two names were on it.

Ten minutes. Four calls. God, the anguish he could have saved us,
himself most of all. "Jimmy," I said, "why didn't you find these guys
when the rumors started—and put yourself in the clear?"

Jimmy squinted at me. "You crazy?" he said. "I find these guys, you
ask right away how I do it. Take you two seconds figure out."

I sighed. He was right. No point dwelling on it, in any case; I had
work to do. "Do you know where they are now?"

Jimmy nodded toward the telephone. "He say they every night in
Purple Onion."

In my mind I could see them—the faces behind the windshield of
the Suburban—but a fleeting glance under such duress wasn't good
enough for an arrest. "How do I identify them?" I asked.

Again Jimmy ground his teeth. I sat there listening to him. A
minute passed. Then abruptly he picked up the phone again and
punched a local number. Without identifying himself, he asked his
contact to meet him at the Purple Onion at ten o'clock, explaining
that he wanted to look the men over before talking to them. Then he
hung up. "Be outside Purple Onion at ten-thirty," he said to me.
"Wait for me. Maybe wait long time."

Yes, it was the same Purple Onion, the lower-budget version of its
neighbor, the Hungry i, where in the fifties and the sixties Mort Sahl

and Woody Allen and Lenny Bruce had led the ridicule of the society they'd inherited. The Hungry i had long since closed its doors, but the Purple Onion, located in a Columbus Avenue basement, had passed through a series of owners, winding up as a dingy nightclub with a three-piece band and a Chinese vocalist, whose patrons were almost exclusively Asians.

Without speaking to him about it, I thought I understood what Jimmy was up to. He would ask his contact to point out the two men to him, and then to disappear, explaining that he didn't want him involved in case anything should go wrong. The contact would understand that. I was equally certain that Jimmy, who had no way of knowing that I'd understood his conversation, had asked me to be outside the nightclub half an hour after his rendezvous so there would be no chance I'd see him with the contact. Fair enough; it was just as well for me not to know the man's identity. I kept my part of the bargain, parking on Columbus, just across from the club, at exactly ten-thirty.

To judge by the behavior of the scattered pedestrians moving along the sidewalk, a chill wind was blowing down the avenue. Their jackets were buttoned or zippered, their collars were turned up and those pedestrians moving up the avenue were bent forward a few degrees from the waist. Only a few of the shops and restaurants had hung Christmas lights in their windows this year—a sign, perhaps, that the country's heralded economic resurgence hadn't reached Columbus Avenue. I'd turned the motor off, and it soon became cold in the car. To add to my discomfort, I was feeling dehydrated and jet-lagged. But I would have endured torture, by this point, to get a break on the case.

At one-thirty the next morning, as I was beginning to wonder if I'd dozed off and missed Jimmy, he finally walked out of the club. Two men had just preceded him up the steps. I climbed from my car to make sure he saw me. As soon as he did he nodded in the direction of the two men, then turned and walked away.

One was skinny and quite young, mid-twenties at most, the other at least forty, probably older, about the average weight of a beefy American but heavy for an Asian. From this distance and in the dark, I couldn't be sure theirs were the faces I'd seen in my rearview mirror, but I thought they were and, more to the point, they fit the descriptions Maggie had given me. They walked south on Columbus, moving slowly and a little unsteadily. I waited until they were a block away, then followed in my car. At Clay, they turned east, walked for half a block and got into a fairly new Lincoln coupe, the heavy one behind the wheel. He pulled quickly into the street, drove to Montgomery, turned south to California, then turned right and headed west. It was easy to follow them because there was almost no traffic, but I had to keep a big distance between us to keep them from getting suspicious.

At Gough the driver turned left toward Geary, then right onto Geary and headed west again. It was obvious that he'd already learned the city; Geary is the best east–west thoroughfare in town. It was equally obvious that he'd had a lot to drink. He kept weaving from lane to lane. At Fifteenth Avenue, he turned left, drove a block and a half and parked in the driveway of a tan, stucco, single-family house, immediately in front of the garage door. To the left of the garage was a small door leading—if it was anything like similar structures I'd seen—down a long outside corridor to an in-law apartment at the back of the house. The two men got out of the car and walked to the small door. As they opened the door I drove past them, flipped on my brights, made a sharp U-turn into a driveway and down the sidewalk, stopped six feet from them and jumped out of the car. "Police!" I said. "Freeze!"

The skinny one took off. I grabbed the fat one, pushed him through the door and down the corridor to the in-law apartment. It was a studio, unfurnished, with a kitchenette. Two pads were on the floor, a blanket on each of them. The rest of the floor was littered with trash. The smell of old food intermingled with mildew. "Hands against the wall," I ordered in Chinese. He looked at me, startled, then did it. I patted him down; he was clean. Then I turned him around. As I did, he pushed me hard. I stumbled on one of the mats, and fell. He darted for a corner of the room, kicked frantically at some clothing, then bent quickly, straightened and spun around, both arms out in front of him. In his right hand was a cleaver.

He was grinning now. I would have recognized it anywhere. It was the same grin I'd seen on the face of the man piloting the power-cruiser that had played tag with me on the bay.

For a heavy man he was quick. He lunged at me, lashed out with the cleaver, missed by a hair, and recovered, all in a second. We circled like wrestlers, first to the left, then the right, each of us feinting several times. Again he lunged and again the cleaver flashed through the air and again he missed and recovered—but this time not quite as fast as the first time. He was panting now, his mouth open, swallowing air. Once more I feinted, causing him to lash out, even slower this time, and slower to recover. Yet another feint, and he lunged at me again, and this time as he recovered, I took a step in, planted both feet, and landed the best punch of my life on the side of his jaw. He reeled backward. His head hit a wall. As he crumpled to the floor the cleaver fell from his hand.

I wrapped the cleaver in a shirt and put it next to the door.

Two minutes later, he stirred. I slapped his face to help bring him around. When his eyes focused on me, he recoiled. "I didn't do it," he said before I could ask a question. "It was the other guy. He cut the girl. I just drove the car."

"Who paid you?" I demanded.

"Sergeant Joe."

There are moments when the mind leaps across years and cuts through thousands of memories to link isolated facts. In that horrific millisecond, with nothing more to go on, I knew the identity of Sergeant Joe.

I pulled the man to his feet and out the door, grabbing the cleaver as we went, and through the corridor to my car. I opened the front door on the passenger side and stood him next to it. Without a gun or handcuffs or a secure backseat, I did the only thing I could. I hit him with a short right, on the same spot on his jaw, and once again he crumpled. I caught him and shoved him into the car. Seconds later, I was racing the car down the street, running every stop sign. I crossed Park Presidio against a red light. In two minutes, I pulled up to Richmond Station on Sixth between Geary and Anza. I raced around to the passenger side, opened the door, pulled the man out and dragged him inside. "Book him to me," I shouted to the desk sergeant. "Captain Tobias, Special Investigations. No warrant. Two forty-three. Hold for Immigration." And then I was out the door.

I have no idea how long it took me to drive to my apartment. I remember them only as nightmare minutes in which I calculated how long it had taken the skinny one to get to a telephone and call Sergeant Joe and whether there had been sufficient time for Sergeant Joe to beat me to the apartment. As I sifted through the events of the last weeks, understanding at last how each followed upon the other, I hadn't the slightest doubt that that was where he'd go. I parked in front of my garage, took the steps three at a time and rushed to my door. It was open. In my living room, I found what I'd more or less expected, an off-duty cop, one of Tony Garibaldi's men, out cold, duct tape across his mouth and around his legs. His arms were behind him, taped at the wrists. I raced through the door to my bedroom, knowing once again that my only weapon was surprise—not the surprise of my sudden appearance, because I knew I was expected, but the surprise of sudden action. Sergeant Joe would expect me to stop at the sight of his gun. My one chance was to keep going.

And there he was—Joseph Pendola, the man I'd fired from the Gang Task Force—standing next to my bed, pointing a revolver at Britt's head. Britt was in the bed, the covers pulled to her chin, as though they might somehow shield her from this nightmare. I knew that if I looked at her I'd be lost; the terror in her eyes would stop me.

I charged without thinking, my body thankfully remembering to do what it had done so many hundreds of times on the football field as I attempted to get past an offensive lineman: stay low, feint, turn sideways. I heard a shot and felt a sudden, overpowering cramp in my gut, as though my bowels had exploded. But my momentum kept me going. I felt my shoulder hit his legs and then we were both on the floor. The force of the fall knocked the gun from his hand. As he reached out for it I brought both fists down on his head with all my might. That slowed him just long enough to enable me to beat him to the gun. And then I was on top of him, with the gun in my hand, pointed at his head, and I spoke through the unbearable pain that had now invaded every molecule in my body. "You've got one second to tell me who put you up to this," I said, "or I swear to God I'll shoot you."

I have to hand it to him; in this moment he showed not the slightest fear. Venom can do that for you. "You won't shoot me, you kike faggot," he said, spitting the words. "You haven't got the guts."

A dam within me crumbled. There spilled through it then such hatred as I had never felt before, hatred for this man and what he and others like him had done to dehumanize my city, to destroy its balance, its openness, its tolerance—hatred of such intensity, I knew in this humbling and degrading moment, that it surely matched his own.

I fired.

25

Britt screamed.

Directly below me, I could hear my tenants shouting. I was sure they'd call for help—the bullet had probably gone through their ceiling—but sure wasn't good enough because I was so overcome with pain I thought I might pass out. "Dial 911," I told Britt, my eyes still on Pendola. "Say '406, officer needs assistance,' and give 'em the address. Then get out of the building."

The absence of sound told me she hadn't moved. "Britt! Please! Do it now!"

An instant later I heard her receding footsteps, and knew she'd left the room.

In the second after I'd reached the gun and before I'd shot him, Pendola had struggled onto his back. I was sitting on his stomach, my knees on the floor, my legs on either side of his chest. My nose told me he'd lost control of his bowels. I could see red where I'd creased his scalp. My shot, meant to scare, not kill, had done its job. "Talk to me," I said, aiming this time between his eyes. I wasn't bluffing; I knew I could kill him. I *wanted* to kill him. The knowledge was as overpowering as the pain in my gut.

But Pendola said nothing. Either he was hanging tough or—as his wide eyes and gaping mouth and rapid breathing suggested—I'd scared him so badly he'd lost his voice.

I could hear Britt on the telephone, down the hall, giving the message, word for word, and adding the address. Within seconds I heard the distant sound of sirens. There were at least four of them. Two sounded no more than half a mile away. They'd reach the building in a minute. It would take them another minute to get from the street to the bedroom. I wasn't sure I could hold on.

A fierce stab of pain, as surprising as lightning, made me gasp and wince. My eyes closed for an instant, but that was all Pendola needed. I felt a hand around my wrist, and then he was pulling me and I toppled to the floor. He banged my right hand against the floor so hard that I lost my grip on the gun. And then he was on top of me with the gun in his hand, its barrel a foot from my eyes.

I heard a shot, but saw no flash.

Pendola's eyes widened in surprise, and then, as blood poured from his mouth, he fell on top of me and went limp. I pushed him off me, turned my head and saw Britt in the doorway, looking aghast at the gun in her hand.

I remember almost nothing of the next hours except the pain. I have impressions, nothing more, of many cops around me, and then paramedics, and of being in an ambulance whose cornering movements made me scream. At some point someone at SF General told me I was going into surgery. I have a hazy memory of a moment in the recovery room, where I shouted to attract a nurse and tried to ask what had happened. But I'm not sure I made sense and whatever she responded didn't register. My first solid memory is of rolling on a stretcher down a corridor and Britt leaning down and saying, "They removed your right kidney, but you're going to be fine."

When I was able to listen, the doctors told me that thousands of people are born with one kidney and lead normal lives, that a single kidney has twice the necessary capacity to purify the body of its wastes, that, in any case, my remaining kidney would eventually gain the functional power of two kidneys as a consequence of its added burdens. But nothing they said could dispel my conviction that forces beyond my control had taken command of my destiny. And no amount of medication could eradicate my pain.

Each time I emerged from my stupor I'd been conscious of Britt's presence, but in those moments I was so overcome by my own agony that it was two days before I recognized what terrible shape she was in. Her eyes were rimmed in black, their whites streaked with red. That extraordinary vitality I had always associated with her had disappeared from her face, her trademark openness replaced by guarded glances each time a doctor or nurse or technician came into the room. Otherwise she stared vacantly, saying nothing, seemingly unaware of my gaze. Only on the third afternoon following my surgery—Christmas Day—did she open up.

"I killed a man," she said.

"You saved my life," I answered.

She went on as though I hadn't spoken. "Jack—the guard—was lying on the floor, all tied up. His eyes were closed. His gun was in the holster. I took it, and ran to the bedroom and saw that man roll you over and take the gun and point it at you. I didn't even think. I just shot him." She looked at me imploringly, as though for absolution. "I'd never killed anything before except an insect, and now I've killed a man."

"You saved my life," I said again, slowly, emphasizing each word.

Britt stared at me for a moment, then closed her eyes, as if to retreat to the privacy of her thoughts.

It's a measure of how spacy I'd been since the shooting that I'd scarcely thought of Joe Pendola. I remembered that he'd been shot, of course, but it hadn't occurred to me that he might be dead—probably because I so desperately wanted him to be alive. Now finally it registered that the answers to a dozen questions had died with him.

I had no answers for Phil Barbera, the lieutenant in charge of homicide, when he appeared on Monday, the day after Christmas, along with two of his inspectors. I'd been expecting him because department regulations require the head of homicide to investigate all shootings involving a police officer, even if no one was hurt. Barbera did the talking; his inspectors listened.

"What the hell was this about, Zack?" he asked. He was a muscular six-footer whose sunny disposition belied his work. A thick salt-and-pepper mustache contrasted starkly with his almost bald head.

It was my first day out of bed for any length of time. I was seated in an armchair next to the window, wearing a robe, still hooked up to a

portable IV. It was a few minutes before ten on a stormy winter morning. Through the window I could see the cars moving along the slick
surface of Potrero Avenue. In the distance, beyond Noe Valley, Twin
Peaks was enveloped by rain. "I don't know enough to tell you, Phil,"
I said.

He was standing a few feet from me, leaning against the wall. "You
had a history with Pendola," he said. It wasn't a question.

"He was part of the Gang Task Force when I took over," I answered
quickly. "I thought he was crooked. So did everyone else. I pushed
him out."

Phil squinted. "Is *that* what this was about?"

I shook my head. "I can't believe that," I said slowly. "It was years
ago."

"Did he say anything at the time?"

Thinking of those days was like turning the pages of a picture book,
each page an image of some unpleasant memory. "I don't recall anything but dirty looks," I said after a bit. "He was pretty bottled up."

"He didn't threaten you?" Phil asked suddenly.

"No," I said, shaking my head again. "I would have remembered
that—and I would have done something about it at the time."

Phil nodded, and worked his mouth, as though chewing on a
thought. "Tell me exactly what happened when you got to your
place," he said then.

"You've talked to Britt?"

"She doesn't know much. She said Pendola got there just before
you did. Told her he wouldn't hurt her. Then he just stood there,
pointing the gun at her. No explanation. She was totally shocked
when you came through the door. Says she didn't know you were in
town."

"That's right."

He gave me a what's-going-on-here look. "Lotta questions, Zack."

"I know, I know," I said quickly. "What about Garibaldi's guy?"

"Name's Jack Demarest. He's a patrolman, six years on the force.
Pendola rang the bell, told him he'd arranged with Garibaldi to take
over the work, wanted to case it out."

"At two-thirty in the morning?" I said incredulously.

"Yeah, I know," he said, nodding. "I asked him the same thing. He
said with Pendola that was no big deal. He'd worked for him before,

and Joe would often make rounds at that hour, checking on his guys. Anyway, Demarest turned his back for a second and it was lights out. Pendola tied him up. I guess he figured Demarest wasn't going anywhere and, being in a hurry, he didn't bother to take his gun."

"Lucky for me."

"I'll say. So take me through it."

I did, step by step.

"He called you a kike, huh?" Phil said.

"A kike faggot, to be exact."

He shook his head. "That guy really knew how to hate. He didn't have a good word for anybody. How'd you know he'd be there?"

The way he'd run the subjects together made me think he'd hoped to catch me off guard. But I'd anticipated the question. I locked my eyes on his, hoping he'd see that I was leveling with him. "I don't want to lie to you, Phil, and I can't tell you the truth."

He watched me carefully. "It's gotta have somethin' to do with Maggie Winehouse and that whole bit."

I shrugged, but said nothing, and hoped my eyes didn't give me away.

"Who's that dirtball you dropped off at Richmond Station?" Phil said, his eyes still glued on mine.

I shrugged again. "The truth is I don't know—but that's not the whole truth. Let's leave it at that for now."

Phil began to suck on the inside of his cheeks, first one, then the other. I could imagine what he was thinking. I was under suspension, and no matter how you sliced it, I'd precipitated a killing. But I still ranked him.

"Can you tell me if he figures in this case?" By his tone, as well as his phrasing, he seemed to want to make it plain that he was asking, not ordering.

"Sorry, Phil," I said. "I understand the spot you're in, but I can't answer that right now."

"I know what you been workin' on, Zack," Phil said almost apologetically. "Is it possible you learned something' that involved Pendola?"

I sighed. "Can't talk about it, Phil. Sorry."

Phil shook his head from side to side half a dozen times. "Have you been watching television or seen the papers in the last coupla days?" he said.

"I haven't exactly felt up to that."

"Yeah, I can understand that. Well, it's a feeding frenzy out there. The speculation's unbelievable."

"They'll just have to wait."

He rolled his eyes. "Do me a favor, will you? You tell 'em that."

In my postoperative daze, I hadn't thought about the story I'd created. Two cops in a shootout. One killed by the other's girlfriend. A feeding frenzy, all right.

Suddenly, thoughts of Gordon flew into my mind. A panic seized me. He was walking around with a conviction about Jimmy Chang's guilt, encouraged by me, that was almost certainly wrong. As reluctant as I was to get involved, I knew I had to warn him off. "Look, Phil," I said, "I'm pretty tired."

"Sure, Zack," he said at once. "I understand. We'll talk again." Within seconds Phil and his two inspectors were out the door.

I waited half a minute to be sure they were out of earshot, then called Gordon at home, thinking I'd leave a message. But he hadn't left for work yet. "You're the only person I'm calling," I said without preamble. "If you say we talked I'll deny it. I can't talk about what happened to me. The only purpose of this call is to warn you not to use anything about Jimmy Chang. If you do, you're going to be very sorry."

There was a long silence. "You've got to tell me more, Zack," he insisted.

"I'll tell you when I can, but right now I can't tell you anything. The only reason I'm telling you this much is to keep you from ruining yourself and other people."

"What do you mean by that?"

"That's it for now."

He gave a bitter little laugh. "You're killin' me, Zack."

"No. I'm saving you."

He exhaled, slowly and angrily. "When will you call me?"

"When I have this sorted out."

Another bitter little laugh. "Am I allowed to ask how you are?"

"Not to use. If anyone finds out I spoke to you, I'll have to talk to everyone. I'm just not up to doing that."

"Okay," he said, resigned. "How are you, just between us?"

Less than a week before, he'd asked the same question in Hong Kong. My response was pretty much the same. "Weak. Shaken. But glad to be alive."

For the next hour, I thought about every aspect of the case, beginning with the night the chief had called me at home. But I couldn't make connections. In the absence of the hard facts Joe Pendola could have supplied me, I would have to rely on reason. I tried to reduce it to the basics and lay it out, step by step.

Pendola had hired two Asians to hit Maggie Winehouse, who had just done a series on Asian migration to the Bay Area.

Someone had to have hired Pendola to do that job, because Pendola had no stake in those events.

Whoever hired Pendola *did* have a stake in those events.

What kind of stake? What was there to gain? What did the hit on Maggie achieve?

It destabilized the city.

Who had a stake in *that?*

I knew the answer by the time I'd asked the question.

I picked up the phone and called Bud Donnelly.

"I think we've got something to talk about," I said. I didn't even identify myself. I figured he'd recognize my voice, having heard it at least half a dozen times a year since I was a child. And in view of what had happened, I was sure he'd been expecting my call; beneath that police commissioner bluster was an extremely savvy man.

"I'll be there in half an hour," he said and hung up.

Sometimes you get lucky.

He *looked* like a man in the throes of contrition. His skin was gray. His hands shook. His eyes were puffy, and shifted about the hospital room as though he expected demons to materialize from the closet or the bathroom or from under the bed. He'd arrived just as an orderly was removing a lunch I'd scarcely touched. "Are you strong enough to walk?" he asked me.

I'd been up and down the corridors several times, at first with a therapist and then on my own. Not an easy undertaking; my right side was so stiff and tender that it seemed powerless, and had to be dragged along by my left side. "I'd just as soon stay here," I said.

"I'd feel better talkin' somewhere else," he insisted.

"If you're worried about bugs, Bud, forget it. No one knows you're here."

"If you wouldn't mind, Zack . . ." He trailed off.

I shrugged. "Whatever you like," I said, then moved gingerly from the bed and put on my robe and slippers.

"Yer not wired, are ya?" Bud said, lapsing into his just-one-of-the-boys brogue.

"Only with the IV," I said, reaching for the stand.

"You'll have to excuse me, Zack," he said. Before I knew what he was doing, he had patted me down. "Sorry," he said. "I got to be careful."

I walked slowly into the corridor, wheeling the IV stand along beside me, then turned right and walked to the far end of the corridor, past a dozen patients' rooms, every one of them occupied. I could see the bodies of the patients in their beds, but not their faces. In some of the rooms TV sets were on; in most, the lights were out, and the patients lay motionless. Doctors' rounds were over, the technicians had come and gone. The nurses were all in the nurses' station at the center of the floor, doing their paperwork. A quiet time.

At the end of the corridor, next to a window, were several wooden chairs that looked as though they'd somehow survived the last renovation. The window looked north, toward downtown, which from this distance and angle and through the rain looked little different from the downtown of any American city. I could see none of the landmarks—the bridges or bay or hills—that give San Francisco its unmistakable identity.

I settled carefully into one of the hard chairs. "Is there something you'd like to tell me?" I asked him wearily.

He pulled a chair next to mine, sat heavily, and came so close I could smell the vapors of alcohol that seemed to swirl around his head. "I never dreamed he'd do what he did, Zack," he said, his voice just louder than a whisper. "You got to believe that. I told him to stir things up. I never said, 'Go out and carve up a girl.' I was horrified, horrified." His bloodshot eyes enlarged as he spoke.

"So why did he do it?"

He threw his head back and stared skyward, as though asking God to provide him with an answer. "It was somethin' that happened," he said emphatically. "A coincidence. He's lookin' around for a way to stir things up, and suddenly here's Maggie Winehouse on the tube talkin' about how all this dirty triad money is doin' bad things to the Bay Area. And he gets it into his head to make it seem like the triads taught her a lesson."

The story was plausible. It fit Pendola's habits. "And he never cleared it with you?" I said.

"Never. Absolutely never," Bud said, turning his eyes on me. "If he'd a mentioned it, I woulda stopped him. Same with that attack on the Chinese girl."

"He set *that* up?"

"Who else?"

"Why, for God's sake?"

"To keep the kettle boiling."

I shuddered, and moved in my chair, trying, I suppose, to distance myself from Bud and what he was telling me. The effort cost me; pain shot from my side through my body. I had to wait for it to pass. "What about Jimmy Chang?" I said then. "How did he get involved?"

Bud threw his arms wide. "Another coincidence," he answered excitedly. "Jimmy's name comes up in a news story. Pendola gets it into his head that makin' it seem like Jimmy was responsible would keep the story hot."

That was consistent, too; Pendola had harbored a special contempt for Asians, undoubtedly why he'd volunteered for the Gang Task Force when it was formed after the Golden Dragon Massacre—and one of the major reasons why I'd removed him after taking command of the Asian detail. "He didn't clear that with you, either?" I asked.

"Never," Bud said with an emphatic shake of his head.

Something odd was happening. The man had arrived a penitent. With each explanation he gave me he seemed to be shedding more and more of his guilt. This wasn't expiation; each piece of the argument he was advancing seemed to persuade him a little more that none of this had really been his fault.

"Did Pendola send me that package with the cleaver in it?" I asked.

"Yeah."

"Did he have someone try to run me down on the bay?"

"The idea was to scare you, not run you down."

"Did he have my girlfriend followed?"

"He had one a them guys from Hong Kong do it."

"He wanted me to think it was Jimmy?"

Bud nodded eagerly, excited, it seemed, that I was catching on. "That's right."

"So he rented a black Mercedes?"

He nodded even more emphatically. "That's right."

"And he planted a cleaver in her door?"

"Yeah." By this point Bud was nodding his assent even during my questions.

"And he had those guys push me down Hyde Street?"

"Yeah. All that was Pendola."

"And he sent the faxes to Vancouver and Hong Kong?"

"Yeah. That's right." Now his upper body was rocking along with his nodding head.

"Where did he get the chief's stationery?"

"From a supply room at 850 Bryant."

"How did he know I was going to Vancouver?"

"He had you followed to the airport."

"And Hong Kong?"

"It figured that if you were going to Vancouver, you'd go on to Hong Kong."

It did figure. Any cop would have made that deduction. "And what about the poisoning?" I said. "Did he arrange that?"

He raised a restraining hand. "Just enough to make you sick. Everything he did, he wanted it to look like there was a conspiracy to keep you off Jimmy's trail."

I glared at Bud. "You knew all about this and yet you're telling me he never cleared it with you?"

Again that cautioning hand. "I knew about it only after the fact. He'd brag about it. I'd tell him, 'No more,' that I wouldn't pay him, but by this point he didn't care about the money. It tickled him, playin' games on you. He figured it was payback time for what you did to him."

"Why did he wait so long?"

Bud shrugged. "I suppose it was because he'd never had the opportunity—or the money."

"*Your* money."

Instantly his eyes narrowed. He looked at me warily, as though suddenly aware that I'd led him into a trap. "A *lot* of people's money," he said after a pause.

"But you didn't try to stop him," I said, fighting to keep my voice calm.

"Because I knew that he wanted what we wanted, a mayor who would give San Francisco the reputation of a city that didn't want no more queers or panhandlers or gangs."

My wound had begun to throb. I changed my position, hoping to ease the pain, but that only made it worse. "So the bottom line is that when you saw Halderman was still way behind in the polls you knew you'd have to create an incident to destabilize the city and discredit Mayor Putnam. And you hired Pendola, telling him simply, 'Do what you need to do,' never imagining the terrible thing he'd do."

"That's it, that's exactly it," Bud said emphatically, leaning toward me, his arms wide again, the innocence of his expression suggesting that because I now fully understood how it had happened he was completely off the hook.

In that moment I was more aware than I'd ever been of how you can actually feel what's pouring through your eyes. The only question was which I felt more, skepticism or contempt. "Why would you expect me to believe that?" I said coldly.

"Because it's true, and because I said so and because yer father and I were close friends."

I'd been sure that at some point Bud would raise my father's memory. I could only imagine with what pain my father would have regarded such conduct by a man he'd played ball with, and done deals with, and cried with at his son's funeral. For my father, integrity was everything; without it, a man was nothing. On several occasions he'd turned away from friends and associates who came up short.

I looked at Bud carefully and squinted my eyes, as though I were sighting down a gun barrel. When I spoke it was with the slow, deliberate rhythm with which you're taught to squeeze off a round. "My father would not have been the friend of a man who did what you did, Bud."

His explanation had pumped him up; the remark crumpled him as if he'd been hit by a bullet. He fell against the stiff back of the chair. His spine sagged. "God spared yer father the pain a seein' what's happened to San Francisco since he died," he said. Then, seeming to regain strength from his own logic, he straightened his spine and said, "The truth is, y'don't know what yer father woulda done. Y'think yer father woulda been happy seein' the city infested with these queers and their diseases? Y'think yer father woulda been happy livin' in a city where the whites were a minority? Y'think yer father woulda been happy walkin' sidewalks where he has to step over good-fer-nothin' bums? If that's what yer thinkin', yer dreamin', Zack."

In his worst nightmares, my father would never have dreamed that a conversation like the one I was having would have occurred in his city, and certainly not with a man he'd believed in. Suddenly the pain from my wound flared again, spreading from my side through my torso, and I figured I had just enough strength left to close off this conversation and get back to my bed. "My father would never have hired some sick, crooked cop to create a racial incident," I said adamantly. "And he would have no more respect than I do for a man who would do such a thing. Now, if you'll excuse me, I'm going back to my room."

As I began to push myself up from the chair, Bud put a hand on my shoulder and pushed me back down. I grunted in pain. Then he stood over me. "You should think twice before goin' public with any accusations against me, Zack."

I stared up at him. "Are you threatening me, Bud?"

"I'm talkin' sense to ya, Zack, fer yer own good. I'm tryin' to tell ya that I wasn't the only one involved. You get careless with yer accusations and a lot a good people can get hurt."

"How's that?" I said, figuring the fastest way to get rid of him was to hear him out.

"Yer familiar, I imagine, with the work of Save Our City, that citizens' group I founded?"

"Oh, yes," I said, not even trying to hide my contempt.

If Bud saw it or heard it, he ignored it. "Well, it was SOC, not Bud Donnelly, that paid Joe Pendola."

"So?" I said irritably.

"So SOC is supported by contributions from its members." He paused, obviously for effect. "And the biggest contributor, by far, is yer sister."

Through the years I have felt just about everything for my sister:

love, awe, respect, tenderness, fear, contempt, hatred, revulsion. But until this moment I had never felt pity. "Well, then," I said, for lack of anything better to say, "too bad for my sister."

"It's not that simple, Zack. The contribution didn't come out of Sari's pocketbook." Once again, a pause for effect. "It came from the family business."

He paused again, presumably to let the information sink in. "Somethin' like that gets out, y'could have a boycott on yer hands. I know how much business the firm does with the Asian community and the Pacific Rim. I read about all the money the firm had to borrow to make those new acquisitions. What's gonna happen when the word gets out that the CEO of Z. Tobias and Company was the deep pocket in a campaign against Asians? A boycott, that's what'll happen." Another pause. "Remember when the whole country stopped eatin' grapes? Yer stretched out, Zack. Yer not in any position to ride out a boycott. Y'could lose it all." He nodded, as if agreeing with his own logic. "Y'could lose it all." Then he stood and walked down the hospital corridor.

I watched him until he turned at the nurses' station and disappeared from view. Then I pushed myself from the chair and stood, an effort that seemed to fire every nerve in my body. I gasped, reached out for a wall and waited a minute for the pain to subside. Then, very slowly, I dragged myself and my IV back to my room.

The next hours passed for me as they must for a condemned man whose execution is imminent and whose appeals have been exhausted. I knew, as surely as he did, what the next event in my life would be.

At five o'clock, as I was resting in bed, still exhausted and in pain from my encounter with Bud Donnelly, my sister walked into my hospital room. Mother followed her, moving as though she was being dragged on a leash. She'd been at the hospital the morning of my surgery and every day since. This was Sari's first visit. Both women were wearing damp trench coats, and holding damp Burberry scarves, which subtly reinforced their powerful mother-daughter resemblance. Only their ages and their expressions set them apart. Mother looked anxious. Sari was wearing her war face: stony eyes, flared nostrils, a rigid mouth. She closed the door behind them, then turned to me. "You'll do anything to get me, won't you?" she said, throwing her wet scarf on the bed.

I laughed. It was all I could do. "Like deliberately losing a kidney and almost getting killed? Is that what you had in mind?"

"You know what I'm talking about," Sari said contemptuously.

"Let's start over," I said. "Zack! I'm so sorry about what happened. How are you?"

"Grow up, Zachary," she said with a look of malice that stirred a thousand dire memories. "I *am* sorry about what happened to you, but nothing that has happened to you excuses what you've done."

I stared at her in astonishment. "What *I've* done? All I'm trying to do is investigate a crime."

"Don't play semantics with me," she ordered. "Bud Donnelly told me about the trouble you're going to cause us."

I couldn't believe what I was hearing. "Did Bud tell you about the trouble he caused Maggie Winehouse and the city of San Francisco?" I asked her angrily.

"It wasn't his fault," Sari said dismissively. "*He* didn't tell that man to hurt that girl—any more than I did." Her mouth was a hard straight line. It was all I could do to make myself confront the rancor flashing in her eyes. "However it happened, it doesn't excuse your ruining the company—and Mother and me in the process. You want to ruin yourself, that's your business. But when your stupid little games threaten your family, that's our business." She turned to Mother. "Tell him!" she said. It was an order, not a request.

I looked at Mother, and she at me. She was shaking, and wringing her damp scarf in her hands. "Oh, Zack, this is terrible. You know how I feel about airing our problems in public."

"Cut the shit, Mother," Sari said, her voice so loud it made Mother start. "Tell him how you feel about losing seven hundred million dollars. Tell him how you feel about losing your house and your place in the community. Tell him how you feel about being a pauper."

Mother stood there, trembling, speechless.

"*Tell him!*" It was a scream as piercing and violent and venomous as any I'd ever heard.

It was just then that Britt opened the door and peered uncertainly inside.

"Get out," Sari said. "This is a family matter."

Britt looked quickly at me. "Come in, Britt," I said.

Britt stepped inside. "I said get out," Sari said, advancing on her. Britt held her ground.

"She'll stay right here," I said.

Sari glared at me, then at Britt. Then she turned to Mother. "Go on," she said.

"I'm very frightened, Zack," Mother said.

"Say what you said to me!" Sari commanded.

I could see Britt wince.

Mother swallowed. She seemed on the verge of tears. When she spoke, I could hardly hear her. "I don't want to be poor," she said.

Sari turned to me. "You bring Bud Donnelly into this, and you're responsible for what happens to Mother."

Even coming from Sari, I couldn't believe what I was hearing. "If you're so concerned about Mother's welfare," I retorted, "you might have thought a little more carefully before you got the company involved with an extremist group like SOC."

"*I* didn't know any specifics, you stupid moron," Sari said. She was shouting now, the veins in her throat visible under her taut skin. "Bud only told me in general terms what he had in mind. He never said a thing about creating racial conflict."

"I'd just like to know which of those 'general terms' appealed to you so much that you'd put the company's money into SOC?" I said acidly. "The campaign against immigrants? Or the homeless? Or the gays? Or all of the above?"

"Yeah, well, let me tell you something," Sari shouted, thrusting her head at me. "I'm sick and tired of paying their bills, and so is everyone else in this city."

My side was killing me, but I had to finish this. "Then let me tell *you* something, Sari. There is nothing, but nothing, that justifies your use of the company's money to indulge your biases. And if you hadn't gotten so greedy, you wouldn't be out on a limb. The company would've had a ton of assets to weather a boycott."

A look came into her eyes right then that was as rare as snow in summer. It was a look of uncertainty, and it was gone in an instant. "Well, think about this, Mr. High and Mighty Liberal," she said. "If this deal goes sour, we won't be the only ones swinging in the wind. Thousands of people are going to lose their jobs and their homes."

At that moment, Britt slid herself between Sari and the bed, so that their chests were almost touching. "I think you'd better leave," Britt said, her voice icy.

"What?" Sari said, startled.

"You heard me," Britt said. "Your brother's just had major surgery. He doesn't need this."

"Excuse me," Sari said. "I said this was a family matter." With that she attempted to push Britt aside.

I have never seen Britt move so fast. With her left hand, she grabbed Sari's hair. With her right, she spun her around, grabbed Sari's right arm at the wrist and wrenched it behind her back. As Sari cried out in pain, Britt marched her to the door, opened it, and flung her into the hallway.

I would have given a lot to see Sari's expression, but it was even better to have her out of my view. "How dare you?" I heard her cry.

"Don't come back," Britt said calmly, beginning to close the door. Sari must have stuck her foot in it, because it remained open a crack.

I don't know that anyone since my father had confronted Sari so directly. For a moment she must have been too shocked to speak, because there was a merciful silence. Then I heard her call out, "Mother! Come on!"

Mother had watched, frozen. Now she moved to the door. There, she turned and looked at me in consternation, as though trying to figure out how sixty-seven years of a worthy life could have led her to this sordid moment. "Is there anything you need?" she asked. Her tone was piteous, an admission, it seemed, of all her shortcomings as a mother, a plea for my compassion, a submission to my judgment.

I searched my mind, desperate to come up with the right thing to say. "Yes," I said at last. "I could use some chicken soup."

When she was gone, I closed my eyes, waiting for my pain to subside and hoping I might somehow eradicate the images of the last ten minutes. No such luck; they flew through my head. When I opened my eyes again a few minutes later, Britt was seated by the window, watching me, just as she'd done for so many hours since I was shot. She looked only marginally better than she had the last time I'd looked closely at her. Her eyes were still dark and sunken, and she seemed utterly withdrawn. There was so much I'd planned to tell her on my return from Hong Kong about what I'd learned and decided. Even if I'd had the energy to talk about it, I sensed that she wouldn't have wanted me to, that she was out of reach.

"I'm sorry you had to see that," I said.

"Don't be," she said, her voice flat. "It was one thing for you to tell me about it. It was quite another to see it with my own eyes."

"Thanks for defending me," I said softly, hoping she'd see the corresponding softness in my eyes. But she seemed to stare right past me, and it came to me that in all her time with me in the hospital, she had seemed to be there not because she loved me, but because she was concerned about me and felt a duty toward me, and that her thoughts were elsewhere. I had a sudden premonition that when I was recovered, Britt would leave me for good. I closed my eyes again, trying to eradicate that image, as well. When I opened them, she was staring out the window. "Britt?" I said quietly.

Before she turned, she moved a hand to her eyes, and when she did turn toward me I saw she'd been crying. "It's very ugly," she said. "It's all so very ugly."

I thought I knew what she meant, but I didn't have enough in me to explore it with her, or console her, or reassure her. I don't know how long we were silent. Finally, I said, "Why don't you go home and rest?"

She, too, seemed at a loss. She stared at me in a manner that made me want to look away. It was as though she was making a final inspection before a definitive judgment. Finally, she walked to the bed, kissed me on the forehead and left without a word.

A chilling idea crossed my mind. Nine years ago, in this hospital, I lost one of the two women I've ever loved. And now, in this same hospital, I was about to lose the other.

Prepared though I'd been for my sister's onslaught, I was totally unprepared for what followed. At six o'clock Mayor Putnam walked into my room, followed by Chief Doyle. By the look on Doyle's face, I was sure he'd accompanied the mayor about as voluntarily as my mother had accompanied Sari. He closed the door behind him and stood across from the mayor, who had pulled the chair up close to the bed.

"We know you need your rest, Zack, so we won't beat around the bush," Putnam said after asking for and receiving assurances about my health. His Brooks Brothers correctness and ruddy cheeks seemed out of place in an environment of uncertainty and illness. "We've got two matters to discuss with you. The first involves Jimmy Chang. The chief has reported on your call from Hong Kong. Have you seen Jimmy since your return?"

"I have, sir."

"And?"

"And I'm satisfied that he had nothing to do with the hit on Maggie Winehouse." Making that statement public was like getting a virus out of my system.

The mayor's relief was obvious, but the chief seemed at a loss.

"What about all that stuff you gave me on the phone?" he asked. "Doesn't any of it check out?"

"It *all* checks out, Chief."

He frowned deeply. Only then did I notice how tired he looked, as though he'd lost a night's sleep, and then I saw that his hands were shaking almost as badly as Bud Donnelly's had, and I could only wonder how much all the charges and countercharges as well as my battle to the death with Joe Pendola had taken out of him.

"Jimmy confirmed everything I'd learned about his past," I explained. "Getting out of China, his hitch with the triads, leaving Hong Kong under a cloud, changing his name, entering the U.S. illegally."

"But what about now? Is he clean now?" the chief asked, his voice husky with fatigue.

"No, but not because he doesn't want to be."

I told them then about Ying Shen and the Golden Door Trading Company and the Pacific Rim Bank. When I finished the mayor sighed and shook his head and said, "What a mess. Have you any idea how it's going to play out?"

"Not at the moment, Mr. Mayor."

"But Jimmy, himself, is blameless?" He seemed desperate to have that assurance.

"He's still an illegal. Technically, he's an accomplice to a money-laundering scheme. He was responsible for some illegal contributions to your campaign—"

"Oh?" The mayor sat up straight. "What's that about?"

"Let's not get into that now," I said, holding a hand up. "What's important is that as far as the Maggie Winehouse case is concerned he seems to be clean."

"Then you're not going to press charges?"

I shrugged. "I've got nothing to book him on. I can't speak for the Feds."

The mayor was silent for a moment. Jerry Doyle seemed to be out of it, too tired to deal with any more information. Then the mayor leaned forward, almost as though he was afraid someone might over-hear. "How much of this does Gordon Lee know?" he asked.

"I'm going to have to give him something," I said. "As far as he knows, everything we learned in Hong Kong is still valid, and for the moment I can't tell him otherwise. I've warned him off the story, but I can't guarantee what he'll do."

The mayor and Chief Doyle exchanged uneasy looks. Then the mayor turned back to me. "How do you propose to handle it?"

Even in my weakened state—or perhaps because of my weakened state—I was struck by the mayor's deference. I could assume that the chief had told the mayor about our understanding. Nonetheless, I was still, officially, a suspended cop. I laughed weakly. "At the moment, I haven't the faintest idea."

"Can it wait until after the election?"

I'd been waiting for that word. "That's more than ten months off," I said. "I can't make any promises."

The mayor looked at Jerry Doyle. "Chief?" he said.

Doyle cleared his throat. "If Jimmy hasn't committed any crimes in San Francisco, we'd like to keep him out of it," he said.

I was certain he'd been rehearsed. "Out of what?" I asked.

Doyle looked at the mayor, who nodded for him to continue. "Out of the campaign, Zack," the chief said.

I sank back against my pillow. "Mr. Mayor, I'm not sure it's within my power to do that. A lot depends on whether Ying Shen forces the issue."

Doyle cleared his throat again.

"Look, I'm getting pretty tired," I said. "You said you had two mat-ters to discuss. We'd better get to the second one before I run out of gas."

"Of course, of course," the mayor said. He got out of his chair abruptly and stood by the bed. "I had a visit this afternoon from Bud Donnelly."

I took a deep breath, then let the air out slowly. I'd suspected it was coming and had girded myself for it, but given how weak and uncomfortable I was feeling, I just wasn't sure I could handle it. "Go on," I muttered.

"The chief and I have just spent a couple of hours together, trying to determine the best course of action," Putnam continued. He was at his smooth, reassuring, conciliator's best. "What I'm going to say has his full support. Right, Chief?"

"Right," Doyle said. I'll give him this much: he made it sound as if it did.

The mayor smiled, as though he were about to share an inside joke. "I'm sure I'm not the first to tell you that there's a lot of speculation out there about the kind of story you're going to tell when you've recovered."

"So I've gathered," I said dryly.

"For our part," the mayor continued as though I hadn't spoken, "we don't know what you plan to do any more than anyone else. But we know what you *could* say, and that we've got some ideas about. Right, Chief?"

"That's correct, Mr. Mayor." Doyle's voice sounded convincing, but I noticed that he kept his eyes on the mayor and didn't look at me.

"We don't think it's in the best interests of the city for you to tell that story. Am I right, Chief?"

"That's right, Mr. Mayor."

"We've checked with the district attorney, and he's told us that, based on our understanding of what happened, it would be difficult if not impossible to get a grand jury to indict. The one man who could make a case against Bud is dead, but even if Pendola had told someone about what he was doing, and that someone came forward to testify, his statements could well be inadmissible hearsay. As a lawyer, that was my opinion, as well, but it's reassuring to have the backup."

"Bud didn't commit a crime, Zack," the chief said. There was an imploring note in his voice, and he spoke with more energy than he had since arriving.

"What he did was a terrible thing, Zack," the mayor said, his face the soul of earnestness, "and he's really suffering for it. But he never told Sergeant Pendola to do that awful thing to Maggie Winehouse."

I pushed myself up in the bed, wincing as I did. I just couldn't lie there and take this. "Mr. Mayor, we don't really know that. We only have his word for it."

"His word is good, Zack," the mayor said at once. "Bud and I grew up together."

"I *know* you did, sir," I said, "but with all respect, his word isn't good enough."

The mayor stared at me. I could see his chest expanding and contracting as he took deep breaths. "We're *best* friends."

I looked at the chief, who still wouldn't make eye contact with me, then back at Putnam. "If I may ask, sir, how can you say you're best friends when Bud Donnelly's been trying to destroy you?"

The mayor raised his right index finger. "Not out of malice. Out of conviction. He *meant* well."

"That's right," the chief said eagerly, suddenly turning his eyes toward me. "He meant well."

What could I say? I said nothing.

"He's had a bitter life, Zack," the Mayor said. "There was a time when he actually called himself a progressive. But losing his boy killed him." The mayor sighed. "There's no point in hurting him any more. He's paid his dues." He nodded. "And the man who ordered the attack on Maggie Winehouse has paid *his* dues."

"Case closed," Doyle declared, sounding like a judge.

"That's what we want, Zack," Mayor Putnam said emphatically, picking up the cue, "to close the case, drop it, throw it in the bay. If this thing goes on, it'll so disrupt the city that there's no telling what will happen. The city needs to heal, Zack." He paused, and looked at the chief. "We want you to help us heal it."

"By shutting up, is that it?" I said. There was no way to keep my voice neutral any longer, and I didn't try.

"By exercising discretion," the mayor said, ignoring my gibe. He paused for a moment, took one more look at the chief, then turned to me. "And by becoming the new chief of police when Chief Doyle steps down after the election. Assuming I win, of course."

I looked quickly at Jerry Doyle. If he was in pain, he was hiding it. He was simply exhausted. "That's right," he said. "I've had enough."

I was exhausted too. My side was throbbing. This can't be happening, I told myself. I didn't know what to think or how to react. The mayor and the chief were waiting for me to say something. Half a minute passed. At last I said to the mayor, "I'm surprised you wouldn't want the voters to know what a terrible thing was done in behalf of your opponent."

"The public will know," the mayor said. "We'll blame it on a dead man." He squeezed my arm. "Think it over," he said. Then he led Jerry Doyle from the room.

26

I'm not going to pretend that I didn't think about the offer. To become what I'd set out to be—what man or woman wouldn't be tempted? Whatever I might accomplish in disclosing the full story had to be balanced against what I might accomplish as chief of the SFPD. All those dreams, all those plans.

Following the mayor's scenario had other benefits. At this point I wasn't sure he was wrong. The city did need to heal. Who knew how it would react to the truth? And then there were all those employees of Z. Tobias and Company and its new subsidiaries, and, yes, my mother as well. My sister had that much right; I didn't want to be responsible for the economic demise of thousands. If the takeover venture failed of its own accord I, at least, wouldn't be responsible.

What I'm about to say will sound pious; I can't help it. Not to disclose the truth was to lie, even if only by omission, and there was no way I could do that. After all these years, I still had my father to answer to. And there was my own conviction, developed through the years, that however much it hurt, truth served the most people.

That night I slept terribly, more from my doubts than from pain.

In the morning the world began to change.

A few years before he died, my paternal grandfather, who would have given anything to be a scholar rather than the head of Z. Tobias and Company, told me that the older he got the more synchronous and serendipitous life became. I was eleven at the time; I told him I didn't know what the words meant. He apologized for using them. What he meant, he said, was that so much had happened to him by that point that every new happening seemed to relate to everything else in his life. Not only that, it seemed to happen at just the right time. He would read a passage in a book or a newspaper story or hear someone say something and, lo and behold, it would be the missing piece in the puzzle, the combination to the vault, the single idea that put all related ideas in order. While I am exactly half the age my grandfather was when he said that to me, I have to ascribe what happened over the next days and weeks to synchronicity and serendipity—the meanings of which I've since learned.

At ten o'clock the following morning—five physically and emotionally painful days since I was shot—Sam, my mother's housekeeper, walked into my hospital room.

"What are you doing here?" I asked him in Chinese.

"Missus send," he answered in his halting English, holding out a hamper.

It annoyed me that Sam insisted on speaking such terrible English when we could converse so easily in Chinese. But I supposed he was trying to take my mind off his immigrant status. One of these days I told myself as I opened the hamper, I'm going to find out how he got into the States.

And then it happened: one of those instantaneous, inexplicable moments in which the mind miraculously tunnels through a mountain of ignorance and breaks through to the other side.

Inside the hamper was a jar of chicken soup—homemade, I was sure. At another time or under other circumstances, the sight of the chicken soup would have aroused warm thoughts for my mother, and that would have been that. But the combination of Sam and the chicken soup made me think of Kurt Muller in Hong Kong, a Jew who, though a world away from his origins, still maintained his religious traditions and undoubtedly his cultural beliefs as well, one of which, of course, is that chicken soup possesses miraculous medicinal properties. And thinking of Kurt Muller made me think of his problems with the People's Republic and Ying Shen and how they had cost him his shipping lines. And that thought, in the context of Sam's appearance, made me reach for the phone and call Jimmy Chang the instant Sam left the room.

I asked him a single question. It took half an hour of coaxing and promises to get him to answer it. When he did, the last piece of the puzzle fell into place.

My next call was to Bob Bein, the chief of the Immigration and Naturalization Service's Reno office. "How'd you like to get yourself promoted out of Reno?" I asked after he'd gotten over his surprise at hearing from me and satisfied himself about my condition.

He exploded with laughter. "That's like askin' if I'd like to have Ed McMahon ring my doorbell to tell me I'd won his sweepstakes."

"What would it take?" I asked him.

My voice must have sounded as humorless as I felt because Bob said, "You're really serious, aren't you?"

"What would it take?" I repeated.

"A miracle."

"Would a spectacular bust qualify?"

"Do you have one in mind?" he said. He was suddenly as serious as I was.

For the next five minutes I filled him in. He listened in silence. "That would qualify," he said when I'd finished. "How soon can we meet?"

"How soon can you get here?"

More serendipity and synchronicity. Thinking about Kurt Muller had made me think of Steve Crown, the former FBI man who ran the Morris Group office in Hong Kong, the man Muller had retained to help him resolve his problems. At five o'clock that afternoon—nine the next morning in Hong Kong—I called Steve. He was as surprised to hear from me as Bob Bein had been. "I was going to call you several days ago, but then I read about the shooting," he said in a voice so concerned it was hard to believe we'd gotten off to such a rocky start. "You okay?"

"I expect to be."

"Did the shooting have anything to do with our little matter?"

"Indirectly," I said, hoping he'd hear what I wasn't saying.

He did. "Give me a call when you can," he said. Not a trace of excitement, although I was sure he felt it.

"You're at the top of the list," I said. "In the meanwhile did you have any luck with that personal matter we discussed?"

His voice brightened at once. "I did, as a matter of fact. That's why I was going to call you. Running down that loan was simpler than I thought. It was made by the Kadoorie family. You know about the Kadoories?"

"The power-company people."

"Among a number of enterprises."

"When was the loan made?" I asked, just out of curiosity, because, as Sari had said, it was a done deal. I'd at least satisfied myself that one of the triads hadn't bought into Z. Tobias and Company.

"Actually, it won't be made for another couple of days," Steve said.

Serendipity. Synchronicity. My grip on the phone tightened. "Wait a minute! Wait a minute!" I said excitedly. "Are you saying the loan hasn't been funded?"

"Not yet."

A picture flashed into my head, of that rare-as-snow-in-summer look of uncertainty in my sister's eyes, and now I understood it. At that moment she'd known what I hadn't—that she wasn't yet out on that financial limb, that she could still back out of the deal. Safety on the one hand, a financial empire on the other. She'd opted for empire.

I thought quickly. "Can I assume that the Kadoorie people and Kurt Muller are on good terms?"

"The best of terms, as far as I know."

"Would Muller be willing to deliver a message to the Kadoorie people for me?"

There was a slight pause. "That would depend on the message," Steve said carefully.

"The message is that they should not fund that loan. In the next few weeks, Z. Tobias and Company is going to take a horrendous hit. What they should do with the money is buy the bonds of the three companies Z. Tobias was going to acquire. If my sister says they're a steal, I promise you they're a steal."

There was a longer pause. "Isn't this unethical?"

"Call it unorthodox," I said, talking quickly. "It can't be unethical if it helps as many people as this will."

A major pause. "You'd better explain, pal," Steve said.

"Gladly," I said, dizzy with hope. "If the deal goes through, and we're on the hook for a billion dollars, that hit could wipe us out, and the new acquisitions with us. If the deal doesn't go through, we're back to our impregnable position, with all the assets we need to recover from the hit. In the meanwhile, the Kadoories—or even Muller himself—can provide the funds those three companies need to survive. In the process, they make a nice piece of change." I paused, waiting for a response. When there was none, I said, "Do you get it?"

"I get it, all right," Steve said slowly. "What kind of a hit are we talking about?"

"A massive boycott of Z. Tobias products and services."

Steve cleared his throat. "What makes you so sure it's going to happen?"

"All I can tell you is that I've never been more sure of anything."

This time, instead of silence, I heard him humming on the line. "Your sister could sue," Steve said finally.

"My sister won't sue," I said firmly. "She'll be too busy counting her blessings."

"Just a minute," he said at once. "Your sister wants this deal."

"Because she doesn't believe there's going to be a boycott. I *know* there's going to be a boycott. When the boycott's on, that's when she'll count her blessings."

Bob Bein arrived from Reno at eight that evening. Credit the chicken soup for inspirational as well as medicinal properties; thanks to the train of thought it had launched, I was feeling so much better that I was able to sit in a chair throughout our ninety-minute talk.

Stanley Colby joined us at nine-thirty. He'd been wary at first, thinking I was calling to ask for another favor, but once he'd heard what I had to tell him he'd been more than happy to give up an evening at home.

A little before midnight Jimmy Chang slipped through the silent corridors and into my room. By then I was running on adrenaline, but it took less than an hour for him to tell Bob and Stanley what he'd told me and then for us to work out a program satisfactory to all.

At nine the next morning Britt arrived with my clothes. She was not so much distant or cool as matter-of-fact. I had the feeling that she'd already moved to another world. There was nothing I could do about it; I was extremely tired and weak from the short sleep, and getting dressed and ready to leave the hospital took all my energy. When she'd done what she could to help me, she gave me a perfunctory kiss and left. In the fifteen minutes she'd been there we hadn't made eye contact once.

Half an hour later, as I was about to be discharged, Jim Mich appeared, along with two other members of the Gang Task Force. The sight of them threw me. If you've ever been sedated, I'm sure you haven't forgotten how disoriented it makes you. You forget events, and if you do remember them, they're often out of sequence. Seeing Jim, I had a dim memory of having seen him earlier that week, but I couldn't swear to it. "What are you guys doing here?" I said, surprised. "I'm out of here in ten minutes."

"That's why we're here," Jim said. "We're your honor guard."

For a second I thought I was disoriented again. Had I missed something? "What are you talking about?" I said.

"There've been some threats."

The single satisfying thought I'd had since the shooting was that with Joe Pendola out of the way, my days of jeopardy were behind me. "Against me?" I said in surprise.

"Not against your Aunt Tillie. Your silence has made a lot of people nervous."

"What kind of people?"

"You name 'em. We've had tips from every sector of the city."

Fifteen minutes later, seated in a wheelchair and surrounded by my honor guard, I rolled through a door of the hospital into the first fresh air I'd breathed in a week. En route to a black-and-white police car waiting for me at the curb, I passed through a mob of media at least as big as the one that had greeted Maggie Winehouse. My eyes searched the crowd for Gordon, and locked on his once I'd found him. He looked desperate. I nodded all but imperceptibly and threw him a thumbs-up sign, hoping to convey that I hadn't forgotten him.

It wasn't until I'd been home for an hour that I realized my honor guard was going to be with me for the foreseeable future. Two months before, I would have told them to get lost because I didn't need them. If the events since then had taught me anything, it was that all my previous assumptions about what was normal and likely to happen had to be reevaluated.

The day after I returned from the hospital I called Britt to ask if she would have dinner with me at my home on New Year's Eve. I should have waited because I was still weak and not even remotely over the shock of having lost a vital organ. But at least several times a day I'd think about that moment in the hospital when I'd concluded that as soon as I was out of the woods Britt would pass from my life. I wasn't about to let that happen without putting up a fight.

She hesitated before answering, then accepted without comment or enthusiasm.

She arrived promptly at nine o'clock on New Year's Eve, wearing a jacket of black lace and flowing black pants. She'd always worn at least a minimal amount of jewelry whenever she'd dressed up. On this night she wore none. Albert Rainer had sent over a dinner of duck breast from his Hyde Street Bistro, along with a salad and a dessert of crème brûlée. We ate in the study, seated on either side of my desk, and drank a wine even my father would have approved of. The light from a single candle I'd placed on the desk flickered on Britt's face, which still showed the strain of her terrible experience. It was not like old times, not at all. She never did get comfortable, and I kicked myself when I realized, too late, that she could scarcely be at ease twenty feet from where she'd killed a man. But at that time I wasn't free to leave my apartment even if I'd been capable of it, so I had to make the best of it.

Throughout dinner I rehearsed my lines, but when the moment arrived, I blanked. Finally, as self-conscious as though I were addressing an audience of thousands, I said, "I've figured out that you don't exorcise your past or bury it. It's part of you, and stays with you, and you have to learn to use it."

Britt's eyes narrowed slightly, suggesting that she didn't know where I was headed.

"What I mean," I went on, "is that I'm at peace with my past, and I'm ready to begin a new life and I want it to be with you."

Her eyes returned to normal size, but she registered nothing, no surprise or joy or even pleasure. I had nothing to react to, no way of knowing whether she approved of or had even understood what I'd just said. But I pushed on; when you're fighting for your life, you make do.

"I want to be married to you," I said. "I know you don't believe in legal marriage, but just being together wouldn't do it for me. I want to be married because that's the only way both of us can say to each other, 'This is it, this is for life.' "

Britt nodded, but said nothing. The only sound I could hear was the hammering of my heart. "Will you marry me?" I asked.

"Perhaps," she said, her voice low and composed, as though she, too, had thought a lot about what she would say when I proposed, as I'm sure she'd suspected I would. "But not now, and perhaps not ever. I have to go away. I may be gone a long time. I may not come back. After what happened, I'm not sure I can live here. Before it happened, I felt like a guest. I wasn't American, I didn't belong. That was the way I maintained some space between myself and everything I saw happening." She shuddered, and drew her jacket together. "It's horrible what you do to yourselves, just horrible. You had the best country in the world, and you've simply trashed it because you're too selfish to spend what it takes to run it. Worse than that, you abuse one another, and kill one another." At that, she faltered, and had to look away, and I could see the muscles in her face quivering as she fought to keep control. "And now I have been caught up in your horror." She shook her head, hard, as if to dislodge the thought, and at last she looked at me again. "I do still love you, Zack, and I can't imagine ever not loving you, and I would do again what I did. But if I marry you, I marry this country, too, and I'm not ready to do that, and I don't know if I ever will be."

I'm sure she said something else after that, but I was in shock and don't remember. A few minutes later—well before midnight—she left, kissing me once on each cheek, and then once on the lips, a soft, lingering kiss, and then murmuring "Happy New Year." Three days later she was in Sweden.

That ache returned, an ache far worse than the incision in my side, that craving for another person that has nothing to do with sex and everything to do with belonging. For several days, it overrode all my thoughts, just as pain can do, and then one day I beat it the only way I could. I decided that Britt would come back. In spite of everything, I believe in happy endings.

On January 2, I began the chronicle you've just read, convinced that the only way I could sort out everything that had happened was to get it down on paper. I talked into a tape recorder. A cousin of Anna Primi's—vouched for by Anna as completely reliable—came to the apartment each day to transcribe the tapes. Each evening I corrected the transcripts. In the first days, an hour's work would exhaust me. But gradually, as my stamina increased, I was able to work for two hours, then four, then an entire day. I worked seven days a week, becoming increasingly impatient with interruptions.

Except for one.

On an afternoon in early February, as I was immersed in work, Bob Bein called. "We're having a little party tomorrow," he said. "Do you think you could come?"

"I'll have to talk to my honor guard," I said.

"Try to make it," he urged me. "It won't be the same without you."

The next morning, my two regular guards, augmented by two others, got me out of the house and down to the Ferry Building, where Bob was waiting in an unmarked car. As we drove away he filled me in on the details. Several hours earlier, an oceangoing freighter belonging to Pacific Rim Lines, a new Hong Kong–based shipping company, had slipped through the Golden Gate and docked at the Army Street Pier. Before the last lines were secured, longshoremen had begun to unload the first of twenty-five hundred weathered twenty- and forty-foot containers of varying colors that had been lashed to the ship's deck. "The ones we're interested in should be coming off about now," he said.

We drove past a security guard and onto the Army Street Pier. While Bob went into an office I stayed in the car and watched the containers being hoisted off the ship and lowered to flatbeds waiting alongside. As soon as a container was secured to a flatbed, it was hauled to a delivery area, where a waiting trucker hooked it to his rig and, after stopping to have his papers checked, drove it out the gate.

Suddenly, Bob was in the car. "Here we go," he said. He drove through the gate, well behind two rigs that I'd watched pass through seconds before. "Now if we haven't been misinformed," Bob said, "those boys are goin' to the East Bay."

Which is what they did, crossing the Bay Bridge to Emeryville, just north of the bridge, then driving to the loading dock of a warehouse a few blocks from the bay. Bob drove past the warehouse, then looped around the block and came through an alley, slowing to a stop just as the two drivers maneuvered their rigs against the loading dock. We watched in silence as the drivers unhooked their cabs from the flatbeds. Then they drove away.

A minute passed. All at once half a dozen men emerged from the warehouse, removed heavy steel locking bars from the twin steel doors of each container and pulled the doors open. Seconds later two files of men, one from each container, walked rapidly across the dock and into the warehouse. "Good-bye, Reno," Bob whispered. He offered his right hand. We shook.

As soon as the last man was inside, Bob raised a radio mike to his lips and said, "Let's do it." And then it was just like a movie—cars racing out of alleys and side streets from all directions, red lights blinking, tires screeching, armed men, at least fifty of them, half of them from the Immigration and Naturalization Service, the other half from U.S. Customs, pouring from the cars, racing up the steps, breaking open doors at both ends of the warehouse and bursting inside, shouting to the occupants to stay where they were or get down on the floor.

Bob and I had left his car for a better view. As we approached the dock I urged him to go ahead. My heart was pounding, as much from the excitement as the exertion, and I knew I couldn't keep up.

By the time I got inside, it was over. Forty Chinese men were lined up against a brick wall, being patted down. One by one they turned around, only to blink in the harsh glare of the lights of the television crews that had materialized out of nowhere. I stood to the side, watching, until the crews had gotten their shots. Then I moved forward for a closer look at the illegals. What I saw broke my heart: forty exhausted, emaciated, filthy, bewildered men, wearing ragged clothes and shivering in the cold. As I looked at them they all seemed to turn their eyes toward me. I suppose they looked at me because I was the closest one to them. But at that moment I had the sudden, woeful conviction that every last one of them knew who I was: the man who had ruined their dreams of creating a new life in America.

I, the descendant of immigrants whose dreams had been no different and journeys no less arduous.

In Hong Kong, minutes after the event I've just described, a detail from the RHKP, led by Dirk Richards, rousted an indignant Ying Shen from his bed and led him off to jail.

The following week I received a call from Steve Crown, informing me that Kurt Muller was in the process of buying back his shipping line for 20 percent of what he'd sold it for.

None of these events could have taken place, of course, without the cooperation of Jimmy Chang, who, having decided that he did not wish to spend the rest of his life in fear of blackmail, had, on our instructions, informed Ying Shen that his contraband shipments would pass unmolested through the Port of San Francisco. Because of the serendipitous and synchronistic appearance of Sam, Mother's housekeeper, at the hospital, I'd correctly guessed what those ship ments would be.

The toughest part for Jimmy had been leaving San Francisco, but he was the first to agree that under the circumstances it was the prudent thing to do. I knew he was somewhere no one could ever trace him, and I knew he would do well, having already demonstrated an ability to prosper wherever he goes and under whatever name he assumes.

It's two weeks now since the apprehension of those illegals, but their faces still haunt me—and will, I'm sure, for the rest of my life. As the days passed, the moral quandary that encounter had illuminated only served to reinforce my convictions about what I had to do to be at peace with myself.

One heavenly winter day, after a cold wind from the north had blown the latest storm away, a day when the smell of the ocean had spiced the air and you could see for fifty miles, the kind of day that reminded you how beautiful life could be, I wrote a brief letter of resignation from the SFPD, and sent it by messenger to Chief Doyle, with a copy to Mayor Putnam.

That evening my honor guard escorted me to the studios of KUBC. Gordon Lee and Maggie Winehouse met me at the door. It had been Gordon's idea to demand that Maggie co-anchor the special program he had built around my appearance, on pain of taking his services— and my story—to another station. As we took our places on the set

Gordon passed behind Maggie and put his hands on her shoulders. She reached up and squeezed his forearms. It was over in a second, as was the tender look they exchanged as Gordon took his seat.

In the moment before she turned her eyes to me, I had a chance to study Maggie. The crisscrossed scars were all healed now, thin white lines cutting incongruously through her freckles. Gutsy woman, after all; she'd deliberately held off on her plastic surgery until after the broadcast so that viewers would get a good look at what hate crimes could do. As I heard the director's on-air warning, I imagined her as she would appear following the surgery, and I prayed for some kindred power to remove the scar this incident had placed on my beloved city.

Excerpt from Mike Winehouse's column in the Dispatch *of Friday, February 24, 1995.*

Everyone's talking about the program. Everyone has a favorite moment.

Mine comes during the question-and-answer period when that woman from Berkeley, sounding like she already knows the answer, asks Zack why his wife killed herself. Gordon and Maggie gasp in unison. "I don't see how that has anything to do with what we're talking about tonight," Maggie protests. Gordon starts to introduce another caller. But Zack holds up a hand and says, "No, no, let me answer that. It *does* have something to do with what we're talking about."

Until that question, he's looked as comfortable as a woman giving birth. Now he turns abruptly and stares into the camera, so intently it's as if he's using the lens as a telescope to search for someone. And when he speaks you just know he's speaking to that person.

He tells us about his wife's depression, rooted in the country's seeming inability to solve its problems. She thinks it's because people are basically selfish. "No!" Zack insists, face taut, eyes burning, "People are both selfish and unselfish. It's our leaders who set the country's agenda by appealing to one or the other of those strains."

He's right, you know. And not just on a national level. All the way down the line—a point he makes unforgettably at lunch four days after the assault on my Maggie. I ask him—among the many things I ask him that day—why he does what he does when he doesn't need the money.

"You've got it backwards," he tells me. "I should be doing it *precisely* because I don't need the money." He knows his rich friends call him a *schmuck*, he says. *They're* the *schmucks*, he insists, spending their lives making more money than they can ever use, building fortresses to seal themselves off from the decaying world around them. They still think their annual check to charity will fix everything, Zack says. It won't fix anything. It will only care for the casualties.

He leans across the table. "Nothing's going to change until these people step up and change it. They've got to tithe their time as well as their fortunes, to apply those great brains and skills of theirs—the same brains and skills that helped them make those fortunes—to the problems all of us share."

Donated time. Full time. A year. Two years. Whatever it takes. An executive peace corps, right here in the city. "If Mayor Putnam would offer some of his downtown buddies the chance to make a difference, they might do it," he says.

They'd never do it for Mayor Putnam, Zack. Not anymore.

They'd never do it for Mayor Halderman. The man's too venal.

They might do it for Mayor Tobias.

ACKNOWLEDGMENTS

I came to know Harold Evans, the president and publisher of Random House, in the late 1960s, when he was the editor of London's *Sunday Times* and I was the European editor of *Look* and we pooled our resources on an important but expensive story. I'm indebted to him for his continuing belief in me and his support for this book and for whatever inspiration caused him to assign the project to my editor, Susanna Porter, whose concern, energy, insight, craft and knowledge have awed me ever since.

Although the characters and events in the novel are fictitious, they are set against a reality described to me by numerous sources, primarily in San Francisco, Vancouver and Hong Kong. Some have since moved on to other positions; I list their affiliations at the time I interviewed them.

I am especially grateful to Inspector Dan Foley, the head of the Asian team of the Gang Task Force of the San Francisco Police Department's Special Investigations Division, who, since our initial meeting in 1992, has educated me about his special branch of police work, answered hundreds of questions and read two drafts of the manuscript in search of errors.

Others in the SFPD who helped me include Lieutenant Manuel Barretta, secretary to the San Francisco Police Commission; Captain Robert Forney, retired; Inspector John McKenna, Gang Task Force, retired; Sergeant Tom Perdue, Gang Task Force; Inspector Armand Gordon, Bureau of Inspectors homicide detail; and Officer David Ambrose, in charge of the SFPD's public affairs office.

Additional sources include Rollin B. Klink, special agent in charge, and Harry Waskiewicz, special agent, U.S. Customs Service Office of Investigations, San Francisco; Vincent J. Weltz, chief, Criminal Investigation Division, San Francisco office, Internal Revenue Service; Larry Wright, public affairs officer, San Francisco District, IRS; Daniel J. Offield, special agent, U.S. Department of Justice; William Imbic, Immigration and Naturalization Service; Anthony Crittendon, criminal intelligence specialist, California Department of Justice.

Additional information was supplied by John Fang, publisher, *Asian Week,* San Francisco; Richard Reinhardt, my classmate at Columbia University's Graduate School of Journalism and later my colleague at the *San Francisco Chronicle,* who has shared his vast knowledge of the city and of California history with me, and counseled me throughout the life of this project; novelist Herbert Gold; William Coblentz, attorney and civic activist; Pat Steger, society editor of the *San Francisco Chronicle;* Frances Moffat, former society editor of the *Chronicle;* Michael Harris, editorial writer, the *Chronicle;* David Kaplan, news editor, and Linda Jue, associate, Center for Investigative Reporting; James Lazarus, chief of staff to Mayor Frank Jordan; Teresa Lee, of the mayor's staff; Henry Der, executive director, Chinese for Affirmative Action; Terry Leary, former senior inspector, Royal Hong Kong Police; Harry Dorfman, deputy district attorney, San Francisco; John C. Gibbons, senior managing director, San Francisco office, Kroll Associates; Malin Giddings; Gary and Yvonne Goddard; Philip Rosenthal; Rabbi William Kramer, an authority on the history of Jews in the West; Morley Singer, M.D.; Susan Harriman; Geoff and Suzanne Ashton; Jack Jick-chi Chan, deputy director, and Melinda Parsons, principal information officer, Hong Kong Economic and Trade Office, San Francisco; Fletcher Knebel, novelist, journalist, former colleague and friend.

For my understanding of the workings of local television stations, I thank Harry Fuller, news director, KGO-TV; Lisa Stark, reporter, KGO-TV; and Sylvia Chase, anchorperson at KRON-TV.

Norman Chapman, chairman of the board of the J. H. Chapman Group, Winnetka, Illinois, a grammar school classmate with whom I was reunited several years ago, generously educated me about his specialty, mergers and acquisitions, in full knowledge that his views and the view of my protagonist were poles apart.

In Vancouver, Frank Rutter, editor of the editorial pages of the Vancouver *Sun*, gave me a thorough orientation and a list of sources. I was helped, as well, by Dan Grant, chief of investigations, and Phil Barter, communications officer of the Citizenship and Immigration Department's regional office. Gerry Maffre, at the department's headquarters office in Ottawa, assisted me in the later stages of the reporting, as did Vancouver restaurateur John Bishop.

Hong Kong sources included Mark Pinkstone, chief information officer, Overseas Public Relations Subdivision, Government Information Services; Dennis J. Collins, chief staff officer, public relations, Royal Hong Kong Police Force; Dr. H. K. Mong, consultant and forensic pathologist, RHKP; Peter E. Halliday, in charge of criminal investigations, Shatin; Kerry Pearce, an RHKP officer attached to the Shatin station; Lloyd Neighbors, public affairs officer, United States Information Service, United States Consulate General; Gilbert J. Donahue, chief of the consulate's political and economic section; Jerry Wolf Stuchiner, U.S. Department of Justice Immigration and Naturalization Service; Thomas E. Gray, senior customs representative, U.S. Customs Service; Elizabeth Bosher, deputy secretary, General Duties, Government Secretariat; Penelope Byrne and Stephen Wong, Hong Kong Tourist Association; Martin Lee, legislative councilor; Paul Cheng, director, Inchcape Pacific Limited, former president, American Chamber of Commerce, member Legislative Council; Lord Lawrence Kadoorie; Michael Keats, vice president and general manager, Asia/Pacific Division, United Press International; Michael "Mackie" Brander, an attorney and tax specialist; Sheri Dorfman, journalist; Robert Dorfman, director, *Hong Kong Herald;* Lynn D. Grebstad, public relations manager, Regent Hotel; Dennis A. Leventhal, chairman, Jewish Historical Society of Hong Kong. At Kroll Associates (Asia) Ltd., in Hong Kong, I had invaluable help from Richard Post, Dick Wheelan, William E. O'Reilly and Fred Yau. At the Mandarin Oriental Hotel, I received assistance from Gerrie Pitt, public relations director; Neil J. Harvey, manager of the Grill; and Giovanni Valenti, chief concierge.

In addition to Dan Foley, critical readings of early drafts were made by Richard Reinhardt, Abe Battat, Malin Giddings, Gillan MacDonald, Morley and Betty Singer, Susan Harriman, Harry Dorfman, Bob Misiorowski, Brenda Miao, Malcolm Stuart and Richard Freed. David Perlman, science editor of the *Chronicle,* scrutinized an advance reader's copy for errors, and found some.

During the final stages my copy editor, Sono Rosenberg, gave long and exacting attention to the book.

To those who did not want their names used, and to those I may have forgotten, I offer appreciation no less heartfelt.

My thanks, as always, to Sterling Lord, my literary agent of thirty-six years, for his encouragement and enthusiasm, and to my wife, Jacquelyn, who has beautified my life for forty-four years, for her forbearance, support and inspiration.

San Francisco, March 1995

ABOUT THE AUTHOR

Leonard Gross is the author of twenty books, most of them nonfiction, including the acclaimed *The Last Jews in Berlin.* He wrote for *Look* during that magazine's last twelve years of publication as a senior editor, Latin American correspondent, European editor and West Coast editor, winning numerous awards for his work. He is a contributing editor to *Condé Nast Traveler. Strangers at the Gate* is his fourth novel. He lives with his wife, Jacquelyn, in San Francisco, where he began his career as a reporter for the *Chronicle.*

ABOUT THE TYPE

This book was set in Photina, a typeface designed by José Mendoza in 1971. It is a very elegant design with high legibility, and its close character fit has made it a popular choice for use in quality magazines and art gallery publications.